"RIVETING, YOU-ARE-THERE IMMEDIACY . . .
ingenious . . . nail-biting . . . fascinating . . . first-rate . . .
Prime is indeed the word for this involving read!"
—*Publishers Weekly*

"THE TRIAL BEGINS and Martini rolls up his
sleeves to do what he does best . . . packs a satisfying
punch."—*Kirkus Reviews*

The Simeon Chamber:

"CHILLING . . . PROVOCATIVE . . .
STUNNING."—*Publishers Weekly*

"A FINE FOOT-TO-THE-FLOOR THRILLER!"
—*New York Daily News*

"INTRIGUING TWISTS AND TURNS."
—*Orlando Sentinel*

"THRILLING . . . a winner . . . Martini demonstrates a
confident hand and deft control of literary suspense . . .
excellent, top-quality adventure."
—*The Sacramento Bee*

Also by Steve Martini

COMPELLING EVIDENCE
PRIME WITNESS
THE SIMEON CHAMBER

**"WE UNQUESTIONABLY HAVE A NEW
LITERARY LION IN THE FICTIONAL CRIME
GENRE."—Vincent Bugliosi**

Praise for the novels of Steve Martini . . .

Undue Influence:

"ENOUGH TWISTS AND TURNS to send a pretzel
maker into ecstasy."—*Seattle Post-Intelligencer*

"MARTINI, A FORMER TRIAL ATTORNEY, IS
FASCINATING ON LEGAL STRATEGY."—*People*

"DIALOGUE AND CHARACTERIZATIONS ARE
FIRST-RATE . . . a slam-bang narrative complete with
astonishingly good trial scenes."—*Library Journal*

"SHREWD, ENGAGING."—*Entertainment Weekly*

"GRIPPING . . . The characters are sharply drawn, the
facts of the case are presented simply and the
courtroom psychology is laid out vividly. . . .
READERS WILL FIND THEIR FINGERS GLUED
TO THE PAGES."
—*Publishers Weekly*

continued on next page . . .

Compelling Evidence:

Undue Influence

STEVE MARTINI

JOVE BOOKS, NEW YORK

Front cover design copyright © 1994 by Corsillo/Manzone.
Front cover photo copyright © 1994 by Fred George.

This Jove Book contains the complete text
of the original hardcover edition. It has been
completely reset in a typeface designed for
easy reading and was printed from new film.

UNDUE INFLUENCE

A Jove Book / published by arrangement with
the author

PRINTING HISTORY
G. P. Putnam's Sons edition published July 1994
Jove edition / July 1995

ISBN: 0-515-11605-X

A JOVE BOOK®
Jove Books are published by The Berkley Publishing Group,
200 Madison Avenue, New York, New York 10016.
JOVE and the "J" design are trademarks
belonging to Jove Publications, Inc.

PRINTED IN THE UNITED STATES OF AMERICA

10 9 8 7 6 5 4 3 2 1

To Leah and Meg

"And the blood shall be a sign for you on the houses where you live; and when I see the blood I will pass over you. . . ." Exodus 12:13

Undue Influence

PROLOGUE

There is a special clarity of thought, an unclouded focus which is granted to those who shed all fear and panic, who in the end stare death in the eye, and who leave this world on their own terms.

It was this clarity of mind that, in those final days, gave Nikki a superiority of will that I could not resist. Lingering as she was on the edge of death, I found myself unable to refuse her a thing. She would merely ask, and it would be as if she had cast some indefinable spell. All I could say was yes. Floating on an ether of immeasurable courage in a sea of white sheets and pillows, in her last days Nikki finally found her own form of undue influence over me.

Nikki's doctors said she had a virulent strain. They called it "small oat cell cancer." Before they could move, it had metastasized, migrating from the lungs to a dozen other organs.

In those weeks after the funeral, when I finally came to dodge my own self-pity, I dwelled most on the irony. That Nikki, who had never touched a cigarette in her life, who on sensing any negligible odor of smoke would turn on her heels and walk from the most crowded restaurant, who swore off as the foulest of vices all forms of tobacco—that Nikki should die of lung cancer.

It was just eleven months from diagnosis to death. It has

become the mirror image of a nightmare where sanctuary is found in the wakened mind. My only peace with Nikki's death now comes when I can sleep. And it seems I am condemned to insomnia.

The lawyer in me demands some explanation, some cause to which I can affix blame—not for the usual reasons of money damages, but to make sense of this, to give our existence symmetry, some rational design. My lawyer's mind turns, even in its rare moments of sleep, searching for some reason, a logical accounting for this loss, this deprivation now shared with my daughter, Sarah, who is seven. But as to the question of why, there seems no answer. When I told them Nikki never smoked, our family doctor and the oncologist both looked at me skeptically. This was the classic case of smoker's cancer, they told me. And by their looks, the expressions they flashed to each other, lighted by the muted glow of backlit X rays, they squeezed out and conferred their benefit of doubt on me, meager as it was.

Our eighteen years had been a rocky marriage at best, more my fault than hers. An affair during our separation, now some years ago, the constant strain of my law practice—the eternal jealous mistress. Each of these brought their own form of anguish to Nikki. Now I read with increased emphasis articles in popular literature linking cancer to stress, and wonder to what degree Nikki's life was shortened by me.

The therapist to whom I trekked for weeks after Nikki's death—a referral from my physician—told me this was normal, the phase of guilt. He tells me disdain for my dead wife will come next, a loathing that she has left me behind to struggle alone. Each, he says, is an aspect through which I must pass, like the portals of life.

Before, when I shared the trauma of her looming death with Nikki, it was always easier. When diagnosed, we entered the phase of denial together. The tests were wrong. She was healthy and young. The doctors, with all of their science, after all, could not test or measure her will to live. We would beat this thing together, subdue the demon inside her body by sheer force of will if necessary. My conversations with Nikki were laced with bravado, though to my own ear my words too often resonated with fear.

In the end it was Nikki who accepted the truth first, leaving me behind to grasp at the haggard images of naked hope, my dreams of last-minute miracle cures from the shelves of science. Toward the end I found myself in silent bargains with a higher being with whom over the years I have not been on familiar terms.

When I finally subdued my panic, I caught up to Nikki in the serenity of her own acceptance. One afternoon she took my hand, and in the dappled sunlight of our yard, she told me that she had two wishes: to die quietly with her family in her own home, free from the contraptions of modern medicine, and another more personal request that I now fulfill.

CHAPTER
1

"Bottom line, she was an unfit mother." Melanie Vega, Jack's new wife, speaks of Laurel in the past tense—as if she were dead.

In this, I suspect, is some inkling of how Jack and Melanie see their case, like blue chips in a bull market. For two days their lawyer has chewed on Laurel's past. He's had her fricasseed and fried, spiced with indiscretions, and served always in the same way, marinated in liquor. In the valleys that have been Laurel's life, this is a common theme, though I've seen no hint of the bottle through all of this.

"Move to strike. Not responsive." Gail Hemple, Laurel's lawyer, is on Melanie in the witness box like mustard on rye.

The judge tells the court reporter to strike the witness's last statement. Alex Hastings, up on the bench, has the look of perpetual irritation carved on his face like a death mask. This is taking far too long.

Laurel is Jack Vega's former wife, Nikki's sister, and the reason I am here, a blood oath that I would look after Laurel. It was Nikki's last request, for a lot of reasons. Our children are close. While Sarah is younger, she dotes on her two cousins, Laurel's teenagers. But in the end, for Nikki, I think it came down to a more basic denominator of nature, an older sibling's watchful eye over her little sister. Nikki was three years older than Laurel.

Though initially I thought I might grow to regret my involvement here, the fact is that Laurel's cause has grown on me. This may be for no other reason than that Jack, my former brother-in-law, is a jerk of the first water. That his experts and lawyers have Laurel on the run merely proves the adage that there is no such thing as justice—either in or out of court.

I've spent this time here in Family Court as a kibitzer in Laurel's corner, for support. Another lawyer is doing her case.

Laurel is thirty-six, an inch taller than I, a sandy blonde with green eyes and dimples that look like they've been press-punched beneath high cheekbones. When she cares for herself she's an attractive woman. In the years when our families spent time together for holidays, and one brief vacation, Laurel always wore the look of leisured money. But the two-hour facials are now faded memories like her leached-out salon-driven tan.

In recent months she has been forced to fend for herself and her children. With a college degree in the arts, when the divorce came Laurel had no immediately marketable skills or experience. To fill in around the ragged edges of support, which comes hit-and-miss from Jack, she has taken a job at the health club where she used to be a member, teaching aerobics and swimming. At night she chases a teaching credential at the university—something with a better future.

Laurel's fall from affluence can be measured with the precision of the Pearl Harbor bombing. It came one morning with the service of process, divorce papers on the front steps of the family home, and like an iron bomb in a powder magazine it has scattered the pieces of her life.

A rational person might not call this a sneak attack. Over the years Laurel has either known or suspected of Jack's infidelities. They came with the regularity of the seasons, as predictable as blossoms in the spring. Like Ferdinand the Bull, Jack's testosterone level always elevated along with the length of skirts in warm weather. And Jack did little to conceal these moments of misdirected passion. If it weren't so painful, I'm certain he would have carved notches in his dick to commemorate the conquests.

Jack adhered to the lofty view that adultery was merely the application of democracy to love. He saw it as simply another act of statecraft. Some might call this the culture of politics in the state capital, where Jack has held a seat in lower house for twelve years. Still, Laurel was dazed when the marriage ended, in the same way one is stunned when a graceless pickpocket murders his victim. Today her face is a map of tension. It is this look that forms the greatest resemblance to Nikki. She and Laurel were not just siblings, but novitiates of that common order—the Sisters of Worry.

Laurel's two kids, Danny, fifteen, and his younger sister, Julie, wander in the hallway outside like the walking wounded, shell-shocked and numb, excluded from this family boneyard by the court's Solomonlike wisdom. During Nikki's illness and later, after her death, Laurel's children have spent a good deal of time at my house. It has been a place to go while their mother is trying to get their lives together.

Laurel sits directly in front of me, just beyond the railing, at the counsel table.

"The witness will answer the question," says Hastings. "Do you understand?"

Melanie nods.

"Speak up," says the judge.

"Yes."

Melanie Vega is a woman who thrives in the eye of a storm, a personality that grows on animus like a reactor with its carbon rods removed. She gives the judge a smile, something between coy and confused, as if it were possible to forget Hemple's last query—whether she was screwing Jack when he was still married to Laurel. The subtleties of Family Court. One of the reasons I do not practice here.

"You don't remember the question, Mrs. Vega?" The judge looks down at her in the box.

She makes a face, a wan smile, like maybe with repetition it will get better.

"Perhaps counsel can repeat it," says the judge.

Hemple nods, only too happy to oblige.

"I asked you whether you had carnal relations with Jack Vega during the time that he was married to, and living with, Laurel Vega."

With the term "carnal relations," Melanie's eyebrows are halfway to the crown of her head. It is an expression that says it all, like leave it to lawyers to reserve the "f" word for what they do to each other—and their own clients.

"Carnal relations?" she says.

"Fine," says Hemple. "Sexual relations. Is that better?"

From Melanie's perspective, a woman on the make with another lady's husband, she's not so sure.

"I might have," she says.

"Yes or no? Were you sleeping with the Petitioner while he was married and living with the Respondent?" Hemple is tiring of the mind games.

A slight shrug, a concession by the witness. "What if we were? Consenting adults," she says. She looks up at the judge and smiles. Cute but still adultery.

Hemple moves squarely in front of the witness box, still far enough away not to be seen as coercive.

"While you were doing all this consenting," she says, "with Mr. Vega—did you ever happen to do any of it at the Vega family home—maybe during periods when Laurel Vega was away?"

"We might have. I didn't keep a calendar," she says.

"Might have?"

"Once or twice," says Melanie. A grudging point. She looks the judge square in the eye, brazen, and shrugs as if to say, since his wife wasn't using Jack's bed, somebody else might as well.

All she gets back from Hastings are deep furrows above bushy eyebrows.

"I see. So you were just doing your duty, servicing another woman's husband?"

"Objection." Jack's lawyer is on his feet.

"Withdrawn," says Hemple.

Hastings is shaking his head as if to say that having scored her point, Hemple is now screwing it up.

"Then let me ask you another question," says Hemple. "Were the Vega children in the home when you were sleeping with their father—during the time their mother was away?"

Melanie's eyes dart. She swallows a little saliva. She finally gets the point, but a little late. Hemple's not interested in Melanie's sexual conquests, but in Jack's poor judgment as a father.

I look at Laurel, now sitting a little sideways in her chair, eyeing me for effect, to assess the impact of this latest dirt. I can guess where this information comes from. The kids have talked; Julie and Danny Vega. It is the single consolation for Laurel in an otherwise disastrous custody battle, that the children have taken their mother's side in this brawl.

Their father, Jack, is of that political ilk from the southern part of the state who has lived for a decade like one of the barons of yore, members of a political class who believe they invented privilege and still hold the patent.

If money is the mother's milk of politics, Jack has nursed his lips to a purple hue. According to election records he's tickled the udders of various special interests for more than a half million dollars in the last six months. This is money no doubt he intends to put in his pocket. Term limits in this state now have politicians eating their elders. Jack must either run for Congress against another prince of patronage more encrusted with incumbency than himself or find another job. He now talks of "the people" with acid bitterness for their stunted vision in derailing his gravy train. Now I hear he is making plans to peddle influence as a lobbyist in D.C., where many of his legislative cronies have gone, to the great political Valhalla on the Potomac.

What motivates Jack's action here in court is not entirely clear. But then most legal family disputes are more a matter of venom than reason. He has unleashed a colony of highly paid investigators and therapists, like carpenter ants, to chew on the dry rot of Laurel's character, to show that she is unfit to raise her own children. My own thinking is that Jack is at a crossroads. If he moves east he must either seize custody and take the children or continue to pay child support to Laurel. This has been drawing down his legislative paycheck in a major way, a terminal hemorrhage for a man who likes to drink lunch at the Sutter Club and vacation at Cabo San Lucas.

Several months ago Jack fell in arrears on support. Laurel, through her lawyer, brought contempt proceedings, and then stuck a lance a little deeper by sending copies of her legal papers to the media in Jack's district. It was just before the last election, a press release with a suggested headline:

DEADBEAT LAWMAKER DITCHES FAMILY

In the end, Jack was forced to muster a loan from his political slush fund to come current, or go to jail. He won the election based on a handful of absentee ballots cast before Laurel punctured him with her journalist's javelin.

But Jack has never been one to miss an opportunity for revenge. It came three months ago when Danny was picked up on juvenile charges that raised questions of parental neglect and seemed to undercut Laurel's continued custody of the children. The kid was caught joyriding with three friends in a stolen car. One of the other boys had a juvenile record longer than Melanie's face up on the stand.

"It's a simple question," says Hemple. "Did you sleep with Mr. Vega in the family home when the children were present?"

"Well, they weren't in the room," says Melanie. "I would have noticed."

Laughter from the few courthouse groupies in the audience, and one reporter in the front row, a paper from Jack's old district, getting the local angle.

The judge slaps his gavel on the bench and the laughter stops.

"That's not what I asked," says Hemple. "I asked you whether the children were in the house?" There's an edge to her voice this time.

"I don't know."

"You slept with the man in the family home and you don't know whether the children were present in the house at the time?"

"No."

"Well, who was watching the kids?"

"Not me," says Melanie.

This brings more laughter, a smile from the bailiff whose eyes are glued to Melanie's dress, something more sedate than her usual attire. I have seen her outside the courtroom in a red satin halter-top stretched tight as a drum at the bodice. Melanie Vega is not a big woman, except in the upper regions. I am told she works with weights to maintain this, a regimen that gives new meaning to the maxim "build it and they will come." She has the complexion of a ripe peach, clear, with the softness of film shot through silk gauze. She is the kind of woman for whom "blonde" jokes were invented. At twenty-six, she is young enough to be Jack's daughter. The two have been married now for five months, and Jack is starting to show a little wear. He keeps yawning in court, something that makes me think he and Melanie are doing things other than discussing courtroom strategy in the evenings.

With the practiced skill of a fly caster, Melanie flings her head to the side and whips the blond tresses that have slid over one eye, back out, past her shoulder.

Hemple is looking through some documents, a quick conference with Laurel, a cupped hand to one ear, client to lawyer.

At the counsel table with his own attorney, Jack smiles encouragement to his young bride, like she's doing a standup job.

Hemple is back to the witness in the box.

"Now earlier you testified that Mrs. Vega had a drinking problem?"

"I'm Mrs. Vega," says Melanie.

Hemple looks at her. "The first Mrs. Vega," she says. Laurel's lawyer refuses to concede the point.

"Is this correct? Did Mrs. Vega—Laurel Vega—have a drinking problem?"

There are mean little slits for eyes from Melanie.

"Like a fish," she says.

"I think your words were, 'She always had her head in a bottle.' Is that what you said?"

"That's what I said."

"And what exactly does that mean?"

"An expression," says Melanie.

"I see." Hemple paces a little in front of the witness box for effect.

"So you didn't really mean that she actually put her head inside a bottle."

A pained expression from Melanie, like give me a break. "I meant she was always drunk," she says.

"Always drunk?" Hemple jumps on it.

A face from Melanie. If the lawyer likes this answer so much, maybe she should change it.

Hemple doesn't give her the chance. The first canon of the courtroom. Never talk in absolutes.

"So if she was 'always drunk,' that means that in all the times that you saw Laurel Vega you never saw her sober?"

"That's not what I said."

"Well, you just said she was always drunk."

"Most of the time."

"Ah. So she wasn't drunk all the time, just *most* of the time?" says Hemple.

"Yes."

"So we've gone from someone who 'always has her head in a bottle,' to someone who is *always* drunk, to someone who is drunk just *most* of the time." Hemple waltzes a few steps over in front of the bench. "Sounds like a picture of the recovering alcoholic," she says.

No reply from Melanie. Hastings appears to be dozing up on the bench. Good point, but no score.

Hemple moves on to a Capital Christmas party last year, at which Jack disappeared with Melanie, leaving Laurel with the office help.

"Might someone who saw you drinking at the party say that you had your head in a bottle?" says Hemple.

"I wasn't falling-down slobbering drunk," says Melanie.

"And Mrs. Vega was?"

"Yes."

Hemple shakes her head as if to say are we going to have to do this again?

"Fine—and how many times did you see Mrs. Vega actually fall down at this party?"

Exasperation from Melanie, a look like "picky, picky." "Okay, so I didn't see her fall down."

"I see. Just a little more license?" says Hemple.

"Call it what you want. The lady was a lush. On her ass," she says.

"Another of your sayings?" asks Hemple.

Wary of having to define the anatomy or describe the posture, Melanie does not respond.

"Were you sleeping with Mr. Vega at the time of the Christmas party?"

"I don't remember."

"Why? Because it was not memorable or because by then you'd done it so many times with the Petitioner that you can't keep them straight?"

"Objection, your honor."

"Withdrawn."

A quixotic look from Melanie, a spark of light in the eyes, then an expression that could kill.

"She did drugs too," she says. This little gratuity is added to her testimony like the last dollop of frosting on a crude cake.

"Objection, your honor." Hemple's now taken up the chorus.

"That's a lie and you know it!" Laurel's halfway out of her chair. "I've never done drugs," she says.

"Some people call it an illness." Melanie ignores her, smiling into the growing rage that is Laurel's face at this moment. This last added as a flourish for credibility.

"You'd know about illnesses, wouldn't you?" says Laurel. "My husband picked you up at a cocktail party like some communicable disease."

"Former husband," says Melanie.

The judge gavels them to silence. Laurel sits down and turns to look at me, a face of anger I have not seen before. Perhaps it is a measure, her own assessment of how this case is going. I lean across the railing and tell her to calm down. She is now clearly hurting herself, giving credence to Jack's shrinks and their weasel words about instability.

"And you personally saw this . . . drug use by my client?" says Hemple.

A look in Melanie's eye like maybe she could say yes and wing it. But what to do about the details? Where and when? Who was there? And what they were doing when Laurel was doing drugs?

"No. I didn't actually see it. But I heard about it enough times to know it's true." With this Melanie looks at Jack, sitting with their lawyer at the other counsel table. The smile between them removes any doubt as to the source of this information.

"Move to strike, your honor." Hemple bears down. Not

that it will do much good. Jack will repeat all of this, the dirt as to drinking and drugs, when his turn comes. No doubt whatever Laurel swallowed or inhaled Jack had bought and probably shared.

"The reporter will strike the last answer," says the judge.

"Now," says Hemple, as if she is finally getting down to it, "let me ask you: In the five months that you've been married to Mr. Vega, and in the time before that when the two of you were busy consenting as adults. During this period how many times did you actually see or meet Laurel Vega?"

"We met . . ." She thinks for a moment. "Four . . . no, three times."

"That's all?"

"It was enough," she says.

"You didn't find these meetings pleasant?"

"No."

"I can't imagine why," says Hemple.

"Objection." Jack's lawyer is up again.

"Sustained. Get to the point, counsel."

"The first time you met Mrs. Vega was she drunk?"

"I can't remember."

"You do remember the first time you met her?"

A long sigh from Melanie. "Yes."

"Can you tell the court the circumstances of that meeting?"

"It was at Jack's home . . ."

"The home he then shared with his wife, Laurel, and their children?" Hemple would like to paint Beaver Cleaver running across the lawn with his school books strapped by a belt, while Melanie was busy humping their old man upstairs.

"Yes—it was at the home." Melanie looks at Hemple like maybe she'd like to meet this bitch in the alley outside after court.

The lawyer is all sweetness and smiles.

"And would you please tell the court what you were doing when you first encountered Laurel Vega in her home?"

A look from Melanie, something between anger and a train-struck deer. "We, ah . . . We were in the living room . . ."

" 'We' meaning who?"

"Jack and I," says Melanie. "And she came in." Melanie nods toward Laurel at the counsel table.

"You mean Mrs. Vega, who was then Jack's wife?"

"Laurel—whatever you want to call her," says Melanie.

"Then we'll call her 'Mr. Vega's wife,' at least at that point in time."

"Fine."

"And what were you doing—you and Jack—when his wife came in?"

"Umm." Melanie is stalling for time. A lot of anxiety focused in the eyes. She makes several false starts on an answer. Then suddenly a smile. Resolution has descended like a chariot from the heavens.

"Necking," she says. "We were necking." She settles back in her chair, satisfied with this.

"Necking." Hemple says this, nodding her head as if she understands. "Can you describe this necking to us, or is this just another of your expressions?"

"We were kissing," says Melanie.

"Kissing?"

"And hugging," she adds.

"Kissing and hugging." More nodding from the understanding lawyer. "And can you describe to the court your attire? How were you dressed when you were doing all this kissing and hugging?"

"I don't understand the question."

"Isn't it a fact that the first time you met Laurel Vega you were completely naked on the carpet of her living room floor, engaged in full-blown sex with her husband?"

This brings a lot of forced indignation to Melanie's expression, a prim posture in the box that speaks loads of denial.

"No. That's not true," says Melanie. "I can state categorically, for a fact, that is untrue,'' she says. ''Because Jack didn't like it by mouth.''

There's a second of dead silence, then open laughter from the audience as it settles in. Vega's head is in his hands. Melanie looks out wide-eyed. Clearly she's misunderstood something.

''Who told you that?'' she says. A lot of fluster and denial, what Shakespeare said about protest.

In a voice marked by uncertainty almost inaudible: ''Jack didn't like it,'' she says, as if maybe this will clear up any confusion. It brings another swell of laughter.

The judge raps his gavel and this subsides to little tiffs, a contagion of muffled barks and hacks.

''We just didn't do that.'' Melanie puts moral tone to her voice this time, leaving it unclear whether like Shakers they didn't do the act at all, or if it's just the oral stuff they shunned.

In her eyes I can tell Melanie's still wondering what it is that she's gotten wrong.

''Well, thank you for that insight,'' says Hemple. She starts to move on. With points like this you don't press.

For the most part, the two days of hearings over contested child custody have been like a legally sanctioned gang bang. While Hastings is not likely to give much credence to the likes of Melanie, a legion of experts hired by Jack have been beating up on Laurel with professional jargon, enough syndromes of dependence to cause real problems for her case, to leave Hastings with a serious doubt as who is best to now take the children.

''How much more do you have for this witness?'' The judge cuts Hemple off.

She asks for a couple of seconds to confer with her client. Hemple's at the counsel table talking with Laurel. Clearly they are concerned about this latest revelation on drugs. Hemple will now have to draw and quarter Jack on the stand to have any chance to get them back to level ground.

"An hour," she says. "Maybe more."

Melanie's expression droops like a basset hound's.

"And how many more witnesses?"

"Just one," says Hemple. She looks over at Vega like maybe he might wish to marinate parts of his anatomy overnight for the roasting he is sure to get in the morning.

"Then we're going to adjourn for the night. And we'll finish tomorrow," says the judge. "Is that understood?"

Jack's lawyer is on his feet, nodding, like the sooner the better. With Jack on the stand, the press will be here in spades.

"Your honor, one more thing," he says. "We would like a conference in chambers with opposing counsel after adjournment."

Hastings slaps the gavel and is down off the bench, trailed by the lawyers to his chambers.

Outside the courtroom I am leaning over the water fountain for a drink when he comes up behind me.

"I guess we've both seen better times," he says.

Jack Vega's voice has the quality of a wood rasp drawn across the broken edge of a tin can, the vocal legacy of cigars and alcohol. He's tracked me to this little corridor and boxed me in between the water cooler and the rest rooms. Jack's idea of a good meeting place.

When I turn he is smiling, standing there with his hand out extended in greeting, a goofy look on his face. To those he has never married, or conceived, Jack is probably harmless.

"What can I say, Bro?" He still refers to me as his brother-in-law, which we have not been for some time now. It's an awkward moment. I give no reply, but stand looking at his offered hand until it is dropped, limp at his side.

I can see Laurel looking, focusing on me over her lawyer's shoulder as she and Hemple talk fifty feet away. Whatever happened in the judge's chambers has them agitated. A lot of hand gestures by the lawyer, manual conversation. But at this moment I am certain Laurel is hearing none of this, wondering instead how I could possibly exchange anything but profanities with this man.

Having his peace-offered hand rejected, Jack is now posturing for defense, circling the wagons around his ego.

His hair has less gray, more color than I remember from our last family outing, a year ago. It seems Melanie has driven Jack to a different kind of bottle. There's a bald patch the size of a pitcher's mound on top. This is surrounded by tufts and wisps in sundry tones of orange. Still, by any measure he is a handsome man in the way middle-aged and austere men can be.

He is like most of the pols I have known; a wannabe statesman, come up rug merchant. Over the years he has managed to learn a little style, and now wears it like the thousand-dollar suit that frames his angular body. The freckles that seem to run over his face like flyspecks seem more pronounced, a kind of ruddy out-of-door look. Jack has been in the sun. He lives for golf, especially the courses peopled by celebrities where they run a water wagon with iced cocktails to every hole.

He passes some pleasantries, that I look good, that life seems to be treating me well. This despite the fact that my wife is now dead, something Jack seems to avoid. He is testing for other more pleasant subjects, anything that might lead to a friendly opening. All the while he is bobbing and weaving, prancing from one foot to the other, up on his toes. This is a nervous tic that Jack has never controlled. In the Capitol, among the lobbyists who ply their trade kissing collective legislative ass and twisting arms, Jack Vega is known as the Dancer, at least behind his back. Like his voting record, Vega's body seems to constantly migrate toward the last loud noise.

"I'm glad at least that you didn't take her case," he says, "for old times' sake."

He's bounding on his toes in front of me like a child facing an urgent call of nature. For those who know Jack, this motion is a measure of his rising anxiety.

"Divorces and family bloodlettings aren't my bag," I tell him.

"I understand," he says. "Still, you coulda stayed a little more neutral."

"Did you want me to sit in the center aisle?" I say.

He laughs a little too much, then gives me a look, the kind of tight smile I've seen on some men just before they call someone out of earshot an asshole.

As I look in the distance, Jack's son, Danny, is on a bench against the far wall studying his mother with her lawyer. He is lost in this setting, looking a little like the cartoon caricatures of Ichabod from *Sleepy Hollow*. For all of his six-foot size he has yet to grow into his ears. He lives for sports, mostly baseball and basketball, watching and playing, and fills a hollow leg with six meals a day.

His sister, Julie, is standing a few feet away from him, waiting for an opening to approach her mother.

Julie would not be here except that her mother has forced her to attend. The girl wanted to stay home with her friends, party and frolic as if nothing had happened. Laurel thinks she is spoiled. I think it is Julie's own defense mechanism.

"It's okay," Jack tells me. "I suppose you gotta do what you gotta do."

"You mean my presence here, with Laurel?"

"Yeah."

"This is a labor of love," I tell him.

He nods like he comprehends this, forming his own favorable interpretation. But Jack doesn't get my meaning, that this has only partly to do with family ties, the fact that Nikki and Laurel were sisters. I stand up for Laurel and the kids now, in the opposite corner from this man, for the same reason I might run over a rattlesnake on the hot pavement in front of my home.

"I understand," he says. "Families. It's the thing about blood and water."

I'm thinking sharks. He's thinking family ties. Jack is giving me absolution, his forgiveness for my bad taste in siding with my sister-in-law. All the while he's doing a number from Busby Berkeley, up on his toes.

He offers his condolences for Nikki. I don't remember him at the funeral. I tell him this.

A few awkward starts and he makes amends. "I didn't know if I'd be welcome," he says.

I make a face, leaving him to wonder.

He asks after Sarah. I tell him she is fine.

To our right, Melanie emerges from the ladies' room as if on cue. I wonder if she's been listening through the lavatory's louvered outer door. She comes up and does her own straight routine next to her husband's soft-shoe.

"Did you meet my wife?" he says.

I look over at Laurel. I'm not sure this is the right time.

Still, Jack makes the introduction. I nod and smile. She gives me a look like a store clerk wondering if I've shoplifted.

She stands silent for several seconds as we pass idle chatter, then finally looks at Jack and says: "Did you ask him?" To Melanie the shortest distance between two points is a direct assault.

"Gimme time." A look from Vega at his young wife. This does not put her off.

"Jack's got something to talk to you about," she says.

He coughs, clears his throat, smiles at me as if to say, "Pushy women." Jack's prance-in-place seems to move to a canter.

"We're wondering," he says. He looks over at Melanie. "We're wondering if maybe you could talk to her?" He nods toward Laurel across the corridor.

I give him a look, a question mark.

"Maybe talk some reason to her. This stuff is really hurting the kids," he says. He's talking about the verbal bloodshed in the courtroom.

"What the hell does she want, anyway?" he says.

I am dumbfounded by this tactless frontal assault.

"Well, you know I could never read her," he tells me. "Maybe that's why our marriage failed. Lack of communication," he says.

That and Jack's dozen mistresses.

"Why don't you read her pleadings?" I tell him. "I think it's all pretty clear. She wants the kids," I say.

"Sure," he tells me. "But you know what I mean? What does she *really* want?"

I am looking at him, unsure that even he is this dense. The confirmation is written in his eyes. Jack's looking for some crass financial bottom line, the price to buy his own children from their mother. For the first time I wonder if maybe Jack has doubts about his case.

"You think she wants something else?" I'm incredulous.

"Sure," he says. "Talk to her. She'll listen to you. We're reasonable people," he says.

I shake my head, not the kind of gesture that says no, but a show of disbelief. "You want me to spell it out for you? Laurel wants one thing—the kids." I say this louder so that maybe half the people in the hallway can hear it. But Jack is impervious to embarrassment and relentless when he wants something.

"She's not capable of dealing with them," he tells me. "Hell, I've offered her the summers." He looks at Melanie and they both nod like this is a deal. Six weeks during the summer, a week at Christmas.

"I'll even fly the kids out and back." He lays this added treat on like the clincher on closure at an auto sale. Melanie's nodding at his side, batting her eyes as if to emphasize the weighty value of this offer.

"Not exactly like having the kids, is it, Jack?" I look at him.

"Well, how the hell do you think *I* feel? They're my kids too," he says.

"Laurel's not taking them out of the state," I remind him.

"What do you want me to do? I gotta make a living." Jack

makes it sound like tassel-loafered lobbying is a blue-collar job.

"Besides, the kids are getting older," says Melanie. "Danny's starting to get into trouble. The boy's picked up with the wrong crowd," she tells me. "We think we could do a better job."

"I didn't know you were so maternal," I say.

She gives me a look, straightens her skirt with flattened palms on curving hips, as if to say, "What do you think this body is for?"

Jack steps in before his wife can get into it with me.

"Did you see the police report?" he says. "On Danny?"

"I've seen it. What can I say? Kids get in trouble," I tell him.

"Come on, Paul." He gives me a hearty smile, then gets personal. He puts one hand on my shoulder—something from the male fraternity.

"You and I," he says, "we know the realities. Laurel lives in a dream world. The woman's had a sheltered life." He makes it sound like he was slaving in the vineyard through their marriage while Laurel was eating bonbons.

"That was fine when she was growing up and her father was paying the bills, when we were living together and I was supporting her."

"And there are some," I say, "who might argue that she was raising three children back then."

Jack ignores this, but the smile fades and his tone becomes more earnest. "She can't take care of Danny and Julie the way we can, and she knows it. You and I know it. Hell, if there's problems, we can give them the proper counseling by professionals, put 'em in private schools. Can she afford that?"

"Maybe you should tell the court to increase your spousal and child support," I say.

He looks at me dead in the eyes. "I thought maybe we could talk reason," he says. "This is your niece and nephew who are in trouble," he tells me.

"And I feel for them," I say. "They are now children from a broken family, with all of the attendant problems." I dump it, the divorce and all of its progeny, back in his lap.

Melanie gives me a look, something defensive, like maybe the subject is shifting to the question of home-wrecking.

"You sound like some touchie-feelie therapist," he says. Suddenly the touted professional counseling he could give the kids sounds like a labor performed by quacks.

"Did you talk to him?" I ask.

Vega looks at me, dense. I've lost him with the question.

"Danny?" I say. "After he was arrested, did you talk to him?"

"Sure. I chewed his ass."

"But did you talk with him?"

"What's to talk about? The kid needs some discipline," he says.

"That's something only his father can give a boy." Melanie gives me a quick up-and-down with her head like this is holy writ direct from the source.

"The kids are getting older," says Jack, "and she can't control them." Then he brings up the issue of Laurel's drinking.

Now I'm getting it, both barrels from the two of them.

"She drank," I say. "Past tense. She hasn't touched a drop since this started, even with all the crap laid on by your witnesses."

"Yeah. Until the next time," says Melanie.

"It's been nice." I start to go laterally to get around the two of them. Our conversation has become too loud, too obvious. Laurel is making overt moves to break away from her lawyer and Julie.

"Yeah? Well, it's gonna get a whole lot worse," says Melanie, "unless she's willing to talk reason."

Prancing in place, shifting his weight, Jack gives her a look that could kill.

Their case is over, all their evidence, their witnesses presented. I wonder what Melanie is talking about. I linger for a moment, an invitation for her to open her mouth, maybe put her foot in it.

But Jack has her by the hand, squeezing her fingers till the ends are white.

"Talk to her," says Jack. "Tell her to be reasonable." They start to move off. Suddenly behind them I see Laurel, coming on like a locomotive at a crossing, her eyes ablaze, two white-hot coals. She swings it over one shoulder with both hands like a misaimed hammer throw in the Olympics, and three pounds of purse crash across Jack's shoulder. The purse misses Melanie's head by an inch and instead catches Melanie's own little bag, a beaded thing carried under one arm, sending it careening to the floor with Laurel's.

There's lipstick, compacts, and wallets everywhere, slapping and sliding on hard terrazzo, the objects women carry scattered for the world to see. A plastic brush caroms across the floor where it ricochets off the polished shoe of a bailiff outside Department 14.

Before I can move, Laurel's into it with the broken strap of her purse, gripping this strip of leather as a handy garrote and seizing Melanie's throat. For some reason this venom is not unleashed on Jack but Melanie Vega.

I grab one arm before she can move.

Jack is caught in the middle between the two women. He has both hands and forearms to his head now, covering up like a prizefighter backed into a corner. He's wearing a woman's hanky near the crotch of his pants. A lacy black thing like a doily, it clings to the wool nap of his suit.

The bailiff's moving toward us.

I grab Laurel by an arm and put myself in front of her, blocking her way. She has an athletic vitality, a sensuous muscularity. As I lean against her I am amazed by the mass of rippled muscle in her arms, and her legs of coiled spring.

"What's going on?" he says. The bailiff's best command voice.

The guy recognizes me and nods.

"Just a disagreement," I tell him.

"Disagreement, my ass." Jack's coming out of his crouch. "Bitch tried to nail my wife with her purse," he says. Not an ounce of fat on her body, thin narrow hips, feeling Laurel's upper arms, Jack's fortunate she didn't take a swing and come up short. He'd be on his ass, cold-cocked on the floor.

"You can use the lawyers' conference room." The bailiff seems interested in avoiding problems, ducking a formal charge that will mean a lot of paperwork.

Melanie with two fingers picks the woman's hanky off her husband's pants and lets it float to the floor. She gives the bailiff an imperious look like he should do something more.

He does. He picks up the handkerchief and hands it to Melanie. "Belong to you?" he says.

It is the closest thing to spit I have seen from a woman. Hemple's picked up Laurel's purse. I take the handkerchief from the cop and stuff it inside. People are picking up objects from the floor.

"You bitch. You stay away from my kids." Laurel is pumping up the venom again, a second wind. "I wish it was a goddamned sledgehammer." She's holding up the purse by a piece of its broken strap.

I'm pushing her away now. The bailiff is giving us one of those dubious law-enforcement looks, perhaps second thoughts as to whether he should ask the victim if she wants to press charges.

"Ask her what she did." Laurel's in my face now as I block her with my chest and move her toward the conference room.

"And you," she says. Laurel turns it on Jack now. "You don't give a damn if she destroys your own children." She calls Melanie a liar, among other assorted and more odious epithets.

I have no idea what she's talking about, but lawyer's instinct tells me it has no place here in a public corridor.

Hemple's now joined us. She's coaxing Laurel along from behind like a tugboat at the stern.

Melanie's talking to the bailiff, all hands and facial gestures, like maybe she can convince him to get out his handcuffs. He gives her a face, lots of sympathy and equivocation. All the while he's backstepping toward the courtroom, picking up things, offering them to Melanie for her purse, no doubt wishing he'd been looking the other way when this started.

Inside, behind louvered blinds and enclosed glass, Hemple gives me the news.

Laurel is still too angry to talk.

"It's Julie's school," says the lawyer. "They caught another girl with drugs. The kid claims she got them from Julie."

To the extent that anything involving adolescents can surprise me, I am startled by this. From every appearance my niece's only narcotic to date is the adulation of her peers. To this she is heavily addicted. I wonder if it has led to heavier things.

"Crack cocaine," says Hemple. "The other girl, her friend, had enough for personal use, not dealing."

Thank God for little favors. "Are they bringing charges?" I ask.

Hemple makes a face likes she's not sure. "They caught the kid three days ago. They're still investigating."

"How did Jack find out so fast?"

"What I'm wondering," says Hemple, like maybe there's some artful device going down here, Jack and Melanie engaged in creative self-help. A kid caught on charges might be willing to fabricate a story, implicate some innocent for a price. The rules of commerce. Jack is not above seeing the social problems of his children's school as an ocean of opportunity, a place with more substances of abuse than the average pharmacist's shelf.

"It gets worse," says Hemple.

"It's a lie," says Laurel. She looks at me stone cold, an edge to the expression in her eyes. We have reached bottom, like the thump of an elevator in the basement. To Laurel this is now something fundamental, a tenet I must believe.

Still, denials are the small talk of the lawyer's venue, more common than discussions of the weather, and Hemple ignores her.

"According to the kid," she says, "Julie made admissions."

"What kind of admissions?"

"The kid says Julie told her the stuff came from home, a stash her mother kept in the house. What's worse, Melanie has confirmed this. She says Julie also told her the same thing, that her mother used drugs."

"It's not true," says Laurel. "She's a lying bitch."

I might expect her to fold, to be fighting back tears, driven to the edges of the glass enclosure by the charge. Instead she is standing, head erect, shoulders squared, shaking her head, and in clear unassailable language telling us that this is crap.

Laurel came to the divorce with a schoolgirl's faith in the justice of courts. It has been rocked by the slow recognition that money speaks here as clearly as anywhere in life. If I believe her, and I do, she is now getting a cynic's first taste of how the scales can tip with the preponderance of perjury.

As I stand and study her, at the opposite end of the small conference table, standing in the glare of fluorescence, there is a cold recognition, like a dark cloud, that passes across her face.

"I'm gonna lose the kids," she says. "Aren't I?"

CHAPTER
2

"Wake up, kiddo." I whisper softly into my daughter's ear, not enough to rouse her. The TV has gone white with snow, a local station that signs off the cable at the witching hour.

Sarah is dressed like some fairy princess—a Halloween party earlier in the evening with some kids from her school.

I'm sprawled in the recliner in the family room, my feet up on the pop-up footrest.

We've fallen asleep, Sarah in my lap. We have done this now three nights running. Without Nikki to impose a regimen on our lives, it seems we are adrift, anchorless, without the hale habits of life.

I shift in the chair and Sarah clings to me, her little fingers digging into my shirt like the claws of a kitten. As I move she gives off a feckless moan, then little mewings.

I look at the clock. It is after one in the morning. There is no chance of waking her. I lift her, dead weight in my arms, and carry her off to her bedroom.

She will sleep in the chiffon of pretend royalty tonight. She can change in the morning, before school.

These days I worry what her teacher, or some of the mothers must think, when they see my daughter. Her clothes are clean but not pressed. Perhaps it is merciful that Sarah, who was born a clotheshorse, has with her mother's passing lost the fascination for things feminine. The dresses she used to wear,

frilly things of pride to Nikki, now hang like listless ghosts in
Sarah's closet. My faculty for color coordination has never
embraced my own tie rack. It is painful to the senses when
applied to a little girl's colored tights and tops. The braids and
fine ponytails that seemed to take Nikki five minutes defy my
thick fingers, so that most mornings Sarah's bountiful hair now
looks like hay in a Kansas windstorm. When we play games
together these days it is not jump rope or jacks, but baseball,
or tossing hoops in the yard, where I hold her up near the rim
so she can do her own version of slam-dunk. When she trudges
off to school each day, backpack slumping across her scrawny
shoulders, I wonder if by yoking her affections to her widowed
father's wagon my daughter has doomed herself to life as a
tomboy.

I pull off her socks, cover her, a peck on the cheek, then
flip on her night-light.

Down the hall in my room I can hear her breathing in the
child monitor on my nightstand. I rummaged through a dozen
boxes in the garage to find this. Nikki had packed it away
when Sarah turned three, when the worries of SIDS and other
parental paranoia had passed. But in the weeks after Nikki's
death, Sarah suffered bouts of crying that tore at my soul. I
would go to her in her room and hold her, cradled in my arms,
while she asked questions I could not answer. Why her father,
who could do all things, could not bring Mommy back? Where
had she gone? Would we ever see her again? Staring down in
her round baleful olive eyes, I soothed her with a litany of
faith—that her mother was with God, that she was happy, that
from the clouds in heaven she watched over her little girl—
and that one day we would all be together again, forever. And
in my soul of souls I hoped beyond all that I knew that this
was true. Then Sarah would sleep, secure in the promise of a
father's wishes.

In a daze I step into the shower tub. Cold water laps my
legs to midcalf. I'd forgotten drawing Sarah a bath, hours ago
now. As I pull the plug I hear the phone ringing on the bedside

table. I run, wrapping a towel around my waist for fear the
phone may wake Sarah. Who the hell can be calling at this
hour? It cannot be good news.

"Mr. Madriani."

"Yes."

"Gail Hemple here."

"What is it?"

"I'm at Jack Vega's house," she says. "You'd better get
over here as fast as you can."

"What's wrong?"

"The police are here," she says. "I got a call an hour ago
from Vega's lawyer."

It hits me like an iced dagger—in the cynical center of my
lawyer's brain—Laurel and her temper. She has done some
foolish act of harassment, broken a window, smashed a wind-
shield, inscribed her initials with a key in the satin finish of
Jack's state-leased $80,000 Lexus. After the allegations of
drugs in court, I knew I should have had her here in the house,
overnight. I spent two hours before dinner grilling Julie and
her mother on the charges. Each in her turn denied them
roundly.

"What did she do?" I say.

There's a stutter on the phone as Hemple regroups. She
knows who I'm talking about. Clearly her client has done
something.

"I can't talk now," she says. "Don't say anything more.
I'm in my car, on the cellular. Just answer one question. Is
she with you now?"

"Laurel?" I ask.

"Just yes or no," she says.

"No. She's probably home."

"She's not," says Hemple.

"Where are the kids?" I ask. "What the hell's going on?"

"Can't talk. Get over here," she says, "now."

"Sarah's sleeping," I say. "I'll have to get someone to watch her."

"Do it," she says, and hangs up.

Mrs. Bailey, the next-door neighbor, may never forgive me—a phone call in the middle of the night, another urgent request for help. She is every family's grandmother, sixty-two, strait-laced, and alone. A churchgoing lady of conservative habits, she lives for the welfare of little children and her weekly Bible classes, in that order. I'm afraid I've taken advantage of her weakness for kids. She's been my perpetual crutch, baby-sitting in every pinch since Nikki died. She will not take money for this, so I wait for her back fence to blow down in a windstorm, or her car to conk out some morning, any way to reciprocate for her kindness by the performance of some manly duty. To date, everything she owns is upright and work-ing, more than I can say for myself at this moment.

I'm wiping sleep from my eyes, gripping the steering wheel with both hands as I drive.

Jack and Melanie Vega live on a cul-de-sac off of Forty-second Avenue, in a large colonial gambrel, white pillars on a setback of manicured lawn larger than some city parks.

Two blocks from their house and there is an ethereal glow to the night sky, fogged by the vapors of early autumn, the ghostly colors flashing blue, amber, and red. Two patrol cars have the intersection leading to Jack's house blocked off, the only way in or out.

I lie to one of the cops at the intersection, tell him I am a relative, present tense. He passes me through, directs me to park on the other side of the street.

A fire truck is at the curb directly in front of Jack's house, its diesel engine droning a dull monotone.

I wonder for a moment. I have never thought of Laurel as any kind of firebug, then dismiss the thought. These days if your kid samples snail bait they dispatch a hook-and-ladder, the vehicle of choice in any emergency.

There's a growing crowd at the curb, a few drive-by rubberneckers and neighbors on my side of the street. Some bold souls are across on the other side, closer to the house, pressing one of the cops and the firemen for information. I look for Gail Hemple, but see no sign.

I park the car and walk, milling with the neighbors, most of whom are in bathrobes and slippers, a guy in pants, his jacket zipped to the throat, and sockless loafers. His collar is muffled up against the cold. He's plying an older woman for the latest rumors wafting through the crowd, what she saw or heard. A lot of shrugging shoulders from the old lady.

"One of the policemen said something about a victim inside," she says.

Suddenly there's a knot in my stomach, cold sweat on my forehead. Hemple's voice on the phone, her tone, was not the siren of concern over some mild monkeyshine cast as vendetta.

The driveway, the only break in a six-foot wrought-iron fence that seals off the front of the house, is barred with yellow police tape. Guys in plain clothes are wandering back and forth between the house and parked cars, the little satchels of forensics in their hands.

The portico of Jack's house is a miniature of the executive mansion, everything but an honor guard and the Secret Service. Impressing the world is what Jack lives for. I have a clear view of the entry, wide open, lit like a Christmas tree, Corinthian columns all around.

There is a message conveyed by all of this—a victim without the urgent care of racing ambulances. The thought, the limited possibilities, leave me with a chill.

I tried four times to call Laurel at her apartment on the cellular on my way over here. There was no answer. I figure the kids must be with her.

"Mr. Madriani." I hear a soft voice behind me and turn. It's Gail Hemple. She's standing with a small group twenty feet away, another woman and a couple arm-in-arm, near some bushes in the driveway of a house. The woman with Hemple looks vaguely familiar, a face I recognize to which I cannot put a name, someone from a past life. The couple, man and woman, young and shivering in the cold, stir no embers of recognition.

I move toward them and Hemple meets me halfway, a little huddle out of earshot.

"What's going on?" I say.

Long sigh from her. "Bad news," she whispers. "There's been a shooting."

She can tell from my look that this does not surprise me, having wallowed in the sea of rumors getting here. I wait for the bottom line.

She reads my mind. "Melanie Vega's dead," she says.

This takes my breath. My mind racing.

"Where's Laurel?"

"You tell me," she says.

"What about Jack?"

She makes a face, a question mark.

This takes a while for me to absorb, all the implications. "Maybe a burglary?" I say this hopefully. Hemple shakes her head. She has no idea. "The cops aren't talking," she tells me. But from the look on her face I can tell she is considering another scenario.

"I called Laurel's house as soon as Vega's lawyer called me," she says, with the same result as I.

"The kids?"

Palms up, shrugging shoulders. She has no idea.

"Wonderful."

While we are talking the woman with the familiar face, the one Gail had been talking to, comes up behind her. Good-looking, auburn hair, dressed in a jogging suit, the look of something grabbed from the closet at the sound of sirens.

I think maybe she wants to talk to Hemple. Then she looks straight at me, smiles, and says, "Paul. It's good to see you again. Sorry it's under such circumstances."

She is now feasting on my blank stare, poorly masked by a witless smile. I give her a nod, something that conveys I haven't got a clue.

She laughs. "Dana Colby," she says. "Law School." A little lilting uplift in her voice. "It's been a long time. I was a year behind you," she says.

"Ah, yes. I remember," I say. But my voice is filled with the distrust of my own memory. The game of names and faces has never been my strong suit.

As we stand and talk, recall sets in like the chills before a flu, vague recollections of this woman kicking my ass somewhere in a courtroom. It's been some years since I've seen her. One of a dozen at the university back before the female rush. If I remember right, she was the one whose bones we all dreamed of jumping. Five-foot-ten, auburn hair, eyes like shimmering amethyst, a face like an angel, with a body that only God could have made. She has not changed. In the genes department she is what every woman thinks of when told that life is unfair.

Right now all I want is to get Hemple alone where we can talk. The couple that seems to be with Colby have moved up a notch, a young man and woman, mid-thirties. They seem to be attached to Colby like the stitched-on shadow of the great Pan.

Dana Colby looks at me, hesitates for a moment as if in doubt. "I'd introduce you," she says to them, "but I'm afraid I don't know your names."

"George Merlow—my wife, Kathy." The guy nods at Colby and smiles. I shake his hand. "We live on the block," he says. "This is very disturbing. Just moved in," he tells us.

Kathy Merlow has a long and sallow face, dirty-blond hair, and a bedded look like maybe she's been sick. She is a small woman, her hand is twined around her husband's arm and lost within the deep pocket of his wool overcoat, a tweed affair, its collar turned up around a five o'clock shadow and dark stringy hair. As he turns and stoops to whisper in his wife's ear, I can see George Merlow's thinning locks, arranged in a short ponytail. He has the grungy look of celebrity on vacation. There is a slight accent to his voice, something east of Omaha, maybe Massachusetts or New York, but not hard or fixed, like maybe the guy is rootless, that he's moved around a lot.

As I look at him there's a lot of agitation in the eyes, nervous posturing. Standing in the street, waiting for the coroner's wagon, I attribute this anxiety to the events of the evening.

Our little group is of a mind. "It's just awful." Kathy Merlow's first words. "Shootings on the news every night since we arrived. A violent town," she says.

It sounds like Capital City has not made a good impression. I think maybe these people are from Mayberry, visions of whistling kids with fishing poles.

"You walk on the street, you become bullet bait," says the guy.

"Like any other big city." Colby's chorus to the couple. "Still, we could have hoped for a better welcome wagon." Colby's looking at the coroner's van, which has just pulled in to the driveway of Jack's house. Two cops ease the tape barricade back in place.

Hemple gives me a look, like "let's hope the cops are having the same thoughts about random violence."

I'm praying that maybe Laurel has an alibi—off doin' Midnight Mass with the Sisters of Mercy. With Laurel, since the divorce, you never know. One night she showed up at our house with a Catholic priest. Nikki was commode-hugging sick, the aftermath from a session of chemo. I was left to entertain Laurel and his eminence in my pajamas at two in the morning. Seems Laurel was feeling particularly sinful that night. She ended up last in line for confession, and afterward with a friend invited their young confessor out to dinner. After doing penance over cocktails, Laurel managed to ditch her female friend and convince her companion in black to loose his collar while they did a few sashays on the dance floor. By the time they reached my house, shit-faced as they were, Laurel was busy putting the bans of celibacy to the ultimate test. There are times when my sister-in-law can be the devil in drag.

Still, I don't think she could kill.

"Understand you're related?" says Colby. She's looking at me, nodding toward the house behind tape, in bright lights.

I look at Hemple. She gives me an expression, like "me and my big mouth."

"One-time brother-in-law," I tell her. "Past tense."

"Oh." Silence like she's stumbled over some aging uncle's peccadillo.

"You live in the neighborhood?" I ask her.

"A few blocks away." She nods in a direction over her shoulder somewhere. The years have been kind to her.

"You?" she says.

"Just passing by." As this escapes my lips I think, at two in the morning Colby must wonder what tavern I'm coming from. Still, I'm not anxious to advertise that I am here on business, in pursuit of the wayward Laurel, or to feed suspicions that she might be involved in the activities across the street.

It seems the two women—Hemple and Colby—have done their thing together on the Queen's Bench, a local club of women lawyers, where they've followed each other through the chairs of high office, part of the network for advancement among the fairer set.

"Dana's with the U.S. Attorney's office," says Hemple. "White-collar unit." She says this with emphasis, like hanging a sign—"prosecutor present."

"Ah." It hits me. Where we did battle, Colby and I. A sentencing matter in the federal courts, back when I was with the firm. Dana Colby cleaned my clock. A federal district judge, another woman, probably one of their clan, put my client away for an ice age. There is not enough good behavior this side of heaven to have seen his release.

"You look cold." Colby's talking to Kathy Merlow.

"She's just getting over the flu," says her husband.

"You should take her home," says Colby.

All of this is going right past Kathy Merlow. Her gaze is fixed on Jack's house.

"Do you think they'll bring her out soon?"

For a moment I'm not sure who Kathy Merlow is talking about. Then it strikes me. She's been bit by morbid curiosity. She wants to see Melanie Vega's body cloaked in its shroud.

"Did you know her?" I ask.

She looks at me for the first time, wide-eyed.

"Oh, no. No. We never met." She seems emphatic on the point. "We didn't know either of them. We just haven't been here that long. We don't know anybody, really," she says, big round eyes looking at me. She seems relieved by the thought that the Merlows and Vegas were strangers, as if perhaps violence is something contagious, and that with distance comes immunity like a vaccine.

"I think we should be getting home." George is looking at his wife like maybe all of this has been too much for her. He looks at Colby, then whispers something in her ear. She nods, but no smile. I suspect he's making amends to get his wife out of here.

"Come on, let's go," he says. He tugs Kathy Merlow toward the street. "Nice to meet you," he tells me. "Wish it coulda been under better circumstances," he says. They wander off toward the street.

"Nice couple," says Colby.

"Yeah." I watch them as they go, across the cul-de-sac and up the driveway to their house.

"But they must be recluses," I say.

"Why's that?"

"They don't know the Vegas but they live next door."

She looks at me, a puzzled expression. "You're right," she says.

Suddenly my attention is drawn to the "south lawn," to the portico that is Jack's fantasy of helicopters and grand trips of state. There's action on the front porch. I see Vega and another man come out. Jack's scanning the crowd in front of the house. Even from this distance his image is one of death warmed. His face haggard, there are bags the size of blimps under his eyes. But my focus is riveted on the guy behind him. My blood runs cold at the sight of Jimmy Lama, the cop from hell.

Lama and I go back a ways, to a time years ago when I had him drawn and quartered on charges of excessive force in the arrest of one of my clients. More recently we tangled in the trial of Talia Potter, when Lama, in violation of a court-issued gag order, leaked damaging information to the press, seeming to link me to the murder of Talia's husband, Ben Potter, the senior partner of my old law firm. Talia and I had been an item. To my discredit we'd had a brief affair during a period when I was separated from Nikki. But Lama's efforts to draw me into Ben's murder came to naught when Talia was acquitted of her husband's murder, and the riddle of who did it and why was solved. On Lama's scorecard I am still ahead. Jimmy was disciplined for violating the court's order, a suspension without pay, and a demotion.

Vega's searching the crowd, looking, shading his eyes against the glare of the lights, police vehicles in his driveway, some with their light bars gyrating with synchronous color. Then suddenly Vega points with an outstretched arm, finger like a cocked pistol, Jimmy Lama at his shoulder taking a bead—dead center on me.

"Counselor. Fancy seeing you," he says. "And I thought life was too short."

The smile on Jimmy Lama's face is nothing less than sinister. Lama's most dominant feature is his blockhouse build. Lama is square, from the angle of his jaw to what is left of the hair on his head, leveled by shears to a flattop. The haircut is a holdover from his days in the military. I am told he once did M.P. duty in an embassy behind the iron curtain. I have often wondered for which side.

Lama and I have a long and untoward history, a level of enmity that rivals things between Arabs and Israelis. Our respective bunkers have been the courthouse and the cop shops of this town. Lama stands about five-nine, though his moral stature is somewhat more dwarfed. He is ambitious to a fault, and corrupted in the way many aspiring people are, not by money so much as by the pursuit of upward mobility. His career has been stunted to a degree by our last outing. He has spent the last three years getting back to level ground following the disciplinary action for which he blames me. Tonight I wear this like a badge of honor.

The young cop, the uniform who hauled me off the street, introduces me like I don't know Lama.

"So it's lieutenant again," I say. "That explains the noise," I tell him, "that old familiar sound."

"What's that?" says Lama.

"The scraping of the barrel downtown," I say.

Mean little slits for eyes. He utters some profanity, something that ends with his ass, and commands me to pucker. He says this low under his breath so that Hemple and the other cops can't hear it. Maybe it is true that one mellows with age. Jimmy Lama has learned a little restraint. Ten years ago my words would have earned a change in the contour of my head, conforming to the ripples in the handle of his flashlight.

Lama's sitting, sprawled in a leather club chair by the fireplace. He's nibbling on a toothpick, a pacifier since he gave up smoking a few years ago.

Gail Hemple has come with me inside Jack's house, though she wasn't summoned. I think Hemple is planning on playing lawyer-client games with Lama, privileges and immunities, trying to draw fire away from me. I could do the same thing, but it would take Lama only an hour and a couple of phone calls to find out that I never made an appearance in court as counsel on behalf of Laurel. Then he would be all over my ass like hot tar under feathers.

"Where's the lady?" he says. This is directed to me.

"Lose somebody?" I say.

"Your sister-in-law, jackass." He shakes his head, grins around the toothpick. "Make it easy and tell us where she is?"

"You might try her apartment. That's where she lives."

"Nobody home," he says.

"Really?"

Lama's chewing the toothpick to a dull point.

Jack's now joined us in the living room. On my way in, the coroner and an assistant were wheeling the body down the curved staircase, Jack following along behind. He gave me only a sideways glance, a look of vengeance.

When he sees me now his eyes flame. Vega's appearance tells me this is more than grief. He's been seeking solace in a bottle. He's looking for more. He heads for the liquor cart in the corner. Halfway there he stops, a thought he can't suppress.

"You son of a bitch," he says. "I told you. I warned you." His finger's shaking in my face. "Laurel was over the line and you knew it," he says. He talks like all the facts are in, the deed done, case closed. All he needs now is to catch Laurel.

It's an awkward moment, wrestling with the spouse. I look at Lama.

He smiles. No relief here.

Finally I offer Jack my sympathies, tell him I'm sorry for whatever has happened, but that he's making a lot of assumptions, jumping to conclusions.

"Bullshit." Vega jumps me verbally. I have given him what he wanted—a target of defense for Laurel.

"The bitch killed Melanie," he says. "She's got a loose screw. You saw her in court," he tells me. "Threats and violence. Went after Melanie in the hallway like an animal." He's trying to persuade now.

"She was emotional," I say. "An argument, that's all."

"An argument!" says Jack. His eyes are glazed over with

anger. "What do you want, Kodachrome?" he says. "You
want it in living color? Laurel pulling the trigger on videotape?

"Oh, you'd love that," he says. "Like all the rest of the
lawyers, you'd chop it up into suey. A lotta freeze-frames and
lies," he says. "So you could charge Melanie with impeding
the flight of a bullet. Well, it ain't gonna happen here," he
says. "Laurel's going down," he tells me. "If I have to pull
every fucking lever in the state." He stands there for several
seconds, waiting to see if I want to offer another line of reasoning.

I want to ask him where he was tonight, whether he saw
anything, whether in fact there is a videotape or if all of this
is merely the wrath-filled ravings of Jack's imagination. But
discretion overtakes advocacy. I stand silent.

There's some mumbling under Vega's breath, finally a victory in a bad day. He passes behind me. The next thing I hear
is the tinkling of ice cubes in a tumbler, bourbon splashing on
rocks. I would ask him for a drink, but I'm afraid he'd throw
the bottle.

Lama's waiting to see if Jack can spray any more bile on
me. One of Jimmy's joys in life, spreading pain. He senses
that it's over.

"You got pictures?" I turn this on Lama.

"You're here to answer the questions," he says. "I'll ask
them."

"We've got nothing to say," Hemple chimes in.

"Who invited you?" he says.

"I'm Laurel Vega's lawyer." Hemple pulls a business card
from her jacket pocket. Hands it to Lama. He looks at it,
smiles, then begins to pick his teeth with one of the card's
sharp little corners.

"Oh, good," he says. "Then you can tell us where your
client is?"

"I don't know," she says.

"Write that down," says Lama. "Her lawyer has no idea

where the suspect is.'' Another detective across the room scribbles in a little notebook.

''Maybe you know where she was earlier this evening— about eleven-thirty?'' says Lama.

Silence from Hemple.

''Seems she doesn't. Write it down,'' says Lama. ''Got anything else you want to tell us?'' he says. A shit-eating grin on Lama's face.

Hemple doesn't respond.

''Gee, thanks for coming.'' He smiles, Mr. Duplicity, then motions to one of the uniformed cops, who escorts Hemple to the door.

Lama turns his venom back on me. ''And where were *you* at eleven-thirty tonight?''

''Gee, Jimmy, do I need a lawyer?''

''Not unless you know something we don't.''

''Could you write that down?'' I say this to the dick across the room, who offers up a little hiccup of a laugh.

''Always the smart-ass,'' says Lama. ''I understand you been playin' guardian angel for your sister-in-law. Guess you kinda blew it tonight,'' he says.

I don't give him a response.

''Guess you'd know her better than most people?''

A concession from my look.

''Then you'd probably know if she has a gun?''

I give him bright eyes like maybe he's hit something.

''What kind?'' I say.

''Nine millimeter, semiautomatic.''

''Wouldn't have a clue,'' I tell him.

Lama gives me a sneer. Now he's given up information with nothing in return. My guess is they don't have the gun. If they did, Lama would have made a make and model. I assume they have loose cartridge casings and whatever ballistics survive when lead meets tissue or bounces off bone.

''When's the last time you saw her?'' he says. Now he's pissed.

"Who?" I ask.

He gives me a look like, "don't fuck with me," snaps the toothpick in half, and spits the broken piece on the floor.

I make a face, think a couple of seconds like maybe it's a strain to consider back that far. "This afternoon—the courthouse."

"And you haven't seen her since?"

I shake my head.

The cop with the little book is making notes.

"Then you wouldn't have any idea where the kids are?"

"I assume with their mother." God's own gift, I think. Two walking, breathing little alibis, for whatever they're worth.

"Goddamn," says Jack. He's shaking, hand with the glass outstretched, booze all over the rug. "She's murdered my wife, now she's running with my children. What the hell are you guys waiting for?" It was one thing when Jack was chewing on my ass, now he's getting on Lama's case.

A head signal from Jimmy and suddenly Vega is being quietly hustled from the room. Condolences from the cop, but he's got to go, official business being done here.

Vega turns to look at me on the way out. "She'd better let 'em go," he says. He's talking about the kids. Jack has visions of Laurel in Rio. I know better. She has no money.

"You hear me," he says. "I'll leave no stone unturned." He says this like he honestly believes I can deliver a message. Then he's history, out the door, straining to get a last look at me over the cop's shoulder.

Lama smiles, puts another toothpick in. "Angry man," he says. "I wouldn't want him mad at me."

"One of life's battles," I tell him.

"Yeah. Talkin' about battles, I understand you broke up a good fight in the courthouse this afternoon?" says Lama.

"Me?" I say.

"Yeah. Laurel Vega attacked the victim—the deceased?" He says this with all the emphasis on the "d" word.

"Like I said, a minor disagreement. Custody matter. A difficult situation. She got a little emotional. I wouldn't call it an attack.''

"Geez—I heard she nailed the woman with her fucking purse.'' says Lama. He snaps his fingers a couple of times, and his colleague with the notebook is fanning pages. The guy finds what he's looking for.

" 'Laurel Vega said she wished it was a sledgehammer,' '' the cop reads from his notes.

"Maybe she found something better than a hammer,'' says Lama.

"Nice thought,'' I say, "but if that's all you've got, I think maybe you should get up off your honkers and start looking for whoever actually killed Melanie Vega.''

"Oh, I think we are,'' he says. He chews on what is left of the little stick in his teeth, then gives a wicked smile.

"Are we finished?''

"For the moment,'' he says. He gets out of his chair like he's going to escort me personally to the door. He touches me at the elbow. I nearly recoil from the contact. Lama looks at me. If I didn't know better I'd think he was offended.

"Now, you will tell us if you see her—won't you?''

"Sure,'' I say. "You bet.''

I know that I won't have to. Vega will have me tailed by his minions.

"We appreciate the cooperation,'' he says. He's almost giggling to himself. I can sense the joy building inside of him, the knowledge that I am now tangled in this mess.

We get to the door. He sees me out onto the portico. Lama steps off the welcome mat and into some dirt, potting soil, and broken shards of clay. He's wearing black boots with low heels—what they call Wellingtons—with little zippers on the side. I have seen these on the CHP and a few drill sergeants, his heroes. He scrapes the dirt off the bottoms on the mat.

"Looks like somebody made a mess,'' he says.

There's a spray of black dirt on the siding by the front door. Lama looks up. My eyes follow.

"Geez—somebody really nailed it," he says.

There, under the ceiling of the portico, ten feet up, is a single security camera, aimed down at the entrance, its lens caked with dirt, its plastic outer case cracked like an egg.

He smiles. Jimmy Lama's giving me a message—that a picture is worth a ream of words.

CHAPTER
3

"Uncle Paul."

Danny Vega is waiting for me at my house, a hangdog expression under the bill of a Giants cap. He is all elbows on knees, the architecture of youth, good for propping up chins when sitting, as he is now on my front porch.

It is nearly four in the morning, and he is about the last person I would expect to see.

"Danny?" I say.

He can read the question in my voice.

"Baby-sitter said we could come over. I put my junk and the scooter in the garage," he says. He looks up at me, brown oval eyes. "It's okay, isn't it?" He says this like maybe I'm going to throw him out into the street.

"Sure," I say. I give him a smile, perhaps the only soft look he's had from an adult in days.

I can see the little Vespa by my workbench, Danny's way in the single-parent world. Next to it is a red helmet and a small daypack.

Laurel and I had given him the little motor scooter as a gift on his last birthday. Danny made a small wooden box that fits neatly on the back where, under hasp and lock, he keeps the mystical items that capture the fancy of a fifteen-year-old.

"Where's your mother? Why didn't she drive you?"

He humps his shoulders and shakes his head, as much as forearms will allow.

"Thought she might be with you," he says. Danny hasn't got a clue where Laurel is.

Chills course through my body, a combination of sleep deprivation and thoughts of where Laurel might be at this hour.

None of this seems to concern Danny. He is glum in the way teenagers often are. Little would excite him short of nuclear attack, and that only because of its brilliant flashes. Despite a desperate home situation, his expression is a map of feckless innocence.

He often seems to be transmitting on a different frequency. In his moments of deepest musing you could lose your ass wagering on what was coursing through that mind. In any conversation it can take half a day to figure what he is talking about, and if you took ten guesses you would no doubt be wrong in nine. The kid is in an adolescent daze, trapped somewhere between puberty and the twilight zone.

Danny looks nothing like Jack. Coloring and eyes, around the mouth, he is his mother's boy. While Danny has noticed, he has yet to undertake any serious forays beyond the gender gulf. He has no serious friends of the fairer persuasion, though I have seen a few girls bat their eyes his way, lashes like Venus fly-traps. In his own way, while not effeminate, Danny is prettier than they are. The gyrations of MTV seem to hold no apparent allure. I have never seen him out-of-doors without a baseball cap, worn to the ears in the image of idols on trading cards from the fifties. By all appearances he has avoided the social disorder of American youth, the affliction of "cool." But he has paid a price. Danny suffers the immutable pain of not being one of the guys. His single attempt at socialization, a ride in a boosted buggy with the boys, was powered by peer pressures more combustible than anything in an engine block. And it ended with a sputtering backfire, in the glare of a flashing light bar and the harsh words of a father who for much of Danny's life was absent. All things consid-

ered, I think Danny Vega would have been happier had he
been born on a farm in a verdant field—sometime in the last
century.

"She said you went over to Dad's, that something happened." The "she" he is talking about I assume is Mrs. Bailey, who's been fielding my phone. Danny is a lexicon of
disjointed thoughts.

"Julie's inside." He offers this up without my asking.

"I think she's asleep," he says.

He doesn't ask what happened at his father's. Instead he's
off again on another wavelength, something about wax and a
model he has to make, a project for school, he says.

I do a double take at four in the morning. Wax.

"Your aunt used to use some for canning. I think there
might be some in the garage," I say. "Can it wait till morning?" I give him a large yawn.

"Okay."

"When did you see your mom last?"

He makes a face, thinking back. "Three—or so. Maybe it
was four."

To Danny time is a fungible commodity. Like grain or pork
bellies, any hour of the day can be traded for any other. He
doesn't own a watch.

"She went out, said she'd be back."

I give him a look, like—"And?"

"She never showed up."

This is not a usual occurrence, the reason the boy is here.
Laurel may be many things, but she is not a dilettante mother.
Her few wayward evenings turned into early dawn, like the
escapade with her confessor, I can count almost on the hairs
of my palm. These infrequent lapses have occurred only when
the kids were safely elsewhere. Laurel is not one to subject
her children to the odious intrusion of quick alcoholic lovers
or fortnight Lotharios.

I ask Danny if he's eaten.

"Some Froot Loops and a banana."

"You hungry?" I ask.

"Sure."

I wave him on into the house and forage in the cupboards of the kitchen for some crackers and a can of soup. These days I am not exactly a dietitian's wet dream.

Mrs. Bailey has fallen asleep on my front room couch. I can see her through the open door of the kitchen, and feel the rattle of her snoring on the floorboards.

"Where were you tonight? I called the house earlier, nobody answered." I put the can in the opener. It twirls like a carousel until the lid collapses.

He rolls his eyes, gives me a kind of dumb-kid smile.

"Julie asked me to go over to a friend's. She uses me," he says, "like for wheels. It's not that I mind," he says. But I can tell he's embarrassed, performing shuttle duties for his sister, who is two years younger, to her boyfriend's house. Unlike her brother, Julie's social plane is pressurized, and designed to fly in the stratosphere. She dates boys older than Danny, guys who think nothing of calling her at ten to have her over at eleven.

Julie is a honey-blonde, with blue eyes, good bones, and a feminine form that is ripening faster than her ability to reason. She is learning all too quickly that good looks, rather than good works, can often get you what you want. The downsides, the temptations of excess and the price to be paid, still elude the telemetry of her radar. At thirteen she is the sexual equivalent of a toddler with a nuclear warhead. Were I Julie's father, I would have my broker investing heavily in a nunnery.

I put the soup in front of Danny, no ladle, just a bowl, microwave hot. I draw up a chair across from him at the table.

"There's something I have to talk to you about."

He's spooning it down, looking up at me with doelike eyes. His cap is politely off, on the table next to his dish with crackers.

"There was an accident tonight at your dad's house. A bad accident. A shooting," I say.

He takes the spoon away from his mouth, and still holding it, rests forearm and utensil on the table. The spoon is shaking at its tip.

"Is my dad all right?" He's looking at me wide-eyed.

With all the anguish of an open custody battle, and Jack's short temper with the boy, Danny still cares about his father.

"Your dad's fine."

He starts to eat again.

"But Melanie is dead," I say.

He stops for a moment and looks at me, swallows hard. There was no love lost with Melanie, the usual friction of kids with a stepparent. But still I can tell that he is rattled by this news. To the young, life is an infinite, never-ending party. Even for kids like Danny, who live outside the loop of their peers, death is a vagrant who wanders another street. I had watched him at Nikki's funeral. To Danny it was something surreal to have known someone, to have talked to and touched someone who was no longer with us.

"How'd it happen?" he asks.

"They don't know for sure. The police are still investigating."

"The cops?" he says.

"They investigate any cause of death that is not natural," I tell him.

"Oh—I guess so," he says.

He's back to the spoon. But I can tell things are rattling around upstairs under that mop of hair.

"I guess Dad's pretty shook up."

"You could say that."

I don't tell him that the police are looking to question his mother. He will find out soon enough. I can hope that in the interim, circumstances might conspire to put her in the clear. Little sense in worrying the kid until I know more.

"Are you okay?" I say. I'm eyeing him as this news goes down with the soup to be digested.

"The wax," he says, "is it white, pretty clear?"

"Emm?"

"For the model," he says.

"Ah. Yeah. In a block," I say. "A white block, as I remember."

"Will you help me find it first thing?" he says.

"Sure. Eat and get some sleep." Earth to Danny. The kid is off on a frequency of his own. What is left of my family is coming apart, and Danny Vega is worried about wax.

This morning I am running on adrenaline and something that looks like the discharge from the *Exxon Valdez*. I take a sip and my tongue curls like a slug in death throes. An hour's sleep in a night can do funny things to your eyes. I wonder if maybe the sign over the little drive-in stall read "Esso" instead of "Espresso."

When I arrive, Harry Hinds is in my office, borrowing my morning paper. Harry has an office down the hall. We share a library and reception services and have talked about a partnership. It's one of those things, we talk, but neither of us is willing to make the first move. Like Harry says, "Why ruin a good friendship with marriage?"

Hinds is almost twenty years my senior, a fixture in the legal community of this city. A balding head and a nose like Karl Maldin's, he has done some heavy-duty criminal work in his day, and now talks a lot about retirement. Those who know him well tell me that Harry has been talking about retirement since he passed the bar forty years ago. I have no doubt that when the end comes they will have to pry Harry's dead fingers from his briefcase, which he packs like a portable office. For Harry there are too many psychic battles ahead to pitch it in. He now feeds on referrals from my practice along with a steady diet of his own clients and acts as my number two in heavier cases.

This morning Harry's on a roll, newspaper in hand, feet propped on the edge of my wastebasket, uttering suppressed profanities, little whispered vulgarities mixed with what for

Harry when talking politics passes for reason. Harry hates all things official, with a special fetish for politicians and their hangers-on. He is not a Republican or Democrat. Harry is of his own affiliation, a party conceived under the tree of distrust for government and fueled by a zealot's devotion to a creed. He is what I would call a "social contrarian." Harry is largely against everything.

Lately he's gone into the clipping services, taping articles from the morning papers to various areas on my desk. It is his effort to enlist the apathetic. Each day I find a new batch of these, his musings penned on square-inch Post-It notes, the travails of the world, all the things Harry can do nothing about but bitch.

His interests are eclectic—world trade; the national debt, which is too big, and the nation's defenses, which are too small; the environment, which is overly protected, except on Tuesdays and Thursdays, when it seems the polar hole in the ozone has its effect on Harry. On those days he joins the Greens. Never let it be said that Harry is bewitched by the forces of consistency. And always there is a side to him floating just above the waterline of humor, when you never know if Harry is truly on the level.

Without even saying hello, Harry is reading to me, a date-line from Lexington, Kentucky. It seems the federal government has sold two truckloads of used computer equipment for forty-five dollars. Harry bitches about the price, the dousing of taxpayers, until he discovers further on that the government wants the equipment back. In an instant, less time than it would take to squeeze a trigger, Harry has chained himself to the bulwarks of free enterprise, shouting the battle cry: "fucking Indian givers."

Another paragraph and Harry discovers why the government is reneging. These particular computers contain confidential information, the names and addresses of hundreds of federally protected witnesses, carted away for their own safety, information which a government technician has failed to adequately erase before selling the computers. Questions of political theory land in the dustbin as Harry sees a wedge of opportunity.

"Can you imagine all the puckered assholes?" He says this with a wicked gleam in his eye, like a schoolboy who's discovered a treasure map.

"You know," he says, "we should hang this on the bulletin board in the county jail. Your government at work for you. A snitch's worst nightmare." Then he giggles in the pitch of a cheap tenor.

This is the Harry I know. He can go every direction at once, with the only true course change coming on the winds of opportunity. The notion of some prosecutor whose case would be creamed because his ace witness suddenly grew legs and walked, or suffered a bout of terminal laryngitis on the eve of trial, these are thoughts destined to catch Harry's fancy.

After all things are said, Harry is a defender, dyed-in-the-wool, sworn to the cause of the underdog. He views any commitment to the objective processes of the law as its own form of treason. In trial before the bar, Harry takes no prisoners. He will seize and hold tenaciously any edge that is offered by circumstance. It is just that Harry's idea of happy circumstance can at times be a little skewed.

For the moment I leave Harry in his negative nirvana, uttering the party mantra over the sacred scrolls.

I pick up the phone to call Clem Olsen, a friend at police dispatch. Clem and I went to high school together. He has always been a straight shooter. When he can he will talk, little musings like the oracle on Delphi—he will tell me what is wafting on the airwaves of the police band.

I get him after two rings.

"Clem," I say. "Paul Madriani here." Light-voiced, I make it sound like a social call.

"Hey, baby." Clem has called everyone he knows "baby" since the tenth grade. I have heard him on tapes do homicide calls like the Wolfman, while frantic citizens scream hysterical gibberish about blood and bullets on the nine-eleven number.

Clem never made it to college, instead he did the woodshop routine and left school without a clue, until the Army got ahold of him in the Vietnam draft. They taught him how to kill, and later radios. From these Clem found his own way to the police department.

"You gonna make the reunion?" he says. This affair, it seems, occurs every five years now, where Clem, for one shining night, rises to the level of some higher aspiration as class MC.

"Gonna try," I say.

"Hey," he says. "You remember the girl, the blonde from homeroom our senior year, the one with the hooters like two dead cone-heads? Do you remember her name?" he says. "Can't find her on the mailing list."

This, a girl's form from twenty-five years ago, is something Clem would etch in his mind like the inscriptions of the Commandments in stone.

I tell him I can't remember. I don't puncture the illusion that nature has by now probably worked its will, and that gravity has no doubt taken its toll. I could tell him to look at his own love handles, which now sag like sodden saddlebags from his hips. But with Clem, memories of the past are always more valid than images of the present.

"Listen, I got a favor to ask."

"If I can," he says.

"Last night there was a shooting—a legislator's wife out in the east area."

He cannot have missed this. Melanie's death, while too late to make the first-edition papers, has hit the A.M. news shows, both TV and radio, with all the cheery dignity of checkout-counter journalism. The video cameras panned the body all the way into the coroner's van. The reporters with their mikes and plastered hair did everything but zip open the body bag to see if she was wearing her nightie.

"I heard," he says.

"If you can tell me," I say, "have there been any APBs? Anybody they're looking for in connection, maybe for questioning?"

A long pause, like he knows but is not sure whether he should tell me.

"Wouldn't be you got a client?" he says.

Clem is a friend, but he has never been close enough to climb my family tree. He has no sense of my kinship to Laurel, or for that matter her former relationship to the grieving legislator.

"Not at this time." I won't lie to him, but I shave the edges of truth a little.

"I'd have to check the overnight dispatches," he says. "Can I call you back?" Clem wants to make discreet inquiries to determine exactly how much he can tell me.

"Sure thing. I'll be here all morning." I give him the backline number so he can call direct, around my receptionist. On items like this Clem doesn't like to talk through middlemen.

Harry's into another incantation, with more gusto now that I am off the phone, still chanting from behind his curtain of newsprint.

"Health-care reform by the same crowd who gave us tax simplification," says Harry. "Why don't I believe it?"

I ignore him and hope it will go away.

"You know they will exempt themselves," he says.

I don't know who he's talking about, and I don't want to ask. But Harry volunteers.

"Fuckers in Congress," he says. "They wanna be able to roll their asses over to Bethesda at the first sign of a sniffle, for the red carpet treatment. A private suite with hot and cold running Navy nurses," he says. "That's so they can have a good grope and get saluted at the same time."

Harry fans a page and looks for more grist for his mill.

"So there's no word on her?" He says this in a different tone. This time I can't mistake the subject of his inquiry. He's talking about Laurel. Harry knows that I am in a family way on this thing. I called Harry early this morning. Got him out of bed and told him about my all-night stand at Vega's house and the attempt at inquisition by Jimmy Lama.

"No word," I say.

"You can always hope," he says. "Who knows? Maybe they've given her up. Found another suspect."

"I might feel better if I knew what the cops had."

"Maybe you wouldn't," he says. "Maybe she did it." This is Harry, soothing you with his blarney one instant and honing the knife's edge on your open wounds the next.

I give him a look, like "thanks for the comforting thoughts."

"Well, hey, it does happen," he says. "Crime of passion, the tangled triangle," says Harry. "Two women doing battle over the same man. Jealous ex and the beautiful younger wife." He gives me arched eyebrows over the press-cut edges of the morning paper.

"Vega would love you for the thought," I tell him. "The women in his life ready to kill for Jack. It's a premise to fatten his ego."

The Capitol dome will float ten feet higher if this notion were to find public expression. But Harry is right. It's a theory not likely to be lost on an eager prosecutor.

"And where did she go?" Harry's talking about Laurel. "You think it's just coincidence?" he says. "She happens to vanish the night her ex's latest squeeze buys it. Doesn't tell the kids where she's going. Just takes off for parts unknown." Harry's playing kibitzer for the devil, musing behind the paper, foraging for something more to raise the level of his bile.

"Irrespective of your feelings," he says, "I think you gotta admit, the cops might have good reason for suspicions."

"Joining the force, are you?"

"My feet aren't flat enough," he says.

"One thing's for sure," I tell him. "Lama must have thought he was having a wet dream the minute he found out Laurel and I were related. Blood, marriage, it wouldn't matter.

It's any way to drive the sword with that one.''

''I can imagine,'' says Harry. ''How's it feel?'' He wiggles his ass a little deeper into the chair, as if to reveal where Lama might have buried this thing in me.

''From what I hear,'' he says, ''whenever Jimmy is in pain, it is your name he takes in vain.''

I don't answer him.

The phone rings on my desk.

''Hello.''

''Clem here.''

''That didn't take you long,'' I say.

''Heyyyy, the Wolfman don't disappoint.'' A voice like somebody sandblasted his vocal cords. ''You must be clair-buoyant.'' Clem's understanding of the language does not come from reading it.

''Like you said, APB went out at oh-two-twenty today,'' he says. ''Issued for one Laurel Jane Vega, age thirty-six, height . . .''

''That's all I need.'' I cut him off.

''And a bad actor at that,'' he says.

''What do you mean?''

''Listed as possibly armed and dangerous.''

This means that Laurel, if she is found, would be taken at the point of a loaded pistol. Some foolish gesture, a wave of a loose hand through her hair, and I could be minus one more family member. More stark than this is the thought that Clem's superiors have allowed this information to come my way. Whatever they have linking Laurel to murder, they see as solid.

CHAPTER
4

Like clockwork I do the gym every Thursday at noon, the place Laurel used to work before she disappeared.

It's a dozen blocks from my office to the Capital Gymnasium and Athletic Club. At twelve-fifteen I get an urgent message delivered on the squash court. I take my leave, to one of the white telephones lined in cloistered booths in the foyer.

"Hello."

"Paul." She is breathless.

When I hear the voice I have a single question: "Where the hell are you?"

"I don't have much time. Where's Julie and Danny?" Laurel's voice is strained and tired. What I would expect from someone who has been on the lam for nearly two days now.

"Half the county is looking for you."

"I know," she says. "But I didn't do it."

"Then where are you? Why did you run?"

"I can't talk."

"Come in, give yourself up," I tell her. "They're calling you armed and dangerous."

She laughs at this. A nervous titter.

"It's no joke. Cops with an adrenaline rush have a habit of shooting," I tell her.

"I'll be okay. Do you have the kids?" Laurel's mind at this

moment is a monorail, single track and rolling with her children on board.

"I did until yesterday. Jack had 'em picked up from school by one of his AA's." These are gofers who do menial tasks for legislators—lackeys-in-waiting.

"Damn it." Silence on the phone while she thinks. I can smell it like burning neoprene coming over the line, the machinations of panic on the run. Still, Laurel has not completely lost her mind. She has found me in the one place where Lama is not likely to be eavesdropping. With Jimmy you can't take much comfort in the formalities of magistrates and judicially ordered wiretaps. I've suspected for days now that my phone has suddenly become a party line.

"Can you get a message to them?" she says. Her kids.

"Why?"

"I want them out of there."

I think her brain is scrambled. "You want them on the run with you?"

"No. No. A friend," she says. "In Michigan."

"That's not my biggest concern at this moment," I say.

"Oh, shit," and she's gone from the phone—a receding voice, sound vanishing like fog on a warming day.

"Hello. Are you there?" I get mental images—Laurel swinging around some corner, enough tension on the phone cord to break it. Then I hear her breathing closer again.

"What happened?"

"Police just swung by in the parking lot," she says. "It's okay. They're gone now. Probably just a coffee break," she tells me. "My picture is everywhere," she says. "Even up here."

I could get a map and play with little pins, my twenty best guesses on where "up" is.

"Use your head," I tell her. "You're no good to your kids dead or in prison. Come in and we'll deal with it." I try to engage her in conversation. I ask her where she was the night of Melanie's death, hoping for an alibi, something I can bootstrap into an argument for our side, to induce her in.

"Can you get a message to them?" she says. She's back to her children.

"They're fine. You're the one in trouble," I tell her. "Come in, I'll meet you, pick you up. I'll make arrangements with the DA to surrender," I say. "It'll go much better at trial. We'll have a shot at bail," I tell her. I've got more closers than a used-car salesman. None of them working.

"Not till the kids are gone," she says. "Out-of-town. Then I'll surrender.

"Listen," she says. "I have a friend in Michigan. Went to college together. She's willing to take the kids, keep them there quietly until this is over."

"Your kids can handle it," I tell her. "I'll take care of them, keep them out of it."

"No." Her tone tells me she's maybe half an inch from hanging up. I take another tack to keep her talking.

"This friend," I say. "Does she know your situation?"

"I told her. It makes no difference. Like I said, she's a friend."

The way Laurel says this it makes me think perhaps at this moment I am not qualifying for inclusion in this group.

"I can't talk," she says. "I gotta run. Gotta hang up now." All of a sudden frenetic noise on the line. "Call you later," she says.

"Laurel. Hello. Hello." What I hear is a melodic noise, like scrape-and-thump, scrape-and-thump. I listen for several seconds until I sense what this is—the pendulum of the receiver on the other end, left to dangle against a wall by its cord as Laurel walked away.

When I return to my office, there's a small pile of messages on my desk. I paw through them quickly. There is one from Gail Hemple, others are the usual, calls on cases, except for the one on the bottom which catches my eye. A pink slip with Jack Vega's name and number on it.

I pick up the phone and dial Hemple first.

Gail warns me that Jack is on the warpath. He is demanding to know from his lawyer why he's compelled to pay spousal support to Laurel, who is now, in his words, a fugitive. Whoever said that alimony is the ransom a happy man pays to the devil has never met Jack.

According to Gail he's demanding that his lawyer go back to court, an order to show cause on changed circumstances, the fact that the kids are now abandoned, to seek temporary custody until the matter of their missing mother is resolved.

"Vega has called me," I tell her. "Any idea what he wants?"

She has scuttlebutt from Jack's lawyer. It seems the attorney-client relationship with my brother-in-law is not all the man could have hoped for.

"Jack found out that Danny and Julie were at your place the night Melanie was killed," she says.

Playing the wounded father, Jack's now busy trying to sever all links. He has left strict written instructions at his kids' school that I am to have no contact.

Vega has an antiquated notion of teenagers and how to deal with them. In an age when kids are packing Mac-tens in the classroom and pistol-whipping teachers who look at them cross-eyed, Jack sees a note from home as something on the order of the Great Wall of China.

"The man doesn't miss a beat," she tells me. "We're noticed for a hearing on temporary custody in five days. Got any ideas?" she says.

Jack has found the soft underbelly. Laurel is not likely to show in court, and her lawyer, having already appeared on the custody matter, can't avoid service. Jack will take a default on Laurel, grab the kids, and cut off support, all in one fell swoop. It is what you notice first about Jack, not his blinding intelligence, but his devotion to the rules of opportunity. Facing Melanie's funeral, and a sea of grief I do not deny, he still finds time in a busy day to sort out the silver lining in his wife's death.

As much as a lawyer can be, Hemple is depressed by all of this.

To Jack there was never anything sacred about taking care of his family. For a guy with a woman in every room, support payments were viewed as nothing but an exorbitant stud fee. I tell her this. But she doesn't laugh. There is a dark cloud, something unstated, hanging over our conversation, the sense that Gail is waiting to unload something more on me. We tiptoe around it for several minutes, mostly lawyer's small talk, adventures in divorceland, a ride on every theory, none of them with a cheerful ending. Then she punches my ticket.

"I may as well tell you," she says. "I'm not going to be able to go on representing her."

"What are you talking about?"

"I'm filing a motion to withdraw as counsel," says Hemple.

A lawyer leaving a case unfinished conjures all the images of Fletcher Christian lowering the longboat to put you over the side—in this case, given my limited grasp of things domestic in the law, without benefit of compass or charts. At this moment there is a sick feeling at the pit of my stomach not unlike what you would get out on the rock-and-roll of the bounding main.

"You can't do it," I say.

She's got a million reasons. A waste of Gail's time and Laurel's money, what it comes down to in the end.

She can hear me fuming on the other end, the silent thought that a lawyer should never cut and run. Though in this case, with Laurel on the lam, I must admit that it is an open question who has abandoned who.

"Listen, if it's a question of money . . ."

"It isn't the money. That ran out a month ago. Laurel passed me two bad checks since," she says. "Bounced and skipped like flat stones on a pond," she tells me. We are siblings under the skin, Gail and I. Like the criminal bar, it seems rubber is the stock-in-trade of divorce.

"I kept going for the reason that a lawyer always keeps going," she says. "I didn't know how to say no."

I tell her to send me her rubber checks and I will give her cash.

"You'd be putting good money after bad," she says. "It's not just the money. It's the case. There is no way," she says. "How do I tell the court that my client hasn't abandoned her kids? 'Your honor, she's a fugitive from justice, the cops can't find her, but she is a good mother. She cares for her children. She just does it long distance.' It isn't gonna wash," she says.

I bite my tongue. I want to tell her about my conversation with Laurel, but disclosure has implications. As absurd as it might seem, at this moment Laurel could claim that she was just traveling, some urgent mission with a purpose, unaware that the cops were after her. I am the only one who knows from her own lips that this is not the case. For the moment I must keep it that way.

"They haven't charged her with anything," I say. "If she turns up, what then? There could be a logical explanation for her disappearance."

Some pained breathing on the other end. Gail Hemple trying one more time to muster the sand to say no.

"Vega's getting ready to turn a paper blizzard," she says. "And right now he's got a monopoly on all the wind machines. If she came back today maybe, with a good story, I'd have time to prepare. After that, anybody appearing on the merits is nothing but a punching bag. There would not even be a basis for the slightest compromise," she says. "In a way she might be better off unrepresented," says Hemple. "If she beats the criminal charges, or they don't bring them, a court on review might be more sympathetic revisiting custody."

I have no answer for this.

"If you hear from her before five, and she has a good

one''—Gail means a story—''give me a call,'' she says and
hangs up.

The State Capitol building is a showcase, historic rooms preserved on the main floor like museums and gilded elevators
with live operators, at least when the Legislature is in session.
The hundred and twenty men and women officed here live
like rajas, with personal attendants to cater their every whim.
There is no money for schools or hospitals, but austerity is
not part of the decorative scheme here. As the boundless party-
line goes, the dignity of the people demands that their elected
leaders operate in opulence. The political class of this state
are about as out of touch as the fops of yore whose heads
rolled from the guillotine.

To get to Jack's office I run the gauntlet of a rogues' gallery,
framed oil portraits the size of small houses, spaced along the
walls leading to the rotunda. These are pictures of former gov-
ernors, mostly robber barons from the last century who bought
respectability with their public office. Mixed in with these are
the feckless oily smiles of a few contemporaries, actors and
the sons of political nobility, official portraits of men bearing
expressions of constipation, straining to look like they belong
to the ages.

What Jack wanted to talk about when I returned his call
could not be discussed over the phone. I trek to his office in
the Capitol, more from curiosity than anything else, the
thought that any information, even that which Jack wants me
to have, is better than none.

His receptionist offers me coffee and a chair to cool my
heels while Jack holds forth behind the closed door of his
office. I can hear the rumble of voices, men belly-laughing.

As a chairman of a standing committee, Vega rates a suit-
able office and a battalion of publicly paid minions, mostly
young, each striving to look more important than the other,
and all off on their own urgent mission to prop up the world.

Twenty minutes go by and the door to Vega's office finally

opens. I hear Jack's voice, but it is lost in a well, behind a bull of a man who fills the doorway. The guy's back is to me. There is nothing fat about him, just big, more cloth on his suitcoat than the *Graf Zeppelin*. The guy's shaking Jack's hand, talking the jargon of this place, something about legislation, a "juice bill," meaning there is money in it. The wonders of politics in the free-market world.

The man doesn't see me sitting here, and Jack's view is blocked by the hulk in front of him.

The guy tells Jack it's time to go see the "guv, down in the corner office. Not the big place out front, the little office in the back, where the real deals are cut," he says.

Jack wishes him luck.

"No need for luck when it's wired," the man says. What every lobbyist would have you think, that his hand is up some elected official's ass, making the mouth work.

Clinton Brady is one of the better-known members of the third house, the unofficial, but many would insist most powerful branch of government, the six hundred or so registered lobbyists in this town.

He pats Jack on the shoulder and turns to leave. In a blue serge suit with sleeves an inch too short, Brady looks like something that climbed down from the beanstalk. He straightens up, noticing that strangers are in earshot, and cants his head to one side in order to clear the transom over Jack's door.

Brady represents insurance interests the way the Führer represented Germany, a lot of blitzkrieg and scorched earth to any who oppose him. With his contacts and high profile he has become more important than the interests he represents. He owns whole committees and sells his services to clients like the mob sells protection. He has by now learned that giving money to Jack and his ilk is like feeding fish to seals. Word has it for the last decade that Jack has been living in one of Brady's pockets. At this moment the lacquered grin on Vega's face would do little to dispel this thought.

"Clint needs some copies. Clint needs to make a call. Clint

needs this. Clint needs that.'' Jack is Clint's own gofer, doing his own form of the soft-shoe between Clint and the secretary. He takes a pile of papers from Brady and hands it to his secretary to be copied. The woman moves with the flash of lightning, like her job depends on this. Brady's then ushered down the hall to some subaltern's office, a detour to make a few phone calls before heading off to see the ''guv''—no doubt a telephone request to his clients to wire more cash. Politicians in this state don't accept reasoned argument, and they don't take American Express.

Jack gives me a wag of his head and no greeting. I follow him into his office, where he closes the door behind us.

Though the consumption of alcohol in the Capitol is a misdemeanor, Jack maintains a rolling liquor cabinet in a walk-in closet, more jingling glass than the dime toss at a county fair.

''A drink?'' he says.

I decline. He would probably have me arrested.

The office is hot, the product of an hour of deal-making behind a closed door. I take off my jacket, hold it in my lap as I sit in one of the chairs on this side of the desk.

Jack is sweating like a bull, but still wearing his coat. He compensates with a tumbler of iced scotch, and dances toward the business side of his desk, where he finally lands in cushioned leather and swivels to face me.

''Been talking to my lawyers,'' he says. ''They told me to stay away from you.'' Jack's contempt for lawyers has him ignoring his own.

The wall behind him is covered with political mementos, plaques and resolutions of appreciation from business and civic leaders in his district. These are mostly people trying to get where Jack is, who figure that planting their nose up his ass can't hurt. There are three large trophies centered on his credenza. Perhaps things other people let him win, little bronze men embedded on marble pedestals with a single arm outstretched. I can read Jack's name engraved on the brass plate of one of these.

He holds up a few papers from the center of his desk, letter-sized, looking like receipts.

"Dealing with the funeral home," he says. "Gonna have to be closed casket." He looks at me to see if I will ask why.

"Her head," he finally says, shaking his own. "One shot to the head. The morticians couldn't do much."

The willfulness of this, a shot to the head, not some heedless act of instant provocation, has its effect on me.

"I suspect there are a lot of things you don't know," he says. "She was executed. There are pictures," he tells me.

I'm thinking coroner's shots. Then he says: "Of Laurel, at the house."

"Shooting Melanie?" I cannot resist.

He shakes his head. "May as well be. Videotape of her arguing with Melanie on the front steps. Neighbors heard it. Security camera filmed it all until Laurel smashed the lens with a flowerpot." The way he says this, Jack clearly imputes a little method to Laurel's madness, a purpose in destroying the camera. Something I suspect he's either picked up from the cops or planted in their minds.

"Where were you?"

"I had a meeting. Didn't get home till late that night."

It was Jack who found Melanie's body in the master bath and called police. According to what he tells me, forensics figures that about three hours passed between the row on the porch and the murder.

"They believe Laurel probably went to get a gun and had to think about it for a while before she worked up the nerve." The "they" Jack is talking about I suspect is Jimmy Lama, who is busy trying to inspire thoughts of premeditation and deliberation to some wily prosecutor.

"How do you know it was her?"

A pained expression, like "give me a break."

"I suppose you still don't know where she is?"

"I don't," I tell him.

"Not a word from her?"

"And if I had, I would tell you?" I smile.

"Touché," he says.

Jack's musing over his drink, talking about Melanie's funeral, which is scheduled for tomorrow.

I had not expected to see him in the office, a period for grieving. I tell him this.

"It's easier to cope if I go about my day," he says. Jack's talking like he's had time to think. The immediate rush of anger so evident at his house that night has passed. This is not unlike Vega. Jack has always lacked the stamina to hold anger for long. He talks about the kids, what to do with their mother. It's not easy. It's not his decision, but he and his children will have to live with whatever happens to Laurel.

"For their sake," he says, "I cannot see her sentenced to death." It's starting to sound like Jack is coming to his senses.

There are little beads of sweat running down his nose. He puts the side of the iced tumbler to his forehead and catches the sweat with the sleeve of his coat.

"They will find her," he says. He is dogged in this. "What I want to know is what you're going to do," he says.

I look at him.

"When they catch her. Are you going to represent her?"

"I hadn't thought about it," I tell him.

He smiles. Bullshit is Jack's native tongue. By nature he is not confrontational. Manipulation is his special gift. I get a lot of penetrating looks from across the desk as he sizes me up for some pitch.

"I suppose it would make sense if she were represented by someone who knew the family well. I mean the whole situation. It would be easier," he says, "for the kids, for all concerned if it was over quickly. And the evidence," he says, "is irrefutable." He goes on at length that there is a certain symmetry and sense to my representing Laurel. At least then I'd be in a position, in his words, "to make it easy on the family."

Jack is taking me on his own sojourn of mercy. If he can't keep me away from the case, Vega's busy mining the circumstances for some silver lining. He would use me like a handy tool to have Laurel cop a quick plea.

"It'll keep her out of the deathhouse," he says. "And the kids. It'll be easier on them." It's like he's talking to himself, thinking out loud. "Of course you'd have to know the circumstances. All the details. How she did it and why." He stops for a moment and looks at me as if perhaps I already know these and will share them with him now.

This is a conversation we shouldn't be having. It is not only premature, it is ridiculous. I tell him that.

"Just keep an open mind," he says.

"You might do the same," I tell him.

"I understand the kids were with you the night Melanie was murdered," he says. "Until this is over I'd like you to stay away from them. I think you can understand. I don't want them in the middle." This from the man who had his two children on the discount rack at the custody mart.

"Whatever you say, Jack."

"I knew you'd understand." It is all very civil, what you would expect from Jack once he's had time to collect himself and find the direction of advantage. He will no doubt be trying to plan Laurel's defense with me if she is arrested and charged. Anything that is short and sweet and leads to a long stretch will do.

He pushes forward and rises from his chair. The button of his coat catches on the edge of the desk. It tears the fabric and pops across the room like a rivet in an earthquake.

"Damn," he says. A stupid smile, like "look at me in my ruined thousand-dollar suit." With nothing to be done, he shrugs and reaches across the desk to shake my hand, leaving his jacket to flop open. In his mind I think Jack's view is that we have buried some mythical hatchet. If he had a peace pipe at this moment he would offer me a smoke.

His is a big, affable smile.

"Like I said the other day. We all have to do what we have to do." He ushers me to the door, one hand on my shoulder, renewing the vows of brotherhood.

He pats me on the shoulder one last time, bids farewell, and closes his door. I wander through the warren of offices like Moses after the promised land, any way to get out. With each step I weigh frantically every word spoken during our meeting against a single question in my mind.

Why was Jack Vega wearing a wire?

"Guess who's here?" she says. Sarah has a big grin. She's just answered the doorbell, and she knows I don't have a clue.

"Danny." She is jubilant.

"Oh."

My daughter dotes on her cousin. Everything that a seven-year-old girl can think about a teenager, the gamut from love to simple fascination. She looks up at him with oval eyes and a painted-on smile, stuttering as the words can't come out fast enough.

She's tugging on one of his hands, dragging him over to look at a picture she's just finished in crayon, yammering about school and a book she is learning to read. She has plans to corral him on the couch while she struggles with the words.

"Uncle Paul." Danny's hat is in his hand. He's wearing a black Raiders jacket that gives his body more bulk than it warrants.

I'm working over the stove, what passes for cooking in this house. I ask him if he's hungry. Is the Pope Catholic? His eyes are looking in the pot as it steams. Nothing he recognizes, I'm sure, but then Danny is a risk-taker.

"Does your dad know you're here?" I ask.

"I'm out with Julie tonight," he says. "Took her to her boyfriend's. Suppose to pick her up in an hour."

I shudder. Plenty of time for the pointed little sperms to wiggle their way upstream. In his own evasive way, Danny has answered my question. His father doesn't know he is here.

"We had a talk today," I tell him. "Your dad thinks it's best, for the time being, if we don't see each other."

" 'Cuz you're helping Mom," he says. Just like that, the kid has put it all together. "I know. He told me," he says. He shrugs his shoulders. "I didn't think you'd mind."

Sarah is fuming, a bundle about to explode. Enough talk between grown-ups. She wants Danny in the other room, and she is not subtle. Sarah has him by a thumb and one finger, pulling with all her weight, about to commit an act of dislocation.

Sarah wants to ride around the block behind Danny on the little Vespa motor scooter, but I scotch this. She has no helmet, and besides it is beginning to get dark. He cons me with requests to stay just for a few minutes. Then looks at me doe-eyed.

"I guess I could sit outside her friend's house."

I give a sigh and a look of concession. "For a few minutes," I say.

They head for the living room as I slice carrots into a pot.

Nikki left me a small binder of recipes, a part of her legacy of love. In her dying days she took hours penning these out in longhand, things that even I could prepare without burning the bottom out of some pan. I watched in amazement as she went about this, pulling together these handwritten pages, a nutritional map for survival. She did it without a thought, almost cavalier, in the same way that she would have once plunked TV dinners into the freezer for me before leaving for a week to visit her mother. My wife had a selfless penchant for the practical.

Sarah's talking up a storm in the other room. Danny's taken to the tube in defense, the disconnected jabber of some quick and dirty channel-surfing. He settles on something, a dull monotone I cannot make out.

More carrots, a little parsley, a spoon of butter, and stir. Something's tugging at the back of my pants. I turn. It is Sarah. Her face is filled with agitation. A wagging finger, she has me bend low for some secret.

"Danny is crying," she whispers.

I wipe my hands and head for the other room.

The kid is hunched in a corner of the couch, knees drawn up, as close to a fetal position as is possible for someone six feet tall. He's staring at the screen, tears streaming down his face.

There on the television, in living color, pictures of Laurel, her hands cuffed behind her, being pulled toward a squad car—a black-and-white with a door shield I do not recognize. Laurel's head is pushed down as she's deposited in the back-seat. I can see only the silhouette of her head through the rear window as the car pulls away from the curb. I reach for the controls and boost the sound just in time to hear: "This is Norm Kendal reporting from Reno."

I stand in a daze, mesmerized by the stench of incinerated carrots and the thought that I finally know where "up here" is.

CHAPTER
5

It is just after noon, and the customary crowd of the tattered and vagrant wander in front of the Capital County jail, waiting for friends or relations to be turned out on bail.

Laurel has waived extradition from Nevada. Lama and his crew have wasted no time in bringing her back to Capital City.

I wait in a small interrogation room on the ground floor of the jail. Apart from minor children I am the nearest relative. So I have retained myself to represent her, something that has raised eyebrows among the jailers, unsure whether they should admit me.

In the hallway outside I can see Laurel through a window as she is led in. One of the female deputies has her by the arm. Laurel is wearing no makeup. Her face is drawn and tired. She has aged ten years in the last two.

I remember her in those halcyon years of my own marriage. She was happy and seemed always to move at single speed, in cork-soled sandals. She wore waistless dresses with a back-pack, the latter filled with Danny in diapers, the former beginning to show the bulge of his sister.

This was the late seventies. My generation was busy slithering through the corporate jungle, trying to shed its social conscience. The Mercedes hood ornament had replaced the peace symbol as the icon of the moment.

It is said that timing in life is everything. Laurel, it seems, foundered under a bad star, having missed the Age of Aquarius. She was a natural hippie.

When she first met Jack, she was a year out of Berkeley. He was older. Sporting hair halfway to his ass, he talked a dialect of liberal gibberish that tickled the cockles of altruism. Jack, who was then working in the Capitol, one of the lackeys-in-waiting, was honing the skills that would make him a politician. He was telling Laurel what he thought she wanted to hear, the prelude to a marriage made in hell.

Whenever we discussed the weighty topics of our time, my impression was always of Laurel searching her soul, agonizing for some ultimate truth while Jack paid lip service, what some speechwriter had crafted in ten minutes at a typewriter. He was too busy enjoying the perks to examine the policy. At home and abroad, Jack was always a ship sailing under false colors. My guess is that from the start, he had been shlepping his mast into other ports. It took Laurel a time to figure this out, and a little while longer to immerse the problem in a bottle.

Through all of this the only constant in her life, it seems, has been the instinct to protect her children. In this she has the maternal impulses of a cheetah with its young, extended claws longer than the spiked heels on the shoes some women wear.

The door opens. Laurel is cuffed. The glint of metal, a chain encircling her waist, runs down between her knees to the locked shackles on her ankles, so that when she moves she sounds like something from the yule season. There are little steps here like a Chinese peasant with bound feet.

She wears an orange jail jumper three sizes too big, and canvas shoes, an indication that she has already undergone the indignities of admission to this place—cavity searches in places only your physician should see, and a shower with antiseptic soap so astringent it could lift paint from metal.

She clears the door, and the first thing I see are Laurel's hands as she holds them out to me. They are a vibrant shade of red, like someone may have cooked them over an open flame.

"What happened to her?" I look accusingly at the guard.

"Ask your client," she says.

"It's all right," says Laurel.

The guard gives me her best cop's smirk.

"You can take those off," I tell her. I'm talking about the cuffs and shackles.

"In your dreams," she says.

"You want, we can call your boss to discuss it," I tell her. "My client has a right to confer with her lawyer without a ton of metal on her feet and hands."

"Not down here on the main floor," she says. Testing the water. How far can she push? Too lazy to work the keys.

I look her in the eye, and she blinks. I start to move to the door, toward a higher level of appeal.

"Your party," she says. If looks could spit. She works with her keys, more locks than a chastity belt. Then, dragging six yards of chain, she stations herself, her back leaning up against the wall five feet away.

"Outside, if you don't mind," I tell her.

Coming to the county jail to talk to a client is like being dropped into a sandbox filled with snarling pit bulls. The guards who can't bite will at least try to piss on you. Generally these are deputies who higher authority won't put on the street for fear of causing a riot among rational citizens. So they are left here to develop their public personas like Quasimodo. She moseys out the door, dragging metal behind her.

They have just booked Laurel, a charge of first-degree murder. She is slated for arraignment tomorrow morning, the reading of formal charges, and an appearance to set a date for entry of a plea. I think Harry was right. It would appear I can take little comfort in the state's case, though I have yet to see any part of it. Harry is busy preparing a motion for discovery. Apparently the cops believe they've got a dead-bang winner based on the evidence already in hand. I have heard rumors of a witness. Perhaps it is something they would like us to believe.

Laurel sits in the chair across the table from me. She is stone-faced, but there are no tears, no frazzled hysteria.

Other women I know would recoil in horror at this place, beefy guards and other inmates with an attitude on the hardness scale of a diamond. But it is the thing about Laurel. She is one of those people who always seem to find a second wind in adversity.

I can see Lama's beady little eyes outside in the hallway, through the window with its blinds. He has finally found a place where he is comfortable, in the company of other misfits, peering through a window on a private conversation. I close the blinds in his face.

Now we are quiet, enclosed and hopefully private.

"Are you okay?" I ask.

"Where are the kids?" she says. She's back to first thoughts.

"They're all right."

"Do they know I've been arrested?"

"Danny does," I say. I can only assume that by now someone has told Julie of her mother's fate.

This is the Laurel I know. She looks off at the middle distance—a woman who moments ago was in cuffs and chains, charged with first-degree murder, and her headiest concern is sheltering her kids from the knowledge.

"Have you talked to Gail Hemple? Will he get custody?" She's talking about Jack taking the kids.

"We'll have to talk about that later," I say.

"No—now," she says. "Will he get custody?"

"The kids have to live somewhere while you get through this mess," I tell her.

"Not with Jack," she says. "You can take them," she tells me. "At least temporarily," she says.

Laurel's looking over her shoulder now, paranoia like

maybe somebody is listening. Here, in this place, this is a healthy attitude.

She puts a cupped hand to the side of her mouth. "Her name is Maggie Sand," she says. "Write it down."

I have a glazed look. "Who's Maggie Sand?"

"My friend from college," she says. "I told you about her on the phone—lives in Michigan. It's all arranged." She's talking quickly, before the guard comes back to take her to her cell. "The airline tickets are purchased." She gives me the airline and flight number. "They're in the last name of Sand," she says. "Danny and Julie Sand." This so that Jack or the cops won't be able to trace them. "All you have to do is get them on the plane. Maggie will pick them up in Detroit."

"You've got bigger problems right now," I tell her.

She brings up her hands and buries her face for a moment in thought, no tears, just a few seconds of private contemplation as if she's making one final stab at getting it together.

"What happened to your hands?" I ask her. The soft pale skin is turned a shade of red more vibrant than any sunburn in a warm shower.

"It's nothing," she says. "I'll tell you about it later."

"I hope I did the right thing?" She changes the subject. "Deciding not to fight it."

My heart skips a beat, images of some fatal admission.

"You didn't make a statement?" I say.

"About what?" Her face is a puzzle. Then she gets it. I'm talking about a confession. Her expression turns to a mocking little smile, severe to the edges of her mouth.

"You think I did it," she says. "You think I killed Melanie." Her face turns to the side. Tight lips as if she were about to talk to someone in the empty chair next to her.

"Well, the fact is she deserved it," says Laurel. Her face whips to the front, eyes boring in on me. "But I didn't do it." She gives herself a pained expression.

"I hope you can believe that," she says, "because if you

can't I'm gonna need another lawyer.''

From the tone of her voice you might think I had arrested her. The look on Laurel's face at this moment brings me down.

"I was talking about the extradition," she tells me. "Giving up my right to a hearing. Was it a mistake?"

Like ships we have passed in the night. "Ahh." I shake my head. "No major mistake," I say.

At most a fight over extradition would have been a skirmish for delay across the state line, a battle that we would have ultimately lost and that the state might have used against us in a subsequent trial. I tell her this. We don't have much time. The guards are shuffling in the corridor outside, anxious to get her upstairs to a cell. I had to pull every string to keep from having this conference delayed until tomorrow.

I give her quick instructions, the basics intended to get her through the night. Seeing Laurel's exhausted condition, and knowing Lama, he will probably house her with some jail-house snitch in hopes that my sister-in-law will unburden her soul to a friendly face in seemingly similar circumstances.

"Can you get me out of here? Bail?" she says.

Without seeing the evidence, I am assuming the worst, that they will charge Laurel with a capital offense, first-degree murder with special circumstances. A lawyer's game of worst scenario. In a death case bail can be denied. I fudge. But there is no need to tell her this until I see the charges.

"It could be tough," I say. "Your trip out-of-state. They will argue you're a flight risk." She may sleep better without thoughts of execution.

"We'll see what we can do."

"You want to know why I went to Reno?" she says.

"A good explanation would help. But there's time for that later."

"I can't tell you," she says. "You have to trust me. Later," she says, "but not now."

Wonderful. She would leave the DA free to fill in the blanks.

"Yeah. Later," I tell her. "We can talk about it then."

I suspect that Laurel is operating on less sleep than I, not a condition that is likely to lead to a lucid rendition of facts. A client's story is always better told from a clear mind. I would like to avoid little slips, errors or omissions in detail, inconsistencies that might make me, or a jury, wonder later whether Laurel is telling the truth. It is always easier to put a defendant on the stand if her lawyer has confidence. And if Laurel is going to lie, I don't want to know. I would prefer that it be a carefully thought-out and credible whopper.

"What about your hands? Do you need something?" I say.

"Oh." Laurel looks at these sorry things, inflamed and irritated.

"It's just laundry solvent," she says. "She said they'd get the dispensary to give me something for it." She's talking about the madam from the Gulags who is now standing outside our door jangling her keys.

I arch an eyebrow in question.

"It's from the rug I was washing," she says. "At the laundromat in Reno." There's not a word as to what she was doing a hundred and thirty miles from home in the middle of the night, washing a rug. But from the look on her face, to Laurel, at this moment it seems a complete explanation.

If her story doesn't get better than this, she may need a lot more time than I thought for creative contemplation.

"They don't have the gun, smoking in her hand or otherwise," he says. "Except for that, there isn't much they're missing." This is Harry's way of telling me we are in trouble on the evidence.

Laurel is still behind bars. Arraigned ten days ago on a sealed indictment by the grand jury, she is charged in a single count of first-degree murder, alleging special circumstances. According to the indictment there is sufficient evidence of "lying in wait," that somehow Laurel entered Jack's house and scoped out the victim before striking. If this can be proved, the state can ask for the death penalty.

A pitch for bail during the arraignment netted me a major ass-chewing by the prosecution and a quick gavel from the judge. Unless we can quash the indictment, or at least wash out the special circumstances in a pretrial motion, Laurel will spend the duration waiting for trial, behind bars. Though that may not be the worst of our worries.

This morning Harry starts with the little stuff, trashing what had been an early dream, some way to attack probable cause for the arrest and spring Laurel back to her kids. At best this would have been a temporary fix, assuming there was cause, until they reconvened the grand jury.

"Even if we succeeded, she fled the jurisdiction on the night of the murder. Laurel was due in court the next day on the custody case. She's given the authorities no explanation for this trip. They claim this is highly suspicious," says Harry.

He is right. They could hold her on this alone.

What is more troubling is that Laurel has given no better accounting to us. She insists that she did not kill Melanie, but refuses to tell me what she was doing in Reno the night of the murder. She says she had a bona fide reason for the trip. Presumably she will share it with us sometime before she is convicted.

"Maybe she'll have an explanation ready for us in the morning," I tell Harry. This is when I am scheduled to see her again at the jail.

"Sure." He cackles, always the artful dodger. Harry has seen clients like this before. People who wonder if they should tell their own lawyer and instead end up doing it for the first time on the stand. I shiver and put it out of my mind.

I've told Harry about Vega and the fact that Jack was wired for sound in his office. He thinks Lama was trying to set me up, some compromising statement that perhaps I had knowledge of Laurel's whereabouts. This could make me an accessory after the fact, or at the very least cause the bar to launch a probe like a photon torpedo into my practice. Either way

Jimmy Lama would have a psychic orgasm.

Harry's fanning through pages on his desk, materials copied by the police and given to him under our application for discovery. At this point, with an ongoing investigation they have supplied everything except the names and addresses of any witnesses, people who may have seen things outside the house that night. These they will hold back until their investigation is complete. Lama would not want us talking to these people until he can cast their stories in concrete. He will tape their words and take signed statements so that they cannot later have some altered recollection.

"There is the rug," says Harry. "The one she was cleaning when they took her down."

I question him with a look.

"Heard me right," he says. "She was not in the casinos pulling handles when they got her." Harry punctures what he knows was my best hope to explain Laurel's trip. There are people who consider travel, blurry-eyed and at the speed of light over the mountains, as a quick fix for the gambling disease.

"She was in a laundromat doing the spin cycle when she was rudely interrupted," he says. "She was washing a bathroom throw rug," says Harry. He gives me a look like this is some crazy lady. What makes this worse for our side, as he explains, is that this particular rug has been identified by Jack Vega as belonging to him, part of the spoils of divorce. Jack has told the cops that it was in the house on the night of the murder, somewhere on the floor near the bath where Melanie was found dead. What Laurel was doing a hundred and thirty miles from home washing a rug is not clear. Harry shrugs his shoulders on this one.

"Did the cops find anything on the rug? Blood?" I say.

He shakes his head. "Clean as a whistle. She washed it in one of those chemical machines, the industrial ones with solvent."

"They'll argue she cleaned it to destroy evidence," I tell him.

"They already are, in a roundabout way," says Harry. "Powder-residue tests on her hands. Came up negative. She'd dipped them into the solvent."

Visions of Laurel's inflamed hands. Powder-residue tests are used to determine if a suspect has recently fired a gun. The discharge of trace elements, chemicals, can be detected on the hands, and in the case of a long gun other parts of the body.

I sit, taking in air, like being sucker-punched. There is little that will ignite righteous indignation in a jury faster than inferences of evidence being destroyed.

"Even assuming she did it, why would she take the rug? If it had blood on it, why not just leave it there?"

"It's one way to clean her hands and have an excuse for it." Harry's tracking on what will surely be the state's line of reasoning.

"Next," he says. "One gold compact, with the initials MLH. This was found in Laurel's purse at the time of the arrest."

This means nothing to me.

"MLH," he says. "Melanie Lee Hannan. The victim's maiden name."

"Oh."

Harry can tell by the look on my face that this is daunting, Lama's case against Laurel beginning to stack up.

He gives me an expression, a tilt of the head, like who knows? "Never circle the wagons in defense too early," says Harry.

We're both beginning to wonder if Jack was not right. That perhaps we should maybe have some early conference with the DA before the tides of temper run high.

"Then we have videotapes," he says.

"More than one?"

He nods.

The most damaging, he tells me, is the security video from the porch of the house, the night of the murder. It has the time and date imposed at the bottom left corner.

"I haven't seen it," says Harry. "We'll have a copy in a few days. But the description isn't good," he says. He reads from a page prepared by one of the evidence techs. They have pictures but no sound, what is described as a lot of angry and threatening gestures by Laurel toward the victim followed by the destruction of the camera by Laurel after the door was slammed in her face. According to the report, at one point Melanie, in the doorway, threatened to call the police if Laurel didn't leave.

"How do they know that with no sound?" I ask.

"Lip-readers," says Harry. He's talking about experts who can read lips with field glasses a mile away. These people can take the art of sounding out words from a tape to whole new levels.

"Do they know what Laurel was saying?"

"If they do, it's not in the report," he says.

"What time was the tape?"

"Twenty-seventeen hours," he says. Seventeen minutes after eight, the evening of the murder.

"Time of death?" I'm making notes on a pad, the critical elements.

"Ah." He's looking. "Eleven-thirty." This is as close an estimate as the medical examiner can make.

A little over three hours between the two events. "You said there were two tapes?"

"Yeah. The courthouse earlier that day," he says. "There was a security camera in the ceiling when Laurel went after her."

"All we needed," I say. It was bad enough that there were a dozen witnesses. On film this attack will take on a whole new meaning. A skillful prosecutor can splice these pictures together with forceful argument. The image for our case is not a pleasant one. A brooding Laurel languishing over thoughts of vengeance for hours before presumably carrying out the deed. Their case is beginning to take form, handed to them on a platter, a blood feud between the two women, with one of them now dead.

"The toughest part of their case," he says, "are the special circumstances." Harry does not believe that the DA can produce hard evidence that the killer, whoever he or she was, actually lay in wait for the victim.

"No lurking in the corners on this one," says Harry. "Whoever did her came straight at her," he says. "And they fought. The evidence in the bathroom shows a scuffle. They're playing it down," he says. "But the evidence is there. There was a perfume bottle shattered on the floor, like maybe she tried to throw it at the killer. A lot of stuff was knocked off the vanity. The scene was more consistent with evidence of a rash act of violence than somebody lurking in the shadows to do the victim quietly," says Harry.

It would be our first break in what is an otherwise seamless case for the state. Perhaps I can tell Danny and Julie Vega that at the very least their mother is not facing death if convicted.

Tonight we will be burning the oil, a first cut on a pretrial motion to attack the indictment, to scuttle the special circumstances. For the first time in a week some of the knots in my stomach begin to unwind.

"What else have they got?" I ask him.

"Bits and pieces," he says. "Very little blood in the tub, where they found the body. What was there is typed to the victim.

"Melanie was shot near the tub in the master bath. She appears to have been unclothed. Probably getting ready for a bath. The cops are thinking she fell in when she was shot or else the killer picked her up and put her in the tub afterward. They're still choreographing," says Harry.

"Any powder burns?" This could give a clue.

"Pathology," he says. "Not in yet." We have a new medical examiner in this county. He is notoriously slow.

"They did find some semen."

"Where?"

"The sheets on the bed," he tells me. "Dried. No biggie. Police lab checked it. A secretor," says Harry.

About sixty percent of the general population are what are known as secretors. These are people who carry in their bloodstream a specific substance that makes it possible to determine their blood group from other body fluids—tears, perspiration, saliva, and in this case semen.

"Blood type matches the husband," says Harry. He's talking about Jack Vega.

"Still, I'd like to check it," I tell him.

It is a problem most often in cases of disputed parentage, fudging on blood in a serology report. It is one of the areas I always check. Move a decimal point a few digits in one direction and the probability that blood belongs to one person or another, to the exclusion of all others, can go from one in a thousand to one in ten million.

I have known some good-time Charlies, working stiffs with a roving eye for the ladies, who are now on an eighteen-year cycle of support payments—paternity cases involving promiscuous mothers with more lovers than a rock band and children who look like the random sampling of a gene pool. It is what can happen in a lab when the candidate is itinerant and Welfare gives a little nudge. They figure the law of probabilities. If he didn't do this one, he surely did another.

Though rarely is it a problem in a murder case, still I ask Harry to check the blood and semen, an independent analysis. Harry has the name of a good lab. I want to know if Melanie was bedding another lover, maybe passion gone astray as a motive for murder.

"You think she was bobbing for apples with somebody else?"

I give him a face, like "who knows?" Harry makes a note to take care of it.

"Any prints?"

"Nothing they've disclosed," he says.

Fingerprints in a case like this can be a blade that cuts both ways. The absence of any prints tying Laurel to the crime, on its face, might lead to the inexorable conclusion that she was not there. On the other hand, if they can show by independent means that Laurel was inside the Vega home on the night of the murder—hair or fibers, a witness, any faint moves on the Ouija board of identification that a jury might buy—then the failure to find her prints in the house might lead to quiet conjecture, the kind you can't counter, that she wore gloves. It is only a short hop from there to thoughts of premeditation.

Harry fanning more pages in his pile of papers.

"All we have left is ballistics," he says. "Single nine-millimeter slug," says Harry. "Thin copper jacket. Badly deformed from the head shot. One copper casing, nine-millimeter Luger, with multiple toolmarks."

"How do they account for that?" I ask. I'm thinking dry fire. I have known shooters, mostly hobbyists, hunters, and marksmen, who will work the slide on a semiautomatic by hand with live rounds to ensure that the gun will not jam when fired. This would leave extra marks on the cartridges where the tiny metal teeth grip the rim for ejection.

"They're saying the casing had been previously fired. Expanded and resized," he says.

"A reload?"

"That's what they seem to be indicating."

"Where the hell would Laurel buy reloaded ammunition?" Their theory starts to have holes.

Harry gives me a look like "take your best guess." "You can buy the stuff at some ranges. Gun shows," he says. Harry plugging the leaks in their case. It might float, but these—gun shows and firing ranges—are not places I would ever expect to see Laurel.

"Anything on the gun itself?"

He shakes his head. "They're still looking for it. Lands and grooves on the bullet are a right-hand twist. Could be any of a dozen models sold. But here's the interesting stuff,'' he says. ''Their lab found some striations not quite as deep as the grooves. Four of them at the edges of the bullet,'' he says. ''Each one about the width of a piece of coarse thread.''

''Do they hazard a guess?'' I ask.

''Without another bullet fired from the same piece to compare, it's tough,'' says Harry. ''But they think it's a defect in the barrel of the gun.''

''It'll make the murder weapon easier to identify than dental plates if they find it,'' I say.

''Let's hope they don't find it in Laurel's apartment,'' says Harry.

CHAPTER
6

This morning Harry and I are doing some cold canvassing. Wearing out shoe leather on the cul-de-sac where Melanie was murdered, a survey of the neighbors, anything they may have seen or heard that night. With the cops holding their witness statements for another day, we have no choice but to go door-to-door.

We have an uphill battle. Like Harry says, "Anyone who ever fended off a murder case knows that shit always flows downhill." We are busy digging up dirt to build a dam.

Two days ago the city's mayor, Lama, and the Capital County DA, Duane Nelson, held a joint news conference on Laurel's case. They cozied up to the camera lenses, basking in the glow of warm strobe lights like they were on some hot beach in Mexico. Nelson told the press he had a stone-solid case, then proceeded to give them no details.

Nelson is a good lawyer and a better politician. Even though he can't stand Lama, having canned him once as a DA's investigator, he bestowed undue praise on Jimmy for netting the defendant so quickly. The event was one of those law-enforcement love fests that politicians crave—victory wreaths all around—a conquest in the war on crime.

There was more than a little hypocrisy in this. The day before Nelson called me to ask for a continuance in Laurel's entry of a plea. A reversal of roles. Prosecutors with a strong case are usually hell-bent for court. He gave me some babble about assigning the case to another deputy, some minor amendments to the indictment. My antenna is up. Something is wrong—hopefully with their case.

I gave him the delay and told him I would get a gag order if he didn't quit with the press. He laughed, good-naturedly, and assured me he would not do it again.

Melanie's murder has stirred particular anxieties in this city of political commerce, "Beltway West."

Government is a growth industry here, and the thought that legislators and their families are not safe is bad for business. Important people can leave to go live in the foothills.

The responsible voices of leadership, the Chamber of Commerce and the City Council, have been busy building on the theme that this was not a random act of violence likely to be visited on another prince of politics.

Laurel's arrest serves a useful purpose. The city is hard at work on the message that a vengeful former wife, no matter how much she is vilified in the press, is not Jack the Ripper. The Speaker of the Assembly can curl up in confidence with his concubines and sleep in peace.

I punch the bell and a woman comes to the door. A pleasant face, maybe sixty-five, white hair like the lady on candy boxes, but with more style.

"Margaret Miller?" I say. Harry's gotten names where possible from voter records.

"Yes."

"My name is Paul Madriani, this is Mr. Harry Hinds. We'd like to talk to you for a moment concerning the death of Mrs. Vega."

The smile fades on Mrs. Miller's face.

"Are you with the police?"

"We are lawyers, Mrs. Miller, hired to represent Laurel Vega. We'd like to talk to you if you have a moment."

"Oh." An expression like leprosy is now stalking her just

beyond the screen door. There's a lot of pained indecision. She would rather not, but doesn't want to be unfair. It is what the criminal defense lawyer sees with the good citizen, the detached witness. I can tell by the way she studies us that Mrs. Miller is uncertain whether by merely entertaining us on her front porch she is now violating some criminal law.

"I don't know. I guess it would be okay. If it's all right with the police," she says.

"Last time I looked, they hadn't repealed the First Amendment," says Harry.

She's giving him an imperious look as I knee him, a good one, in the thigh.

Mrs. Miller gives me a smile. She unlatches the door and swings it open.

Like a brush salesman I am busy giving her a full complement of teeth, artless smiles, and assurances that the law permits her to talk with us.

Harry, properly rebuked, gives her a business card and a ration of happy horseshit. "It's all part of the process of getting to the truth," he says, something Harry's shown no interest in except for those few times in open court when it has reared up and kicked him in the ass.

From the look on Mrs. Miller's face, it is against her better judgment, but she invites us in.

The Miller home is no hovel. Her living room has more bird's-eye maple than some palaces, enough antiques for a museum. It is festooned with trinkets from around the world, figurines carved of ivory, masks on the wall with the look of Polynesia. The lady, in her time, has the appearance of a global traveler. There is a picture propped on a table, of a man, she looks younger, his arm around her. They are in some far-off place, a lot of stone steps and jungle vines. There is no Mr. Miller. Or if there is, he does not vote. Harry's guess, given to me on the street, is that the man has gone on to the great cul-de-sac in the sky.

She offers us the couch, then fidgets, not sure whether we're the kind of guests to whom she should offer coffee. She finally decides that the right to talk does not include beverages.

"Mrs. Miller, we have a number of questions we'd like to ask you." I make it sound like I'm working from a questionnaire, some marketing survey, all very clean and clinical, "just the facts, ma'am."

"Why don't you take a seat?" I say. Prerogatives in her own house. She could throw us both down the front stairs and we would have no recourse. Except for unusual circumstances, the law does not permit a criminal defendant to depose or otherwise take a sworn statement from a witness unless they agree to cooperate.

She sits on the edge of a chair, the last two inches supporting only her spine. Her posture conveys the thought that she doesn't intend to stay this way for long.

"Have you talked to the police about the events of that night?"

She nods.

"Can I ask you how many times?"

She has to consider this for a moment. Bad news.

"Three times. Once here. Twice at their office," she says.

"The police station?" I say.

She nods.

Only serious customers go there.

"Did you call them?"

"Oh, heavens no! They came here. Knocked on the door. Like you," she says. "The morning after she was . . ." She reaches for the "m" word, but can't say it. Like perhaps this might be offensive to us.

"The morning after she passed on," she says. Sweet and a little singsong, she makes it sound like some shifty-eyed embolism sneaked up and took Melanie in her sleep. We should wish for her on the jury.

"Can you tell us what you told the police?"

"I'm not sure I'm supposed to."

"Did the police tell you not to talk to us?"

She shakes her head.

"That's because under the law, they can't. The police are forbidden to tell a witness not to cooperate with the defense in a criminal case. That's the law," I say. It is also a quantum leap from the inference I would have her draw—that she *must* talk to us.

"It's how we get to the truth," I say. "Everybody talking to everybody else." I make it sound like a social tea. "I'm sure you'd like to cooperate?"

"Oh. I don't want to be uncooperative."

"Of course not. And we appreciate it. Now can you tell me, as well as you can, what you told the police?" The devil at work.

"I guess you want to know about the woman," she says.

"The woman?"

"The one who came to the house."

"You saw someone come to the Vega house the night of the murder?"

"Yes."

Harry and I look at each other. Bingo. The cops have a live one. The first neighbor who has seen a thing.

"Can you tell us what time you saw this person come to the house?"

"Actually I saw her twice," she says. "The first time about eight o'clock or thereabouts. A lot of noise. Arguing on the front porch," she tells us. From the way she says this the cops may not need a lip-reader to peruse Jack's security tapes.

"Were you able to identify this woman?"

With this she looks at me. "I think it was your client," she says. "They showed me a picture. Actually several pictures. I was able to pick her out. It was hard to miss her. She made so much noise and all."

"And did you see this woman leave?"

"I did. A few minutes later."

"About what time was that?"

"I think I told the police about eight-twenty. She got in her car and drove off. I may be wrong, about the time I mean. The police thought it was closer to eight-thirty. They're probably right," she says.

"Why do you say that?"

"I'm not very good on time," she says. And because they're the police. She doesn't say the latter, but I can tell from the look on her face, like every good citizen Mrs. Miller is anxious to defer to authority.

The next item I tread on carefully, not anxious to reinforce something that may not be helpful.

"You say someone came to the house a second time that night. Was that later?" I ask.

"That's correct."

"You saw this person?"

"I did."

"And what time was this?"

"About eleven o'clock. Maybe a few minutes after. I saw her out on the street."

"Did the person arrive in a car?" I say.

"You mean the second time?"

"Yes."

"No, I didn't see a car."

"Did you see which direction she came from, the second time?"

"No. She just seemed to be standing there, near the driveway at the front of the house. And she'd changed."

"Changed?"

"Her clothes."

"What makes you think it was the same woman you saw earlier in the evening?"

"The build. The way she walked. Her face," she finally says.

"You saw her face?"

She nods, soberly, like she knows this is bad news for our side.

"What was this woman wearing when you saw her the second time?"

"Sort of a sweatshirt, with a hood. It looked like running clothes to me. Like perhaps she'd been out jogging or was getting ready to go."

"But you did see her face?" says Harry.

"Pretty well," she says.

"Enough to identify her?"

She thinks for a moment. The ultimate issue. "Yes."

"You're sure it was the same woman you saw earlier in the evening? The one on the Vegas' porch who was making all the noise?"

"Oh, yes. We've established that," she says.

"We?" I say.

"The police and I." Jimmy Lama's conquest. Mrs. Miller's views are no doubt now cast in stone.

"Have you signed a statement?" I ask this in clinical terms, like no big deal. You can change it at will.

"Last week," she says.

"And they taped their conversation with you."

She looks at me like she's not sure. But, knowing Lama, this is a certainty.

"The first time this woman came to the house, did you see the car she was driving?" Harry is now double-teaming her.

"Yes. It was green, large. A Pontiac, I believe."

The lady has a good feel for cars. Laurel has a late-model metallic-green Pontiac.

"But you never saw this car later that night?" Harry looking for a point.

She looks at him grudgingly. "She could have parked it around the corner," she says. In the role of good cop, bad cop, it is clear who is going to get the confidence of Mrs. Miller.

"Still, you didn't see it?" I ask.

"True."

"Had you ever seen that car in the neighborhood before?"

"No."

"Had you ever seen the woman before? The one you identified for the police?" I say.

"Not that I can recall."

"But the second time you saw the figure"—Harry's not
conceding it was Laurel—"the second time there was no
car."

"I said I didn't see a car."

Harry's just checking. Hostility rating high.

"Did you think this was strange? No vehicle?"

She makes a face. "Lots of people run," she says.

We probe for openings, any concession she might be willing
to throw our way.

"Did you actually see this person, the second figure—did
you actually see this person enter the Vega house?"

"No. And I told the police that." She's nodding to us, like
"isn't that fair?"

"Thank you," says Harry. Now if she will only retract her
identification of Laurel on that second trip, Harry would kiss
her behind.

"How well did you know Melanie Vega?" I ask.

"Not at all. We had nothing in common." There is no
equivocation here, abrupt, like the two women lived on different planets. I get the sense that there is something of disapproval lurking just under the surface, like Mrs. Miller is just
egging me to ask. She sits on it like a pincushion.

"You never saw her in the yard, over the fence, maybe
gardening?"

"I don't think she would have known a rose if it stuck her,"
she says. A lot of imperious looks. "If we passed we didn't
talk. She kept to herself—and her few *friends,*" says Miller.

"Friends?"

"She had a few."

"Women in the neighborhood?"

"They may have been from the neighborhood, but they weren't women. At least not that I noticed."

If we had tea and little sandwiches we'd be heading toward the lady's dirt session.

She fumes about a little, searching for the words. Then she says: "Mrs. Vega had callers."

I give her a look.

"Mostly at night, when her husband was away." She looks at me, waiting to see if I will roll with her in this hay. But I am taking notes, the dispassionate clinician. She takes to the defense, like a gossip scorned.

"Well, when men come at night they're not usually selling vacuums. I told the police the same thing."

She looks at Harry, who is smiling. I can tell his mind is back to Melanie and the thought that, in his words, "She was bobbing for apples."

"Well, I may be older, but I've been around."

"Oh, indeed," says Harry.

She's not sure how to take this, but she lets it pass.

"You told the police she had gentlemen callers?" I say.

"Absolutely. They wanted to know everything, so I told them." She gives me a solid nod, like "done my duty."

A buzzer goes off somewhere, the clock on a kitchen stove.

"Will this take much longer? I have some errands to run," she says.

"A couple more questions," I tell her. I could ask her about the hood, how much of the woman's face it covered. Just how well she could see that night. What the light on the street was like. A million questions to set up doubts. But if she is going to equivocate, I want it to be on the stand, in front of a jury. Probing these issues will only serve to prepare her, perhaps quicken images already planted in her mind by Lama and his minions. I want to keep her as much in the middle between our sides as possible, reinforce the view that the good witness does not belong to any camp. With Mrs. Miller it may be the best I can do, at least for the moment.

Harry grills her on a few more points, what she heard on the steps as the two women argued. Lama might have hoped for more on this. It seems all she got was a lot of shouting, with very few intelligible words, most of which she does not wish to repeat. "Foul language," she says. She could jail Laurel for this alone, I think.

"Could we hurry this up?" she says. "I have a phone call to make before I leave on my errands."

I seize the opening, some time to prepare and another session.

"If you're in a hurry, maybe we could continue this at another time, more convenient."

"That would be better," she says. Like a patient out of the chair in some dental office, she is now all smiles.

"When would be convenient?" I ask.

"Why don't you call me?" She gives us her number. Harry writes it down.

We head for the door. I can see large windows in the dining room. These look out directly onto Vega's front porch. She would not need field glasses to see who was there.

"One more question," says Harry. "That night, did you hear anything that might have sounded like a gunshot?"

She shakes her head, soberly, like she's thought about it before, something on which she is adamant. The cops must have grilled her on this.

"No gunshot?" he says.

"No."

"No popping sound?"

"I know what a gun sounds like," she says.

Harry looks at me. We have already hit three of the five houses in the cul-de-sac. Mrs. Miller's house is next door to the Vega residence. The Merlows live on the other side. Except for Kathy and George Merlow, who we will do next, and who I met that night, Miller is closer than any other house in the neighborhood. So far, the bathroom trashed, glass bottles thrown and smashed, a nine-millimeter round fired, and no one heard a sound that night.

"You don't suffer from any form of hearing impairment?" Harry can't resist.

She stops and looks at him. "No one has ever accused me of that." If we get her on the stand I will keep Harry outside.

I thank her, tell her I will call in the next day or so, and we are gone.

We're down the steps, out on the sidewalk. Mrs. Miller's front door nearly hit Harry in the ass on the way out.

"Bad news for our side," he says. "We could have her eyes checked. Subpoena the records of her optician," he says. "A fucking jogging suit," he tells me. "She can see through a hood. Better eyes than Superman. Why the hell didn't she just swallow the speeding bullet and save us all the trouble of a trial?" Harry has a bad attitude with witnesses who are not helpful, particularly if he thinks they are embellishing what they saw for the benefit of the boys in blue.

This is clearly his thought with Mrs. Miller. "If it walks and it wears a badge," he says, "it's right."

Four down, one to go. We head for the Merlows'.

Their house has a deep setback, forty yards of grass and dying shrubs.

George Merlow lacks inclinations toward a green thumb. Or else his gardener's been deported. The lawn hasn't been mowed in a month. It's covered by a carpet of leaves, and weeds sprout in the planter beds like tulips in Holland.

We head up the walkway through the front garden. The double front door is one of those arched affairs, something that looks like it belongs under a steeple, in a church. Except that stuck in the crack between the two doors is a single sheet of colored paper, a handbill that is weathered and brittle. An advertisement for a Halloween sale that ended three weeks ago.

There's a newspaper, still wrapped in its rubber band. It's been watered by the automatic sprinklers or the morning dew and left to dry in the sun. I have seen parts of the Dead Sea Scrolls in better shape. I roll the rubber band down and open it to the front page. The lead story is about Melanie Vega:

LAWMAKER'S WIFE MURDERED IN EAST AREA

It has been here, forgotten under some bush, since the day after the murder.

I climb the steps and look through the glass on the door. It is leaded and beveled, a view like a kaleidoscope, glittering light with more angles than one of Harry's clients. I pick a facet and look. Clear carpet as far as I can see. No furniture. Nothing on the walls.

I ring the bell. We wait patiently for the sound of footfalls. The only thing that arrives is a cat, calico and hungry. It bounds down from the railing on the porch and begins to make love to my leg.

"Nobody home," says Harry.

We ring again. Same result.

It isn't until I turn that I see it. At the far end of the porch, propped against a windowsill, a sign—"For Sale"—a realtor's logo emblazoned across the background. I walk the distance and look at it. Some agent's name and number, home and office, dangle from a separate metal placard below the main sign. I take these down on the back of a business card and slip it in my pocket.

"Moved," says Harry.

"Looks like it," I say.

As I turn I can see directly into one of the windows that looks in from the porch. A bedroom, empty space. If you hollered it would echo. The only thing remaining is the curtain on one side of the window, like maybe whoever left did so in haste.

I head down the porch and around to the side of the house, Harry on my heels.

"Maybe you were mistaken. Maybe they went into another house. Lot of confusion that night," says Harry.

"No mistake," I tell him. "I watched them walk all the way down this driveway and disappear into the backyard."

Some confusion. Harry tramps to the sidewalk and checks the street number painted on the curb against his copy of the voter rolls, the Merlows' address. They don't show up.

"Good citizens," he says. Given Harry's attitude toward government, I might question his criteria for demerit points in civics.

He pulls out a little cellular phone and flips open the mouthpiece. Harry and the electronic age. Some fool in a company has given him this thing to use for six months, part of a promotion. Harry has already dropped spaghetti sauce on the dialing pad, which he bitches is too small for his lumpy fingers.

Phone directory has no listing for the Merlows, new or old. He's talking to himself as I head through the gate toward the backyard.

"Nosy neighbors may call the cops." Harry's worried.

"We're house shopping," I tell him.

I don't have to worry about running into Jack. Since the murder he and the kids have moved into a condominium downtown, closer to the Capitol. Word is that Julie and Danny were spooked by the house. Danny would not stay there after he saw cops tramping through with questions, brushing fibers off the carpet of his dad's bedroom. The condominium was a concession, part of the deal for tempo-rary custody, to lure the kids back into Jack's nest pending Laurel's trial.

"What are you looking for?" says Harry.

"I don't know. Just something about them that night."

Maybe it was Kathy Merlow, her wide-eyed preoccupation with the remains, wanting to know when the coroner would bring out the body. Perhaps it was her fragile condition, not so much physically ravaged as psychically stressed. Whatever—Kathy Merlow had a look that night, an aspect that in twenty years of criminal law practice I have seen enough times to recognize. She wore it in her eyes, the stamp of someone who was witless with fear. Not some idle vague anxiety, but more specific, some reason to be afraid.

Harry humors me as we survey the yard.

The Merlows' house, or what used to be, is one of those modern Victorians, a lot of gingerbread sold as style—half a million dollars of house on a million-dollar lot.

Like Harry said when he saw the neighborhood, "Area is everything."

In the back there's a pool and sport court, fenced in black chain-link, surrounded by faux gaslights like a London street, in the motif, so that in a fog you might have visions of Jack the Ripper.

"These people live nice," says Harry. He'd like to know what George Merlow does for a living.

"That may be our best chance to find him," I say. "His work." Though I don't have a clue what it is. I try to remember the tenor of our conversation that night. But it wasn't a meeting where small talk predominated. Kathy Merlow was too busy looking for bodies.

On the far side at the back of the house there's a low deck. This leads to a small dining area off the kitchen. Harry tries the sliding door. It's locked.

I look at him, raised eyebrows.

"I just want to look," he says.

Upstairs there's a balcony, turned spindles, and glossy white handrailings, what every little girl would like on her dollhouse. This runs the entire width of the house, to the second-story turret, where the balcony becomes a descending staircase, spiral and wrought-iron to the ground.

Harry and I climb. On the balcony, the slider between the large bay window and the stairs is locked. Harry has checked this. He's now wiping little smudges from his fingers off the glass with the bottom of his coat.

I peer through a small window by the stairs. As vacant as below, a bedroom. My guess is the master. I can see a large adjoining bath.

The bay on the other side, closest to the Vega house, is a small den. A man's room. A wet bar, brown wallpaper with ships. There's a built-in entertainment center on the far wall, a cabinet with one door not closed. There's a built-in desk in the bay of the window. Depressions in the carpet tell me that furniture was placed in front of this. My guess is a swivel desk chair, something to take advantage of the views from the window over the desk, that could be turned to the TV.

"Nothing here," says Harry. "We can run 'em down from postal records." He's thinking change of address.

I'm thinking three strikes and you're out. Something in my bones tells me that George and Kathy Merlow will not be that easy to find.

We turn to leave, and I stop, dead in my tracks. Harry's halfway to the stairs before he realizes I'm not behind him.

I'm looking from the balcony, the view from the bay window, Merlow's study. Like a seat in the bleachers at Dodger Stadium, it looks down, over the fence, and directly into a large window in Jack Vega's house. This is not just any window. It is one of those greenhouse affairs that could house a small family—a glass wall curving from roof to foundation, bigger than the bubble on a B-29.

Set in the window is a massive bathtub, Jacuzzi heaven, white porcelain on a platform of tile. Strands of yellow police tape bar the door to the bathroom. Something left in Jack's wake of departure.

Harry's finally joined me back at the railing, tracking on the view.

"It's still preserved," he says. "We oughta get a court order for Jack's house." Harry wants a look at where it happened. Leaning against the railing, he looks over his shoulder at the gaping glass of what we must assume was George Merlow's study.

"And we need to find your friend George Merlow," he says.

CHAPTER
7

The fourth floor of the county courthouse accommodates the probation department, the cafeteria, and the master calendar of the municipal court. Muni court in this state does small-dollar civil cases, misdemeanor trials, and gets most of its publicity by serving as the clearinghouse for arraignments on major felonies.

A further arraignment is why I am here this morning, facing a bank of lights and running with my briefcase under one arm through the loading chute of pack journalism, trying to avoid being roped and branded.

There are a dozen questions shouted my way. The cameras hold back, a lot of long shots with the strobes, file film they can use on another day, when some notorious event occurs, when your client has been drawn and quartered in legal fashion, and you are seen on the tube grinning and cavorting like it's all in a day's work.

Some asshole sticks a mike in my face and asks if my client did it.

Criminal confessions—film at five.

From the tenor of his question I'm not sure the guy has a clue as to specifically what *it* is, other than one of the usual infamous acts certain to nourish an inquiring mind. Otherwise why would his producer have sent him? The information highway, all the shimmering depth of quicksilver.

I passed Jack Vega on the steps on my way in. He seemed more hostile than usual. Perhaps he was just skulking, trying to find his own way in around the press and cameras.

I get inside the courtroom door and shut out the din of the unwashed. It is quieter here, more subdued, muted tones, a humming undercurrent of courthouse gossip. Some of these are the legal groupies. What used to be all guys, and now some women, regulars who live in the court's bullpen, the pressroom downstairs. They have more access to the judges than any lawyer. Some of them have their own keys to the clerk's office so they can burn the midnight oil.

They'll do a filler on page ten from a probate case one day, some Daddy Warbucks who left ten million in trust to his pooch, a shar-pei with a face like somebody's other end. They'll do a big-bucks tort the next. But give them a choice, and murder among the tony set will always hit the top on their charts. Rumpled reporters who know how to rifle a clerk's file. The people you gotta watch. Turn your back, a loose word in the wrong ear, and you become news, not the kind you want to read about.

I hear my name, the topic of banter. Somebody breaking from one of the cabals in the front row.

When I turn I am staring Glen Dicks in the face.

"Glen," I say.

"How you doin', Paul?" Everything is first-name here, but we don't shake hands. These are secondary relationships. Not ugly, just business.

Dicks writes for the *Herald*. One of two papers in this city. He has the edge on the out-of-towners who have come to see because of the political fallout of the case. A legislator's naked wife found shot has potential.

Dicks is gray curling hair to the lobes of his ears, and a mustache to sweep your porch with. He wears a sport coat with more things sticking out of pockets than a porcupine's ass, and bears a gut like a Victorian bustle, which has opened and jettisoned a button on the belly of his shirt.

He gives me the old saw about a lawyer defending himself. Then he asks me: "Is that anything like defending a relative?"

"I don't know. You should ask my sister-in-law if she feels like a fool," I tell him.

He laughs a little. Dicks is shrewd enough, a goer to events, the watcher of a thousand courtroom brawls, to know there is a tactical downside to my representation of family. Played to the jury in the right tone, a backhanded compliment by a prosecutor, it could sound as if I don't believe in her case so much as feel an obligation.

Glen inserts a few delicate probes, looking for anything to get a pencil into. The time frame for trial. Whether it's likely the defendant will take the stand. Ideas on the number of defense witnesses. He gets quotes he can print, but no information.

"What's happening here today?" he says.

"You should ask the DA."

"Amended indictment," he says. "They didn't tell you anything?"

I pass it off as minor stuff. "I assume it's mostly technical. T's and I's," I tell him. "Crossing and dotting."

"Emm." He is writing this down.

"Any theory of a defense?" he says.

"Sure. And I'd like to share it with you, just as soon as I have confirmation that the DA is deaf, blind, and doesn't read Braille."

A nervous grin. A look like he had to try.

"How is she taking it?" He's talking about Laurel. If he can't get a real story he'll go for the human interest angle.

"Except for the bars and the ladies who do the screaming meemies at night, she tells me it's just like home."

He would laugh, but Glen is sensitive enough to get the picture. He's nodding like he understands, so I give him something he can write.

"She's facing serious charges," I say.

Little squiggles in his book.

"She doesn't have a clue as to what happened. And like any mother, she misses her kids."

"The children, they're with their father," he says. Not a question so much as seeking confirmation.

I nod. "They're not orphans yet. They have their dad."

"At least for the moment," he says.

A look like maybe I should depose him. My turn for information. He misses only a beat.

"Well, you hear things," he says. "Courthouse bureau talks to the Capitol bureau. Things like that," he says.

"Things like what?"

"Stuff on the assemblyman." He tells me this, and then, like speak of the devil, his notepad is up to the corner of his mouth, shading it from any lip-reading, a nervous eye to the door.

Jack Vega has just entered the courtroom.

Dicks screws up his face a little, like maybe he's not sure whether I've undone this particular family knot. Maybe Jack and I split poker pots on Thursday nights.

I let him know, in a few words under my breath, that there is no love lost.

"What are you hearing?" I say.

"That he's coming under some intense scrutiny—of the federal variety." He gives me a face like some Frenchman judging a foreign wine. "FBI, and the U.S. Attorney," he says.

There has been talk of a hot federal probe for months, a lot of smoke but no fire. Everybody figured the air was clear when a state senator, the acknowledged subject of the inquiry, was given a clean bill of health. It came in a bland statement by the Justice Department, like a medical press briefing on the condition of the legislature—the patient has cancer coming out its ass, but we can't find it on the X rays.

Still, maybe Jack's power party is about to end. He has been doing business with an ardent passion lately, shaking the givers out of the political money tree. With his term ending,

Jack's running out of time, trying to sell his ass before it sinks to the value of Confederate currency.

"What are they looking at, the feds?" I ask him.

"If we knew that, we'd be doing a story," he says. "But word is he's under investigation," says Dicks. "We hear rumors, no sufficient confirmation yet, just rumors, of another federal grand jury."

I would not want to shatter Dicks' illusions, but if Jack is wearing a wire, he is no longer the one under investigation. Suddenly Vega's electronic connections are beginning to make sense. It had nothing to do with Melanie's murder. My guess is that Jack is aboard the good ship justice, chained and manacled, and in the brig. With a full federal court press, the squeeze on, if they got him on film taking a bribe, some hotshot agent looking for an Oscar, Vega would whittle in his pants on show night.

He would convince the feds that the Capitol is a den of thieves, not that they would need much convincing. And if anyone whispered the word wire, there is not a doubt in my mind Jack would show up with cables coming out his ears and a car battery strapped to his ass.

I see a guard bringing Laurel in through the steel door that leads from the holding cells. My conversation with Dicks comes to an end. He drifts off to circle again with the pack. Having planted this seed in my curiosity patch, he will no doubt watch to see if it sprouts during trial.

Laurel is sans the shackles and chains, though she is still wearing the orange jail jumper, like some farmer's daughter in papa's overalls. With no jury in the box, for the moment, her looks are irrelevant to the interest of justice.

She sits down at the counsel table and I join her.

Not a word, she takes my hand on top of the table. Her look over at me is only fleeting, a smile, forced in bad times. In our few conversations she has seemed embarrassed that her grief has been laid on my plate. There have been repeated promises that she will pay every dime of her legal fees. At one point she even told me to bring on the public defender. She would qualify for services.

"What's going to happen?" she says. "Here today."

"Just conforming charges to evidence," I tell her. It is hard to imagine that they could do more damage. I am thinking maybe some legally ham-handed effort to shore up their special circumstances, to bolster the theory that Laurel was skulking around Jack's house that night, hiding in closets, waiting for Melanie to come around a corner.

Harry has his own theory. He is guessing that they will charge Laurel with robbery—the theft of the bathroom rug that she was washing in Reno, and which she has yet to explain. The crime of robbery in connection with a murder falls under the felony-murder doctrine, its own form of special circumstances that justifies a death sentence.

I have told Harry this is garbage. Robbery would require evidence that Laurel formed the intent to take the rug before she confronted Melanie. No one has ever accused Nelson and his staff of being mentally wounded. It would take such an assumption for the state to try this case on the theory that Laurel murdered Melanie over a scrap of carpet.

Commotion, bodies moving, shadows in the corridor beside the judge's bench. First I see Jimmy Lama, then a feline form coming out ahead of the bailiff. Duane Nelson has made his assignment of counsel, the prosecutor who will do this case.

Morgan Cassidy is part of Nelson's A-list, one of four or five top trial deputies out of nearly a hundred lawyers in the office. She does only heavy-duty stuff, a woman with a death wish for every defendant. Five-foot-six, trim in the way only frenetic people are, a Dutch-cut brunette, she is not a lawyer to inspire trust among the defense bar. She has been known to win a few cases at any cost, a woman who will tangle with a judge, and in the best two falls out of three will come up wearing his balls.

She is driven, obsessed with the chase, one of those people who flail themselves hourly for their few missteps in life, who are haunted in their quest for success, but once victorious find no enjoyment in it. A trial against her is like milking a cow in competition with a machine. She has a plug on every leak in your case, with the suction turned on supercharge.

What is as distressing as her presence here is the fact that she comes to the courtroom from the direction of the judge's chambers. With anyone else I might not care. With Morgan I am wondering what plot she hatches.

Cassidy doesn't look at me, but Lama gives me a smirk as he passes in front of our table. He does a little shifting of the eyes above this shit-eating grin, to Cassidy then back to me as if to say, "Looky what warped soul I brought you."

They get to their table and arrange a few papers. Lama will sit with her during the trial, the people's representative. They are entitled to one, and as the detective in charge, Jimmy would be most familiar with the evidence—real, and, at times in Lama's career, manufactured.

I would get up and talk to Cassidy, ply her a little, but there is no time. On their shadow is Tim Bone, presiding judge of the municipal court. He is up on the bench swinging wood and coming to order.

"The matter of the People versus Laurel Jane Vega."

The clerk reads the file number. The stenographer hitting the keys, taking notes.

Bone is tight-lipped, a skinny little man, bald as a baby's ass, and not to be screwed with. He has a face like yesterday's wash left too long in the dryer, a lot of wrinkles, and cold.

"I believe the defendant was informed of her rights at the initial arraignment," says Bone. "So we can dispense with that here.

"Ms. Cassidy, have you delivered a copy of the indictment to counsel yet?" The way he says this makes me think that it has been the subject of some conversation in chambers between the two of them. Like maybe Bone is not happy that we've received no notice. As a legal principle it doesn't matter. The purpose of the arraignment is to identify the defendant and to advise us of the charges pending. But Bone is a stickler for courtesy.

"Doing it now, your honor." Cassidy snaps her attaché case open, takes out a sheaf of papers, and waltzes over to hand it to me. It is stapled, numbered in the left margin, and looks about the same as what we received in the first arraignment.

"Mr. Madriani, you should take a few moments." Bone is beckoning me to read. "I've told Ms. Cassidy that this is not to happen again. Not in my court. In the future you will deliver copies of charging documents to opposing counsel in advance of arraignment," he says.

"Yes, your honor." About as chastened as a hooker caught with her john.

I am reading down the page, the single count of murder, followed by the allegations of special circumstances—lying in wait. So far so good. If Cassidy has goosed it for advantage, I don't see this. I flip the page. Nothing new. Turn it over. On page three, centered in the middle, big bold print:

COUNT TWO

As and for a second and separate count, it is further alleged and the defendant is charged with violation of Section 187 of the Penal Code in that on October 19th of this year, she did unlawfully take the life of John Doe, an unborn male child. . . .

For an instant I sit there glazed, my eyes no longer focusing on the page. I slide it at an angle so that Laurel can read over my shoulder, my finger moving under the operative words "unborn male child."

By her expression she is wondering why it is necessary for her to be reviewing technical revisions of the indictment. Then the words settle in. Big eyes, she is reading, swallowing air.

"Oh, my God," she says. Hand to her mouth, she is suddenly ill, like a sucker punch to the gut. She retches, a deep convulsion, but comes up dry. Hand to stomach, she is still reading, like maybe the words on the page will change. Vanishing ink.

I am thankful that at this moment there is no jury in the box to witness this. There is a lot of satisfaction spreading across Cassidy's face, she and Lama busy studying the defendant for affect. In their eyes Laurel's actions possess all the confirmation of guilty knowledge, the ultimate import of her dark deed. I am struck in this moment by the irrefutable fact that a trial with these two is not likely to be a religious experience.

I stumble to my feet to object, without much purpose, and before I fully comprehend. What can I say? "They have surprised us. We respectfully request that the court dismiss the charge"? Cassidy knows her tactics constitute a wrong without a remedy.

"Your honor. This is the first we are hearing of this. The state has declined to produce its pathology report."

"It's simple," says Cassidy. "The victim, Melanie Vega, was four months pregnant when she was murdered by your client." Smug, righteous indignation. A morality play for the press.

I don't turn, but I can see Glen Dicks' pencil flailing out of the corner of my eye. Tomorrow morning's headline: CLIENT HAS FOOL FOR LAWYER.

"But the state's pathology report . . ." I say.

Bone is looking at her, eyes that could kill from the bench.

She pops Pandora's box once more, and this time has Lama span the gulf to hand me a copy of the coroner's medical report, five pages single-spaced, little drawings on every page.

I scan it quickly, and nearly weep. Medical evidence of a potentially viable fetus. It is the stuff that Cassidy lives for. A cause. She will have pro-life groups stacked in the halls outside, placards and chanting, amidst pictures of pale and washed-out embryos floating in mayonnaise jars.

We have not yet started, and Cassidy has headed me off at the pass. She has crushed one of the few advantages of our case, that if placed on the stand, my client on a single shining issue would ring true and loud, a beacon to the jury, the picture of Laurel, the image of the good mother. She sits here now sullied and seemingly with the blood of some unborn child on her hands.

I am told that going to trial against Morgan Cassidy can be a little like a honeymoon: every day there's a new surprise, and all the while you are constantly being fucked.

Having been ripped in the arraignment, I waived a formal reading of the charges, scooped my slackened jaw off the floor, and retreated to the relative safety of the holding cells and the more amiable society of career felons.

On my way out I fired my only bullet, a motion to keep sealed the grand jury transcripts, the details of the evidence away from the prying eyes of the press and public, and a request for a restraining order to gag the prosecution and the cops.

Judge Bone, who was already in an ugly mood, having been transported there by Cassidy and her conduct, granted both, though only on a temporary basis. We are to return in ten days to argue the merits of a permanent restraining order. Cassidy may be able to screw me in court, but if she talks about it on the air or to the scribes in the front row, Bone will put her butt behind bars.

Laurel and I sit at the little table in the client conference area, door closed, a guard outside. I am struggling to put the pieces of our tattered case back together, my brain trying to communicate with damage control. In the courtroom I was unable to finish reading all the details of the indictment. I get to this now, language at the bottom of the page, further allegations of special circumstances. This is Morgan's coup de grâce.

The unlawful killing of a woman carrying a potentially viable fetus constitutes two murders—what is known in the law as a multiple-murder special. This is true even if the perpetrator did not know of the pregnancy, and a single act kills both mother and child. In points and authorities delivered to me, Cassidy cites chapter and verse, case law directly on point. The only way Laurel can beat death now is to convince a jury that she didn't do it, or if she did, that there were mitigating circumstances, some excuse that does not warrant the death penalty. With Cassidy stamping around in the blood of an unborn child, this will be no mean feat.

"This is awful," she says. Laurel's talking about the fact that Melanie was pregnant. "A baby." She's shaking her head, looking at the tabletop as if maybe there's an answer in the scarred metal surface.

"I may have been capable of killing her," says Laurel. "God knows I hated her enough."

Thoughts I would keep from a jury.

"But not with a child," she says. "Never with a child."

Laurel is one of those people to whom the young always seem to gravitate. Every family has them, aunts and uncles who speak a special language of love. These people know what makes kids move. On family outings Laurel would spend endless periods talking to Sarah, off in quiet corners. She knows more about my own daughter, her secret desires, the things that terrify her in the night, than I do. So this dead child, and the thought that others at this moment think Laurel is responsible, is a blow of staggering proportions.

"They really think I did this?" she says. For the first time she looks at me.

I don't respond, but she knows the answer.

"You didn't know that she was pregnant?"

Laurel's head is back in her hands, supported by fingers at the forehead. Eyes focused down once more.

"How could I?" she says. "Melanie didn't share such things with me. Did she look pregnant to you?" she asks.

"I thought maybe Julie or Danny . . ." I say. Like perhaps

Melanie talked to one of the kids during periods of visitation at Jack's house.

"No. They would have told me," she says.

I have been wondering why this didn't tickle Jack's rage earlier, the death of an heir. His male ego, the fact that his seed was snuffed before it had a chance to come to full flower, is not something Jack could easily walk from, even if an extended family was not something high on his agenda. The reason for Jack's seeming heightened hostility this morning now makes sense. Jack got his own surprise. The first hint that his wife was pregnant came from the medical examiner, after the autopsy.

"One thing doesn't make sense," I tell her. "Why would she keep it from Jack? Another child on the way. Seeds of a new family. Domestic tranquillity. With what they were doing in court, they could have used it in the custody fight."

"You're assuming the child was Jack's," she says.

"I know there was no love lost," I tell her.

"It's not a matter of animosity," she says. "I know the child could not have been Jack's."

"What?"

"It was not something we talked about, even to the family," she says. "But Jack had a vasectomy twelve years ago," says Laurel. "Right after Julie was born. He could no more father a child than I could."

CHAPTER
8

She arrives wearing beige pants, a white blouse, and a long flowing caftan, yards of shimmering silk and open down the front. It is the feminine counterpoint to the rough cowboy's duster on an abandoned street with guns slung low on the hip.

Dana Colby looks from across the room, the smile of recognition as she negotiates the small tables of the crowded restaurant, mostly couples paired off. She is a contrast in striking features, amethyst eyes against pale skin, and hair the color of burnished copper. She moves with a saucy confidence that screams divorced and in demand.

A score of male eyes wander from their dinner companions to stare at this electric beauty, the lusty-eyed look of children who have suddenly spied something better on the shelf.

I rise. She does the thing that is chic, takes my hand, then leans across the table and plants a kiss on my cheek, nothing amorous. To those initiated in the ceremony it says we are merely friends.

"Sorry I'm late," she says. "Friday night. Traffic was hectic," she tells me. "Have you been waiting long?"

"A few minutes." Looking at her, I know it was worth it.

Dana's hair, like Rapunzel's, if undone could lower a family from a burning building. Tonight it is braided in a single course, shimmering to the center of her back.

We are standing in the middle of the Chievas, the most

expensive restaurant in Capital City, on the main level, off the dance floor, a legion of envious eyes on her, male and female. I feel like the winner of the last jackpot on bingo night.

She sits. I slide her chair in.

"Thanks." In her smile there's enough heat to fire a boiler.

The waiter is on us. Something to drink?

"A glass of white wine," she says.

A dozen choices, she picks Gewürztraminer.

I order a liter. I will ply her with wine.

I called her yesterday and asked if she could meet me for lunch, a couple of items I wanted to discuss, perhaps renew an old acquaintance. I have a more specific agenda, but I kept it to myself. She was busy for lunch, so tonight we do dinner. It is business, and I am still feeling married, a daughter at home who expects me before the witching hour of her bedtime, at nine. I would lack the confidence to ask this woman on a date. Still Dana has the grace to make this look social.

In law school she had a boyfriend, four years ahead of me, a prophet who'd already crossed over into the land of milk and honey, a lawyer with all the accoutrements, Porsche Carrera, and a condo at the Point. While it turned out later to be an exercise in futility, he'd given her a ring with a stone the size of a glass doorknob. It was our semester of "Equity," and to this day the thousand maxims born of the ancient law of chancery are a mystery to me. I spent my time, like a dozen other guys, dazed by the kaleidoscope of the colors radiating from the prisms on her finger, and dreaming at my desk.

"You look spectacular," I tell her.

She blushes just a little.

Men are funny. Do a thousand trials, some silver-toned Cicero on the jaded edge in front of a jury, and a woman in a caftan, dressed for adventure, can steal your tongue.

"I'm sure we both look better than we did the last time," she says. She's talking about the street out in front of Jack's house the night of the murder.

"I love this place. Have you been here before?"

"A few times," I tell her. "You?"

"Once or twice."

No doubt on the arm of sterner stuff than this.

The waiter arrives and pours our wine.

"Lately I see your name in every newspaper," she says.

"Mostly taken in vain," I tell her. "It's hard to turn an arraignment into disaster. But it seems we managed."

She laughs a little. "Morgan has a positive talent for other people's disasters."

"You know Cassidy?"

She nods.

"We belong to the same club," she says.

"Ah." I'm a thousand expressions, all of them bad.

She has both hands on the stem of her wineglass, holding it just off her lips, the pose of meditation.

"And no, it is not 'bitches anonymous.' " She's smiling at me.

"Hey—did *I* say it?" But she can smell my thoughts.

"Not in so many words."

"Am I that transparent?"

"Window to your soul," she tells me. "Though on the subject of Morgan it's not difficult to read the mind of another lawyer who's crossed her path. She has been known to play the ball out of bounds," she says.

"Where were you last week, before the arraignment?"

"Hey, she's not all bad. Has some good points."

"I guess I haven't seen that side."

"She does people without discrimination. In terms of gender," she says. "Half the women lawyers in Queen's Bench, the club we belong to," she says, "won't talk to her. Fortunately I've never been on the receiving end of one of Morgan's free kicks. So I guess we're still friends."

"You sound like an admirer."

"In my own way. It's a tough world out there."

"Tell me about it."

"You should try it in a skirt and heels sometime."

"Somehow I don't think it would help," I tell her.

She smiles, little laugh lines forming around the eyes.

"We do lunch once a week," she says. She's talking about Cassidy. "Maybe I can put in a word."

"Not on my account," I tell her. I have known people like this before. To those on a crusade, efforts to influence are often taken the wrong way.

"Maybe you just haven't seen her softer side."

"Not so I noticed."

"I'll talk to her," she says. The smile on her face tells me this is a fruitless gesture. Idle chatter over lunch is not going to get Cassidy to ease off on multiple murder. Maybe with some other deputy DA, if the victims were homeless vagrants and the press weren't in attendance. But with Cassidy the juices of obsession run fast and furious, like a white-water ride down the Colorado.

"This is really an excellent wine," she says.

I agree. The Gewürz is going down smooth. Something to give you that light liquid buzz, jelly in the stomach and knees when you go to rise.

"So what's this thing you wanted to talk about?" she says. "I suspect you did not call me simply for a session of Morgan-bashing."

"No. Not that it hasn't been fun," I tell her.

She smiles again. "I'll tell her you said that." She winks at me over her glass.

"I wanted to talk to you about the Merlows. George and Kathy," I say.

A blank stare, searching her mind, like maybe the Merlows are players in some coffee ad on the tube.

"You remember?" I say. "The young couple out in front of Jack Vega's house the night of the murder?"

"Oh, yes," she says. The light of recognition.

"I thought you might know where they moved."

Head slowly shaking. "No. I didn't know they had."

"Small neighborhood, little cul-de-sacs backing up onto

each other. I thought maybe you might have talked to them,"
I say.

"No, can't say that I have. The east side is full of strangers.
People who commute but never talk. Fact is, I'd never met
them before that night. And haven't seen them since. When
did they move?"

"Soon after the murder. Like maybe the next day," I say.

"And you're thinking this is highly coincidental?" She's a
smirk across the table from me. I can tell what she's thinking.
The desperate defense attorney grasping at straws.

"A little strange," I say, "that they didn't mention it."

"You're thinking maybe they saw something? Or at least
hoping?" She is now a full smile. The prosecutor as cynic.

She hasn't seen Jack's bathroom window.

I make a face, a concession that it's a long shot, but unwilling to convert her to a laugh.

"Good luck," she says. Then, all serious, "If I knew I
would tell you. Are you sure they've moved?"

"The house is empty. There's a for-sale sign."

"It does sound like they've moved," she says. "Listed with
a realtor?"

I nod.

"Well, there you are. I'd talk to the realtor. They must
know something."

"We're checking. I just thought maybe if you knew them
you could save me some time."

"If I could," she says. "But the fact is they wandered up
and introduced themselves that night. First time we ever met."
She shrugs her shoulders, like "wish I could help, but can't."

"You're in a box on this case, aren't you?"

"A firefight," I tell her, "and I'm low on ammunition."

"Gotta be tough," she says. "Is it correct what I hear, that
she is family?"

She's followed the case closer than I thought.

"My wife's sister."

She sips her wine and nods like she understands.

"There are children, I hear."

"Two. Teenagers."

She's shaking her head. "That is awful. Hard on them."

"Tell me about it." I sneak a look at my watch. Not carefully enough.

"Do you have to be somewhere?" she says.

"Oh, no. My daughter," I say. "I told her I'd be home in time to say goodnight. But I have plenty of time."

"Oh." She softens, little crinkles around the mouth.

"How old is she?"

"Seven," I say. "Going on twenty. The price we pay for living in the global village. MTV and the loss of innocence," I tell her.

"It must be difficult," she says. "Raising a child, alone."

"It has its moments."

"Do you miss her a lot?"

"Emm."

"Oh. Never mind." A lot of flailing hands across the table, looks of embarrassment.

"I'm prying," she says.

Then I catch her drift. "You mean Nikki?"

"Yes. But it's none of my business."

"I don't mind," I say. "Yes. I do miss her. More than I like to admit. Especially to myself. It's the thing about the people we know best. The ones we love. We take them for granted. I never realized how much I would miss her until she was gone."

She nods like she understands. But I can tell she doesn't have a clue.

"You spend a lot of time preparing, and then it's over, you're alone, and you discover that all that preparation was a waste of time. Because there's really no way to get ready. No matter how much time you have. In the end there's just a great big hole left in your life."

"It must have been a very special relationship."

"I wasn't a particularly good husband," I say.

"You're being modest."

"No. We had more than our share of problems. My obsession with work. A wandering eye during a period of separation," I tell her. I could tell her that more than my eyes wandered.

She looks at me, a little startled by my frankness.

"But I suppose if the measure of a good marriage is how much you miss someone when they're gone, then ours was a good marriage."

I notice that we are no longer making eye contact. It is getting maudlin. A session of true confessions.

"The story of my life," I say. "How about you?"

"Oh. Three years of marriage. No children. One divorce. And for the record, I don't miss him."

"The advantages of dying," I say. We laugh a little, but for me it is bittersweet.

We pick up our menus and scan the entrées. The waiter arrives with a list of specials, a dozen more dishes given to us like a pop quiz in physics. We order, and afterward there is small talk, mostly about work. My venue being mostly state and hers federal, there is wide latitude for talk without breaching confidences.

Dana is a comer, on the move. There has been talk of a federal district judgeship, not from her lips, but I have read it in the papers, her name on a short list. She would be the youngest appointment in the history of the district.

I'm cutting a ravioli with the edge of my fork when I finally broach the subject.

"I'm hearing some rumors," I say, "about Jack Vega and a federal probe."

She is good. Her eyes never leave her plate. A face like a stone idol. Not the slightest hint that I have bushwhacked her.

"Some pretty good sources," I say. "They tell me that he's the target of a federal investigation."

She says nothing, but puts down her fork, wipes her lips with her napkin. I can tell by the look that she's preparing to stonewall it. I play the trump card before she has a chance to dig herself in deep with any lies.

"Your man's wearing a wire," I tell her.

Suddenly her look becomes more serious.

"Who told you that? Have you been talking to Mr. Vega?"

"We have talked. But he didn't tell me. He didn't have to. Jack's a natty dresser," I tell her, "and fargos tend to make a bulge. He shot a button—into the next county," I tell her. "And I got a glimpse."

"Oh, shit." She's looking at me from the corner of one eye, like she only half believes this. Then she starts to laugh at the mind picture drawn here, her napkined hand in front of her mouth.

"You aren't kidding, are you?"

"No, I'm not." I go along with her, and we both end up laughing.

"I can't believe this. What an idiot," she says.

"Well, Jack wouldn't be my pick for an informant," I tell her.

If she thinks he's bad now, wait until she gets him on the stand. In front of a jury, Jack is likely to possess the credibility of Jell-O—a lot of wiggles and all transparent.

"You understand I can't confirm or deny," she says.

She already has, but I tell her I understand.

"Who else *suspects* this?"

"Some of the press believe he's the target of an investigation. They're just a little behind the curve," I tell her. She looks at me, and I can tell she's wondering how long the secret is good with me.

"How long has this been going on?" I ask her. "Jack's part in your investigation."

"This is very awkward. You put me in a spot," she says. "Who would have thought that his wife would be killed in the middle of it?"

"See it from my perspective. The man's married to the victim. He's a principal player. I suppose I could get a subpoena," I tell her, "but it would be easier for both of us if I didn't have to."

"On what grounds?"

"On grounds that if Jack was turning state's evidence in a major federal undercover investigation, it's conceivable he could have been the target of a murder attempt the night his wife was killed."

"You're not serious?" she says. "It's only a white-collar investigation."

She says this like these people are all uppercrust. Like they do all their crimes only with pen and pad, and only on starched white linen.

"Like none of them ever panic?" I say. "Maybe snuff one another to keep a secret?"

She's shaking her head in disbelief.

"The jury would certainly have a right to hear it," I tell her.

"You believe that's what happened?" she says.

I make a face. "Whether I believe it or not is not the issue. To get a subpoena all I have to do is show relevance. And I think a court would agree that this is relevant."

"I should have known better. He couldn't even turn it on and off at the right times." She's talking about Jack and his electronic hip pad. "Half his conversations are things we didn't want or need. Calls to check on his laundry and have his hair styled."

"Sounds like Jack fell early?" I say.

"First fish in the net," she says. "So he got a good deal."

"And let me guess. You've been turning the screws on him pretty hard?"

"He folded like a house of cards. Told us things we would never have discovered in two lifetimes. And when he fessed up, he cried like a baby. Seems he was having some personal problems of his own," she says.

I raise an eyebrow.

"Marital," she says. "I almost felt sorry for him."

"And how did you know this?"

"I can't say any more. Until I get authorization," she says. "Do I have your word you won't say anything to anyone until I talk to my superiors?"

"I'm not interested in saving Jack's bacon. But I need to know what's going on."

"Do I have your word?"

I nod.

"Maybe we can cooperate, wrap up our investigation quickly before you go to trial," she says. "If we can get indictments, it won't matter if Vega's cover is blown," she says.

"Can we meet tomorrow night?" she says. "It'll give me a chance to talk to my people."

I nod. "Whatever," I say.

This is fine with me. I have no stake in Jack. They can have his ass, roast it over an open flame for all I care. What I want to know is what kind of pressure they were putting on him. At this point I have two theories of what might have happened that night, only one of which I have told to Dana.

CHAPTER
9

"The Resolution Trust Corporation," says Harry.

"What?"

"The RTC. The agency that took over the bankrupt savings and loans."

Harry is driving as I am looking at him from the front passenger seat of his car. He is telling me who holds the mortgage on George and Kathy Merlow's house. Harry's run up a dead end with the realtor.

"What's more, the agent said they never heard of George or Kathy Merlow. The sales listing was signed by some swag from the RTC, part of the excess real estate the agency picked up when they were shutting down the thrifts," he says.

According to Harry, this property, the Merlows' house, has languished on their rolls of unsold assets for some time.

"How did the Merlows come to live there?"

"Your guess," he says. "The realtor thinks it was probably rented out. He says that's not uncommon. Public agencies often do it, he says, while trying to sell property they hold. It defrays expenses."

"Where do we go from here?" I ask him.

"I got a call in to the RTC," says Harry. "Left a message on their voice mail. They'll probably call us back in the next life," he tells me.

In the meantime Harry is driving me to the old downtown

post office, the place where, according to neighbors, Kathy Merlow worked.

"This employment is past tense," he says. Harry's talked to a supervisor. "They haven't seen her in almost a month," he says. "Not a word. She just didn't show up for work one day, and hasn't been back since."

"Let me guess. Right after Melanie Vega was murdered?"

"Next day," says Harry.

Kathy Merlow vanished like a ghost.

I'm not sure what we hope to find at the post office, but Harry thinks it might be worth nosing around. He's made an appointment.

"What about George Merlow?" I ask.

"If he worked, it was out of the house. Neighbors said they never saw him leave. Once in a blue moon," says Harry. "Like the guy was a recluse."

"That house," I say. "Pretty expensive digs for a guy without a job and a wife who works at the post office."

"Maybe he clipped coupons," says Harry. "Big stock portfolio."

"And his wife needed to work at the post office? It doesn't make sense."

"Maybe with the government for a landlord the rent wasn't much," says Harry. "You don't expect 'em to charge fair rental value?" Harry sneers at the mere thought of a rational act by a government agency. A lot of maybes, but no answers that make any sense.

We pull up and park in front of a meter at the curb. Harry pumps three quarters and watches as the dial barely budges. He hits me for some change. I give him two more.

"We'll have to work fast," he says.

We're up the stairs, through the heavy bronze doors.

The old post office is one of those structures built during the time of the WPA, when only the government had money and wage scales were on a par with the pay for the pyramids. Dark, with dated artistic touches, more marble than a mauso-

leum, it is now a tomb for the unknown bureaucrats who toil
here.

We take the elevator to the second floor. Harry's reading
from a scrap of paper, a note with the man's name and room
number. He finds the number, 224, a door with a translucent
window, lots of chicken wire in glass, and a transom over the
top of the door that looks like it's been stuck open since the
forties. It's too dark to tell if they've painted the corridor since
then, but my guess would be no from the state of the dingy
walls.

Harry opens the door and we go inside. The room is immense, and mostly empty. There are two metal government
desks, one of which is vacant. At the other sits a thin black
man, pencil mustache, maybe in his early fifties. Short-cropped
graying hair. He looks up at us.

"Looking for Mr. Goldbloom," says Harry.

"You found him." The guy gets up and Harry introduces
us.

"Oh, yes. You called. Lawyers," he says, "about some
case."

Harry gives the guy his card and plucks one from a holder
on the man's desk, government issue recycled stock, the gray
cast of cardboard: "Cyril Goldbloom, Postal Inspector."

Leave it to Harry to find a cop.

"What's this about?" he says.

Harry refreshes his recollection, their telephone conversation.

"Oh, yeah. You called this morning. Something about a
criminal case. Looking for one of our people. A personnel
matter," he says. Relief on Mr. Goldbloom's face. He's found
the right pigeonhole for our problem. He sits back at his desk
and motions for us to join him. I take a chair on the other side
of the desk. Harry opts to put one cheek on the empty desk
across the way and watch from there.

Goldbloom opens a top drawer and pulls out a form, more
small print than the Bible.

"Employee's name?" he says.

We're going to do this by the numbers. Harry looks at me. I can tell he is thinking profanities.

"Kathy Merlow," I say.

"That's right. I remember," he says. He writes her name in the block at the top of the page.

Now he's writing Harry's name, address, and phone number from the business card, putting it in a little box on the form.

"Purpose of the inquiry?" he says.

I look at Harry, shrug my shoulders. "Legal investigation," I tell him.

"Your relationship to the employee?" He looks at me, then to Harry.

"Strangers," I tell him.

"Emm." There doesn't seem to be a little box labeled "strangers." He labors over this for several seconds, then finally scribbles a note at the bottom of the form.

He has a dozen more questions, most of them inane. Then he looks up. Task done.

"We'll file this," he says. "As I explained when you called"—he's looking at Harry—"Mrs. Merlow no longer works here. We'll check her personnel file to see if there's any information that we're free to disclose."

"Can we look at the file?" says Harry.

"No. No. Personal and confidential," he says. "Federal law. There could be all kinds of stuff in there."

That's what Harry's hoping for.

"What *can* you tell us?" I say.

"That's about it," he says.

"What position did she hold? You oughta be able to tell us that," says Harry.

He makes a face, thinking, like maybe what he's considering is against his better judgment, giving information to citizens. Then he reaches for one of the lower drawers of his desk and pulls out a series of typed sheets, stapled together in the upper left-hand corner. This is an impromptu phone directory of some kind, what is given to employees to find each other. He flips through some pages.

"Here it is. Kathy Merlow. Customer Relations," he says.

"What's that?"

"Customer complaints. That kind of thing."

"Did she transfer in from another post office?"

"That I don't know."

"She was only in town a short while."

"Wouldn't know."

"She worked in this building?"

"Uh-huh. Downstairs," he says. "Now that's about all I can tell you."

"How long before we get a reply?" says Harry. "To your form. Maybe a forwarding address for Mrs. Merlow?"

Goldbloom makes a face. "Could take a while. Has to go over to the main branch. Postmaster will have to review it. Personnel Department," he says.

"So we could die of old age?" says Harry.

Goldbloom laughs. Staring all day at four dingy walls, his humor threshold is low.

Harry's getting hot. "If we were the cops you'd show us her personnel file today, wouldn't you?"

"That'd be a different matter," says Goldbloom. "An official investigation," he says.

"Would a subpoena do any good?" I ask him.

"Oh, sure. Then we'd be free to show you the file." He smiles at us. "One of the exemptions in the law, a court order," he says. "I'd like to help, but my hands are tied," he says. Dark eyebrows arching.

"Sure," says Harry.

We say good-bye and head out.

We're halfway to the elevator. "We get a subpoena," I tell Harry.

He has a better idea. We're down the elevator and out the door, and Harry's not headed for the car. Instead I'm tracking him down the street, along the side of the building, which covers half the block. In the rear is an alley that cuts the block in two. From Seventh Street this runs downhill and back up to Eighth Street on the other side. At the lowest point in the alley is a loading dock, several small postal vans backed up to this.

"No law against talking," says Harry.

We're down the alley and up on the dock before I can say a word. A couple of carriers are loading mail. They ignore us, maybe hope we will go away, pain-in-the-ass citizens looking for mail.

Harry walks up to one of them.

"We're here to pick up a package," he says.

"You go to the window out front," says the guy. He's not even looking at Harry, still loading his crates of letters, his back to us. He flings the little flats of letters into the back of the truck like some Bedouin flipping camel dung into a fire.

"They told us to come here. It's a big package," says Harry. "We got a call some time ago from Kathy Merlow," he says. "I think one of her friends here, I can't remember the name, is supposed to be holding it for us. Could you check?" he says.

The guy finally straightens up, gives Harry a look and the government-service sigh. You can tell what's going through his mind. "Like world crisis, national calamity, a package lost at the post office."

"Gimme a minute," he says. He loads two more crates in the back of the van, empties the little hand dolly, and turns for the building and another load.

Harry's on his heels.

The guy turns.

"Stay here." He freezes Harry with a look. Then he disappears through a swinging door into the building.

Harry gives me a devilish grin. Even in the short time that she worked here, Kathy Merlow must have made at least one friend, somebody this guy will run to who would come outside to see who is using her name.

It's a couple of minutes, Harry and I killing time on the dock, dodging other carriers with crates full of mail, happy to ignore us so long as we reciprocate.

Finally the carrier comes out. I think he's alone. Then I see her, a woman, more properly a young girl, lost in his shadow. She could be anything from sixteen to twenty-two, not so much slender as gaunt. Dressed in the blue uniform shirt of the Postal Service a size too big, the shirttail hanging outside of her dark trousers nearly to the white tennis shoes on her feet. Her mousy brown locks are braided into two pigtails that jet from either side of her head and explode in a frizz of hair just beyond the rubber bands holding them together. In a rational world someone might be pressing the Postal Service under the child labor laws. She has a pale complexion dotted with a few freckles, and all the hope she can muster resides in oval brown eyes that seem to belong to somebody else. She has the look of an urchin from a Dickens fable that ends badly. But one glance and I know, that whether locked in hell or the bowels of the federal post office, from what I remember of Kathy Merlow, this woman and she are likely soulmates.

"You lookin' for Kathy?" she says.

Harry nods.

"She don't work here anymore."

"You knew Kathy Merlow?" says Harry.

The woman has wary eyes. "Whadda ya want?" she says.

"We'd like to find Mrs. Merlow," says Harry.

"He says you was lookin' for a package?" She's looking at the carrier, who's wandered back to his chores.

"We need to talk to Mrs. Merlow." Harry softens like he's talking to a young child, coaxing information.

"Seems everybody wants to find Kathy," she says.

"Who else has been asking?" says Harry.

She looks at him but doesn't respond.

I step forward and hand the girl my business card. She studies it for several seconds.

"We're lawyers," I tell her. "We'd like to talk to Mr. and

Mrs. Merlow in connection with a case we're handling. We think it's possible that they could be witnesses in the case.''

"They do something wrong?"

"No. No. We just want to talk to them."

"I can't help you. I don't know where she is." She starts to walk away.

"Ma'am."

She turns.

"It's very important. A woman's life may depend on it."

She locks her oval eyes on me for a moment.

"A mother with two children." I turn the screws a little deeper.

She looks at the carrier, who's paying no attention at this moment. She moves a step closer to us.

"How could Kathy save a life?" she says.

"It's a murder trial. We represent—"

"Marcie!" A booming voice from the doorway behind her. The woman shrinks to half her already minimal size. There, outside the swinging door, is a man, maybe thirty-five, a tie, white shirtsleeves rolled to his elbows, close-cropped hair, the look of management in his eyes. "Are you on a break?" he says.

She turns. "No, sir."

"Then you're supposed to be sorting," he says. "This is what we talked about in your last performance evaluation," he tells her. "Do we have to go through it again? Put it in your file," he says. "I don't have to remind you that you're on probation," he says. "One more unsatisfactory report and you're on the street. I told you. I warned you."

This woman, Marcie, is now shaking, though I cannot tell if it is from fear or anger.

"I just stepped out," she says. Her voice is of sterner stuff.

"Do you want to talk about it or do you want to have a job? If you want to talk about it, you can do that from out there, on the street," he says. He points to the sidewalk.

She stands there frozen in silence, with her back to him,

and mouths the word for us to read, "asshole."

"Well, which is it gonna be?" he says.

Marcie looks like she could squeeze between the door and its frame when it was closed. But in passing this guy she has difficulty. And he won't move an inch to let her by, but makes her walk around him.

Shaking his head as she skulks past, hands on his hips. He could be the Master of Tara after some worthless pickaninny fieldhand. All that is missing is the broad-brimmed hat and the whip.

Before I can say another word she disappears through the swinging doors. The hot breath of opportunity, gone.

The guy in shirtsleeves is standing there looking at me now, but a different posture, a lighter tone, dealing with the public, somebody not so easily cowed.

"What are you gentlemen doing here? This area's off limits to the public," he says.

Harry's moving as if he'd like a piece of this guy. In his face, solidarity with the workers, a budding assault on the ramparts of management.

I grab him by the arm. "Another time," I tell him.

Harry growls deep down in the throat, like some mad mongrel about to rip the ass end out of somebody's pants. I would swear that there's a little foam at the corner of his lip.

Before we hit the steps down to the alley, the guy's chewing on the carrier.

"What are you doing letting them back here?" he says. "Why do you think we have rules? You can't deal with it, you call security. How many times we have to talk about it? We go over, and over, and over this stuff and you people, you never listen."

Five-nine to six feet, he's looking across at the carrier's chin, shouting into his throat, a dressing-down in front of others you would not give a schoolchild caught shoplifting.

The mailman looks at him like he could deck the son of a bitch. The only thing holding him back is the need to feed his family in what the politicians euphemistically call a downsized economy.

We're down the concrete steps from the dock and up the alley and I can still hear the guy ranting, ragging on the carrier, who could kill.

"What an asshole," says Harry.

"She knows something," I tell him. "She knows where Kathy Merlow is."

He looks at me. "How do you know?"

"She was gonna talk. I could smell it. When I told her there was a woman's life in the balance. She leaned," I say. "She was falling into our arms. In that instant before Simon Legree showed up."

"Maybe we could look on Goldbloom's list and find the name Marcie," he says. "Call her on the phone."

"What, and fill out another form?" I ask him. "We'll find another way to run her down. Come back after work if we have to."

"It raises another question," says Harry. "Who else do you think is looking for Merlow?"

"My guess? Probably Jimmy Lama."

Harry gets the picture. If Jimmy did the neighborhood like us, he couldn't miss the Merlows' empty house.

"He'd check where they worked. Lama and his cronies probably lined up all the help in the mail room and did the third degree. A point for our side," I tell him. "If it was the cops who were asking. Marcie's a friend. If she thought Kathy Merlow was in trouble, you think she would talk?"

Harry's shaking his head like a village preacher asked if the devil goes to heaven.

"That's what I think," I tell him. We do a mutual smile, grins all around.

We're to the corner when I see the expression on Harry's face turn grim, then angry.

"Shit." It is the only thing he says.

The meter maid is busy writing Harry a ticket.

• • •

"Racketeering, mail fraud, and extortion," she says. "Six counts. He pled out two months ago to a sealed indictment." This is Dana Colby's rendition of what the Justice Department has on Jack Vega.

I whistle, low under my breath. He could do a dozen years for this. These are no doubt all activities that Jack would lump under the term "fund-raising."

"Mr. Vega doesn't have good money manners," she says.

Knowing Jack and his ability to draw attention, he was probably working the rotunda of the Capitol, threatening tour groups with new taxes unless they gave him their pocket change.

It is nearly seven-thirty in the evening. I am at Dana's house out in the avenues. Two blocks from Jack's. It was Dana's choice to meet here. To do it in the office, she says, would have raised questions. She has talked to her people and is now able to tell me some things.

"So Jack's now doing his civic duty," I say. I'm talking about Vega rolling over on his unsuspecting friends in the Capitol.

"He had something to offer. We were interested," she says. "Sit down. How about a cup of coffee?"

"Sure." I settle into the couch in the living room, where I can see her through the opening to the kitchen while we talk.

Dana's still dressed from work, white blouse, a gray tight wool skirt, hemline above the knees, pinstripes. What the well-dressed female lawyer wears. The skirt clings to her form as she moves about the kitchen in bare feet, having ditched her heels by the chair across the way in the living room.

"We offered him eighteen months at Lompoc," she says. "And a quarter-million-dollar fine."

This will no doubt draw down Jack's kitty. And while he will do his time in one of the federal country clubs, the place where the junk-bond kings made muscles, grew beards, found God, and turned over new ethical leaves, it is still a penitentiary. When he comes out he won't be doing any lobbying in D.C. The thing Jack lives for, power, will be drained from his bones like some leaking, dead battery in a discarded toy. For someone like Jack, who doesn't know how to do real work, he would view this as the first step on the road to homelessness. A man who is suddenly under a lot of strain, getting his psyche steamed and pressed.

"His lawyers made a big pitch," she says. "First offense. A man with a family. A long and distinguished public career."

"Long I will concede," I tell her.

"And children," she says.

Suddenly Jack's rush to get custody is making more sense. The kids were a foil, a shield that he could throw up to a sympathetic federal judge. No place to go, they need a father.

"He must have given up quite a bit in return?" I say.

"Some members of the House," she says. No names, but from the way she speaks I am certain these are ranking politicians.

"And a few lobbyists." She talks like they are trading pieces on a chessboard—my knight for your majority whip.

She's out with the coffee, two mugs, and a little dish of cookies. She hands me a mug, offers a cookie, and I take one. I am doing without dinner tonight. Then she kneels down on the couch, legs slightly spread and curled under herself so that we are now two endpieces with a single cushion between us. Her skirt has hiked up a little so that I am now getting a lot of open thigh with my coffee and cookies. She sees me looking, does nothing to adjust her skirt, but gives me that knowing look that some women do so well when they know they are being ogled but don't mind.

"It's a pretty good deal—for Jack, I mean. Given the charges, if the evidence was solid."

"Ironclad," she says. "We had him on tape, soliciting and accepting bribes. Still, he's not finished dealing."

I give her a look, a question mark.

"His lawyers are arguing that the murder of his wife, the

absence of any available parents for the children, changes the circumstances of his situation. His lawyers are making a pitch for straight probation. Another hearing before the court.''

One thing is clear. Though she doesn't yet know it, the name of Dana Colby will be appearing on my list of witnesses for the defense.

''You don't sound like you're putting up a pitched battle over this.''

''He was a corrupting influence, poisoning the system,'' she says. ''Whether he does jail time or not, we've effectively cut him out like a cancer. The terms of probation will be long and severe. No lobbying, barred from public office. Sometimes there is only so much you can do. Diminishing returns,'' she says. ''We had what we wanted. Vega's cooperation, the man out of the process. His testimony against others more corrupt,'' she says.

I don't think there is such an animal. And Dana sounds more than a little defensive. I wonder if there are other reasons they backed off to let Jack walk, something she is not telling me. Some other leverage that has gotten Dana to call off her dogs.

Still, this is the Jack I know. The king of Teflon, even in the jaws of justice. A tragedy in the family, and Jack doesn't miss a beat. His lawyers ever on the lookout for the silver seam, he appears to have found it.

''How far are you from closure?'' I ask. ''For Jack to finish his chores? Indictments?''

''Ahh. Well, these things take time,'' she says. ''A few weeks, maybe a month—could be a little more.''

It would be easier to get federal cooperation, to go public with the information on Jack's criminal involvement and avoid a messy battle with the feds if they can wrap their case and bring indictments quickly. It would also shed a new light on the grieving spouse, perhaps take a little of the edge off of the state's case against Laurel. After all, the victim was, at a minimum, living with a felon. I wonder how much Melanie knew.

The favored tactic on defense. Put the victim on trial.

"There's no doubt that his wife's murder adds a complication," says Dana. "Still, I'm not sure we see any connection between the two, our investigation and Mrs. Vega's death." Dana's look at this moment is more questions than answers. She wants to know if I have anything specific linking the murder and Jack's problems with the feds.

"That raises a question," I say.

"What's that?"

"Would you have told me about the sting with Jack if I hadn't stumbled over the wire?"

She smiles, little crinkles at the corners of her mouth.

"Probably not. We would have seen no connection to the murders. No foul, no crime," she says. "Unless you know something we don't."

I give her a stone face.

"You don't really think that somebody tried to kill him that night to silence him?"

I am a shrug, a downturned mouth.

"Tell me about his marital problems," I say.

She looks at me over her coffee mug.

"The other day, over dinner, you said that on top of everything else, the screws you folks were turning, that Jack had marital problems."

She takes a sip. "Hmm—that," she says. "No offense. I know he's your former brother-in-law and all."

"You can put the emphasis on the word *former*," I tell her.

"I suspect if his wife was sleeping with other people she probably had good reason," says Dana.

"You sound like you're not a fan of Jack's."

"I take a hot shower with lots of soap every time I have to deal with the man." She tells me it's not just Jack's corrupting ways.

"Every look you get from him, it's like he's having optical intercourse with you," she says. "I'm not talking mild glances. The guy would zero in on cleavage, a gap in your knees, any open opportunity,'' she says. ''And it didn't stop with looks.''

''I've never noticed,'' I lie.

''You're not a woman,'' she says.

I can believe that having set his eyes on Dana, Jack would have developed eyes that could fuck.

''Was Melanie doing it with somebody else?''

''More like everybody else,'' she says.

There's a long sigh, like she's not sure she should be getting into this. Then she finally looks up at me.

''You didn't hear it here,'' she says. She reaches across the gulf between the couch and the coffee table and puts the mug down. Little pockets of fabric open on her blouse and I can see a lot of lace underneath, then I divert my eyes. The ravages of the guilty male mind. She's sitting up again, straight. I lock eye contact to keep my own from wandering.

''He allowed us to put a tap on his home phone. I don't think his wife knew.''

''You heard her talking to other men?''

''I didn't. But agents who were monitoring did. Liaisons out of the house, and some there.''

''Did Vega know?''

She nods.

''How do you know?''

''The guy was awful with the wire,'' she says. ''He'd leave the thing on for hours. Forget to turn it off. Then twice when it was off and there were important conversations, he forgot to turn it on. We know,'' she says, ''because the people showed up on the video in his office.''

The image of this, like some silent movie, pictures and no sound, somehow is chilling. I make a mental note not to be seen in Jack's office again.

''We had to send him back,'' she says. ''I mean, it was terrible. He mealymouthed his way back into some guy's office and told him he forgot what they'd discussed ten minutes before, about the contribution, wink, wink, and what piece of legislation was the quid pro quo. Can you believe?'' she says. ''Like talk into my tie clip.''

''And I'll bet the guy repeated it all.''

''Oh, yeah.'' Dana is all big eyes. A face filled with expression. Incredulous. ''These people believe in trust,'' she says.

Why not? I think. They're talking to Jack Vega, the patron saint of political corruption. Who was dirtier than Jack?

''It was impossible for Vega to have a secret from us. Even things we didn't want to know.''

''So he suspected that his wife was having an affair? He said this?''

''At least twice,'' she says. ''Once to one of the young aides in the office. A woman. It was pretty bad,'' she says. ''He was producing a pity play for sympathy, complete with sound and cameras. Crying on a soft shoulder. The gal was in her early twenties, didn't know what to do. This slobbering guy all over her, arms around her neck. I couldn't tell if he was serious or if it was just a pitch to get into her pants,'' she says.

Knowing Jack, I can form my own conclusion. He always operated on a double standard. If it moved, Jack would fuck it. But let Melanie step out with some other man, and you can imagine Jack—capable of almost anything.

''And there was one other time,'' she says, ''on the phone to somebody. We don't know who. It was all very cryptic.''

''Do you know what they talked about?''

She shakes her head.

''You have the tapes?''

''At one time,'' she says. ''I don't know if we kept them. Policy is to get rid of anything not relevant.''

''Could you check?''

''Is it important?''

''Could be,'' I tell her.

She's looking at me, intense. Wheels turning inside of

wheels, then they click, and lock, coming up all bars and bells. The dawning of light.

"You're thinking he killed his wife," she says.

"I'm considering the possibilities."

CHAPTER
10

Harry and I are on the way to the county jail, a meeting with Laurel. We're doing the seven blocks on foot. It's easier than trying to find a parking space.

"You sure there's not just a little family venom propelling this thing?" he says. Harry's talking about my ruminations that maybe Jack killed Melanie.

I've been beating this drum in my head all night, even in my sleep.

"Don't get me wrong, I'd love to hang the fucker," he says. The fact that Vega is a politician is enough for Harry. The fact that he is dirty is to Harry merely part of the job description.

"I admit I bear a little enmity," I say. "But there are things I haven't told you."

"Like?"

"Like the fact that Jack lied to the cops the night of the murder."

I look over and Harry is a half stride behind. His interest piqued, he is now catching up.

"He told them that he never owned a gun. That was a lie. A sloppy one. But then that's Jack," I say. "The question and his answer were in the police report."

"He owns a gun?"

"At least at one time he did. In his office, on the credenza, behind his desk, there are three trophies, a lot of marble and chrome," I say. "If you look, you'll see they're for target shooting. Pistols," I tell him. "One of those legislative tournaments where all the lobbyists and the people who hire them let the pols win."

Jack was heavily into the gun culture. He took trips to the big national gun shows, paid for junkets, one in Dallas, another in Miami. Jack got trophies just for showing up. He also got a pistol, nickel plated in a walnut box, a lot of tooling and scrolling engraved on it. From one of the manufacturers. Tokens of appreciation for a vote against a gun control bill. He showed the thing all around the family a few years back, twirling it on one finger. "A semiautomatic," I tell Harry. "Nine millimeter."

Harry whistles. "The cops went over the place with a tooth comb. They didn't find it. You think he did it and got rid of the piece?"

It is a possible scenario, but I am reading other tea leaves.

"What troubles me about the theory," I tell Harry, "is that I do not conceive of Jack as a doer. Don't get me wrong. I can see him, with enough motivation, planning a murder. But doing it is another thing. It is not Jack's style. He is somebody who would brood over the justifications. Think about it for a while. Then go to some middleman, somebody he trusts, someone with connections in sleazoid circles to job it out."

"A crime of passion once removed," says Harry.

"Passion? Maybe. Maybe it was more than that."

"But why would he lie about the gun? If he hired somebody, they wouldn't have used Jack's gun."

"I think that was Jack's mistake. He probably panicked. When the cops asked him if he owned one, Jack thought they were zeroing in on him. Guilty knowledge makes people do stupid things. He lied for no reason. He wasn't thinking. If he'd turned it over, my guess is they would have checked it and ballistics would come up negative. Now we've got him in a lie."

"It might look better for our side," he says, "if Jack can't produce the gun." Harry likes it, then a point of concern: "Can we prove he knew she was having an affair?"

"If I can get the tapes from Dana."

"Even if the feds destroyed them," says Harry, "we could subpoena the agent who monitored the conversations. Put him on the stand," he says.

"And hope that he has a good memory for family dirt," I tell him.

"A lot of hearsay," he says.

"Perhaps with exceptions," I tell him.

"State of mind?"

I nod. Statements made which reveal a person's state of mind, what they believed to be true or untrue, are not considered hearsay when testified to by others. They are admissible in court.

"What we don't know," says Harry, "is if Vega knew she was pregnant. And if so, when he found out. That might have sent him over the top. A catalyst for murder would be a nice present to hand to the jury."

"Maybe," I say.

For me the trigger was Jack's lack of *passion* when it was revealed that his wife was pregnant at death. I would have expected this to fuel his anger. But there was nothing. It was like he already knew about it.

"Maybe Jack was more calculating," I tell Harry. "You have to remember he'd already taken the fall with the feds. Now he finds out his wife is unfaithful. He knows he's headed for prison. What's going through his mind?" I say.

"She ain't gonna play the dutiful wife and wait for him." Harry finishes my thought.

"Exactly. So Jack bides his time. Thinks through a plan. He makes a play for the kids, an end run for custody. Pisses off Laurel, gets her juices flowing, maybe does some things to direct Laurel's venom toward Melanie. My young wife would like to play mommy for a while, so we'll take your children. He sets the stage for a cat fight in court. Then he has Melanie popped and points the accusing finger at Laurel. She becomes the prime patsy. Jack gets custody of the kids and uses the tragedy of the murder to get the feds to reconsider his sentence. Voilà. He's out on probation.''

"Minus one wife," says Harry.

"You got to admit he cuts his losses," I say.

"You think the guy's that devious?"

"Knowing Jack?" I give Harry a lot of arched eyebrows.

"Still, it leaves some questions. Like what was Laurel doing up in Reno?" he says. "And how did she come by the rug, the one from Jack's house that she was doing in the laundry?"

"Only one person can tell us that."

From the outside it looks like some tony downtown hotel, eight stories of curving concrete—the Bastille Park Regency, Capital County's newest addition, a sixteen-million-dollar jail.

Each of the seven floors above the main level is divided into sections by looming walls of acrylic, several inches thick and two stories high, floor to ceiling, a transparent matrix, set in a steel gridwork. These give the place the feeling of an aquarium without water. Behind the acrylic are the attractions, fifteen hundred inmates at any one time. The jail was built three years ago and is already beyond capacity.

The people incarcerated here are not in cells as you would think of them. There are no bars. They sleep behind doors of solid steel, in a room six-by-ten, walls, floor, and ceiling made of concrete with air pumped in from ducts in the ceiling.

Those who reside here are the sand in the gears of society, charter members of the "five percent club," that minority who always seem to cause the majority of problems. Most are not archcriminals. They lack the intelligence, drive, or discipline to do anything well, least of all the commission of any gainful lawless act. Their lives are a mix of madness and mirth, sometimes in lethal proportions. Sad cases every one. The man who torched his business for the insurance and lit himself up like a roman candle, and who now hangs patches of synthetic skin like little yellow flags from the handles of the weight machine after showering; the guy they call the Phantom of the Opera, who tried to commit suicide with a shotgun and flinched; the Asian immigrant so disgraced by a drunk-driving arrest that he performed a fatal swan dive onto concrete from the second-tier balcony; the swimmer who sealed the crack at the bottom of his cell door with a towel and stopped up the toilet until things were deep enough to dog paddle; and the hapless guard who saw the little puddle outside the cell door and decided to open it. All are members of the cast who have walked the corridors of this place, our own local version of the cuckoo's nest.

I wonder if there is hidden significance to the fact that Laurel, whose psyche is stretched more taut than piano wire, is now here.

We enter near the booking area, which has the efficiency of a cattle chute. We are in the age of stardust. Fingerprints are now taken on a glass strip and imaged on a computer screen where copies can be made and sent to state and federal agencies for cross-checking in other crimes. Inside this building everything is monitored by computer: meals the inmates eat, who is going to court on any given day, the time and department, who gets suits and who goes in jail togs, who's in the detention of isolation and for how long. Drop out from the computer's mighty RAM, and your sentence becomes eternity. The machine is God, a brazen idol whose gaze is a luminous blue screen. On the few occasions that it has gone down, this place has been its own version of administrative hell.

They have searched our briefcases and put Harry and me through the metal detector on the ground floor. Open your mouth to complain and the price of admission may become a cavity search.

The only defense attorneys who garner any trust in this place are the public defenders, who see less daylight than many of the prisoners. They are often on a first-name basis with the guards, something that does not engender much confidence among their clients.

This morning we are headed upstairs to what the guards in this place call the pods, one of the holding areas that resemble cargo bays from the starship *Enterprise*—sleek and foreboding. Being new, it is all very clean, surfaces that would require a diamond to scratch your initials.

The elevator has slick walls of stainless steel to which even spit will not adhere. Once inside you discover there are no buttons to select your floor. To get to your destination you have to talk, as Harry and I do, while looking at the camera mounted on the ceiling, twelve feet up in the corner of the car. I tell the guard in some unseen monitoring station: "Seventh floor."

Seconds later the doors open, a temporary reprieve from the onset of claustrophobia. A guard waiting for us.

A few of the inmates, all females on this side of the tower, are exercising beyond the acrylic wall. Two more are playing Ping-Pong, while others wander, read, or watch television in the "day room," a large open area on the level beneath us. Here they are monitored by guards watching video screens in a control room, cameras in every crevice. With all of this, it is a monument to the ingenuity of man that drugs and other contraband still make their way into this place.

Harry and I are like cattle with our ears punched, wearing tags that mark us as visitors. We are ushered to the lawyers' conference room, a concrete closet on the tier above the day room. Laurel is waiting when we arrive. There is heavy plate glass between us, with a small mike embedded so we can hear each other.

She wears a hopeful expression, with the "B-word" of passage for every prisoner on her lips before I can sit: "Any more word on bail?" she says.

We have been up and down on this three times on separate motions to obtain bail in the last month.

She's dressed in blue jeans and a blue work shirt. There's

a haggard look about the eyes that says she has not been sleeping well. Laurel is a person who fairly hums with physical and nervous energy, who finds it difficult to be still even for a moment, who always takes the stairs, never the elevator. Being locked in a six-by-ten cell with no windows must to Laurel be a living nightmare. The view from beyond the glass is of slowly crumbling human wreckage.

I have to dash her hopes. Our final attempt at bail has been denied, a hearing in which Morgan Cassidy played up the fact that Laurel was apprehended in another state. The court has bought into the concept that my client is a flight risk.

"I could reopen the issue if I knew what you were doing in Reno," I tell her. This is a sore point, as Laurel has not been forthcoming.

"That again," she says. "I can't tell you." She's looking at the ceiling, a pained expression. "Have you decided yet whether you will help me with Danny and Julie?" she says.

This whole exercise is becoming circular. Somehow these things, her trip to Reno and the children, are wedded, but I haven't yet figured out the connection.

"I'm trying to help you," I say. "You've got to trust me. What is it you want?"

"You know," she says. She makes a face but doesn't want to say it out loud, wondering if others are listening over the microphone. It is a cryptic little dance we have done over two sessions now. She wants me to help her get the kids away from Jack, to usher them out-of-state, probably to her friend in Michigan, the one she told me about on the phone that day before her arrest when she called from Reno.

"You know I can't," I say.

"You mean you won't."

"We've been through this before. I'm an officer of the court," I tell her. "Jack has a temporary custody order. Do this," I say, "and the court will make it permanent."

"Help me and he'll never find them." With all of her problems, lashing out at Jack—a preemptive strike involving the kids—still seems to be at the top of her agenda.

I shake my head in frustration. Dealing with Laurel is becoming a cross to bear.

"The answer is no."

"Then I can't tell you what I was doing in Reno." She turns her head away from me. This is her final answer. Unless I help her with the children, she is holding this information hostage.

"You can't do this. When we get to court, we have to be able to explain to the jury what you were doing there. That you weren't on the run. That you weren't fleeing from the crime. That your trip to Reno had nothing to do with Melanie's murder."

A long silence. Nothing from her.

"It didn't—did it?"

She looks at me, fire in her eyes. "No."

But still she won't tell me what she was doing there.

"Let's come back to that later. Let's talk about the bathroom rug," I say. More ground we have been over.

"Jack says it belongs to him. He says it was in the house, in the bathroom on the night of the murder."

"Jack's a liar," she says. "He would say anything to make it look bad for me. The man is plainly vindictive." Coming from Laurel, this is like Typhoid Mary warning of a plague.

I have not told her about my theory that Jack himself may have had reason to murder Melanie.

"Then where did the rug come from?"

"I've told you," she says. "It was mine. It came from my apartment."

"What was it doing in Reno? Why were you washing it?"

"We've gone over all of that."

"Let's do it one more time."

"Fine," she says, like I'm wasting her time.

"My cat slept on it. He used the rug as a bed. It was full of cat hair. It needed to be washed. How many times do I have to tell you?"

"So you went to Reno to launder the rug? Is that what you want us to tell the jury?" says Harry.

She gives him a face, a lot of sarcasm.

"No. I went to Reno for other reasons. I figured while I was there I would wash the rug. I was killing time."

"Let's hope that's all you were killing," says Harry.

"Screw you," she says. "Why don't I just get the public defender?" She's up off the stool on her side, pacing as much as the space will allow.

"Hot as a pistol," says Harry. "We gotta get her out of here. The place is having a bad effect," he says.

"Fuck you," she says, "and the horse you rode in on."

My sister-in-law is no wilting daisy. She is reaching the snapping point. If it weren't for the glass I think she could tear out Harry's throat. She has lost ten pounds since being jailed, weight she could not afford to give up. Still, she could take Harry two out of three falls.

"Sit down," I tell her.

She looks at me, an expression I have seen on Sarah when she is certain not a soul in the world loves her.

"Please," I say.

She sits and looks at me, a petulant child. It is the problem with Laurel, embattled, fighting wars on so many fronts she can no longer distinguish friend from foe. She is giving us a harder time than she gave the cops, forcing us to do the third degree.

"You have to admit on its face it doesn't make much sense. People don't take dirty laundry on a trip."

"This person does." She says it matter-of-fact, like this is it, final answer on the subject.

Maybe it's the problem with real life, but there are some things you just can't tell to a jury—not and possess any credibility when you are finished. I tell her this.

"Fine. Then make up some other explanation."

"Even if I were willing, my imagination isn't that facile."

"Then the truth is the best answer." On this she has me.

For the moment we are dead on bail and no closer to a credible explanation of her conduct on the night of the murder.

We talk about something else. I want to know why she went after Melanie that day in the courthouse.

She looks at me. "I don't know that I did," she says. "Did I hit her?"

"Like she was a railroad spike and you were John Henry," says Harry. We have viewed the tape from the courthouse.

"Well, I guess I didn't like what she said on the stand."

"What in particular?" I say.

"What she said about drugs."

"But you said something that day. Something about Melanie staying away from your kids. What was that all about?"

She fumes, looks at the floor. "Oh, hell. I suppose it will all come out. Jack knows about it. He's probably already told the cops."

My chest starts to tighten. Like burnt toast, I smell some damaging admission on its way.

"It happened the week before she died." This is Laurel's characterization of Melanie's passing, like some geriatric who slipped away in her sleep.

"I was supposed to take Danny to a concert in the city."

"San Francisco?" I ask.

She nods.

"Pearl Jam was playing—"

"What's a Pearl Jam?" says Harry.

"Rock group," she says.

A rolling nod like now he understands.

"Except I couldn't afford to buy the tickets. Jack was late with support payments as usual. I was short. It was either pay the rent or buy the tickets for the concert. I had to tell Danny. He was disappointed, but he took it well. Somehow, I don't know how, whether Danny mentioned it to Jack, and Jack said something to her, but somehow she found out."

"Melanie?"

"Right. The next thing I know she's bought two tickets and

they're off to see Pearl Jam. She drove Danny to the city in the new Jag Jack bought her. It was the last straw.

"I didn't know about it. Julie told me in the corridor outside the courtroom. I just snapped," she says. "I just lost it. When I saw her standing there with you and Jack, talking like nothing had happened, I could have killed the bitch," she says.

I look at the microphone and pray that no other ears are listening.

She fades a little beyond the glass, her shoulders drooping like some wilted flower.

To Laurel her kids were everything. More than a soft place in the heart, they made the world go round. She would have left Jack years before, in the flash of an eye, but for Julie and Danny. She stayed, putting up with the man and his nights of wandering lust, because of the children. Now Jack had left her for a younger woman, a manipulator who at least in Laurel's eyes was making moves to entice Laurel's children away, buying them the things she could not, while Jack bludgeoned her over custody. Embattled and alone, fighting for everything she valued in life, to the reasoned mind Laurel's flash of anger in the courthouse that day might seem perfectly plausible. But to a jury weighing charges of homicide, it could also provide the specter of a motive for murder.

Downstairs, Harry and I drop the visitor badges in a box at the front counter and head through the lobby of the jail. I'm five steps from the door when he walks through and almost into my arms. Baseball cap drawn to the ears, the only kid I know who wears the bill to the front, Danny Vega sees me and smiles.

"Uncle Paul. Did you see Mom?" he says.

"What are you doing here?"

"Visitors' day," he says. "First time they would let me in."

Looking at the tattooed crowd of tough faces, Danny is a little taken aback, but seems a bit relieved to have run into us.

"Do you wanna come up with me?"

"I'd love to, but I have a client waiting at the office."

I introduce Harry, but Danny's not looking. Instead he is studying the escalator to the mezzanine, the route taken by most visitors to see friends or relatives. He scans the ceiling, nearly three stories over his head, light fixtures like star bursts.

"Whoa. What a place," he says.

To Danny, whose generation has lived out their school life in portable classrooms, that taxpayers would foot the bill for a structure on this scale is, I suppose, a novelty. He is lost in other thoughts, checking it out, I can tell by the look, fantasies of hang-gliding down from the ceiling dancing in his mind, or the raucous ride a skateboard could do down the escalator.

"I haven't been here before," he says.

I can tell.

"How did you get here?"

"Vespa's across the street at the library," he tells me, "in the bike rack."

"Does your father know you're here?"

He gives me a look, Tom Cruise in *Risky Business*.

Jack doesn't have a clue. What's worse, I know, is the only thing that would bother Vega is that the kid is here to see his mother. But for this, I suspect Jack couldn't give a damn where Danny was.

"How's Mom?"

"She's fine. A little tired," I tell him. "Otherwise she's okay."

"Are you gonna get her off?" There is an urgency in his soulful eyes. This is Danny. Cut to the quick, bottom line, why mess around?

"We're going to try."

"How does it look?"

"We're still collecting evidence," I tell him. "It's going to be a tough case."

"It looks that bad?"

"Not to worry," I tell him. "We'll deal. We'll cope. Your

mother is a tough lady.'' A lot of brave talk without an answer to his question.

''I know,'' he says. ''But she didn't do it.''

''I know,'' I tell him. ''We're gonna do everything we can.''

''Can't you talk to the judge?'' he says. To Danny the elements of justice are simple.

''It's not that easy,'' I tell him.

''I know,'' he says. The boy's hands are suddenly everywhere, nervous gestures like he doesn't know what to do with them. Finally he reaches out to Harry. Shakes his hand.

''Nice to meet you,'' he says. ''I gotta go.'' He nods to me, a big smile, the same one I remember as being toothless when he was seven. He turns and saunters toward the line leading to the escalator.

I watch for a moment as Danny walks through the metal detector. Beepers go off and they send him back. A guard passes a hand-held magnetometer over the boy's jeans. Danny empties his pockets, a handful of loose keys and a folding knife that they take in return for a claim check.

As I watch him disappear up the escalator, I want to spit at the self-indulgence of my generation. My guilt as a father simmering deep inside, vapors of shame. We are a society that sheds spouses and takes on new lovers faster than a rajah can work through his harem. We dissolve entire families on a whimsy of lust. We pursue bald ambition as if it were the true religion, leaving our children to come home to empty houses, to fix their own meals, to cope with the crippling insecurities of adolescence, while we engage in an endless chase after the grail of possessions. And we have the audacity to wonder who killed the innocence of childhood.

CHAPTER
11

This morning is what they call an early-dismissal day at Sarah's school. Class is out at eleven so that teachers can attend a conference. I am doing lunch with my daughter, a treat at one of those pizza places with big singing dummies where they dispense tokens to play games and take all your change.

We're sprawled at a table over a twelve-inch disk filled with cheese, the processed kind a cow would never recognize, sharing a pitcher of Coke. Sarah is big round eyes and smiles, struggling with a string of cheese that has stretched longer than the reach of her arms.

It snaps and she chews. She rubs her mouth with her sleeve. I hand her a napkin.

"Kevin's been kissing me again." She says this out of the blue with her mouth full, reaching for her Coke.

Kevin is the little second-grader in her class who has taken a shine to my daughter. He hasn't heard that girls are yucky yet. I am told that disease sets in among the boys about the third grade. I can't wait.

"Tell him to stop," I say.

"It's okay," she says. "I kinda like it."

"Well, I don't."

"We're not French kissing," she says.

I roll my eyes skyward. Nikki, I need you. "Where did you hear *that?*" I say.

"Hear what?" A face of toothless wonderment, her two front ones gone.

"About French kissing."

"Courtney showed us, at the sleep-over. She knows all that stuff." Courtney is one of her little girlfriends, a foot taller than Sarah but the same age. She is the authority on everything. It seems size at this age is a big thing.

"We will talk about this later," I tell her.

I need some time for perspective. I will talk to Laurel.

"Why do we have to talk?"

"Never mind. Just tell Kevin to stop kissing you."

"All right. I'll try to remember," she says.

She grabs a bunch of tokens, still chewing on cheese and half-cooked dough, and heads for the helicopter ride. She's been waiting for ten minutes to get her chance.

I take the opportunity to call the office from the pay phone near the rest rooms. I can see Sarah across the way as the thing lights up. She pulls the control stick and the little chopper lifts on its hydraulic arm, maybe four feet off the ground.

I dial and get the receptionist.

"Hello, Sally, it's Paul. Any messages?"

"Let's see." I hear her pawing through slips at the other end.

"Your one o'clock canceled. He wants to reschedule next week. Department twelve called, motions in Vega are due the fourteenth."

"Who's the judge?" These are the pretrial motions in Laurel's case. Whoever hears these is likely to be our trial judge.

"Don't know," she says.

"Check the court roster."

"A new one's due out. Reassignments," she says. "Do you want me to call over there and find out who it is?"

"Yeah. And put a note on my desk."

"Will do. And one more message. Marcie Reed called."

"Who?"

"She says her name is Reed."

"I don't know any Reed. Did she say what it's about?"

"No."

I'm racking my brain. Then it hits me. Marcie—the woman from the post office. Kathy Merlow's friend.

"Did she leave a phone number?"

She gives it to me and I write in on the back of a business card.

I thank her, hang up, and dial.

"Postal Service. Can I help you?" A man's voice.

"Marcie Reed, please."

"Who's calling?"

"Paul Madriani, returning her call."

"Just a minute."

I hear him hollering Marcie's name. He calls out several times. Several minutes go by, a lot of shuffling and noise on the other end. Then suddenly a voice, in the female timbre and very tentative.

"Hello."

"Hello. Ms. Reed? This is Paul Madriani."

"Oh, yeah. You're returning my call."

"That's right."

"I uh . . . I saw your name and your picture in the paper," she says. Dead silence on the other end.

I wonder for a moment if the line's gone dead.

"Hello? Are you there?" I ask.

"Yeah. I'm still here," she says. "The woman you're defending, is she the one you told me about, the one you want Kathy Merlow to help?"

"She is. Do you know where I can find Mrs. Merlow?"

"Maybe. I might be able to help you."

"How?"

"I can't talk on the phone. They monitor our calls," she says. "They keep track of the time we're on the phone. If they catch us making personal calls—"

She leaves the thought hanging, but I can hear the swift glide of the guillotine blade in its runners. The sweatshop school of management. They spend two million designing a chic logo for better image, an eagle's head with a beak like the Sunset Limited, but still they can't resist shoveling metric tons of psychic guano on the help.

"Can we get together? I can meet you wherever you say," I tell her. "My office?"

"No. No—I don't want to do that. Besides, I can't leave here during the day."

"After work?" I say.

"I have to pick up my kids from the sitter. How about over here?"

"The post office?" I say.

"Yeah."

"Are you sure you won't get in trouble?"

"Mr. Haslid is off today." For Marcie Reed trouble starts with an H.

"He was the shouter on the loading dock?" I say.

"Yeah. But he's gone today."

And the mice will play, I think.

"Why not?"

"I take my lunch at one. I have forty minutes," she says. "We can talk in Kathy's old office. There's nobody in there right now."

I look at my watch. It's nearly twelve-forty.

"Do I come to the front counter?"

"No. Don't do that. I'll meet you on the loading dock. One o'clock. Gotta go now," and she hangs up.

Sarah's run out of tokens and is grounded playing with the stick, a little blond boy eyeing the craft jealously. I pluck her out of the helicopter and make his day. I will have to cut short the date with my daughter, drop her at day care a little early.

•   •   •

On the loading dock two mail carriers are putting letter crates into the back of little jeeplike vans. There's no sign of Marcie Reed, so I hang back at the end of the alley. I'm about five minutes late, and I begin to wonder if she has already come and gone, or had second thoughts about talking to me.

I lean against the wall of a building, one eye on my watch, the other on the loading dock. Several minutes pass and finally the door opens. It's Marcie. I move down the alley until she sees me. She says something to one of the guys working on the dock.

He stops long enough to look at her, hands on his hips. He shakes his head.

As I get closer I can hear part of their conversation. "You get caught, it's your ass," he says.

She appears undaunted and waves me on.

"You're late. I thought you weren't comin'," she says.

"I had to drop my daughter at day care."

"I don't have much time." She's carrying a sack in her hand. I assume her lunch.

The two men on the dock are sizing me up, the look in their eyes, like get caught inside and you're dead meat.

"Are you sure this is all right?"

"Yeah. It's okay, but let's not stand out here," she says. To Marcie okay means not getting caught. There's the gleam of excitement in her eye. The boss is gone, time to play.

I climb the dock. The looks I get from the two mail handlers tell me I am probably violating several sections of postal regulations, thoughts of the inspector upstairs with his badge and gun.

"Are you sure it's okay? There's a coffee shop down the street. My treat," I tell her. Last gambit to do it off-site.

"It's all right." She looks at me, like grow some balls. Marcie strikes me as one of those impish characters, hammered all her life, always in trouble, capable of feigning great fright but never truly afraid, something from never-never land.

I'm on her heels and we're through the swinging door, the one with the big red sign on it:

AUTHORIZED POSTAL PERSONNEL ONLY

Inside is a maze of tables, canvas mail bags tied open to metal hooks, rolling dollies and carts. Maybe a dozen people, dressed in various versions of the uniform, blue-gray shirts with the postal emblem on the shoulders, jeans, and sneakers.

"How old's your kid?" she says. Small talk as we walk, under her breath.

"Seven," I whisper. I feel like some teenager sneaking onto the driving range after hours to steal balls.

"Same as my boy," she says. We are doing a circuitous course at a quick-step that seems to take us the long way, around mail carts and stacks of sorting trays, skirting any contact with other employees. I can see hands flipping letters, and midriffs as they work at tables one aisle over, the upper bodies concealed by cabinets that I assume on their side contain pigeonholes for mail or parcels being sorted.

Near the front of the building Marcie stops. She's fumbling with several keys in the lock of a door—dark, mottled glass in the upper part of the frame. Stenciled on the glass the words

CUSTOMER SERVICES

She finds the right key, flips on the light, and we are inside, with the door closed. She finally takes a deep breath.

"There, that wasn't so bad," she says. She turns to look at me. The excitement of a mission accomplished written in her eyes. The frizzled ends of her pigtails look like she's stuck her finger in a light socket. Freckles on her face. If she were a little shorter, she could pass for one of Sarah's friends.

She sits in the chair on the other side of a clean desk, just a little dust on the surface of green metal, and catches her breath.

I drop my attaché case on a chair in the corner and slide the other chair over, in front of the door, and sit. Inside my briefcase I have a little tape recorder in case Marcie knows something and is willing to talk on tape. If not, there is a note pad.

"I take it if they catch you here with me, you could lose your job?" I say.

She doesn't answer. Instead she's looking at me, studying me up and down, taking stock before she talks. I'm waiting for the pitch. How much is this worth? Marcie's information market.

"Is this Kathy Merlow's office?"

She nods. "It was," she says. "For two months and four days. Before she left."

There's a sweater hanging on a hook on the back wall. A few directories on a bookshelf. The look of an abandoned office.

"You must have got to know her in a short time?"

"Soulmates," she says. "Kathy and I had some things in common. Management didn't like us," she says.

"Did she go on to another job?"

She shakes her head and continues to look at me.

"What exactly did she do?" I nod toward the stenciled letters. "What's customer services?"

"A title."

"That's all?"

"That's what they gave her. An office and a title and a paycheck," she says.

"She must have been civil service?" I say.

"Not exactly."

"How do you get a job—"

"We don't have time for this," she says. "We can talk

about all that later. Right now I need to know a few things. This charge against your client. I need to know whether there's anything you can do to get her off without Kathy's help.''

The way she says this makes me wonder who's asking the question, Marcie or Kathy Merlow?

"I don't know," I say. "A trial is a crap shoot. This one I wouldn't want to bet on.''

Maybe she's testing the ante, I think, trying to find out how much her information is worth.

"Do you know where the Merlows are?" I say.

She turns to the bag she's been carrying. It's on the desk. I think maybe I'm finally going to get some answers.

She opens it. Takes out a package, wrapped in waxed paper. Peanut butter and jelly on white bread.

"You want half?"

"No, thanks.''

"How much do you know about Kathy and her husband?''.

"I know that they lived next door to the house where the murder occurred. I think they saw something that night.''

She gives me a face, no confirmation. But she has told me enough already for me to put the pieces together.

"Then they haven't told you," she says.

"Told me what? Who's 'they'?''

She seems mystified, like there is something manifest, an obvious item I have missed. Part of the equation.

"What do *you* know?" I ask her.

"I know your client didn't do it.''

"How do you know that?''

"Because I know who did it, and why.''

"Kathy Merlow told you this?''

Her expression is a stone idol, but I can read yes in her eyes.

"What did she tell you?''

"Someone was hired to do it.''

"The murder?"

She nods.

"Who hired the killer?"

"You want more, you gotta talk to her, to Kathy."

"Fine. Tell me where she is."

A lot of deep sighing from across the desk, nervous hands all of a sudden, fingers to the mouth. I notice that her nails are chewed to the quick.

She studies me for a long moment, quiet contemplation. Then she reaches down and slides open the center desk drawer. She pulls out a small white envelope, the kind that carry little thank-you notes. I can see a penned scrawl on the outside.

"I got this about a week ago," she says. "It's a note from Kathy. Nobody else knows about it. I don't think George even knows she sent it. She wanted something she left behind. I mailed it to her yesterday. I have to have your word that if I tell you where she is, you won't tell anyone else. You'll talk to her yourself. You won't send somebody else."

I give her a face, consternation. "Depends where she is," I say. "I'm preparing for a trial. Usually we use an investigator."

She starts to slip the envelope back into the drawer.

"Okay," I tell her. "I'll talk to her alone. Nobody else. But I may have to subpoena her."

She gives me a smile. "Good luck."

There's a rap on the glass behind my head. Cramped quarters. I look at her.

She is white as a sheet, more than a little fear. She's looking at the shadow through the glass.

She silently mouths a single word: "Haslid."

I read her lips.

But the light is on. Whoever is outside can see us through the translucent door.

He knocks again.

She gives me a little shrug, a concession like we may as well open it up and take our licks.

I do the honors. I get the door open just enough for the guy to stick his head through. It's the mail carrier from the loading dock.

I can hear her breath of relief from this side of the desk. Marcie is hyperventilating.

"Goddamn it, Howard—you took five years off my life."

"Good," he says. "Maybe you'll get the hell out of here and go back to work."

"What do you want?"

"Courier with a package for you."

"For me?"

"That's what he says."

I get up, move the chair away from the door. Outside is a guy in another uniform—dark blue, with white running shoes, a white stripe down the side of his uniform pants, a private courier. He is young, maybe late twenties, good-looking, square jaw, hair cut close like something from the military. He's either wearing an undersized shirt or maybe he does weights in his off-hours.

"Got an express packet," he says.

"This is looking like a fucking convention." Howard is pissed. "I'm supposed to be in charge when the man's gone, and you put me on the spot," he says. "Finish up and get the hell out of there. He's not supposed to be in here." The guy's looking at me. "And you're not supposed to be in that office."

"Just a couple more minutes," Marcie tells him.

Howard is the kind who screams and yells a lot, uses profanity like it is a second language. But he lacks a command presence. In any shouting match I suspect that infants probably throw up on his shirt and dogs lick his face.

Marcie looks at the courier. "Who's sending me a package?" she says.

"Sign here." The deliveryman is in the middle. He just

wants to do his job and run. He can't get through the door, so he hands me the letter pack and a clipboard with the form to be signed.

"She's number eighteen." He puts an X on the line for her signature.

The package is heavy, bowing out the seams of its cardboard container.

"And you"—Howard, the postal employee, is looking at me—"somebody wants to see you at the loading dock."

"Me?"

"Is there anybody else in there?"

"Nobody knows I'm here," I tell him.

"Good for you," he says. "All I know is that somebody wants to talk to the guy who's inside meeting with Marcie. Somebody knows you're here."

"Who is it?"

"What am I, Western Union?" he says.

Marcie's finished with the clipboard and I hand it back. The deliveryman is gone like a shot. At a quick jog he's headed for his van. Howard looks at him, shakes his head, a mocking grin, like he's seen the kind before, some butt-licking hustler looking to make an impression with his employer. Howard's civil service. Besides, he knows there isn't a hope in hell of his owning the post office one day.

I follow him out toward the loading dock. This time we take the direct route, through the center of the sorting area. Employees looking at me. Little sniggers. I can see Howard's head shaking from behind. Like he's running a tour-and-escort service.

We get to the dock. Howard's friend is still loading the other van. Except for Howard and me, he is alone on the dock.

"Where did he go? The guy who wanted to see me?"

Howard scratches his head, walks to the edge of the dock, and looks down the alley. Nobody. He asks the other carrier.

"I dunno. Here a minute ago. Musta got tired waiting and left," he says. He gives us the government-issue shrug.

I look up the alley the other way. The courier is at the curb, standing at the open door of a vehicle, looking back over his shoulder in my direction. There's no one else in sight, just an old lady and a vagrant walking down the sidewalk that cuts the alley at Seventh Street.

"If he comes back, tell him to wait." I'm looking at Howard.

"What am I—your messenger?"

"I'm going back inside. Unfinished business," I tell him.

Howard gives me the look, the face of authority, withering like blossoms in a drought. He makes no effort to stop me. Alas, the man is not management material.

I head back through the door, wondering who could have been looking for me here. I didn't tell the office where I was going. It couldn't be Harry. One of those nagging things, like a ringing phone in the night, with nothing but heavy breathing on the line. An annoyance. I try to put it out of my mind.

As I clear the mail-sorting area, I am still filtering the sights from the loading dock, like light through a camera lens set on a quick shutter speed, fading images being processed, the man's silhouette at the curb. Why, I think, would a private courier be getting into the backseat of a dark sedan?

The thought is fused in my mind by the searing blast, the flash of light followed in an instant by heat that toasts my face. The concussion sends me reeling against the wall. Splinters of wood, particles of glass spray my body like gravel shot from the barrel of a gun. In a dreamscape I find myself sprawled, supine, bathed in the warmth of glowing embers. Dazed, things move about me, over my head, white and blue butterflies.

My eyes focus. Little shards floating in the air, not butterflies, but pieces of papers, singed at the edges, drifting down.

One of these settles on my nose, balanced perfectly, then teeters toward one eye. I close the lid, surprised that I can muster that much control over any part of my body.

Slowly I stagger to one knee, then two. Hands and knees, I feel for the wall, warm sweat running down my face. I can hear nothing but the ringing in my ears. People are moving about me now, soundless emissions coming from agitated faces. One of them takes my arm. He says something in my face, but I can't hear. I shake my head, motion with my hands, like speak up. Only the ringing in my ears. He steadies me against the wall and moves toward the door, the office where Marcie is.

I'm holding my head with one hand. Wet warmth. I look at my palm, glistening with blood. It is not warm sweat that is trickling down my cheek.

The door to the office where Marcie is has disintegrated. The glass blown out of the upper portion. The lower panel of wood is a fringe of splinters. What is left of the chair that I had been sitting in has been blown through the door.

Two guys kick out what's left of the lower panel. One of them steps through.

Mouths are moving, people trying to shout, but they have all lost their voices.

"Somebody call 911," I say. But I don't hear the words.

Two of the clerks have come from the front counter.

I steady my legs and push myself forward to the doorway. My head is ringing. The pounding in my ears. A wave of nausea. I turn toward the wall like I am going to retch, but force it down. I fight for control.

From the doorway I can see nothing of Marcie. The chair where she was sitting has been blown over backward. It rests partially embedded in the wall behind the desk. One of its wooden arms splintered. No sign of Marcie.

I move inside the room and steady myself with my hands on the desk, little droplets of blood forming with the dust and shards of paper on its surface.

Then I see her. On the floor, sprawled on her back. The clothing gone from her upper body. Only her bra, which is singed, and a few strings of fabric from one sleeve remain to cover her frail torso.

I look at her face, singed and burned, even more innocent and childlike now, gripped in the sleep of death. One man at the pulse of what is left of her thin wrist, looking up, shaking his head, a universal message requiring no words.

People are beginning to congregate at the door. I see my briefcase, flattened against the wall, its surface scarred like a pistol target, a half dozen nails through its thick latigo.

Then I see it on the floor, near the chair and my briefcase. The little envelope. The note that Marcie pulled from the drawer of the desk. The one sent to her by Kathy Merlow. Its edges are charred.

I move in a world of ringing silence. People are milling toward the desk, at once curious and recoiling. Their thoughts for the moment fixed on the fragile form on the floor. Tiptoeing over to look.

I slip behind two of the women who have pushed their way to the edge of the desk. I reach for my case, tattered, its cover imploded by the force of the blast, studded with nails.

In as fluid a motion as I can manage, I reach down, trapping the little envelope on the floor between two bloodied fingers. As I rise up, no one seems to notice that there is one less scrap of paper on the floor. Another wave of nausea. I catch the bile in my throat and swallow hard. My hand to my mouth. Bloodied prints on the little envelope. Slowly I back from the room. I can see over the front counter, two federal cops in blue uniforms and shiny badges. They're headed for the door that leads back here.

I walk, stumble, pick up my pace, try to make a straight line to the rear of the building.

On the loading dock I am alone. Everyone is inside. I manage to get down the stairs, tripping and dripping as I walk, moving as quickly as I can toward the safety of my car, clutching the little envelope in my hands, my only link to Kathy Merlow and what she knows.

CHAPTER
12

"I need your help," I tell her.

I'm in the office with Harry, picking at one of the bandages on my forehead. There are three stitches and a score of lacerations on the right side of my face. A young doctor picked glass out from under the skin at a surgicenter, one of those walk-in doc shops where with enough plastic you can have anything from your tonsils out to your tubes tied, no questions asked. My face feels like hamburger pounded into shape on a gravel driveway.

I'm talking to Dana Colby on the phone. It's a little after six in the evening. The city is beginning to die, surface streets emptying. I've caught her just coming through the door from work. She's a soft voice on the phone and I can't hear her.

"You gotta speak up," I tell her. "The blast got my ears." I've told Dana that the trail of George and Kathy Merlow led me to the post office and the deadly letter bomb. She's heard about the explosion. It's a hot topic on the news—every channel and the local radio stations are laying it on thick to the commuting crowd. Dana now senses she's on the cutting edge, listening to everything I say, eyes and ears to what happened.

Harry's shaking his head. He thinks I am being foolish to involve her. To Harry, gender and good looks notwithstanding, Dana is just another prosecutor. He's trying to talk in my other ear.

"Big mistake." Harry writes this note on the pad on my desk and slides it under my face to read.

We've been over all this, Harry and I. He thinks I did the right thing by running, not staying to talk to the cops. Now he thinks I'm blowing it.

I ran because I wanted to avoid the police and their questions. Lama alone would hold me for a week for questioning. Cavorting with the feds would be bigtime for Jimmy. And to Lama the opportunity to spread pain my way would be better than sex. They would want to know why I was there talking to Marcie Reed. One thing would lead to another, Kathy Merlow and her note, which the cops would want. It is my only lead to the Merlows and what they know about Melanie's murder.

I wave Harry off. He's in my ear.

"Please—I can't hear myself think," I tell him.

He turns and walks toward the window, a lot of motioning with his hands, talking to himself.

"No, not you," I tell her. I'm back to Dana. "I've got to talk to you. Can we meet at my house?"

"I can be there in twenty minutes."

"No. I need at least an hour," I tell her. "One errand I have to run."

"I'll be there in an hour," she says.

We hang up.

"You're outta your mind," says Harry. He's still facing the window, away from me. "You tell her you were there, and she's gonna call in the fibbies." Harry's term for the FBI. "They'll have you in a chair with bright lights in your eyes before you can sneeze. You may as well have stayed there and talked to 'em at the scene. At least it would have looked better."

Harry gives me one of his better expressions, the ones that tell me when I'm being a dumb fuck.

"You gotta admit, I mean, you go to talk to this girl, Marcie Reed. You leave the office for two minutes and she's turned into Spackle, all over the walls.''

"Oh, shit!" Suddenly I'm staring off at the middle distance, right through Harry.

"What's wrong?" he says.

"I'd forgotten," I tell him. "The package. The one the courier delivered. I handled it. I handed it to Marcie," I tell him.

"How did you manage that?"

"The room was too small. He couldn't get in. So I handed it to her."

"Oh, great." Harry's a quick-step, pacing between the window and my desk, slapping his thigh, going, "Oh, great! That's great. Why didn't you finger the fuse while you were at it?" he says. "You're gonna need one helluva lawyer," he tells me. "I hope you know one." Harry's not offering.

I'm wondering if forensics can lift prints from tattered and singed bits of paper. Not that it matters, I suppose. It's only a question of time until they place me in the room. Fingerprints on the desk, witnesses who saw me.

"I just need to buy some time. Long enough to check out the note. Try and run down the Merlows."

"And you think she's gonna give it to you?" He's talking about Dana.

"I'm hoping."

"Good luck!" Harry's face says it all. "In your dreams."

He's standing, staring out the window, looking at the lights of the city, the Capitol five blocks away, lit up like a crown by incandescent lights that arc up the sides of the dome, setting off the cupola topped by its golden sphere.

There is a gray cast that has us in its grip. The central valley in winter, where they know how to do fog.

I sit at my desk, studying the contents of Marcie Reed's little singed envelope. There is a snapshot, its edges charred. In the photograph, what looks like a small one-room church, green clapboard over starched white plaster, set in lush greenery, tinges of a brilliant blue sky. There are glimpses of a few headstones, a small graveyard next to the church.

And there is the note, written in a feminine hand:

Dear Marcie:

I'm sorry, but I need to ask a favor. Left my Mom's ring in the top drawer to my desk. Could you send it, general delivery, care of "Alice Kent." Thanks for all your help. You have been the only friend I have had in two years. This place is the end of the earth. One day when this is all over, I will call. Take care. All my love.

K.

My guess is that Alice Kent is a name of convenience, something quick and easy that Kathy Merlow could use to collect a package at general delivery. By now she would have some plausible ID, maybe more than one. Given the speed with which they lost themselves after Melanie's murder, and the absence of any tracks—Harry still has no word from the Resolution Trust Corporation on the house rental—these are resourceful people, the Merlows. I look at the envelope, the little circular postmark.

Then I turn the snapshot over. On the other side a note, scrawled in a faint pencil, Kathy Merlow's hand:

"If I take the wings of the morning
and dwell in the uttermost parts of the sea."
It is a special place, where I spend my afternoons.

I flip the picture over, study the little church.

Whoever took the picture was careful. No place-names or signs in the frame, nothing I could use to blow up, to get a fix on where it is. Nothing I can see, anyway.

Harry's looking over my shoulder.

"My guess it's part of a poem," he says.

"What's that?"

"The wings and the sea," says Harry. "Lyrical stuff."

"Your heathen roots are showing," I tell him. "Sunday school does have its benefits."

"Why's that?"

"It's part of a passage from the Bible. One of the Psalms."

The doorbell rings. I haven't had time to even take off my coat. Dana's made it in less than an hour. I open the door to greet her.

"Hey, man, you the lawyer? Danny Vega's uncle?"

On my front porch are three kids, maybe sixteen, dark-complected, coal-black hair, shades dangling from their shirt pockets. They are wearing khaki pants and oversized black shirts with long sleeves, part of the uniform, Pancho Villa's army of revenge, gang-bangers all.

"Who wants to know?"

One of them has his hair tied in a tight bun, a black hairnet drawn over the top. He's the one doing all the talking.

"Hey, man. Just answer the question. Don't give us no shit. You know Danny Vega? You know where he is?" The kid has sixty-year-old eyes set into a face that is at best sixteen, but mean.

His two companions are giving me faces of resolve, expressions of enforcement.

I'm looking at the security chain, hanging limp from the frame of my door. The only thing between us is the tattered screen door, which has been mauled and ripped by one of my neighbor's cats.

"I think you should go."

"We goin' noplace till you tell us where Danny is. We don' wanna get into it with you, man. But you push us—"

One of them pulls a butterfly blade from his pocket and whips it open. For the moment he's cleaning his fingernails, making sure I see the razor-sharp edge.

"We're not lookin' for no trouble—" The kid with the hairnet is back in the lead.

"Sure. You're just standing on my front steps threatening me."

"Hey, man, did we say anything that was threatening?" Big eyes all around, a chorus of shaking heads.

"Not me."

"You hear anything threatening?"

"Nada."

"What do you want with Danny?" I say.

"Hey. I think he's inside." One of them smiles. "Hey, Danny—you in there? Come out, come out, wherever you are." His friends are laughing. They think this is cute stuff. The hairnet grabs the latch on the screen door. It's locked.

A look on his face, crestfallen, like his feelings are hurt. "Hey, man. I tole you we just friends over for a visit. You let us in, okay?"

"No, it's not okay. I'm gonna suggest you get the hell out of here." The level of my voice is beginning to rise, signs of fight or flight.

"Hey, not very friendly, man."

The guy with the blade starts to whittle on my screen, near the handle.

"Just send him out. We can talk here. How 'bout it?" The hairnet flashes me a full load of pearly whites. "Come on out, Danny. Or else we're gonna have to come in. Up to you." He's singing through my screen door.

"I don't know where he is. He's not here."

"You sure?" He pulls on the door handle one more time, like maybe it will give. He's bouncing on the balls of his feet now, looking over his shoulder to make sure there are no nosy neighbors. Visions of the blade slashing through my screen door.

"Danny doesn't live here."

The kid with the hairnet looks at me.

"Oh. Then you know where he lives. You can tell us."

"I think you ought to leave."

"Hey, man, no trouble, just tell us where he is."

I know Danny well enough that these are not friends. If they are looking for him, it is because he is in trouble. It could be nothing more than an indignant look that Danny flashed their way, an offense to their macho dignity. With what is now standing at my front door, anything other than downcast eyes could earn you the kind of greeting that comes in a muzzle flash from the window of a moving car.

Headlights pull up out in front.

One of them turns to look. He tugs on his talking buddy by the shirtsleeve. The hairnet takes in the car.

Dana's getting out at the curb. She sees the crowd at my front door, stands for a moment, and looks at them over the roof of her vehicle.

A woman alone. The hairnet gives me a smile.

"Your woman maybe?" he says.

I don't respond. I sense an ugly scene about to start. Me in here, Dana out there.

When they turn and look again, she's on the phone, the cellular receiver from her car. The cocky smiles suddenly evaporate.

One of the seconds is at the hairnet. "Hey, man, let's go."

The leader of the pack isn't happy. He's bouncing on his toes. "Okay for now, man. But we'll be back," he says. "You got it?" He's pointing a finger in my face, an inch from the screen, like it will have to do until he can find something more lethal to aim in my direction. All the charm of the seven plagues.

"See you around," he says.

"It's been a pleasure."

"Yeah. A pleasure, man." He spits in my roses.

I make a mental note to call Harry, to have him talk to Laurel. Perhaps she is right. Maybe Danny would be better off someplace else for a while.

They're down the steps, through the front gate, and across the street to a low-slung wagon, a cherry-red Impala with a sound system to rouse the dead. Around the corner I can still hear the *boom-boom* of base with no treble as they drift away.

"Friends of yours?" Dana's up the steps.

"Not exactly."

Before she clears the front door, a black-and-white cruises down the street. She turns in the light of my porch lamp and waves. Then she points in the direction of the boom box, and the cruiser picks up speed, nearly taking the turn on two wheels.

A screaming visit behind red-and-blue lights from those sworn to serve and protect may not cause these guys to widdle in their pants, but they will know they've been tagged.

"I hope they're not carrying any contraband in the car." The way Dana says this makes me think these kids will be talking with bright flashlights in their faces for a while. The professional courtesies of the law-enforcement fraternity.

"You look awful," she says. She touches the side of my face with the softness of her gloved hand, gentle, feathering, like a local anesthetic to my skin.

"Does it hurt much?"

"Only when I laugh."

"Then we'd better talk about serious things," she says.

"Cup of coffee?" I ask.

She looks at her watch. "Why not? The night's shot. I have a feeling this is going to take a while."

Twenty minutes later, over the scent of a freshly brewed French roast, Dana is studying the contents of the note written by Kathy Merlow and the envelope it came in.

The little snapshot I have left in the inside coat pocket of my sport jacket—my trump card—for the moment I keep to myself.

"It isn't much to go on," she says after reading the note.

"It's a lead."

"Still, she could have had someone else mail it." Dana's looking at the postmark. "I mean, if this woman Kathy Merlow really wants to stay lost, she might have a friend carry the note on vacation and mail it, then wait to collect the item from general delivery and bring it back. That's what I would do.''

"Good thing I'm not looking for you," I say.

She makes a face, smiles. "Just telling you what I'd do."

"Anything's possible. But for the moment the note and that envelope are all I have."

"What makes you so sure Merlow knows something?"

"Because of what I was told by Marcie Reed."

"What's that?"

"Kathy Merlow knows who killed Melanie."

"This Marcie told you this?"

"She didn't give me a name. But she did say that it was a hired killer. That Kathy Merlow would have to give me the rest."

A gray cast comes over Dana's face. "A hired killer? How would Kathy Merlow know that? I mean, I can understand if she saw the killer she might be able to identify him—"

"Maybe she didn't see anything," I tell her. "Maybe she was told something."

"I don't understand," she says.

"Think about what we know," I tell her. "We know that Melanie was pregnant at the time of death, and according to Laurel, Jack is not a likely candidate for father."

"So Melanie was getting it on with someone else. One or more," she says.

"I'm only concerned about one in particular," I say. "Someone who lived close to her. Who could slip in and out of the house with apparent ease. Who might know when Jack was out. Who might have been Melanie's principal sideline squeeze. A friendly neighbor," I say.

"Kathy Merlow's husband," she says.

"Enter George Merlow."

"But how would George know about a hired killer?"

"What if Melanie was getting worried, concerned that Jack was on to her and George? I know Vega," I tell her. "He would not put up a good front. Planning something like this, under stress you could read Jack like a book. And Melanie may have had more than a hint. Maybe she stumbled across a note or a phone message that put her in a panic. Not enough to call the cops, but something to keep her up nights. Who is she going to tell? Who would she take into her confidence?'' I say.

"George."

I nod. "So George is keeping watch, the dutiful lover. And that night he gets an eyeful. He sees the murder. Too late to do anything about it, the thought enters his mind, if Jack was willing to do his wife, he'd be fairly itching to do her lover. George gets scared. He's got to tell his wife something. He comes clean, tells Kathy, she's either forgiving or suffers from low esteem, whatever,'' I say.

"And like that, the two of them are gone," she says.

"You got it."

"Why not stay and tell the cops what he knows?"

" 'Cuz all he knows is that Melanie had suspicions before she was killed. What can he say? 'I was screwing his wife and she suspected he was getting jealous'? While the cops were investigating, if there was a contract already out, George could end up in the crosshairs. Especially if word gets out that he saw the killer. The Merlows weren't heavily invested in the community. Smart money says to run,'' I tell her.

"So you need Merlow as a witness?"

"That's it. Without him all I have is a lot of circumstance. Attempts to shine some light on another suspect. If that collapses, it's gonna be a cold hard hunt for mitigation."

"If it comes to that, I don't envy you," she says.

Dana's right. Laurel's no sobbing spouse or molested child to claim she was battered, the defense of choice in modern America. My sister-in-law is just an ex, after the fact, allegedly out for revenge.

"There is another possibility. A reason why they might have run," she says. "How do you know Kathy Merlow or her husband aren't involved in Melanie's murder?''

"I wasn't sure until today. Think about it. The courier de-livers the package. At the same time somebody asks to talk to me at the loading dock. The tooth fairy? My guardian angel?'' I say.

Dana's a quizzical look.

"Someone wanted Marcie Reed dead so she couldn't tell me something. Something about Kathy Merlow. They also wanted me out of harm's way. People who send letter bombs are not generally that considerate. If they want me alive it's for a reason. They know I'm looking for the Merlows. I think they're doing the same thing, and they're hoping I'll do their job for them. A lawyer up to his haunches in a murder trial, with access to judicial process to compel the appearance of witnesses. That's not a bad bird dog,'' I tell her.

"So you think they want to kill the Merlows?'' she says. "Why?''

"I think whoever killed Marcie Reed pulled the trigger on Melanie Vega and got caught in the act. Somehow the killer found out that he'd been compromised. Now he's trying to cover his tracks.''

She looks at me, big round eyes.

"It's Jack's style. Trust me. He'd hire somebody to do Mel-anie. When we check, I'm sure he'll have six alibis for the night of the murder. Think about it. His wife is pregnant. She's got a young lover. Jack's getting ready to do hard time. She wasn't going to wait for him. A washed-up politician, no fu-ture, his money siphoned off by criminal fines. To Jack, Mel-anie was more of an asset dead than alive. If he could get the kids, a murdered wife, he'd make a bid for sympathy. He was getting ready to play you folks like a piano.''

"And the bombing? You think Jack had a hand in that?''

"No. I think matters are now spinning out of control. I think the killer panicked and tried to engage in some free agency to cover his tracks. He got desperate.''

"And a little sloppy at the post office,'' she says. "If what you say is accurate, a few people saw the courier there.''

"True. Desperate people do stupid things.''

"And where's Jack in all of this?''

"I don't know if he knows what's going on at this point. He probably paid the tab, whatever the going rate is these days for a hired hit. My guess is he doesn't know they screwed up. That there's loose ends, a witness to the murder. His tight little ball is about to unravel.

"One thing is certain,'' I tell her. "In a few hours your people will know I was at the post office. It won't take them long to make me. Fingerprints at the scene, descriptions from some of the employees. My picture has been in the papers almost daily since the start of Laurel's case. Once they get ahold of me I'll be a week answering questions, looking at mug shots in hopes I can ID the courier.''

"And you won't be able to find Kathy Merlow,'' she says.

"You got it.''

"Why not just send an investigator after her?''

"It's something I have to do myself. I made a promise.''

"To who?''

I don't answer the question, but she reads my mind.

"Marcie Reed,'' she says.

More silence.

"She's dead.''

"Sorta seals the vow, doesn't it?''

"It makes no sense.''

"Maybe. But I've got to do it myself. One person, somebody I drew into this, is already dead.''

"What you're doing is dangerous,'' she says. "You said it yourself—desperate people.''

"I don't have a lot of options,'' I tell her. "And I don't have much time.'' I'm looking at my watch.

"What do you want from me?'' she says.

"I've got a flight out in less than an hour. I couldn't wait till morning. Your people may have a net out by then. My chances of getting on a plane tomorrow would be less than fifty-fifty. So our conversation here is a little CYA. Because I trust you I'm telling you what I know. Cleansing my soul," I say. "If your people catch up to me while I'm over there, I want to be able to say that I gave you all the details."

"Great. And what am I supposed to say?"

"That you couldn't stop me. You tried and I slipped away."

"But there's another reason?" she says.

"That's it."

"You're telling me in case you don't come back you want somebody in a position of authority to have some clue as to what happened."

"Never entered my mind," I tell her.

She smiles. "Nice try."

"Well, if it happens, clean their clock, the courier included. I left a written description with Harry. Right down to the pimples on his bony ass. At least one other person got a glimpse of him at the post office. Guy named Howard. Somebody ought to be able to ID a mug shot. If he's of record."

"What about your daughter? Where is she?"

"She's with friends since earlier this evening. A couple Nikki and I were close to. They live in the country, have a pony, and a little girl Sarah's age. She'll be fine."

I don't tell her, but Sarah would have gone there whether I left tonight or not. After the surprise in the letter pack, I am taking no chances.

"You shouldn't be doing this. We shouldn't even be talking about this. I should be calling the FBI, and you should be answering questions, looking at pictures."

"I don't have a choice," I tell her. "If I don't find Merlow—Kathy or George—I'm going to trial on a case that is at best shaky. A long time in the joint for a nice lady, or worse," I say. "So I'm going. Don't try to stop me."

She considers this for a long moment, silence over her coffee, flipping Merlow's envelope in her fingers, one side up and then the other, finally laying it on the table, the canceled stamp facing up. She looks at the postmark. The clear lettering inside the circle:

Hana HI 96713
USPS

"Is your flight full?" she says.

"I don't know."

"If it is, I can use my credentials to bump somebody. Government business," she says.

"Not a chance," I tell her.

"Then you'll never board the plane," she says.

"Why not?"

"I will stop you." Visions of the cops rolling by in their cruiser. There's not a hint of mirth in her eyes. She is dead serious. Unless I take her, she will have her people pick me up at the airport or pull me from the plane.

"We're talking a federal crime," she says. "A postal employee has been killed in a federal facility. I can't take the responsibility of letting you go off alone to hunt for someone who, according to your own theory, is a target—a witness to another murder. According to your own words you're being tracked.

"And if something happened to you, how would I live with myself?" she says. "Besides, what would I say to Sarah?" She smiles, soft feline looks, head canted just a little to one side, auburn hair coiling at her shoulders.

"Do we have a deal?"

My options are closing.

"If we catch Merlow I get her as a witness?" I say. I'm trying to stave off Dana's good looks, struggling to maintain my lawyer's wits under the laser intensity of her oval eyes, the wafting fragrance of her scent.

"Why not? At this point we have a mutual interest. You solve your crime, maybe I solve mine."

She can see my resolve beginning to wither. Not that I have much choice.

"Let me call to get a ticket," she says. "Then we can go to my place while I pack—unless you have an extra toothbrush and a nightie," she says.

"I can meet you at the airport. You go home and pack."

"Not a chance." Her grin widens. "You don't leave my sight until we're on the plane."

I start to say something and she stops me, her finger to my lips.

"Shhh. You talk too much," she says. Her smooth palm, ungloved this time, comes across the table to soothe my battered cheek. Like a balm easing the tension and fire of pain-racked nerve ends, Dana is warm, tender looks through bedroom eyes.

CHAPTER
13

Six hours on a plane, some of it with Dana's head on my shoulder as she sleeps, is not an entirely unpleasant experience.

Dana stirs on my shoulder, stretches, and arches her back in the chair.

"I'm gonna use the phone," she says. "Try to get us accommodations." Dana's been here before, so I leave this to her.

"Here, catch up on your reading," she says. She hands me the evening paper from Capital City, pulled from the side flap of her briefcase under the seat in front of her.

I watch her move down the aisle toward one of the cellular phones up front.

The bombing at the post office is the lead on the front page, a banner headline with a three-column photo, police tape on the loading dock, a human tide of the curious in the alley behind the building, fire trucks and police cars in view.

They are withholding the name of the employee killed until next-of-kin can be notified. I think about Marcie's children, the seven-year-old son she talked about, and wonder: Does he have a father? What will become of the boy now? And I think about Sarah, who but for a few more feet down that shattered hallway . . .

So far there are few details on the bombing. What is published is a lot of conjecture, quoted statements from postal officials talking about the constant risk of bombs being sent through the mails, the difficulty of security precautions given the volume of letters and packages. Speculation, most of it wrong. I scan the page, two columns, and turn to the inside. There is not a word about the private courier or the package he delivered. I am wondering what has happened to Howard, Marcie's friend who ushered the courier back to the office. Have they questioned him? Figured it out?

I turn the page, nothing more.

Up front Dana has her back to me, pressing more buttons on the phone. I think maybe she's having trouble getting a hotel.

When I look up again, she's coming down the aisle.

"I think you'll like the place," she says. "I stayed there once with my husband, years ago."

"I'm sure it'll be fine," I tell her. This is no vacation.

She swings into the seat and buckles up.

One hand is in my sport coat pocket. I feel the photograph of the little church, now wrapped in a plastic cover—what I have kept back from Dana.

My eyes are still running over the paper. At the bottom of the page there is something of interest, speculation on a federal court vacancy in Capital City, Dana's name mentioned prominently on a short list of candidates. The lady has juice.

I show it to her, point with my finger at her name.

She makes gestures of modesty.

"The press," she says. "Once on their 'A' list you never get off. They have to have something to fill in around the ads," she says.

But I know better. Dana's in the power set in Capital City. Well-thought-of and a serious contender for higher office.

We talk for a while, doze on and off. My head is spinning. The blast from this afternoon, the pressure of the cabin, the droning of the engines, all combine to make for fitful sleep.

By the time we do the interisland flight it is nearing midnight Hawaiian time. Stars so bright you want to reach out and grab them as we do the last few miles on the road to Wailea and our hotel. I'm driving the rental car as Dana navigates.

I would have slept in some fleabag near the airport, but Dana insists that we will both need a good night's sleep for the road to Hana in the morning.

"You've been there?" I say.

"Once."

"What's it like?"

"Everyman's dream of paradise," she says. "Azure seas, blue skies, puffy clouds, and the hills are green, very, very green."

She smiles. "And then there is the road to Hana," she says.

"What's that supposed to mean?"

"You'll see in the morning."

The highway suddenly comes to an end and I make a sweeping right turn down a winding drive toward the sea. We dead-end at the driveway to a shopping center, upscale. I see signs with arrows in every direction, golf courses and clubhouses at every point of the compass.

"You want to go left," she says.

I turn, and about a hundred yards up the road I see the sign for the hotel.

We turn in and stop at the kiosk. A woman in a flowing silk sarong greets us.

"Welcome to Grand Wailea. Are you staying with us?"

"The reservation's under 'Colby,' " says Dana.

"Of course," she says. "We got the call."

The woman gives me a parking pass and sends us through, down the broad curving driveway, past cascades of water backlit by colored lights. We turn and stop under the massive carport at the front entrance. A car hop gets the keys. A bellboy takes our bags. If they had six stars, this place would get them all.

We are lei-ed about the neck as we enter the lobby, something from *Elephant Walk*—open air and lush vegetation, a reflecting pond larger than some lakes, and an enormous covered bar in the center, its blue-tiled roof floating on concrete spires fifty feet in the air. We are greeted by a girl in starched white livery at reception, a white tunic with gold buttons, Asian eyes, and an accent that rings with intrigue.

They are doing impressions of our credit cards, and I am wondering how mine will hold up.

Dana leans in my ear. "Not to worry. I got us a good rate," she says.

The girl at the counter smiles.

Great. Three hundred a night, I'm thinking.

They bring us hot hand towels and little glasses of papaya juice. The girl hits the bell twice and our luggage appears on a cart. We follow the bellhop to the elevator, and outside, under stars and flickering tiki torches, past giant banyan trees and a sea of bamboo, palm fronds clacking in the trade winds.

He stops with the rolling cart in front of a door, glossy white enamel with brass fittings, and with the card key opens it. He shows Dana in, drops off her bags, and takes me to my room next door.

I tip him and he's out the door.

The place is palatial but muggy. I open the plantation louvers and the sliding door behind them, walk out on the balcony overlooking the sea, surging white surf on a curve of beach shimmering in the moonlight.

I hear knocking.

It's Dana at the adjoining door.

I unlatch my side and she comes in.

"Like it?" she says.

"What's not to like? The government rate must be a little better than when I worked for the DA," I tell her.

"Pulled a few strings," she says. "Some people in Honolulu owed me a favor."

"Who's that?" I say.

"Some people. Relax," she says. "Enjoy the evening. Tomorrow comes . . . the road to Hana.'' She makes it sound ominous, then smiles at me.

It's a warm night, but the breeze off the ocean carries its own chill. I shiver, more from exhaustion, leaning on the railing at the balcony.

''Do you want to order something in the room to eat?''

I shake my head.

''So this is how the other half lives,'' I say. A world away from the gray-cast skies and freezing ground fog of Capital City in the winter.

''The place really is something, isn't it?'' She's reading my mind. ''You must think I'm awful. The pampered woman. Tagging along and demanding only the best,'' she says.

''Why?''

''I should have let you make the arrangements,'' she says.

I turn and look at her. A smile. ''Why would I think you're awful? Because you have good taste?'' She is shimmering hair, and the magic gleam of night light dancing in amethyst eyes.

''Now you're patronizing,'' she says. ''Believe me, if this trip had taken us to any other place, it would have been government per diem and a travel allowance. Like I said, tonight is a special deal.''

''Why?''

She looks at me, strokes my face with the side of her hand. ''You had a rough day. I thought you needed something . . . special,'' she says.

''Your husband took you to nice places. He must have been well-heeled.''

''You sound jealous.'' She winks. A schoolgirl's grin. ''You never took Nikki anywhere like this?''

I shake my head. ''The anxiety attacks waiting for the bill would have stolen all the pleasure,'' I tell her. ''We're both blue-collar, down to the third cervical vertebra. Vacations, the few times we took them, were a rented mountain cabin that belonged to a friend, meals in, and vacuum before you leave.''

I turn to the railing. She is behind me, the contour of her body pressed to mine, shielded against the breeze of the trades. I feel her knee in the crook of my own.

"My husband's family had money." She's musing, almost talking to herself, leaning on me, her chin nestled on the back of my shoulder.

"Problem was, Darrel only knew how to spend it. He would have been the prodigal son, except he never really left home. Never grew up," she says.

"Sounds like you had a child to raise after all," I say.

"You could say that. Oh, as a woman I always felt good on Darrel's arm. He wore the right clothes, made all the proper gestures, he was tall, good-looking in a charming sort of way. He had the kind of humor that can make a woman forgive a lot, and a first impression that lasted longer than the crease in his pants.

"It took me the better part of the first year to figure out where all the money was coming from. Darrel couldn't hold a job if he owned the place. Daddy kept buying him businesses, and Darrel kept treating them like hobbies."

"Is that what brought it to an end?"

"In part. One night he got drunk and I saw the darker side. He'd had an argument with his father over money, and took it out on me. Slapped me around until I got the car keys. And that was that," she says. "I never went back."

"You left him?"

"Quickest divorce in history. Still like how the other half lives?" she says.

"I suppose the grass is always greener," I tell her. I'm nodding, swaying in the cool breeze, listening to the rollers as they crash on the beach below, white foam glistening in the moonlight.

Three fingers of her right hand are through the buttons on the front of my shirt, twirling through the hairs on my chest, the tip of one foraging over a nipple, like searing heat.

I wonder for a moment if I should move, but there is nothing uncomfortable in this. It feels so natural. A woman's hand on my chest, something I have not felt in months.

The soft whisper of her lips caresses the nape of my neck. I turn, and I am looking into her eyes, dazed, wondering what is happening.

Shattering glass and death, the explosion at the post office, seem something from another decade, another century.

I am mesmerized by the glow in her face. My hands, clasped at the small of her back, take on a life of their own. She is soft and warm, her hands at my shirt, suddenly inside, buttons undone, the soft slide of silk as her blouse driven by points of ecstasy grazes my chest.

The throbbing in my ears is no longer from pain. My fingers at the buttons on the back of her blouse. A trail of fabric in our wake as we grasp and grope each other, moving through the room. My knee gripped by silken thighs. Her hungry mouth pressed on my own, the whisper of her tongue.

There is the slickness of nylon against my naked leg as I ease her onto the bed. I am captured by the reality of her near nakedness. She lies, her hair cascading on the pillow, stripped to the waist, the soft tenderness of her breasts like two beacons, her thin waist encircled by the lacy gauze of a black garterbelt. The tender bare flesh of thighs, above nylon.

She looks at me, her eyes glazed by lust, a mirror image of my own.

She beckons, her flesh moist with the scent of the tropics.

I sink, our bodies two melding pools of pleasure.

She is in my ear, hot whispers of passion laced with my name. Lower regions pressing, the slick wet heat of desire moving, roiling, undulating ancient rhythms of bliss, her fingers everywhere. My mind a sea of confusion, lust, or love. My lips, the edge of teeth jagged at her nipple. She arches her back, and between quick breaths of passion, grinding bone to pelvic bone, she pleads for the pleasure of release.

CHAPTER
14

Shafts of light pierce the louvered shutters of the room like golden arrows. The songs of exotic birds erupt from the verdant bush outside my room, along with the rush of water over rocks in the gardens. There are random voices, people walking on the path beneath the balcony.

My senses, dulled by half-sleep, detect a shadow moving in the distant reaches of the room. I am wrapped in rumpled sheets, sprawled on the bed, feeling the warm humid air of morning in the tropics.

As I open my eyes and focus, she's sitting in a chair, her eyes locked on me, smiling. Dana is wrapped in two bath towels, her hair wet from a washing.

"Did anybody ever tell you that you make these little noises when you sleep?" she says. "Little mewing sounds." She mimics something like a kitten complaining to get out of a box.

"Lovely," I say. The bright daylight outside the window finally registers.

I roll over and sit up, a sheet wrapped around me.

"What time is it?"

"Almost ten," she says.

"What! Why didn't you get me up?"

"Oh, I did," she says. "Last night. At least three times."

"Cute," I say. I can still feel the yen for Dana climb in my groin, a frolic on the edge of hedonism, and wonder what God-made substance can possibly flood the brain to produce such pleasure.

"You were tired. I thought I'd let you sleep."

I feel the scratches on my face from the flying glass of yesterday. Two of the bandages have come off during the night. I wonder how much of the soreness that racks my body is from the explosion and how much derives from our antics of the night.

"We oughta be halfway to Hana by now," I tell her.

"I'll be ready in ten minutes," she says.

I'm up, sheets of modesty dragging on the floor, tripping, grousing through the trail of discarded clothing, looking for my pants. I have distant memories of someone taking a shower in the middle of the night. I feel my body. Sticky. It wasn't me.

"They're on the other chair," she says. My pants.

I grab them and start to put a leg through, then discover that I have nothing on underneath.

She's laughing, out loud.

"Your suitcase is over there," she says. "By the table."

First things first. I rummage and find a clean pair of Jockeys.

She's out of the chair and into the bathroom in her room. I can hear the sound of the hair dryer.

"There's croissants and coffee on the table in here," she shouts over the drone of the dryer. "I ordered from room service."

In two seconds I'm hovering over the table in her room, scarfing with both hands.

"Hungry?"

"Famished like a bear," I tell her.

"And just as fuzzy," she says.

I am hairy chested and without a shirt.

"How long will it take to get to Hana?"

"Depends how dangerously you want to live," she says.

• • •

The way to Hana seems its own form of paradise, verdant sugarcane fields and plantation villages, a rocky coastline, the many surfaces of the sea, cresting emerald waves crowned by white froth. Lava ridges rise from white-sand beaches, forming a dark tawny color to match the tanned brown thighs of girls in thong bikinis as we whisk along the highway.

Then forty miles in heaven turns to hell. Single-lane bridges on hairpin turns, white concrete walls, and plummeting waterfalls that drop a thousand feet out of virgin jungle; switchbacks so severe that half the time we are going in the wrong direction.

The locals drive like someone has loaded their java with testosterone. Life on the road to Hana, it seems, is a perpetual game of chicken.

The road begins to narrow until at one point I have to back up a hundred feet, to a soft spot on the shoulder over a vertical cliff, to let a cement truck pass in the other direction. The driver, a big Hawaiian, beams me a grin like some sumo wrestler who's bounced my ass out of the circle. Like what's amatter, haule? No balls? Even Dana gives me a look, like if I'd pressed it I could have slid between his tires and under the axle.

I offer her the wheel but she declines.

It is after two o'clock by the time I see the dark basalt landing strip of the Hana airport. It lies on a flat point of land over the sea, chopped out of the jungle and carved lava stone. A couple of miles on is the town of Hana. Two churches, the post office, a couple of grocery stores, and a gas station.

''The road gets worse on the other side of town,'' she tells me.

''How can it?''

''I've been there,'' she says. ''Trust me.''

There's a single hotel. Dana points me in the direction, and a couple of minutes later we roll into the circular drive of the Hotel Hana-Maui, single-story bungalows with plantation roofs of tile and tin, old Hawaii before American and Japanese megabucks tried to marble it over like ancient Rome.

But one thing is certain. Hana would be the place of choice for anyone wanting to get lost from the prying eyes of this world.

A woman directs us to the registration desk. We are already registered, adjoining rooms in a bungalow on the grass. I figure Dana was busy on the phone from the plane last night.

"Mr. Opolo is in the bungalow across the way," says the clerk.

"Good," says Dana.

"Who's Mr. Opolo?"

"I'll introduce you in a minute," she says.

I sense there's some surprise coming. "Tell me now," I say.

"You're going to meet him in just a minute."

"Then humor me."

"He's a friend. From Honolulu."

"What kind of a friend?"

"Professional colleague," she says.

"Dana."

"Okay. He's with the FBI. Agent in charge of the Honolulu office."

"Son of a bitch," I say. "I thought we had a deal."

"Listen, you're not going to get anywhere on your own. Jessie can help."

I'm shaking my head. "Wonderful."

"He knows the people. This is an insular place," she says. She makes it sound like the Ozarks of Polynesia. "The locals want to run you in circles, they'll do it. There's a thousand houses in these hills, from estates to the stars to one-room stone huts. The Merlows could be in any one of them."

"And they could be here in the hotel, in the room next to us," I say.

"They're not. We already checked," she says, droll.

"Great."

The clerk hands me a map of the hotel grounds. At this

moment I could spit on it. A bellhop grabs our bags and loads them into an electric cart, Dana giving me a million and one reasons why I should thank her for calling in the FBI.

I'm beginning to think Harry was right, and wondering who fucked who last night.

She's still talking at me minutes later when the phone rings in her room.

"Jessie." Relief in her voice. The troops are here.

"Where are you? Come on over," she says.

Two minutes later there's a knock on the door, and Dana opens it.

Outside is a man, maybe late forties, hair like white silk, skin the color of burnished wood. He's barrel-chested, a big man, a face like a totem, austere. He's wearing one of those loud print shirts, flowers in every color of the rainbow.

"Hey, girl. It's good to see you," he says.

"It's been a long time," Dana greets him.

"Let's see. Since San Francisco," he says. "What—five years?"

She agrees with him, puts her hands on his shoulders, and gives him a peck on the cheek.

Opolo has to bow his neck a little to get under the low lintel of the door.

"Jessie Opolo. Paul Madriani." She makes the introduction, unsure how I'm going to respond.

"Glad to meet you." He smiles. I wonder if it's as artless as it looks or the face of Polynesian guile.

I won't be an asshole, so I take his hand.

"A pleasure," I say.

"How long have you been here?" she says.

"Since this morning," he tells her. "Coptered in about nine."

"Anybody with you?"

"Two agents," he says.

It's a fucking army, I think. I'm waltzing away, rolling my eyes.

Dana can read my mind. "I assume you're keeping a low profile."

I have visions of Humvees with recoilless rifles mounted on the back.

"The other two agents are in the room," he says. "The only thing we've done is check the post office for the package."

"What package?" I ask.

"The ring," he says.

I'd forgotten about this. The ring Kathy Merlow mentioned in her letter, the one she wanted Marcie to send to her.

"It was picked up yesterday afternoon," says Opolo. "Unfortunately we were too late."

"Did anybody sign for it?" I ask.

"Yes." He pulls a small notebook from his pocket and opens it, then unfolds a sheet of paper that's been placed inside it. It's a copy of the postal receipt.

"It was addressed to Alice Kent, and the receipt was signed in that name."

"Can I see it?"

He hands the sheet over.

I flatten it on the table, then take out the note from my pocket, the one sent to Marcie Reed by Kathy Merlow, and compare the handwriting with the signature on the form. Like peas in a pod.

"She's here," I say. "She signed for it herself."

Dana looks at me. "Maybe we're halfway home."

Dana and the agents are huddled in the next room around a coffee table, discussing methods for locating the Merlows. The adjoining door between the rooms is open, so I watch from a distance. They've already exhausted several avenues of search. Utility records, telephone, and power show no new hookups under the names Merlow or Kent. If they're living in the area, they're using another alias. They've checked the rental car agencies, figuring that the Merlows would need wheels.

"If they rented a car on the island, they used some other identification," says Opolo. "No record of a rental in the name of Merlow or Kent, and no charges on George Merlow's credit card since the couple disappeared from Capital City."

Dana was right about one thing, Opolo and his agents have been able to gain access to information that we could not: personal credit-card data.

"I think we talk to the carriers." Opolo wants to concentrate on the mail carriers who service the area around Hana.

"It's a small place. Even if they don't deliver mail to these people, they might know who's new and where they live."

"There's six carriers. Five are out on their routes. We can't get 'em all until later this afternoon." One of the agents has already checked this out.

I've drifted into the room, standing in one corner like the proverbial potted plant.

"There's the grocery store, and the little ranch market," says one of them. "The only places to buy food for two hours in either direction. They gotta eat," he says.

"Maybe," says Opolo. "People may have seen them in the stores, but will they know where they live? The Merlows aren't going to volunteer this information."

"We could stake out the stores," says one of the agents. He's young and eager.

Opolo looks at him, wrinkled eyes of skepticism. "An army of strangers loitering outside the market?" he says. "We'd stand out like bumps. Word'd be out in an hour. This is a small town."

"That's charitable," I say.

"Okay, so it's a village," he says. He smiles at me.

"Still, if one person talks," he says, "a clerk at the post office, one of the employees at the hotel. In an hour everybody in town's gonna know who we are, that we're looking for somebody. The word won't take long to spread. If Mr. Madriani is right, the people we are looking for know how to lose themselves. We won't get a second chance," he says.

Despite Dana's going behind my back, I'm warming to Jessie Opolo. Maybe she was right.

"What about the realtors?" he says. "The ones who rent out houses and cabins? The Merlows would have to obtain accommodations from somebody. Do we have any pictures of them?" he says.

This sends one of the other agents scurrying through an open attaché case.

"Not a great copy," he says. "We got this from the mainland. State DMV. Faxed this morning." He hands Opolo two poor-quality fax transmissions, tortured pictures like Rorschach cards of human images, so bad the subjects would not recognize themselves.

"Nothing better?" says Opolo.

"We can try to get wirephotos," says the agent. "It would take a while."

"Fine. In the meantime we run down a list of realtors in the area," says Opolo. He looks at his watch. "We meet back here in an hour to go talk to the mail carriers."

They're up on their feet, going over a few last-minute details. Dana and Opolo in one corner talking privately. I take the opportunity to slip back into my room.

I've ditched my coat in the closet. Even in winter the Hawaiian sun is too hot. I slip my hand into the patch pocket and remove the photograph of the little church. Two seconds later I'm out the door, heading up the path toward the office. It's a five-minute walk, and by the time I reach the shade of the lanai near the office I am wet with perspiration.

One of the employees, a young woman, is sitting at a table, like a concierge, tour books and pamphlets spread before her. She greets me warmly, a paying guest.

"I have a question."

"Of course. If I can help," she says.

"I have a picture here. A little church in the area. I wonder if I showed it to you whether you could tell me where it is?"

The smile fades a little from her face. "I could try," she

says. "There are a lot of churches."

"I noticed." Dana and I passed a half dozen on the way in, none of them resembling the one in the picture.

I show her the photo. She studies it for several seconds. Looks at me, up and down, a tourist on the prowl. There's a spark, a fleeting moment where I think she's going to say something, then hesitation. She changes her mind. "I don't think I recognize that one," she says. "Sorry."

"Is there a phone where I can make a long-distance call and bill it to my room?"

"In the library. Just pick up and wait for the operator." She points the way.

It's a large room, a couple of club chairs and some rattan furniture, tasteful, quiet, and cool. One wall, from wainscot to ceiling, is a glassed-in bookshelf. I find the phone, take a seat, and wait for the operator, perusing titles on the spines of books stacked on the shelves, and a framed picture on a shelf behind the glass, a black-and-white glossy print.

The operator comes on the line, and I give her the number in Capital City. Harry answers on the second ring, the backline. It's after hours on the mainland. He's been waiting for my call.

"How's it going?" he says.

I don't tell him I'm camped with the FBI. I wouldn't need a phone to hear Harry's ridicule.

"Fine," I tell him. "Anything from Mason's?"

Charles Mason & Co. is an old-line photographic studio in Capital City. In days past they did daguerreotypes of whiskered gents from the gold rush. Today they do family portraits, wedding pictures, and in my case, large poster-size exhibits that I use in court, enlargements of documents, and in this case a major blowup of one photograph. It is the errand I ran on my way home from the office yesterday afternoon before meeting Dana.

"They took it out to twelve magnifications. Nothing," he says. "Just a lot of dots."

"Any name on the church?"

"No. The picture's of the side of the church," says Harry. "The phototech at Mason's figures any name would be on the front."

"Great."

"The enlargement did pick up one sign," he says. "But nothing helpful."

"What does it say?"

"White letters on black paint. Hard to read 'cuz it's in script. Best we can make out, it's just telling people not to go tramping around on the graves. Doesn't really make much sense," says Harry. "A churchyard in the middle of nowhere. Does it look like a place where you'd draw crowds?"

"Far from it," I tell him.

"I dunno," he says. "From what I can see, the picture's a big zero."

A woman has come in. She's straightening some of the books on a shelf, replacing a few others.

Harry wishes me luck and we hang up.

The woman is dusting, opening the center glass panel.

I get a closer look at the framed picture propped on the shelf. A man in a leather flying cap, standing in front of a plane. A face recognizable to any schoolkid of my generation.

She sees me looking.

"He lived in the area for a while," she says. "In fact, he's buried just down the road—a little churchyard."

I'm doing almost sixty, looking at my watch. It is nearly four o'clock, and I'm wondering what the parameters of Kathy Merlow's afternoon are. Her note said she spent her afternoons in the churchyard. I am praying that she is still there today.

It hit me with the intensity of a moonbeam through an open window, the inscription on the back of the snapshot. Something about the wings of the morning.

When I showed the woman in the library the snapshot, she said, "That's it. That's the place he's buried."

Directions were something else. Reluctant at first, she said they'd had a lot of problems right after he died, the curious flooding the little church, taking pictures and picking flowers. But that was twenty years ago, and things are now quieter. Still, the locals are protective. After assurances that I was supposed to meet somebody there, that I was late, she finally told me where it was.

Past the Seven Pools, not to be fooled by the little church out on the highway, "most tourists are," she says. A left turn off the road, and then a dogleg, another left.

Dana was right. The road is worse on this side of town, beyond Hana. It is more narrow, overgrown with vegetation that brushes both sides of my car in places as I rocket past. I come to the top of a hill and nearly careen down a private driveway before I see the turn in the road. By now Dana and the agents are probably wondering where I am, looking for the car in the parking lot.

A few camera-toting tourists are crawling on the highway at the bridge, near the path to the Seven Pools. A couple of them give me dirty looks as I rocket across the bridge ahead of a line of cars coming the other way.

Two miles on I see a church on the right. False lead. I pass it. A mile down is an open gate, on the left, a sign. I turn in. Gravel and lava stone, chained-off private drives two hundred feet in, so I turn left, under a grove of giant banyan trees that transform the driveway into a cave of foliage, dead moss hanging from their limbs.

Then I see it. The little church from the snapshot, green clapboard over white plaster.

I dead-end in a dirt parking lot under the shade of the trees. Two mangy dogs lying like they are dead a few feet away. One of them raises his head enough to look at me as the dust from my wheels reaches, then settles on him. He sneezes, then puts his head down and goes back to sleep.

There are two other vehicles in the parking lot, a small pickup with gardening implements and a sedan. A guy is loading a mower into the back of the truck, along with some plastic bags of cut grass.

A man and woman standing, looking at a headstone in the cemetery at the side of the church, under a large banyan tree. Some distance off beyond the cemetery, through a gate, an old lady, cloaked in flowing garb, a broad straw hat, sits at an easel painting. The signs of serenity. Fronds clacking in the dwarfed palms that line the open grass.

I take the little path through a gate in the low stone wall leading to the church. The door is not locked, but I peer through one of the windows. A few wooden pews and a raised pulpit up front. There is no one inside, so I take the path to the right, toward the graveyard at the side of the church. Here the sun's rays are warm. The humid air hangs heavy. In the distance is a fence, maybe a hundred yards away, where the world drops off, land's end, blue water to the horizon, white breakers crashing on the few rocks that have clawed their way up from the depths.

There is the rumble of a junker engine and the sound of rubber on gravel as the gardener in his beat-up pickup pulls out.

Headstones and other monuments line the narrow path that zigzags toward the open grass and the cliff beyond. I wend my way through.

The couple, Asian tourists, seem finally to lose interest in the headstone. They make their way across the grass toward the parking lot.

I take their place. Under the banyan tree at the near edge of the grass is a grave, a plain flat marker, nothing fancy, no shrine. The name engraved there had been its own monument during life, flashed 'round the world before the information highway was a deer track in the electronic brush.

We make idols of rock stars and bobbing heads doing gangsta rap, people whose contribution to life is as fleeting as the pixels that carry their image to our televisions screens.

Nothing enduring. It is a measure of our spiritual poverty. He was from a different time.

A rectangular pile of lava rocks ringed by a piniosed chain just a few inches off the ground. The headstone, unpolished gray granite, a soft cursive script:

Charles A. Lindbergh
Born, Michigan, 1902   Died, Maui, 1974
*"If I take the wings of the morning
and dwell in the uttermost parts of the sea"*
C A L

As I look up, the aspect of the little church looms before me through the hanging frowns of trees that ring it. Whoever took the snapshot had done so from this location.

There is no sign of Kathy Merlow. I turn and walk toward the fence, the cliff fifty yards away; undulating blue waters, and the glint of sunlight on crested waves.

The old woman is packing up, folding her easel, the afternoon's work done. She is in on a section of grass beyond a gate, a sign hanging on the fence:

KIPAHULU POINT PARK

This seems to merge with the grass of the cemetery.

I plant myself by the fence and wait, looking at the sea, hoping that Kathy Merlow will appear. I look at my watch—after four-thirty. I wonder if Opolo has had any luck with the mail carriers, whether Dana is frantic looking for me.

I see a big blue sedan out on the highway. It cruises by at a slow speed. Stops at the gate. The driver, his head a dot in the distance, stops to read the sign on the gate. Then he drives off.

The Asian couple have made their way to the car, the *thunk* of doors being closed, the engine started. Pretty soon they will be closing the gate on the road. My chances of slipping back here tomorrow are not good. Dana and Opolo will want to know where I've been, the third degree.

The old lady is drifting by on the grass, thirty yards away, struggling with her easel and a small stool, a wooden box of painting paraphernalia. I look at the parking lot. Except for my car it is now empty. I watch as the old lady moves away from me now, toward a small opening in the fence, near the entrance to the park, and suddenly it hits me—not the gait of an old woman.

I am off the fence, moving toward her at a good rate. Ten feet away, staring at her back.

"Excuse me."

She turns. Not the wrinkled and weathered countenance of age, but tan and more vigorous than our last meeting, the vacant gaze of Kathy Merlow.

CHAPTER
15

She looks the part of the chic art set from the thirties, a loud silk kimono with wide sleeves, open down the front, like the academic gown on some Oxford don. Underneath she wears white cotton slacks and a blue top. Capping it all is a broad-brimmed straw hat, cocked at an angle for the sun, and over-sized dark glasses.

"Yes?" Kathy Merlow's smile is somewhat artless. "Can I help you?" she says.

She's burdened by the folded artist's stool and easel hanging heavily in one hand. The box of paints and brushes in the other.

"You don't remember me?" I say.

Wary eyes.

"I'm Paul Madriani. We met the night Melanie Vega was killed. Out on the street in front of her house."

"I think you've mistaken me for someone else." She turns and starts to walk.

I take her gently by one arm. "I don't think so. But maybe you could take off the glasses," I say.

"Take your hand off of me," she says.

I let go.

"I have to meet someone and I'm running late." She gives me the look of uppercrust arrogance, done so well behind dark glass, and dismisses me.

"Can I help you with that?" I reach for the stool and the easel.

She pulls them away.

"I can manage," she says. "Now leave me alone." She takes a step backward, full retreat, and walks out of one of her sandals. She trips, drops the easel and stool.

I grab her arm again.

The lid to the box of paint supplies has opened as she jostles for balance. Tubes of paint and tiny brushes all over the grass.

"Now see what you've made me do."

I let go, and she steadies herself.

"I'm sorry," I tell her. "I'm not here to cause you any problems. I just need information."

"I've told you, you've got me mixed up with someone else."

"You aren't even curious as to how I found you?"

She's picking up the paints. I help her.

"Marcie Reed," I tell her.

She gives me a look. If there is any curiosity written in her eyes, it is hidden by shaded glass. But she curls her upper lip and bites it a little.

"I don't know any Marcie Reed," she says.

"The ring on your finger," I say. "The cameo. Is that the one Marcie sent to you general delivery?"

She stops picking up tubes of paint and covers the back of her right hand with the long sleeve of her kimono.

"We could ask the people at the post office," I say.

The outside of one of the tubes of paint is sloppy with green acrylic paste, and what appears to be the drying swirls and ridges of the owner's thumb. She's looking into my face at this moment. I pick the tube up by the cap and deftly slip it into my jacket pocket so she doesn't notice. Last month she was going by "Merlow." This week no doubt she is called by another surname that I do not even know. It would be nice to have her real name.

She says nothing.

"I think you remember me," I say.

"How did you get here?" The first crack in the wall of denial.

I gesture toward my car in the parking lot.

"I think you should get back in it and go," she says.

"Not till we talk."

"We have nothing to talk about," she says. "You shouldn't be here. There'll be trouble if they find us together," she says.

"Who's 'they'?"

"Never mind."

Having captured all the colors of the rainbow, she closes the latch on the wooden box.

I pick up the easel. She grabs it from my hand and starts to walk away, across the thick grass, as fast as sandals will allow, like some geisha in flowing gowns.

"Do you have a car?" I ask.

No answer.

"I could give you a lift."

"No, thanks." She's opening the gulf between us, twenty yards away.

I start to run, trailing in her wake. "I have to talk to you."

"No," she says. "I've got nothing to say."

"Marcie Reed is dead," I tell her.

Suddenly she stops. I nearly run over her from behind. She turns to look at me over one shoulder.

"Marcie?" she says.

I nod. "Yesterday afternoon in Capital City," I tell her.

She doesn't say a word, but the news of Marcie's death, a woman she claims not to know, has suddenly turned her composure to mush. The easel and stool are back on the grass. As if in slow motion the handle of the box slips from her fingers, the sound of wood on wood as it clacks down on top of the easel. One hand comes up, so many fingers in her mouth I think she's going to swallow them. Deep in thought, she turns away from me. I can no longer see her face. But with a hand she reaches up and takes the glasses off.

"How did it happen?"

"A letter bomb delivered to the post office by a private courier."

When she turns I see her eyes for the first time, tired, dark edges, tracks like a thousand birds in the dried mud at some watering hole on a parched savanna. She's calculating the barbarity of death in this fashion, looks at me, searching eyes, the sense of one tortured by fear, now rendered fearless by fatigue.

"Poor Marcie," she says. "I should never have involved her. She was only doing me a favor."

"I know."

"Why did they have to kill her?" she says.

"Why don't *you* tell me."

"Oh, God. None of this was supposed to happen," she says. "They promised us."

"Who?"

My question draws her from her reverie over Marcie.

"Why did you come all this way? What's your interest?"

"I represent a woman who has been charged with the murder of Melanie Vega. She didn't do it. I think you know that."

"Ahh." Her head is now making big lazy circles, nodding, the way people do when they are dazed. The pieces slowly beginning to fit for her.

"And you think I can help you?"

"Before Marcie died she told me some things."

"What things?"

"That whoever killed Melanie Vega had been hired to carry out the murder. That you knew something about this."

"I'm sorry that your client is in trouble. But I can't help you."

With this she adjusts her glasses back on her head.

"I think you can. Just tell me what happened."

In the distance there's the sound of rubber on gravel. The blue sedan I'd seen moments ago out on the highway, coming this way like there's no tomorrow. Some tourist in a hurry, a lot of speed and dust as the car slides to a stop in the lot.

For several seconds my question lies dormant, punctuated only by the sound of the car's engine rumbling in the distance.

"Mrs. Merlow?"

She's frozen in place, looking at the vehicle, which is stone-still, its motor running, no one getting out.

"We have to talk," I tell her.

"Not now." Her eyes are on the car.

"When?"

She's ignoring me.

"All I want to know is what happened. Give me a hint."

"I didn't see a thing," she says.

"Then your husband?" I say. "He knew something, didn't he? And he told you?" I'm thinking Melanie and her carnal welcome wagon. Maybe she and George, Jack and Melanie, were doing a foursome, some erotic swap-meet. Maybe that's why Kathy Merlow doesn't want to talk.

"Leave us alone," she says.

"No. I won't leave you alone. A woman is being charged with murder in a crime she didn't commit. Sooner or later you're going to have to tell me what you know."

"I don't know a thing, and neither does my husband."

"You expect me to believe that the two of you left Capital City in the middle of the night immediately after Melanie Vega's murder because you didn't like the weather?"

"Frankly I don't care what you believe." As she says this she's giving me eyes-right, less than her undivided attention, her gaze glued to the car in the parking lot.

"Is he with you?" she says.

The vehicle's occupant is now standing beside the car, its motor still rumbling. He's leaning against the open driver's door, looking this way, lighting what looks like a big cigar, a large stogie with a glowing red tip.

I squint in the sunlight. I had been particularly careful driving, watching the rearview mirror for other cars.

"No."

"He's looking at us," she says.

"I don't think so. He's looking at the cemetery," I tell her. "A tourist, probably trying to find Lindbergh's grave," I say.

"Listen. I can't talk to you now."

"Later?"

"Perhaps. But I do have to go now."

"Tell me where I can find you."

"Maybe tomorrow."

"Maybe doesn't cut it," I say.

She looks at me, reading my mind. The road back to Hana is narrow and slow. I could follow her and she knows it.

"Tomorrow afternoon. Two o'clock. Here," she says.

"You promise?"

"I promise."

Like some pesty insect, it settles first on her right temple, a tiny red prism of light, a dot no bigger than the point of a pen, dancing like reflections through the facets of a crystal. She stoops to pick up the paint box, and the light disappears, only to find its way into her hairline as she straightens up.

It takes an instant before the image registers. Like a cigar with hot embers at the tip, but different, a beam of light, one moment it's there, the next it's gone, red glowing like some diffused demonic gaze.

With all the force my body can muster from a standing start, I shove Kathy Merlow. I send her sprawling onto the grass and land on top of her.

The crack of the speeding bullet snaps the sound barrier overhead and passes into the brush beyond. Silenced. Guided to a near miss by the deadly accuracy of its laserscope.

"What! Are you crazy?" She's pushing me off, clawing at my face like I'm some sexual predator.

"Get up." I grab her by the arm.

"Get away from me!" She's pushing at me, trying to dust off her clothes with one hand.

I'm on one knee, crouched. She's on her feet, standing upright. And it hits me—she doesn't realize a shot has been taken.

I've got a grip on her arm like a vise. She will be black and blue if she lives. I'm pushing her along ahead of me, moving laterally toward granite headstones and the church.

"Let—let—" She repeats this three or four times. "Let me go," she says. Waving arms and flailing hands trying to shake free. "Are you crazy?"

Another crack through the air, no more than an inch from my chest, and something buries itself in the grass near her left foot. With this, her eyes go wide, twin saucers. For a single beat she's frozen in place. A few tentative steps, then she breaks into full flight. Sandals flying from her feet, she leaves me kneeling on the grass.

In two seconds I overtake her. We are now running, stride for stride. From the corner of my eye I can see the guy setting up over the windowframe of his car door for another shot. Behind the banyan tree, Lindbergh's grave between us, I can hear the guy swear, fifty yards away, a list of expletives to make a sailor blush. Movement in my peripheral vision as he raises the muzzle of the gun and starts to move parallel to our flight. He's crouching behind a low stone wall, looking for one more opening.

A flash. Something nicks my cheek. Sparks off stone as he squeezes off several rounds, the gunman spraying and praying. They ricochet off tombstones like pinballs in a machine.

Off the grass, Kathy Merlow is hopping gingerly, barefooted, over the sharp lava pebbles on the path. We run through a fusillade of bullets, targets in a penny arcade, until finally we are covered by the shrubbery surrounding the church.

Behind the building we stop. She is down on one knee, wincing, picking a rock from the bottom of her bare foot.

"Are you okay?"

She nods. Winded but not wounded.

"Where's your car?"

But before she can answer I put a finger to my lips. The crunch of gravel, footsteps at the front of the church. The slide and click of precision metal. Our man is reloaded. The wonders of modern methodical murder.

She points away from the back of the church to a fence overgrown with vegetation, a small gate leading away. She moves toward it, then looks for me to follow.

I shake my head, then point emphatically for her to go.

She waves me on.

I shake my head one more time.

Left with no choice, she disappears through the jungle of vines that cover the gate. I see it open. Her form disappears and the gate closes. I will draw cover. One woman is already dead because I pursued my questions.

I am alone now at the back of the church, my only companion a weathered wooden door. I suspect that this leads to the sacristy, the area behind the small wooden altar inside.

More footsteps. This time they come from the area around the side of the church. He is working his way through the graveyard toward where I am crouched.

I try the door. The knob turns, but I look at the rusty hinges and think twice about noise.

An engine starts in the distance. Kathy Merlow has reached her car. The footfalls on the gravel turn to a run. By my estimation he is no more than a dozen feet from the back corner of the church, coming fast. No time to think. Running, I reach for the door, and suddenly I'm inside, enveloped by the cool shadows of the church, the door closed behind me. I move quickly to a position behind the wooden altar, lost in its shadows.

Outside I can hear a vehicle moving on gravel, toward the church. More epithets from the man with the gun as he races for the gate in the fence.

I grab the only object in reach, a candle and its holder on a shelf behind the altar, and fling it hard against the interior wall of the church. It clunks, heavy metal on wood, and lands on the floor.

The footfalls outside suddenly stop. The sound of wheels as they veer in gravel, turning away from the church. The acceleration of the engine, and Kathy Merlow's car is gone, the growl of its engine receding down some unseen road.

Hesitation. The noise from inside the church has cost the killer his quarry. And now he looks for other game.

On the door, behind me, there is a hook for a lock, halfway up.

Quickly I move, in a whisper of sound I slip the hook through the eye in the door, and before I can move back to the altar someone grips the knob from the outside and jerks. The door rattles in its frame but does not open. I am pressed against the wall next to it, the hook jiggling in the eye. I stop breathing. Another tug. Several seconds pass. I can visualize an ear to the wood of the door, an eye to the keyhole, then finally, after several seconds, receding footfalls.

As quickly as they started, they stop. Maybe he walked onto grass, I think, somewhere in the graveyard along the side of the church. Dead silence.

I am braced against the wall by the door, standing upright. I don't know if it is the shadow of a tree limb on the window, but something moves.

Without a sound, I am back behind the altar, on hands and knees, the cold sweat of fear seeping through my shirt.

Through a crack in one of the boards I can see a form as it approaches the glass, backlit by the bright afternoon sun. One hand cupped to the window, shading, to peer inside. Hair that bristles in the sunlight, close-cropped, the face of the courier who delivered the deadly bomb to Marcie Reed.

I pull away from the crack in the boards and press my back to the altar. I am stone-still. Seconds pass without a sound, my breathing almost stopped, my head pounding from lack of oxygen, rivulets of sweat making their way down the sides of my face drip onto the floor. Time passes, an eternity. I lose track, unwilling to move for fear of casting a shadow on a distant wall.

My eye back to the crack in the boards. The figure at the window is gone.

I wait, look at my watch. Several minutes pass. I'm afraid to move. I listen for the sound of his car, tires grinding gravel. But there is nothing.

I could go the way of Kathy Merlow, the gate through the overgrown fence behind the church. But my car is in the lot out front. Then it settles on me. He's waiting. If he's followed me, he knows my car. Sooner or later . . .

Then I hear them. Footfalls again. This time at the front of the church, from gravel, to the wooden porch, a hand on the doorknob, and it opens. A shaft of bright sunlight. I press my back harder against the altar. Hard heels on the rough wooden floor, quick steps coming this way. With each I count the seconds left of my life. I think of Sarah. Life as an orphan. Bitter recriminations. I should not have come and left my daughter to pay the price. The irresponsible things parents do. What I would give for one more hug before I leave her. . . .

A long shadow approaching, growing shorter on the wall. In this instant of blind panic, my mind reaches for an out-of-body experience, floating somewhere over this scene, above this altar of death.

"May I ask what you're doing?"

From the corner of my eye, a head of dark hair peers at me over the edge of wood that is the corner of the altar. A lean face, stern in its bearing, middle-aged, a touch of gray at the temples, the face of peace, framed in black and white, a broad clerical collar.

"What are you doing back here?" he says.

"Oh, God!" I grab my chest, gasping for air.

"Are you all right?" The minister looks at me, suddenly solicitous, one of his flock with a coronary.

I'm hyperventilating, making up for life's deficit of lost breath.

"Fine," I tell him. "I'm fine." My looks must convey otherwise. He's around the altar, helping me to my feet, propping me against the altar.

"Do you need a doctor?"

"No, no. Just give me a second."

Sweat running down my face, my knees trembling. He plies me for my story, some testimony of what I'm doing here, something for a Sunday sermon. Man's ultimate "come-to-Jesus meeting" behind the altar.

"It's a long story," I tell him. I look at the windows, the ebbing sun, the lengthening shadows of late afternoon. I fight to find saliva in a dry mouth.

"You'll have to excuse me, but I was praying," I tell him.

"That's good," he says. "This is the right place. But you're supposed to do it out there." He points toward the pews.

"Somehow, back here," I tell him, "I felt closer to God."

He considers this for a moment, then nods as if to say, "If it's right by the Lord, it's fine by me."

"Is there anyone outside?" I ask.

He shakes his head.

"I mean a car . . . in the parking lot?"

"One driving out when I came in, and another, a small red sedan parked," he says. "I was coming to look for the owner. I have to lock up."

"You found him. Where did you come from?" I ask.

"I live across the road. I walk here each afternoon to lock the church and the gate out on the highway. Can I help you to your car?"

"No. There's no need." I'm around the altar, making my amends, telling him I am fine, my shirt dripping with perspiration, more dust and dirt on my pants than a coal miner.

He gives me a strange sort of look, a shake of the head, something designed to measure my soul, that says it's been a long time since anyone in this little church has worked so hard at prayer.

• • •

On the road back to Hana my eyes are glued to the rearview mirror. If the courier is following me, he's doing a good job, sans lights, taking the hairpin turns in what is now approaching darkness.

I'm past the turnout to the Seven Pools when a car comes from someplace off a dirt road, a lot of dust, and headlights on high beam, close enough that if I brake, he will be sitting in my trunk.

My first thoughts are ones of panic. I goose it and take a turn on skidding wheels.

Suddenly there's the flutter of lights in my mirror, flashing red and blue, followed by a quick siren. Pangs of wondrous relief. I'm about to get a speeding ticket.

We stop. The widest spot on the road I can find, a private driveway. The cop gets out, blue uniform. In the beam of his spotlight it is all I can see. In this instant it hits me. A courier one moment. How hard would it be?

Then his flashlight is in my eyes. He lowers the beam for a brief instant and I can see him. One of the local boys, Hawaiian through and through.

"Can I see your driver's license?"

"How fast was I going, officer?"

No response. I fumble in my wallet.

"Take it out, please."

I hand it to him.

He looks at the license, then flashes light in my eyes.

"Mr. Madriani. Stay in your vehicle and follow me, please."

With that he hands me my license and heads back to his car.

I have had roller-coaster rides with less G force than the trip back to Hana behind this guy. Like some Toon-time character with an anvil for a foot, the cop drives as if the road will stretch like ribbon to hold his tires in the turns. We high-ball through town like a rocket sled, no siren or lights, nothing that might give the odd pedestrian or stray dog an even chance.

Two miles on the other side, he turns down a road to the right, onto the flat plain leading to the airstrip. A second right and a few hundred feet up a dirt road he comes to a stop behind another police car and two unmarked vehicles. A small group is gathered, talking in the headlights. I see Dana, and Jessie Opolo. They're both wearing blue nylon jackets with the letters FBI emblazoned on the back.

As soon as Dana sees my car, she moves quickly toward me, a tight expression on her face.

I kill my lights, and before I can get out she's posturing at my door.

"Where have you been?"

"Pursuing a lead," I tell her.

"You had us worried sick," she says. Dana's face is a map of fury at this moment, but her voice is restrained. "We didn't have any idea where you'd gone. Taking off like that."

"So you sent the troops?" I point to the cop car that brought me in like I was on some kind of tractor beam.

"Jessie had them put out an all-points for your car," she says.

"Discreet," I tell her.

"Well, you should have told us where you were going."

"What's happening?"

"Jessie and his men got a lead on the Merlows. One of the mail carriers saw them driving to a house up the road here. We think it's where they're holed up."

"Wonderful. What are they waiting for?"

"Jessie wants to go in carefully. We're not exactly sure what we're dealing with."

I'm trying to move toward Jessie and the agents. She's got her hand on my arm.

"What did you find?" she says.

"Nothing. Dead end," I tell her.

There is little sense telling her about meeting with Kathy Merlow or my close call with the netherworld at the hands of the courier. It would only make her more angry. If they have

found the Merlows, Dana will know the story soon enough.
We can get them on a plane and I can grill them both for five
hours to the drone of jet engines.

We've made our way to where Opolo and the cops are
standing.

"Hey, man, we were worried about you. She chew your ass
good?" A big smile on the Hawaiian's round face.

I don't answer.

"Where's the house?" I ask.

"Up there. About a hundred yards," says Opolo.

Just then one of agents comes down the road, a steep in-
cline. He holds his voice until he reaches us.

"Lights are on, but no movement. If they're inside they
must be sitting down doing something. We can't see a thing."

"Should we go?" Opolo quizzing his men. There's a de-
bate.

"We don't have a warrant." One of the agents is worried.

"Hell, we're not looking to arrest them," says Opolo.

"I'd like somebody to hold them," I break in. "At least
until we find out what they know."

"No problem," says Opolo. "We got cause to hold them.
To talk to them about the bombing at the post office. If what
you say is true, they know something about whoever sent the
bomb."

"Yeah. We just want to talk." One of the agents chiming
in. "If it turns out they're witnesses, we'll bag 'em and ship
'em," he says. "We'll hold 'em until you can get a subpoena
or an order of extradition if they're involved."

"Well, let's do it," I say.

Opolo looks at me, makes a face like okay.

With the appearance of the courier, the shooting at the cemetery, the longer we wait, the greater the risk that Kathy and
George Merlow are going to run. My biggest fear at this moment is that we will find an empty house, the Merlows and
their bags gone.

A minute later we're up the road, cars screaming to a halt

in front of the house, a small bungalow built off the ground on pilings, a corrugated metal roof. What the locals call a plantation house.

The cop cars have their light bars blazing. Opolo and the two agents are up the front steps. One of them is carrying a small battering ram from the trunk of the car.

The cops hoof it around the house to cover the back.

Opolo pounds on the door hard enough to cause it to bow in its frame. His gun isn't drawn, but he's holding it inside his coat by the grip.

Dana and I have been told to stay at the foot of the steps.

"FBI. Open the door."

No answer.

He pounds one more time and waits just a few seconds. He tries the doorknob. It's locked. He motions to the other agents.

They take the battering ram, a four-inch-diameter metal pipe loaded with concrete, and swing it between them. The forces of momentum send the door flying in an arc on its hinges, splintered wood and broken metal at the lock.

Caught up in the rhythm of the chase, Dana and I move to the top of the steps.

Opolo looks at us. "Stay here."

He and another of the agents are inside, guns drawn.

"FBI. Federal agents. If you're in here, let's hear it." They're moving through the rooms, flipping on lights. Through a window on the porch I can see them edging for angles with drawn pistols in doorways. A few seconds later one of the cops comes through from the back of the house.

"Nobody," he says. A lot of frenetic movement as they hit the last few cubbyholes where anyone could hide.

Opolo waves us in, holstering his pistol.

"If they were here, they're gone," he says. "And it looks like they left in a hurry."

My worst fear.

He leads us into the kitchen. One of the cops has turned off the burner on the stove. A pan of rice is burned to a crisp, long grains charred the dark color of some exotic African ant.

One of the agents comes down the hall. "I don't get it. If they left, why didn't they take their clothes?"

I look at him.

"Closet's full," he says. "Their bags are on a shelf, up in the closet, empty."

"I may have the answer." A voice from the other room, deeper in the house, down the hall. We move toward the sound. One of the cops is in the doorway to a small room at the end of the hall, the door half open.

He steps aside and lets us through, Opolo first, followed by Dana and myself.

I hear the guy whispering to the other cops outside. "No bodies," he says, "but lots of blood."

The room is streaked with it, what forensics would call spatter evidence, on the walls and the ceiling. The bed has a dark pool at the low point where the mattress is worn in the middle. This has yet to congeal, though most of it has soaked into the mattress.

At the foot of the bed is a single item of clothing, stained with blood. One of the arms is ripped, jagged tears in the upper back, like maybe it has been punctured by a knife or some other sharp implement. It is a coat of many colors.

Besides the brown hue of drying blood there are specks of pastel and dried blue acrylic on the silk kimono, the duster worn for painting this afternoon by Kathy Merlow.

CHAPTER
16

It was only by my plea of ignorance to things domestic in the law that I was allowed to remain on the spectators' side of the bar in Laurel's brawl with Jack over custody. This morning I find myself in the unenviable position of being dragged to the other side and up onto the witness stand.

The veins in my eyes look like threads of red dye that someone spilled into egg whites. I've been back three days from the islands, but with little time to sleep. Harry and I have been burning the oil trying to piece together a defense. It is a patch quilt of theories, what we know from my conversation with Marcie Reed, and what I can surmise from the facts as we know them.

This without the critical information that might have been obtained from George or Kathy Merlow. According to the FBI, their best guess is that the Merlows are now serving as fish food, somewhere at the bottom of the Pacific. I have been given little information other than this.

For two days Dana has been grilling me on my meeting with Kathy Merlow. Over coffee and at lunch she has been relentless, going over every aspect of my recollection of the brief conversation. The FBI has interviewed me, obtained descriptions, and had me look through endless mug shots on the off-chance of finding the courier who delivered the letter bomb. On all counts we have struck out.

Dana was not so much angry when I told of my foray to the little cemetery near Hana, as probing for an opening, something to get her teeth into on the bombing, some lead. This crime now looms big in Capital City as details have been made known in the press. She demanded to know what Kathy Merlow had told me, and at first seemed skeptical when I told her that she never had time to tell me anything. On matters pertaining to her office, Dana is dogged.

Yesterday she had a long telephone conversation with Jessie Opolo in Hawaii. She now seems more convinced than I that Jack is at the root of Melanie's murder, and that the bombing and the fate of the Merlows are the tangled result of some witless crime, a daisy chain of inept violence, what some people do when confronted by panic. She seems so convinced of this that I wonder if Dana knows something that I do not.

"Raise your right hand.

"Do you solemnly swear . . . ?"

We do the routine and I take the stand.

Alex Hastings is on the bench, the judge of mangled marriages.

Jack's lawyer, Daryl Westaby, is eyeing me with beady dark pupils. He is an out-of-towner from the Bay Area, a major hired gun, one of the legal thugs of family law who can transform the most rational parties to a divorce into a raging funeral pyre of domestic animosity. At this moment Jack is at the counsel table, whispering in his lawyer's ear, pouring verbal venom like liquid nitrogen into Westaby, about to light the fuse and send him my way.

Laurel is not here for these proceedings, but she is represented. Harry is at the counsel table. The only man in Capital City who knows less about family law than myself. Still, if Harry doesn't know the law, he has a willing fist to pound on the table and the wits to drop sand in the gears at the appropriate time.

I am subpoenaed here this morning because Danny and Julie Vega have disappeared, gone, kaput, vanished. They left with only a note to Jack telling him that they would not return until this mess over custody between their parents was finished. Between the lines Danny made it clear that he would not live with his father.

I have no idea where they have gone. My only complicity in this is that somehow Danny's Vespa, with its locked wooden box on the back, has been left in my garage. It is a sore point since Sarah asks me about Danny each time she sees this, and has been playing, sitting up on its seat at every opportunity.

Hastings is concerned. His initial order for temporary custody seemed the only rational recourse, given that Laurel is in jail. Today the judge seems shaken by the disappearance of the kids.

Jack is frantic, not so much out of worry, as with knowledge that, somehow from her cell, Laurel has engineered this. Jack has spent a million dollars in legal and expert-witness fees to screw her, and Laurel has, with a quarter and a phone call, creamed him. If I had to venture a guess, which I am not required to do here under oath, it is that the kids are probably playing in the snow—visions of Laurel's friend in Michigan, the one she told me about when she called on the phone that day from Reno.

I should have seen it coming—Danny's visit to his mother at the jail that day, the last time I saw him, coming as it did on the heels of my refusal to help her. I suspect that it was there that Danny got his marching orders from Mom.

"State your name for the record, please?"

"Paul Madriani."

We go through the basics. Westaby establishes my relationship to Laurel, family and legal; that I was married to her sister and represent Laurel in a murder case. He draws the details of this out, quotable items of presumed bias for the press, who Westaby has invited, a half dozen reporters, getting color and background for the murder trial. If nothing else, Jack knows this may poison the jury pool a little more. If he keeps it up we may be pushing for a change of venue, though I have my reasons for avoiding this.

"You're aware, are you not, that the legal custody of these children has been granted to their father, Jack Vega?"

"I wasn't served with a copy of the order, but I'm aware of it."

"You do not represent Laurel Vega in the child-custody proceedings, is that correct?"

"That's right."

"Have you ever represented her in those proceedings?" Westaby's skirting the question of attorney-client privilege.

"No."

He smiles. Closing the net.

"Mr. Madriani, do you know where Danny and Julie Vega are?"

"I do not."

"You have no idea?"

"I don't know where they are." I don't give him a direct reply to his question. Instead I dodge it with another answer. Perjury is a crime constructed around specific words. The games lawyers play. Westaby thinking for a moment, should he follow through?

Harry waiting, primed with an objection that the question calls for speculation.

Westaby thinks better of it.

"Have you discussed the matter with Laurel Vega?"

"What matter is that?"

"Where the children are?"

"No."

And I don't intend to. But I don't say this.

"You're not interested? This is your niece and nephew we're talking about. You're not concerned for their welfare?"

Hemming me in. Damned if I do. Damned if I don't.

"Objection. Irrelevant. The issue is whether the witness knows where the children are. He's answered that." Harry and his sand machine.

"I'll allow the question." Hastings is worried about the kids. A good judge.

"Certainly I'm concerned about them," I say.

"But you won't tell us where they are?"

"Objection. Argumentative. Assumes facts not in evidence. The witness has already stated that he doesn't know where they are."

"Sustained."

"Have you ever had conversations with Laurel Vega concerning these custody proceedings and the children?"

"Ever is a long time." Harry is getting into the spirit of things, figuring out that Family Law is, after all, a lot like crime. In the end it all comes down to kicking ass in a courtroom.

"Maybe counsel could put his objections in a proper form," says Westaby.

"Fine. The question is overly vague as to time." Harry would rather put the point of his shoe up Westaby's ass. "Why don't you try at least limiting it to a specific century," he says.

Westaby and Harry are into it.

"Hold on." Hastings from the bench. He repeats this two more times without effect and finally hammers his gavel on wood.

Harry wants to know what Westaby was doing during Evidence in law school. "Obviously it was over your head," he says. The parting shot.

This draws furrowed eyebrows from the judge, like two furry mice kissing on his forehead. Hastings is a gentlemen's judge, not someone used to the likes of Harry in court. For the moment the two are quiet, looking up at the bench.

"Mr. Hinds, if you have an objection you will address it to the bench. Do you understand?"

Harry nods.

"I don't want to see your head, I want to hear your voice," says Hastings.

"Yes, your honor."

"And you, Mr. Westaby—you will allow the court to rule on any objection. That includes any questions as to form. Is that understood?"

"Absolutely, your honor."

A lot of nodding from the lawyers. Harry does something that looks like a curtsy to the bench. Hinds has an attitude when it comes to judges. Always on a thin edge.

"Now, is there an objection?"

"Vague as to time," says Harry.

"I've forgotten what the question was," says Hastings. He has the court reporter read it back.

"Sustained. Would you like to restate the question, counsel?"

Westaby regroups.

"During the last month," he says, "have you discussed with Laurel Vega any matters, any matters at all, pertaining to this custody proceeding?"

"I'm going to object to that, your honor." Harry's up again.

"On what grounds?" Westaby's into him before the judge can move.

"Mr. Westaby—" Hastings has his gavel halfway off the bench.

"On grounds that any conversations regarding these custody proceedings are now intimately connected with the criminal case involving Mrs. Vega. As such we would contend that communications between Mr. Madriani and Mrs. Vega are protected by the attorney-client privilege."

There's stirring in the press rows.

"That's garbage," says Westaby. "There's no attorney-client relationship. How are they connected?"

"We don't have to disclose that," says Harry. "To compel an answer to the question would be to force the defense in a capital case to disclose vital information concerning its strategy."

"And we're just supposed to take your word for it?" says Westaby.

"I'd appreciate it," says Harry.

"Well, I'm not prepared—"

Hastings cuts him off. "You're telling this court that issues regarding these proceedings, the custody of the Vega children, bear directly on Laurel Vega's criminal defense?"

"I am, your honor."

"I'd like to hear it from Mr. Madriani," says Hastings.

"That's correct, your honor."

Harry and I are talking about the theory that Jack cooked up the custody petition as part of a scheme, coupled with Melanie's murder, when he found out she was having an affair with another man. And now he is using his children and the demise of his wife to dodge doing time on the federal corruption sting, a conviction that Hastings knows nothing about. I wonder what he would say if he knew that Jack could be headed for a federal penitentiary. No doubt the kids would be wards of the court.

"I don't believe this, your honor. A smokescreen," says Westaby. He's in Jack's ear at the counsel table. We clearly have Vega's attention. He's looking at me, eager eyes, wondering where we're headed, what I know.

"I used a chartered gamblers' special," she says, "and a bus to get them there."

This is Laurel's explanation of what she was doing in Reno the night Melanie Vega was murdered.

"I had to get them away." She's talking about the children, Danny and Julie. "They couldn't deal with that house any longer, or with their father."

I think she is coloring it, in shades of her hatred for Jack.

"And don't try looking for the kids. You'll never find them."

"I wasn't thinking of it."

This morning Laurel is a new woman, bright-eyed and intense when I visit her in the glass-walled cubicle of the county jail.

Harry has carried out his threat made some weeks ago: the news article about the sale of the Justice Department computers and the compromised federal witnesses. He has given copies of this thing to one of his clients downstairs. It has made its way like some political tract onto the bulletin board of the dayroom on each floor of the jail, a kind of cryptic warning to those who would trust the state and might be tempted to snitch on their compatriots. As Harry says, "If necessity is the mother of invention, government is the father of fuckups."

There are no rings of fatigue under Laurel's eyes. She talks of the impending trial as if it is something to savor, like "whatever doesn't kill you only serves to make you stronger." A lot of bravado now that her kids are beyond Jack's reach. What a good vendetta will do for the spirit.

This is the story that I am to sell to a jury as to Laurel's whereabouts on the night of the murder—the image of a woman trekking over the mountains to obtain plane tickets to spirit her children away from their father while the question of custody is pending before a court. That she sees nothing wrong in this illustrates the poverty of judgment that settles like ground fog in a bitter divorce. Morgan Cassidy would no doubt remind the jury that it is inspired by the same venom that leads to murder.

"We weren't going to win the custody case," she says. "I had to do something. I won't say where they are." She is adamant on this. I don't tell her, but I have no desire to know, particularly after my last curtain call from Jack and his lawyer. For the moment I am off the hook while Harry and Westaby brief points and authorities on the law of attorney-client privilege.

"They are safe and well cared for." Laurel giving me assurances about her kids.

"I'll tell the judge. He'll be relieved."

This has never been my concern. Knowing Laurel, it would have been the first item on her agenda, that her children be taken care of.

"Why didn't you just buy two plane tickets in Capital City?" I ask.

"Yeah, at a thousand dollars a pop," she says. "What was I supposed to do, go to Jack and ask for the money? Try getting two tickets at anything approaching fair price without a fourteen-day wait," she says.

"You could have waited."

She looks but doesn't respond.

"What were you afraid of?"

"I wanted them out of that house. Just leave it at that," she says.

I have the thought that crosses every mind. But while Jack may be many things, I have never pegged him as a pedophile.

"So you went to Reno?"

"I had a friend. She works at one of the casinos. She has access to tickets on charter flights."

Laurel makes a face, a little embarrassment. "Freebies," she says. "People fly into town to gamble, they drink, they get carried away, and they miss their flight out. It happens almost every time," she says. "So there's open seats." What's more important, she tells me, there's no record of the names for the substitute passengers, no flight list that Jack's lawyers or a PI can scrutinize to find the name Danny or Julie Vega. The woman is not stupid.

"They're probably going to subpoena you to answer questions in the custody case."

"I'll take the Fifth," she says.

I try to explain to her that unless we can convince the judge that in some way the custody issues are related to the criminal charges, the privilege against self-incrimination does not apply.

"What can he do if I refuse to talk, put me in jail?" She takes in the concrete walls around her and gives me one of her better smiles.

"The first time in my life I've felt completely invulnerable," she says.

It is as if she is drawing strength from her circumstances, nothing to lose, the kids out of harm's way, toe to toe with Jack and the fates. At this moment when I look at Laurel I am moved by the fact that she is consumed with the fervor of the battle, in the way Joan of Arc led the troops before being fried at the stake.

"The hell with him," she says. She's talking about Jack.

She gives me a look, something that says: "And to hell with you too for not helping me with my children." This last I read whether from my own guilt or the demon look in her eye.

I'm afraid Laurel at this moment is not considering the consequences if we lose.

But she is right about one thing. Jack is running out of options for finding the kids. As for myself, the judge seemed satisfied that I had no personal knowledge regarding the whereabouts of the Vega children. He seemed reluctant to allow Westaby to explore what might be privileged communications with a defendant facing capital charges. He has sent the lawyers off to do what judges always do when they can't make a decision—churn more paper. All in all, Jack has hit a stone wall when it comes to finding his children. No doubt he will play this, too, for sympathy when it comes time for sentencing on the charges.

I don't tell her about Jack's fall from grace, his sealed indictment, or plea of guilty to dirty politics. This would no doubt buoy her spirits. It might also lead her to talk, tales of jubilation. Jails have ears. At this moment Jack's travails and the fact that a curtain has been thrown over them by the federal court is like my card facedown in a game of blackjack—something that, if the gods are with me, Morgan Cassidy does not know.

"Tell me about Jack's operation." I'm talking about the vasectomy.

"What do you want to know?"

"Why did he do it?"

"To clear the decks for action." She gives me a little laugh, as if to say, "Why else?"

"You know Jack. He never saw a skirt he wouldn't chase. And he didn't like condoms. Jack had a saying, usually reserved for the cronies he ran with, but I heard him more than once. Jack used to say that rolling latex was for housepainters. That was back before AIDS was part of the lexicon," she says. "Jack had a special talent for rubbing my nose in his affairs."

"How did you feel? About the operation, I mean."

She laughs. "You think he consulted me? He went off and had it done, an hour in the doctor's office. He didn't tell me until later, months later.

"By that time it probably didn't matter," she says. "We were married in name only. He'd leave me and the kids all night and go off with his friends, lobbyists with a license to take their limit of trollop."

I remember these nights, Laurel and the kids, Julie younger than Sarah is now, coming over to visit with Nikki and me, Laurel on a constant search for social interaction, confirmation that she could still relate in an adult world. Jack would come home with the morning paper, smelling like a brewery, wrinkled clothes, his underwear inside out, telling Laurel that he'd been at a meeting. Vega was always transparent. To him, being a legislator meant that people had to believe your lies.

And Jack could get in trouble. For a man with a wandering eye, he was intensely jealous. Twice he'd gotten into fights over women he had not seen before that night. To Jack, commitment was always geared to the cut of the tush and the size of a bra—double D stood for dueling. Sniff in the wrong place and Jack could rack horns like a moose in heat. When it came to women, Vega had a herd instinct. Possession was always nine-tenths. I'd seen his nose bloodied and his eye blackened after one of these brawls.

"Do you know who the physician was who did the vasectomy?"

"I'd have to look in a phone book, but I think I could find

it. If he's still in practice," she says.

"And he'd have the medical records?"

"I suppose. I could call it to your office tomorrow," she says.

"No. I'll have Harry come by in the afternoon with a notepad." I don't trust the telephones in this place. Conversations have a way of getting to prosecutors.

"One other thing, then I've got to go," I tell her. "Do you remember the gun that Jack had? The chrome pistol in the walnut box?"

"That was a long time ago," she says.

"But you remember it?"

"How can I forget? He spent more time with that thing than he did with me. Until the novelty wore off."

What she means is like everything else in Jack's life.

"Do you know what happened to it?"

"Last time I saw it Jack had it. Made a big deal out of it in the property settlement agreement."

This would be like Jack. Give up half his retirement benefits for a shiny gun.

"Do you have a copy of the agreement?"

"At home with my papers. The box in my closet," she says.

I have the key to her place, Sarah and I watering her plants, taking care of the place.

"Maybe he sold it or lost it?" I'm thinking out loud.

"Not likely. Why?"

" 'Cuz when the cops asked him, the night Melanie was murdered, if he ever owned a gun, he told them no. They searched the house pretty well. If it was there they would have found it."

"You think that was the gun?"

"No. But I'm wondering why he lied."

It's four-thirty in the afternoon, Harry and I locked in a heated argument over the strategy on pretrial motions. My intercom buzzes. I pick up the receiver.

"Dana Colby. She says it's important." The receptionist.

"What line?"

"No. She's here in the office." I tell Harry, make a face like "search me," and excuse myself for a moment.

I find her out in the reception area, looking at one of the prints on the wall, Harry's pride, a black-and-white daguerre-otype of two riverboats locked in the dead heat of a race, steaming under streams of black smoke up the river from the Delta, before the turn of the century.

She hears me and turns. "Sorry to bother you."

"No problem, what is it?"

"I've got something I have to show you," she says. "Can we talk someplace private?"

I lead her to the library and close the door. I offer her a cup of coffee. She says no. I pour myself a cup.

Dana breaks open her briefcase on one of the library tables and pulls out a manila folder.

"I have some pictures I'd like you to take a look at."

I've been doing this on and off for days at the federal building, looking for the face of the courier in FBI mug books, broken down by specialty: people who do bombs.

The fact that Dana has brought this set to my office tells me that maybe they think they have something hot.

"Bear with me," she says.

She arranges the photographs, various sizes, facedown on the coffee table.

"I want you to look carefully at each one," she says, then flips over number one, an eight-by-ten glossy. A guy, cauca-sian, in his twenties, white numbers on a black plaque jammed under his chin, a lot of dead in the eyes. I shake my head.

Number two is a little older, military haircut, no numbers, more clean-cut, but he rings no bells.

She turns over the third picture. Still no prize.

The fourth picture is a tiny one. She turns it over. Color on a blue background. Not a mug shot, but something from Motor

Vehicles. I have to squint to see it, hold it in my hand, and suddenly I am standing bolt upright, big eyes like someone has fed me cyanide.

Dana sees my expression and stops.

"That's him. The courier," I tell her.

"You're sure?"

"I could not forget that face."

Thin lips, hair clipped like someone ran a mower over it. Eyes as cold as an Eskimo's ass. As for age, it could be the picture of Dorian Gray, anywhere from twenty to forty-five, but in good shape, like he works out. He looks more mature in the picture than he did that day at the post office. I attribute this to the uniform he wore. The eye sees what the mind expects. A lot of couriers are college students making ends meet.

"Who is he?"

She reaches for a notepad in her briefcase.

"Name is Lyle Simmons, alias Frank Jordan, alias James Hays, and so on and so forth. Former Green Beret, sometime soldier of fortune. Hires himself out for odd jobs." The way she says this I know she's not talking about gardening.

"He's under suspicion in two unsolved murders in Oregon. No convictions. Fancies himself a high-tech security type. That's what he claims to be his legitimate business. When you can find him."

"Any record?"

"He's been arrested three times on weapons violations, two convictions. It seems they always catch him on the way to or from work, never at it," she says.

"How did you find him?"

"It wasn't easy. We backed into him, based on your theory about Jack. The thought that maybe he hired somebody to murder his wife."

I'm all ears.

"We had an informant. A hanger-on around the fringes of politics in the Capitol." She makes a face like this is not someone you would take home to meet your family.

"This informant saw Jack in some sleazoid bar across the river some time ago. A real dive," she says. "Not one of the places your brother-in-law usually frequents. We know. We've watched him. He was in tow with another man, the two of them talking over a table, guzzling beer.

"A state legislator in a thousand-dollar suit, Vega stood out," she says. "The guy, our informant, took notes."

"Why would he bother?"

"He'd been netted in the Capitol probe. A sometime lobbyist, one of the guys who ultimately led us to Jack. He was low on the political food chain and was looking to play, make a deal. He didn't know what we were doing, but he knew we had an eye on Jack. So among other things he got the license off of Mr. Simmons' pickup truck. It was in the notes on Jack's case. We hadn't pursued it at the time."

I am sitting, saying nothing. Letting it all sink in.

"This informant. Where is he?"

"That's the bad part. The man seems to have slipped off the edge of the earth. At least momentarily. The agent who was his point of contact hasn't seen him in at least three weeks. Word is he's on vacation, but nobody knows where. We're looking."

"And where's this Mr. Simmons?"

"We don't know that either. He gave DMV a false address."

Wonderful. Having seen him kill once and try on a second occasion, he is probably staking out my house at this moment. I mention this to Dana. She tells me not to worry. They have already thought of this. Agents have the house under surveillance twenty-four hours a day, she says. They are also watching Sarah at school. If Simmons shows as much as a hair on his ass they will take him down.

Then to more professional concerns. "This meeting between Simmons and Jack. When did it take place?"

"I'm glad you asked," she says. "Five days before Melanie Vega was murdered."

I am stone cold, the kind of shudder that courses through your body and chills your brain, like a double shot of adrenaline. My theory about Jack has just taken on the flesh of reality.

After meeting in the office, I called it a day and asked Dana to join me for dinner at the house. She is fixing the salad. Sarah is helping, standing on a stool in the kitchen like she used to do with her mother. I cannot help being bothered by this. Thoughts of Nikki and the hole that is left in my daughter's life. I have my work. Sarah has a lot of loneliness, kids at school who ask why her mother doesn't come to class on Monday mornings, teacher's helper, as she used to do. At seven, children don't have a solid concept of the finality that is death. Sarah is starting to learn, a long, painful lesson.

"Maybe you'd like to pour the dressing while I toss the salad?" Dana's trying to take Sarah under her wing.

"No. You do it," says Sarah. "I want to help Daddy with the corn."

Like most children Sarah takes a while to warm to strangers. She is starved for a mother's affection, a real hugger. Sarah would spend twenty minutes every morning cuddling with Nikki on the couch in the family room before dressing for school. I have the corner on this market now, giving her what she craves, a father's love, her last sanctuary against life's insecurities. Though when my daughter now looks at me, it seems too often that she is measuring me with wary eyes, fearful that I too might leave her.

Sarah holds the bowl while I put the hot cobs of corn in with metal tongs.

"The steaks will be a couple of minutes," I tell them.

"Quick. We'd better set the table," Dana moving toward the cupboards. "Show me where they are." She looks at Sarah, trying to make this a game.

But my daughter doesn't budge, instead she is clinging to my side. Since Nikki's death I have found that Sarah is possessive, of the house and its contents, but most of all of me. She does not like change. The few times I have talked about moving to a smaller place that is easier to take care of, she has thrown a pitched battle. It is as if as long as we stay here, Nikki is present, at least in spirit. It seems that she has taken a turn for the worse now that Danny and Julie are gone. Danny had, at least once a week, and regardless of his father's objections, slipped by to visit with us, to tease and play with his cousin.

With a little coaxing I finally get Sarah to help with the dishes. She's in the dining room. We can see her over the pass-through, setting place mats and dishes, mine at one end, her own dish nearly on top of it, and another lonely plate, by itself, at the far end.

Dana looks at me. "Now who do you suppose is sitting way down there?"

"It's a tough time for her," I say. Though I have to admit that at times Sarah is awful. We both laugh.

"Hey, I understand. She's a little doll."

The steaks are well done, we sit down, pour the wine, and Sarah makes a show of grace. It was always her treat when there was company. Ten minutes and Sarah is full. She eats like a bird, weighs fifty pounds, with spindly legs that now represent two-thirds of her height, like a baby gazelle. But she will have two snacks between now and bedtime.

"Two more bites," I tell her.

She argues a little and makes a face. When this doesn't work, she fills her cheeks and excuses herself, disappearing into her bedroom to play.

"You're a lucky guy," says Dana.

We talk about children. Dana lamenting that she's missed her chance, the biologic clock.

I scoff. Somehow I think the only clock that is keeping Dana from having kids is the one that beeps hourly with the appointments of her ambitious schedule. The idle speculation on a judicial appointment, the so-called A-list, has suddenly turned real. It has been whittled down to two candidates, a fifty-four-year-old white male and the woman now sitting across from me at my dinner table. According to today's paper, their résumés are being shipped to a special evaluation panel for a thorough review of qualifications and background. Word is that Dana has already met the political litmus test. She has the backing of higher-ups in the Justice Department in Washington, and the two United States Senators from this state, both women with aggressive gender programs.

On the couch we're doing coffee. Sarah is now asleep. My invitation to Dana this evening is only partly social. She would have to be sedated not to sense this.

"Something's wrong," she says.

"Nothing," I say.

"What is it?" She puts her coffee on the table and gives me her undivided attention.

"I suppose you're packing boxes in your office," I tell her. "Doing fittings for a black robe."

"Is that what's bothering you?"

"Not really bothering me. Just curious."

"Ah." She gives a knowing tilt to her head.

Now I'm embarrassed. Dana must think I'm part of the testosterone troop, the guys who can't deal with women in black.

"You're thinking it would change things," she says. "Between us, I mean."

"Do you?"

"I asked you first," she says.

I make a face, something thoughtfully Italian, stretching the cheeks a little and shrugging.

"Actually I think it might be fun. I've always had this fetish."

"And what's that?"

"I've always wondered what it would be like to do it to a judge, from behind, up on the bench," I tell her.

"Maybe I won't allow you to approach," she says. Then a smile as she drags a single nail of one finger, like some predatory claw, across the worsted fabric of my thigh.

I clear my throat, hoping that when I speak again my voice won't be an octave higher. I'm using a napkin to keep the perspiration from being noticeable on my upper lip.

"Actually I was going to ask you for a favor," I say.

"Have I ever refused you anything?" She gives me a look that could defrost my freezer. At this moment I think neither of us is certain whether we should laugh or just jump each other's bones.

"I'm not worried about your taking the bench," I tell her. "I'm worried about when it might happen."

"No, you're not. You're worried about when my office is going to take the wraps off of Jack's sealed indictment, and his plea."

"Always the lawyer." I smile at her and sit back a little in the couch.

"I think Jack Vega deserves whatever he gets," she says. "It's no secret that I didn't embrace the notion of letting him walk based on hardship. That decision was driven by higher authority.

"And it is true we cut a deal with him. Of course, exactly when we release the news concerning that deal, well, that's more of a housekeeping matter."

"Can I take it that I'm talking to the upstairs maid?"

"Monsieur. Perhaps you will allow me to polish the knob of your gentleman's walking stick." Dana is quick.

If state prosecutors find out that Jack has copped to a couple of felonies, they will never put him on the stand. If I subpoena him into my case-in-chief, it won't take Jack and his lawyers long to figure that I am grooming him for the lead role in Melanie's murder. He would refuse to testify, take the Fifth, and leave the jury thinking that he was merely worried about more political carnage, additional uncharged crimes involving corruption.

In trial, as in life, timing is everything.

No doubt Cassidy, the prosecutor, is building a good part

of her case around Jack the victim—Jack the psychically martyred widower. What could be better than a community leader bereft by the loss of his wife and the murder of his unborn child? With any luck, and if the gods of timing are on my side, there will be a mugging on the way to Jack's canonization. But if I have my way, Vega will end up just a few miracles shy of sainthood. As I gaze into Dana's gleaming eyes, I get a shiver of excitement that shutters all the way down to my sphincter, what for a defense lawyer is the equivalent of an intellectual orgasm—the prosecution is building its case around a convicted felon and they don't know it.

CHAPTER
17

Judge Austin Woodruff is from an old-line GOP family in the valley, more conservative than God, but without the compassion. He is fifty-four, with a ruddy complexion and an aristocratic bearing made more patrician by his utter lack of humor. Woodruff is a stone-face that could slay a dozen comics.

He has the look of authority, like some aging anchorman from the network days of yore—a flowing gray mane and eyebrows like spun silver. He is what the average citizen thinks of when he or she hears the word "judge."

He can be called fair in every way that the word is defined and spelled, from lack of bias to ability on the bench. Though at times I have wondered if he has ever seen a defendant he likes or a golf course he does not. He is stern, with the personality and warmth of a bronze bust, which has moved some cruel observers to lay on a few monikers. I have heard cursing references to the Ice Prince and Old Marblehead issuing forth from stalls in the men's room, but the one I like best, and which seems to have stuck, is Chuckles.

For better or worse, Austin Woodruff is our trial judge. At the moment he's shuffling papers on the bench.

Harry and I are in Department Twelve to argue motions intended to prevent the state from putting its own spin on the various faces of truth. Dana has joined us today, just behind the railing. She is here early for a luncheon date. Since Hawaii she has taken a particular interest in the case.

This morning Morgan Cassidy sits at counsel table with Jimmy Lama, the cop from hell, and a young assistant DA, a kid getting his first glimpse down into the volcano of crime.

Laurel is not present, as is the custom when a defendant is in custody. I have tried to impress upon her the significance of these motions. Lose on a critical piece of evidence here, and half of our case can be flushed before the judge impanels the first juror.

The state's case is one of circumstance. The prosecution will argue that Laurel is a woman consumed by jealousy, a former spouse shed like old clothes, who was embittered and furious with Melanie for stealing her husband. They will insist that this rage was stirred and rekindled when Jack made a grab for the kids. Among suspects, they will show that Laurel had the best motive, as well as ample opportunity to kill. The state will argue that that is exactly what she did.

To the idle observer all this might seem the barest of suspicions, and they would be right if it were not for a few items of evidence that put the cloak of credence on this theory. Cassidy has these, items of evidence, fixed into her case like screws in a coffin lid.

Two pieces of physical evidence presumably purporting to show that Laurel was at the scene the night of the murder could be viewed as highly incriminating; the small rug that Laurel was busy laundering when she was arrested in Reno and which Jack insists was in the master bath the night Melanie was shot, and a gold compact with Melanie's initials found in Laurel's purse after the arrest.

The police also have a witness, Mrs. Miller, who will testify that Laurel was seen in the neighborhood, near the Vega house, about the time of the murder.

Woodruff's voice has the tonal qualities of an aging baron of broadcast, like a bullfrog who swallowed honey, mellifluous and deep, as it is this morning when he asks us if we are ready to proceed.

He doesn't wait for a reply, but immediately launches a series of questions, like torpedoes under the waterline of our first motion.

"What is this about the rug?" he says. "You want to keep it out? On what grounds?"

"No, your honor." I am waving him off. "That's not our motion." Something more defensible, I tell him.

"Well, what is it?"

Not an auspicious start. Woodruff hasn't read any of the moving papers, our written agreement.

"The rug can come in," I tell him. "Though I would alert the court that there is a factual dispute as to its ownership and where it came from."

"That's a question for the jury," he says. "Not for this court. Not for a motion."

"I agree."

Our motion is more subtle, not exactly home turf for Chuckles. So I lead him through the argument. Jack's testimony that the rug came from the murder scene is damaging enough, though Laurel will insist otherwise. I can hope for some neutral pitch on this, a jury that is at least in doubt as to who they will believe.

What I want to avoid are the unstated inferences by Cassidy that might allude to Laurel destroying evidence when she washed the rug or dipped her hands in solvent.

I am a believer in the adage that facts seldom settle an argument. It is the implications drawn from them that most often win the day or cause the damage.

This is the case in the state's lab report given to us in discovery. It refers to gunpowder-residue tests which were "inconclusive because of chemicals into which the defendant *intentionally* dipped her hands."

I make my pitch to Woodruff, and we go at it tooth and tong, Cassidy and I. She is insisting that the rug speaks for itself. A talking rug is one thing. What I'm afraid of is that left to her own devices in trial, Cassidy may try to jump on this thing and fly.

"What other reason could the defendant have for taking it to Reno and washing it," she says, "but to remove blood or other evidence?"

"That's what I'm afraid of," I tell the judge. "That kind of speculation."

"It's a natural conclusion to be drawn from the evidence," says Cassidy.

"Did the state find any blood?" I say. "Or any other evidence?"

"How could they? Your client washed it off."

"That's speculation," I tell her.

Woodruff is becoming a potted plant. He finally notices.

"Address your arguments to me," he says.

"Your honor. The rug is stolen property," she says. Morgan Cassidy has a positive gift for torturing facts. In her hands evidence can take on more twists and embellishments than wrought iron.

"According to who?" I ask.

"According to the victim's husband."

"Stop. Stop. One at a time," says Woodruff. "First you." He points to Cassidy. Morgan doing what she does best, seizing the initiative.

She argues that the rug is stolen property, that the state is entitled to a reasonable inference, that mere possession of this item by the defendant is evidence of her guilt.

I bellow like some wounded bull before she can finish.

"There's no evidence that the rug was stolen."

Woodruff is scratching his head, a blizzard of dandruff on the bench blotter. They don't pay enough for these decisions, he's thinking.

I lead him to the affidavit signed by Laurel under penalty of perjury that the rug was hers, that it was never at the victim's residence.

"So what?" says Cassidy. "We have a counteraffidavit signed by Mr. Vega to the contrary. It clearly puts the rug in the victim's house at the time of the murder."

"Fine. There's a dispute of fact," I say. "There is nothing approaching established evidence that the rug was stolen. That's for the jury to decide."

"And if they decide that it is stolen, are we entitled to an instruction?" says Cassidy. She's talking about a jury instruction so that they can infer guilt from the mere possession of the rug.

"That's an argument for another day. We're not here to talk jury instructions. Or am I wrong?"

"Good point," says Woodruff. He's finally on the same page with us.

Cassidy is making an effort to frame the issues to her own liking. Enough sand thrown up and maybe I'll lose my place on the sheet, start singing out of tune. We've done a complete circle and we're back to square one. Woodruff points to me.

"Your turn."

"The problem is not what the jury might be allowed to deduce from fairly presented evidence," I tell him, "but what the prosecution might be permitted to infer when talking about that evidence—the rug and the solvents on her hands," I say.

Like a light has come on behind Woodruff's eyes. He finally gets it.

"They wouldn't do that," he says.

I read to him from the lab report, the supposition that Laurel *intentionally* frustrated the powder-residue tests by immersing her hands in the chemicals.

"Oh," he says.

Cassidy, sensing the hammer about to fall, starts to argue.

"Enough," says Woodruff. He looks at her. "Did you find any powder residue on her hands?"

"How could we, your honor?"

"Anything on the carpet?"

"It was washed clean."

"And you want to infer that this involves intentional destruction of evidence?"

"We should be given the latitude," says Cassidy. "What's so speculative?" she says. "The defendant fled the scene, took the carpet, washed it to clean away any evidence. What could be more clear?"

I don't think Woodruff is going to buy this, but he is listening—a dangerous sign.

"Is that a reasonable inference?" I ask. "Think about it, your honor, if the state's theory is correct. Let's assume you commit a murder. So you grab a soiled rug from the scene, splotched with blood, and drive a hundred and thirty miles to another city to wash it. If it's evidence of a crime, why not leave it at the scene? If it's true what the state says, that the carpet was in the house, then its discovery there after the crime would in no way implicate or incriminate you, would it? Unless the killer had a fetish for cleanliness, why take it?" I say.

"Maybe she panicked," says Cassidy.

"Fine. Then why not dispose of it somewhere on the road, after panic had subsided?"

For this Cassidy has no response.

"If any inference is to be drawn from possession of the rug, from its washing in a public laundromat in full view of other patrons, that inference should not be one of guilt, but innocence," I say. "People with guilty knowledge don't act in this way," I tell them.

Dead silence. Woodruff looking at me.

It is hard to argue with the stupidity of this act. If Laurel murdered Melanie, the antics with the scrap of carpet defy all logic.

"Seems pretty clear," says Woodruff. He looks at Cassidy. "You can introduce the rug into evidence. But I don't want to hear any inference about nonexistent bloodstains or powder residue on the defendant's hands that couldn't be found," he says.

"Your honor—"

"Is that clear?"

"Yes," she says.

"Next." Woodruff looks at me.

"What about the statement in the lab report?" I ask him. Why settle for a half-loaf if I can get it buttered? "We would move to have it stricken," I say.

An imperious look from the judge.

"Maybe you can soften the language." He looks at Cassidy.

"She put her hands in the solvent. How many ways are there to say it?" she says.

"Take out the word 'intentionally' and we can live with it," I say.

"There. How about that?" says Woodruff.

Cassidy, shaking her head. "Fine," she says.

"Why couldn't you two have stipulated the point before coming here?" The judge looks at me.

He has never tried the word "compromise" on Cassidy.

"Now . . . what's next?"

Woodruff is poring over the papers.

"Looks like a witness-identification problem," he says. "What do we have, a bad lineup?" He looks down his nose at Cassidy. She's not winning any points here: what happens when you circle the wagons and make an issue on every point.

"The lineup was tainted," I say.

"How?"

"We've subpoenaed witnesses," I tell him.

"Is that necessary?" says Woodruff.

I think maybe he's got an early starting time on the links.

"I think we could handle it in oral argument," says Cassidy.

She would.

"Is the prosecution willing to stipulate?" I ask.

"To what?" says Cassidy.

"To exclusion of the identification evidence." I'm talking about the witness who claims she saw Laurel at Vega's house the night of the murder.

"Not on your life," she says.

"Then I'd like to call my witnesses."

A lot of grousing from the judge. I do some groveling, assurances that I will move it along.

Looking at his watch, Woodruff gives me the nod.

"You got twenty minutes," he says.

I call Jimmy Lama to the stand and have him sworn to testify.

Lama has prepped for this as well as he can under the circumstances. True to form, he has tried to sandbag us on a witness.

Margaret Miller is Jack Vega's neighbor. Harry and I had talked to her in the weeks following the murder. She had given us dirt about Melanie's male visitors and the fact that she had seen Laurel twice at the Vega home on the night of the murder, the first time when the two women argued on the front porch. The second visit was closer to the time of the murder, and Miller has told the police that she saw Laurel in a sweatshirt and hood out on the street in front of the house.

The problem here is one of procedure and fundamental fairness, something as alien as moon rocks to Lama.

I turn to Jimmy in the witness box.

We establish the facts, that he heads up the investigation in the case, and that he interviewed Mrs. Miller.

"How many times did you interview her?"

Lama's counting on his fingers. "Three . . ." A glazed look in his eyes as he thinks back. "Three interviews and a lineup," he says.

"And at this lineup did Mrs. Miller identify Laurel Vega?"

"She did. She said the defendant was at the house twice that night."

"This lineup—it was the one attended by my colleague, Mr. Hinds?" I look over at Harry.

"Yeah. He was there. He didn't object, say anything was wrong at the time," says Lama. Getting in his digs.

"Was that the only lineup you conducted for this witness?"

He makes a face. "How do you define lineup?" he says. Knowing Lama, he is not above a little perjury—it's just that if he's doing it, he wants to know it.

"I'm talking about a live appearance of the defendant with other potential suspects before the witness."

"Then that was the only lineup," he says.

Harry has advised me that Laurel was picked out of a group of five other women, all dressed as she was, in jail togs. The women were all of the same approximate height and coloring. Each one was asked to step forward and one at a time to don a sweatshirt with a hood, and to give a full profile, both sides of her face, to the witness, who was in a booth, behind a glare screen. It was a textbook lineup, no suggestions by Lama or the other cops who were present. The problem, it appears, developed earlier.

"Before you scheduled the lineup for the witness, did you have occasion to show Mrs. Miller some photographs?"

"Yeah."

"How many photographs did you show her?"

He makes a face. "Four, five, maybe a half dozen?" He leaves a lot of wiggle room.

"And was Mrs. Miller able to identify the defendant from the photographs shown to her?"

"She was."

"Did you bring these photographs with you?" I know that he has because I have subpoenaed them. It is reversible error, grounds to exclude Mrs. Miller's identification if he cannot produce all of the pictures used.

Lama's holding a large manila folder, an inch thick, overflowing with a couple dozen photographs, various sizes, black-and-white and color.

He hands me the folder. Jimmy's starting to play games—hide the trees in the forest.

"This is all very nice." I start to chew his ass. "But I subpoenaed the photographs used in the identification by Mrs. Miller, not your entire file."

"They're in there," he says, like "you find 'em."

I hand the file back to him. "Show me."

He makes like a table with the railing in front of the witness box and starts propping up pictures, first one, then another.

"I think it was this one. No. No. This one here." He goes through twenty shots and finds two that look familiar.

The law is clear. A defendant has an absolute right to the presence of counsel at a lineup, something that doesn't attach to a photo identification. But there are rules. The police are free to show a witness pictures of a suspect who is in custody, as a prelude to a more formal lineup. The problem develops when the photo identification is so suggestive as to single out the defendant and therefore poison the whole process.

It is the kind of game that Lama lives for—sear some picture of your client into the mind of a witness, with all the finesse of a branding iron on a bovine's ass, and then run the suspect through the loading chute of a lineup. This is Jimmy's kind of sport.

It takes Lama three minutes, and he is certain only about the picture of Laurel, an eight-by-ten color photo with bright lights in her eyes and numbers jammed under her chin on a placard. As for the other four shots of women he pulls from the file, he thinks they are the ones used in the photo lineup.

These are harmless, all color shots, the same size as Laurel's, of women in booking poses with white numerals on black placards.

Lama wiggles and twists like a worm on a hook when I ask him if he's absolutely certain that these are the photos. I press him.

"Pretty sure," he says.

This gets the eyes of the judge looking at him.

"Lieutenant, I ask you for the last time—are you absolutely certain that these are the photographs used in the identification of Laurel Vega?"

Cassidy's looking at him. A critical piece of evidence hanging in the balance. If he says no, the fate of the witness is sealed. The law is clear. The identification must be excluded. The defense has an absolute right to see the pictures used to identify a suspect, to test the validity of the process. If the state can't produce them, that's all she wrote.

Sweat on Jimmy's head. Looking at me, then to Cassidy.

"Yeah," he says. "They're the ones." He leans as if he'd like to say it—"I'm pretty sure"—but I'm waiting to kick his ass and he knows it.

The sigh from Cassidy at her table is nearly palpable.

"That's all for this witness," I say.

"Anything on cross?" says the judge.

Cassidy begs off.

Lama starts to leave with the folder of pictures.

"I'd like to keep those for the moment."

He starts to pick through, to hand me the five he identified.

"All of them," I say.

A look that could kill, then he hands me the folder.

I ask the court if another attorney can join Harry and me at the table.

Cassidy is all eyes.

"Any objection?" The judge looks to her.

She steps into it with trepidation, the two women locking eyes.

"I know Ms. Colby well," she says. Some light banter— what Dana's doing slumming in the state courts. The two women exchange stiff smiles. "Though I would like to know what a Deputy U.S. Attorney is doing in these proceedings."

"Here in an unofficial capacity," I tell the court.

"What's the purpose?" says Cassidy.

"Professional courtesy," I tell her.

The court allows her to come inside the railing and sit in the chairs behind us but not at counsel table.

Close enough for my purposes, I think.

Miller has been outside, sequestered in the hallway. We had a cordial conversation by phone a week ago, a follow-up to our earlier meeting. We talked about the lineup and the photo

ID, a conversation that proceeded with regularity until near the end, when she asked a question.

Lama takes his seat next to Cassidy. He's whispering in her ear.

"I hope this won't take long," says Woodruff.

"A couple of minutes," I tell him.

Margaret Miller is on the stand and sworn, the picture of fairness, what you would think of as womanhood if someone said "apple pie." She wears a print dress and an attitude like portraits on a candy box, hair like spun silk, all smiles and maternal warmth. Sitting next to Woodruff, the two look like the "before" ad for some aging-hair elixir.

I ask the court for a moment in private, and I spend my time turned away from the witness, talking in Dana's ear, idle chatter, but obvious so that Mrs. Miller cannot miss this. Then I turn my attention to the witness.

She identifies herself for the record, and we take up the details of the photo ID. I ask her if she remembers meeting with Lama on the day in question.

"Very clearly," she says.

"And did he show you some pictures?"

"He showed me one picture first, by itself, the night that Melanie—Mrs. Vega—died, and then later several others."

"That one picture, do you remember it?"

"Oh sure. Your client," she says. "I've seen plenty of pictures of her in the paper since."

I have wondered what Jack was doing with a picture of Laurel, the ex-wife he loathed, unless there was some design in this. It appears that he and Lama found a purpose for this photo in poisoning the wellspring of Mrs. Miller's recollections, planting the seed that it was Laurel that Miller saw that night—an onslaught of suggestion.

We talk about Lama's photo lineup. I'm shuffling some of the prints in my hands, images down so she cannot see them.

"Do you think you would remember those pictures if I showed them to you again?"

"I think so. I could try," she says.

I show her the first in the series, one of the shots offered up by Lama moments before.

"Emm." She asks if she can hold it in her hand, so I give it to her. She's shaking her head. "Maybe I don't remember as well as I thought," she says.

I try the next. No luck.

It's not until the third picture, Laurel's, that she finally smiles. "That's the one I identified," she says. She looks at me. "Your client, I believe," she says.

I nod.

She's squinting at Dana in the distance.

Finally Cassidy gets it.

"Your honor, I'm going to object to the process being used with this witness." Cassidy's out of her chair. "This is deceptive," she says.

"A fair test of the witness's memory," I say. I ask the court if I can approach for a sidebar, a conference at the bench.

"What's the problem?" whispers Woodruff.

Cassidy wants Dana outside the railing. She's leveling assertions that I'm intentionally confusing the witness.

"Lawyers are routinely allowed inside the bar," I tell him.

He makes a face. "Fine," he says, "but no more private conversations with the lady." He gives me a look.

"Fine, your honor."

We're back out.

"Mrs. Miller, can I ask you to look at a few more pictures?"

"Certainly."

I give her the last two that Lama culled from the file. No cigar. She has no recollection of these. "But then I only saw them once," she says.

"How many times did you see the picture of my client?" I keep it facedown so she can't get another look.

"Oh. At least twice, maybe three times," she says. "The officers showed it to me the first time they came to the house.

They asked me if I ever saw the woman before.''

"This was in connection with the death of Melanie Vega?"

"Oh, yes."

"Did you assume from this that the woman in the picture might be a suspect in the crime?"

"Objection," says Cassidy. "Calls for speculation on the part of the witness."

"I'm asking about her state of mind at the time," I say, "not what she thinks now."

"I'll allow it," says Woodruff.

"And they kept showing you this picture, the one of my client?"

"Yes," she says.

"Fair game," says Cassidy. "That's a permissible process during the course of investigation."

"And a very good way to alter the memory of a witness," I tell the court.

Woodruff wags his head from side to side. Maybe, but not sufficient to exclude the identification.

I'm wandering in the courtroom. I end up leaning against the railing, a few feet from Dana, where we look at each other but say nothing.

Lama's talking to Cassidy, but she sees what's going on and tears herself away.

"Your honor, I'm going to object. This is a clear deception. Counsel would have this witness believe that Ms. Colby, the lawyer sitting there, is the defendant." She points toward Dana. "It's a clear effort to confuse the witness, and I think it should be put on the record."

"What are you objecting to?" says Woodruff. "I didn't hear a question," he says.

"I'm objecting to where counsel is standing."

"Give me a break," says the judge.

"Fine," says Cassidy. "Withdrawn." She smiles, damage done.

Lama has the back of one hand halfway down his throat,

suppressing a high-strung cackle.

Mrs. Miller gives me a look like "you nasty man." Still, she reserves a goodhearted smile. A woman who enjoys a contest of wits.

So we'll do it the hard way.

"Mrs. Miller—did you think that the woman sitting here looked like the defendant? Like the woman in the photograph?" I ask. It's a fair question.

Cassidy's expression is little simpers, like "good luck."

"I thought maybe she changed her hair color," says Miller. "It's different," she says. "But I think there is a little resemblance."

Apart from the fact that they share a gender, there is virtually no likeness between Laurel and Dana. What mischief suggestion can play with the human mind.

"Now, you've looked at five photographs of different women, Mrs. Miller. Apart from the picture of my client, do you recognize any of the other pictures in the group?"

"I can't say that I do," she says.

"Are these the pictures that Lieutenant Lama showed you at the time of the photo identification?"

"I can't be sure of some of them," she says. "But two I know are missing," she tells the court.

"Which are those?"

"The black woman," she says.

Woodruff is incredulous. "He showed you a picture of a black woman?"

She nods to the judge.

Lama's ducking for cover, slinking in his chair.

"Lieutenant. None of these pictures, the ones you picked out, shows a black woman." Screw the fact that Lama isn't on the stand. The judge wants an answer.

Shoulders and a lot of shrugging from Lama.

"What about it?" says Woodruff.

"I think the witness is mistaken," he says. Left with an alternative, admitting to perjury or impeaching the memory of his own witness, Lama's made his choice.

"You also missed the one that looked like my granddaughter," says Miller. "Remember? We talked about it." If the devil is in the details, Lama's on his way to hell.

It was the question about the black suspect from Mrs. Miller on the phone that alerted me. Why would a police officer show her a picture of a black woman when she had told him repeatedly that the figure she saw that night outside the Vegas' house was white?

I offer her the folder and ask her to look through it. She finds the black woman in twenty seconds, a mug shot of a face with cornrows, a severe birthmark going up the side of her face into the hairline. There would be no confusing this with pictures of Laurel. It takes her a couple more minutes to find the other four photos. Like debutantes at a ball, these are not mug shots, but black-and-white glossies, like something from a high-school yearbook. Lama must have scoured the files of some local modeling agency for these. If you were going to pick a doer from among the bunch, it would not be this lot.

"I told him that this one here looked like my granddaughter," says Miller. She holds up one of the photos, proud of the good-looking girl in her hand, all-American youth, a good twenty years younger than Laurel.

"Your honor, I move that the identification of the witness be excluded."

Cassidy is hissing profanities into Jimmy Lama's ear, feeling victimized by his shoddy practices. She breaks off in mid-sentence to salvage what she can.

"Your honor, the witness may have an independent recollection of the defendant, untainted by the photographs." Morgan's out of her chair, open palms to the bench, the supplicant. "It could be harmless error," she says.

"You have a strange notion of error, counsel." Woodruff bearing down from the bench. It is one thing to argue legal points, another to mislead a court. Lama has crossed the line.

The only question for Woodruff is whether Cassidy was along for the ride.

Woodruff, for a show of fairness, allows her a chance to redeem the evidence. A token gesture. I think he's already made up his mind. What happens when you drag lies before a court.

Cassidy's off-balance. She throws a few softball questions at Mrs. Miller. Whether she had a firm recollection of the figure she saw that night in front of Vega's house. Whether she had a clear view.

Rattled, and now unsure of what is happening, thinking that perhaps she has done something wrong, Mrs. Miller is filled with equivocations, not certain of her recollections. It's been a long time; it was dark that night; the woman wore a hood—enough backstroking for an Olympic medal. Try as she will, Cassidy can't get the witness to hurdle the fence back to the land of certainty.

Finally she puts an end to a painful process.

"Your honor, we would argue that any error is harmless." She makes a final stab. But no gold ring.

"The motion is granted," says Woodruff. "The identification of the defendant by this witness is excluded."

"Is there anything else?" he says. Woodruff is looking at Cassidy. He is clearly angry, a sense that he has been badly used by Lama. What a judge feels when he knows he's been lied to. If jeopardy had attached, and I had some plausible grounds for dismissal, I would lay them before the court at this moment.

A pained expression on Jimmy's face. Woodruff wants to see him in chambers after lunch. Lama had better hope that the judge takes his from a bottle and that Woodruff is a happy drunk.

CHAPTER
18

"Hey, baby." Clem Olsen is speaking to me while he is ogling Dana with lupine looks and yammering in a gravelly dialect.

"Long time no see. Got a shake for the Wolfman?" he says.

All the while his eyes are eating up Dana.

We've both come here in separate cars, directly from other engagements, me from the office, Dana from some political soirée across town. She has accepted my invitation, but says she can't stay long.

"Gonna introduce me?" Clem wants to know. His hands are doing a quick routine of a shake in moves I cannot follow, all variations on a common theme, aping that half of the social order Clem feels is cooler than himself.

I do the honors, introducing Dana. She gets an embrace and one of Clem's sloppy specialties on the cheek, which she rubs off with the back of her gloved hand as soon as he turns away.

Clem has formed a one-man reception line at the door tonight, greeting everything that moves, looking down the front of a lot of dresses, and copping a few good feels under the aegis of kisses and hugs whenever he can.

Some things never change. Clem is one of them.

McClesky High's Twenty-fifth Reunion, and we are gathered in the main ballroom of the Regency, downtown, across from the Capitol. Olsen is decked out in ruffles and formal wear. What little hair he has left on his head is slicked back and thinning, a younger version of Mel Ferrer. He is tall and slender, but with a cop's gut. From the bulge under his coat I know that he is packing. Cummerbund or not, without a hunk of case-hardened steel wedged in his armpit, Clem would have a terminal identity crisis.

There are people in stretch limos pulling up outside, women in furs so toxic with moth repellant that these could only have come from some rental warehouse, men with beer bellies and callused hands in alien suits and ties, craning and twisting their necks like cheap imitations of Rodney Dangerfield. Some of these bear faces recognizable from adolescence under unfamiliar domes of balding heads. People putting on the dog, covering the warts of their lives from others they haven't seen in years, and won't see again for many more, still hustling the peer groups that eluded them in youth; others striving to recapture the popularity they haven't known since.

A slap on the arm. "Later on, buddy. I'll catch you for a drink." Clem gives me a wink and a wave. He has already moved on to the next group coming through the door, rationing the charm. I see one of his hands has slipped low on the silk-encased rump of a woman, one of the pom-pom girls of yore.

"How about if we find a table?"

"Great," says Dana.

She takes my arm and we walk, heading toward the back so we can leave early. I steer her past the punch bowl and the no-host bar, spouses of alumni who don't know anybody, all jockeying in an effort to put themselves into an early alcoholic buzz, their port in this social storm. Anything to get through the evening.

Some guy sticks his hand in my gut, stops me in midstride. "Mike Wagner, city fireman," he says.

Vague recollections of football, some animal of intimidation from my youth who at fourteen had a beard, and a body like Attila, who towered over me, but who hasn't grown a millimeter in a quarter century. I now have twenty pounds and three inches on him.

I shake his hand. "Paul Madriani, lawyer," I say.

No conversation, but he introduces his wife, brunette and twenty-eight if she's a day, dressed in a slinky black outfit, chewing gum and shifting weight from one thigh to another like some taxi dancer with her meter running. I have vague recollections of his first wife, a high school sweetheart who, if she is here, is no doubt throwing daggers from across the room with her eyes at this moment. I move out of target range.

Dana and I take seats at a round table, like Arthur's knights. I shake hands, and we extend a few greetings with three other couples already there, none of whom I recognize from school, a place where we can talk, uninterrupted.

My only reason for being here this evening is the price of a favor from Olsen, though I haven't told Dana this.

Lately she has taken a few hits from Morgan Cassidy for her presence in the courtroom during motions. I have heard tales of some quiet backstabbing, palace intrigues in the darker corners of the fairer kingdom, Cassidy moving in the shadows to get the Queen's Bench to pull its judicial endorsement from Dana. Morgan no doubt views her presence on our side of the aisle as a mortal breach of fealty in the guild of cops and prosecutors. Though Cassidy's efforts would appear to be in vain. From all accounts, when it comes to the appointment, Dana seems to have already pulled this sword from the stone. According to reports, her name alone is headed for Washington.

Tonight she is shimmering in a black evening dress, hair up, spiked high heels of patent leather. The ever-enigmatic smile on her lips. Two of the other women at our table are looking at her as if they might like to corral their husbands' eyes to keep them from roving.

We exchange a little small talk, people settle back into their chairs, and Dana looks over.

"How did the jury go?" she asks. Dressed to kill, and she's

into shop talk. It seems lately that we are either in the sack or talking trials, hers or mine. We have yet to find that middle ground of intimacy, though there is enough growth to the relationship that we are both still looking, chopping our own paths through the jungle of lust.

I have finished eight days of jury selection in Laurel's trial. Eight women and four men, with another guy and three more women as alternates. I am happy with the gender gap. I tell Dana this.

With a victim and a defendant who are women, men on the panel are an enigma. A bad marriage and they could hate their ex, taking it out on Laurel. And guys in a stable marriage would not feel threatened by Melanie as a sexual predator in the same way as women.

The fairer sex will either love Laurel or hate her, see her as the avenging angel in a bad marriage or as a vengeful shrew, depending on their own life situation. The jurors I have gone for are in their late thirties and older. Three are divorced, like Laurel, raising families alone, people who know there's a ragged edge to real life, who will form a chain of empathy with my client.

Pitching a theory at trial is not unlike the pursuit of marketing leads in the world of commerce. You pick your pigeon and fling your seeds. My particular bag of popcorn has Jack as a man with an ego, familiar with the exercise of power and the perks of privilege. If he's on his way out, maybe looking at a term in the joint made more modest by his cooperation with Dana and her friends, his psyche would be stretched to the limit. You have to wonder what a man like this would do under these circumstances if, apart from his other travails, he suddenly discovered that his younger wife had another lover.

My candidate of the week for Lothario at this moment is the late George Merlow, the man feeding fish. I think maybe Melanie had warned George that Jack was on to them. If he was keeping a watch when Melanie took the dive in her bathtub, and saw the killer, my guess is Merlow decided he'd rather not play family feud.

"It would help," I tell Dana, "if your people could come up with the informant." I'm talking of the man Dana told me about, the one who saw Jack in the bar across the river doing business with the courier, over beers.

"They're looking," she says. "It takes time."

"If he's on vacation, he ought to be coming back soon."

"It's more complicated than that," she tells me. It seems this man they are looking for is facing some time of his own, on an unrelated state charge. He may have reasons for an extended holiday.

"You're telling me he's a fugitive?"

"No. Not yet anyway," she says. "We'll find him."

"Let's hope it's before the trial's over."

The band is striking up, strains from the sixties. I go to get us some drinks, tickets in hand. It's a mob scene at the bar.

Some gal sashays by, dark hair to the shoulders like Cleopatra, first name Sharon, but it's all I can pull from the recesses of pubescent recall. It's what sticks in the memory of the fifteen-year-old male—a big chest and a first name. She's wearing a black crochet dress that with a candle from behind you can see through, and from the view I am getting, not much else. The way it hugs her body would be enough to stop most grandmothers from knitting. She pretends she doesn't notice all the gawking from the bar, until some guy, three sheets up and blowing, gives her a catcall, something wild from the northern woods that for an instant suppresses all the chatter at the bar. Then it picks up slowly, snickering laughter and the drone of voices. Not nine o'clock and it's already getting rowdy.

I squeeze my way in and order two drinks. Some kid with pimples who doesn't look old enough to be handling the bottles is pouring.

"Hey—those are mine!"

I turn and it's Clem, a hand on my shoulder.

"Put 'em on my ticket," he says.

The kid makes a note on a napkin.

Leave it to Clem to open a ticket at a no-host bar. He turns for a second and is busy making introductions with the other hand, two guys who want to meet the woman in black. As if by royal command, night of nights, he reaches out, sticks his own hook into a loop of crochet. Got an itch and wanna scratch, Clem as facilitator.

Just as quickly he is back to me.

"Great night, uh? Good crowd." Clem pats his stomach through the cummerbund, a satisfied smile, while he looks around taking in all that is his, like he invented the species.

"Havin' a good time?"

The way he says this makes me think that if I say no, Clem would add another day to the creation, one devoted entirely to the making of merriment.

"Wonderful," I tell him.

"Good to see the old crowd, isn't it?" he says.

"Yeah. Couldn't wait," I tell him.

"Nice threads," he says. "He's feeling the lapel of my suitcoat. Musta set you back."

"Thanks." I don't tell him that I'm on my way from work and haven't changed.

The drinks are on the bar.

"I know you're busy," I say, "but I got a couple of favors."

"Heyyy, anything for a pal." He's looking around. I think he's wondering who I want to hit on, and, given the dazzling looks of Dana, why.

I reach into my inside coat pocket and take out an envelope, open it, and remove the little picture, the DMV shot of the courier from the post office that Dana had given to me the other night.

"I need you to run a make," I tell him. "On this guy."

A look on Clem's face. "If I didn't know you better I'd think ulterior motives," he says.

"Hey—you kidding? I wouldn't miss this for the world."

"I hope this can wait," he says.

"Well, you don't have to do it right now."

"That's good of you," he says. "I thought I was going to have to get my cape and find a phone booth."

"You can wait till Monday," I tell him.

"Wonderful. And this is all you got, I suppose?" He's looking at the picture.

"That and a name. Try Lyle Simmons, alias Frank Jordan, aka James Hays. There may be others. I don't know. The guy's got more faces than Eve," I tell him.

"What about a birth date, social security number?"

"Try DMV," I tell him. "That's where the picture came from."

"What is it ya wanna know?" He's making microscopic notes with a ballpoint pen, light ink-squiggles on the back of the picture.

"Any addresses. Whether the guy did time, either here or in another state, when and where. Anything you can tell me about his background, military, civilian. Whether he's got any family."

"What the fuck did he do, shoot the Pope? Skip out on a legal fee?"

I ignore him. "And one more item." I pull a little plastic Baggie from my coat pocket, the acrylic paint on the tube now hard as cement with the ridges and swirls of Kathy Merlow's thumbprint.

"Can you get the computer guys to run a check on this?" I point to the print.

"You don't want much," he tells me.

"It's important," I tell him. "Do this and I'll owe you big time."

"Fuckin'-a," he says. Clem knows that by doing this, sharing information off of CI & I, the state Justice computers, possible criminal-history data, he is putting his head on the block. Such items are confidential by state law, available only to law enforcement for specified purposes. Criminal sanctions would flow for a violation. His ass could be grass.

I'm running a gambit that Dana's people may not have given her everything on the man known as Lyle Simmons. It never hurts to check another source. It could be something that came their way, something they didn't think was significant. Clem may be many things, but on an errand like this he is above all else discreet.

"No promises," he says, "but I'll see what I can do."

"Thanks," I tell him.

"What's a buddy for?" he says. "Besides, you may need all the friends you can get."

I give him a look.

"Word is that Jimmy Lama's got his sword out for you, sharpening it on a fine stone," says Clem. "That business over pretrial motions."

Lama's embarrassment, the fact that he was called on the carpet by Woodruff, is the talk of the cop shops in town.

Lama's enmity is nothing new. I tell him this.

"Yeah. Well, just don't turn your back," he says.

We talk for a few moments, I grab my drinks and head back toward the table. Halfway there I notice that a guy has moved in next to Dana, the empty chair on the other side. He's looking nervous, little glances to the side, wondering how to open conversation.

"My old high-school special—double rum and Coke," I tell her. "What fueled my engine on Saturday nights." I put the drink in front of her.

The guy on the other side is crestfallen, the look of some wasted auto worker facing life on the line after missing superlotto by one number.

Dana takes a sip, makes a face.

"Like it?"

"I've tasted better paint thinner," she says. "You must of been a real ace in school."

We make talk for a few minutes and the guy on the other

side does what could pass for a discreet exit. The other couples from the table are all on the floor, dancing, Dana and I alone.

"Come on, let's blow this place. I'll mix something special back at the house."

"Can't tonight," she says. "I'm going to have to go in just a few minutes. I've got to fly to D.C. in the morning."

"What, are these coronation bells I hear?"

"For the moment just little tinkles," she says. "First in a series of interviews. Checking for any skeletons that might make an entrance come confirmation in the Senate," she tells me.

The first verification from Dana that this thing, her appointment to the bench, is in fact going to happen.

She reads concern in my face.

"You were hoping for something more tonight," she says.

"That too," I say.

"Oh. It's Jack's case."

I make a face, like I can read between the lines. If she leaves her positions, what assurance is there that I won't have to do blitzkrieg with her office to get the dirt on Jack into evidence in my case?

"Not to worry," she says. "I made a promise. I'll keep it. Besides, I have something else."

She takes another sip from the bitter cup and curls her tongue, like maybe she forgot.

"Fit this into your puzzle and see if you get a picture," she says. "Yesterday afternoon I'm going over transcripts of the telephone tapes from Jack's house."

These are now a few months old, she tells me. Most of it is drivel. According to Dana, Jack kept most of the darker side of life away from the house.

"But there was one conversation, on the eighteenth of August," she says. "A physician called—Melanie's doctor. She wasn't home, so Jack took the call. The doctor simply wanted to leave a message to have Melanie call him back. But Vega became very insistent. It was one of those calls where you read between the lines, that something wasn't right. He wanted to know what it was. The doc tried to assure him that everything was fine. You know Jack,'' she says.

I can picture Jack; nervous Nelly threatening to have the state medical board revoke the guy's license for maintaining a confidence.

''The doc finally relented,'' she says. ''Said it was against his better judgment, but under the circumstances they should be quite happy, being as they were about to become new parents.''

Dana's painted eyebrows are doing heavy arches at this moment.

''The message,'' she says, ''the pregnancy test was positive.''

''Holy shit,'' I say. ''How did Jack take it?''

''I don't know who the telephone carrier was, but I'll bet it's true.''

''What's that?''

''That you could hear a pin drop,'' she says.

CHAPTER
19

Laurel has had a friend, a woman from work, assemble these things, a few more outfits from her closet, and put them into a hanging valise for me.

Tonight, on the eve of trial, I deliver them to the county jail, where they will be stored in a wardrobe warehouse on the main level, a thousand automated hooks like a mechanical snake on the ceiling that moves with the press of a button to produce the exact outfit for the right inmate. One of the many assembly lines of justice.

It is all in the inane belief that the defendant, who has been locked in this hellhole for months, labeled with the scarlet letter of crime and told to scrap for her very existence among the castoffs of this world, will look like you and me when the guards drop the shackles and waltz her into court in the morning. One of the fictions of our system.

I drop the valise with a matron on the bottom floor. They rifle my briefcase and search me, pat-down and metal detector, hand me a clip-on badge, and lead me by the nose upstairs, all without a single word that could be called civil, to the pods, to see Laurel.

I wait in one of the little booths, behind glass. She has not yet arrived. I kill time tapping my fingers on the metal shelf in front of me. Pretrial jitters.

When I see her, it is on the floor down below, coming this

way. A group of women heading for the day room. Laurel's talking and milling, jousting in the body language of this place with another woman. Laurel seems to lose more weight each time I see her, replaced by muscle mass, hours on the treadmill and weight machine downstairs. She could author a book, *Forced Fitness.*

She exudes a lot of sexual energy, but in a package like a female gyrene. As I watch her climb the stairs, I wonder if in this place, Laurel has not in fact found her own element. Like so many locked away here, my sister-in-law is one of the scrappy underdogs of life.

I am reminded of something that Nikki once told me, when the two were girls in high school. They had attended a party out in one of the rural areas of the county. Nikki had wandered off with some guy, who under the influence of a few too many beers, wanted to force the issue. He'd managed to get her into a small gardening shed on the pretext of a walk in the moonlight, and was intent on having his way. She was struggling, fighting him off, hands all the way to her crotch, sprawled on some sacks of potting soil, when Laurel went looking and found them. Without a word, little sister picked up a lawn rake, a dozen sharp metal teeth, and spiked the kid's ass in ways that no doubt he is still explaining to this day.

In a tight situation, most women I have known are talkers. They will, if allowed, rely on their wits to deal. Laurel is the exception. She is merciless in protecting her own, and to Laurel, Nikki was very much one of her own.

For this reason I was taken aback when Nikki asked me to look after her. Through all the years that I have known her, Laurel never seemed like one who needed much looking after, much protection, except perhaps from herself.

She is one of those people who through force of character you take for granted, that you think you know. Lately I've been spending increasing amounts of time wondering just how well I really do know her.

Through the door, she looks at me and smiles.

"If you ever need any referrals," she says, "I've got a lot of friends with hard-luck stories," she tells me.

No doubt most of these are dealing with the public defender. Laurel is a client of status in this hotel, private counsel, and the subject of more than a few news stories.

"They said you wanted to talk to me. More instructions for tomorrow?" she says.

I shake my head. She has weathered Cassidy's opening statement well. Laurel did not blanch or break contact, but stared Morgan in the eye, going toe-to-toe when Cassidy pointed and called her a killer. No glimmer of guilt, no psychic confessions from this woman.

"We need to talk," I tell her.

Ominous eyes. "What's wrong?"

It is something I do with most clients on the eve of trial, one last shakedown cruise to explore all the available courses and headings before sailing into heavy seas.

"Tomorrow we go toe-to-toe," I tell her. "Where possible we try to tear up their witnesses, shred their evidence. In a capital case there is no choice but to get nasty."

The women who do what I do for a living are uniformly called bitches by the men who try cases against them. This is not only a measure of the double standard in life, it is a solid barometer of the air of animus that blows through most criminal courts. In the inferno of a trial, egos get attached to arguments in the same way that patriotism and national pride are fired in warfare. A few angry exchanges, and compromise becomes a four-letter word.

"I need to know if you're comfortable with our case," I tell her.

This sets her back on her stool. "Brother, I don't know if you mean to, but you're scaring the hell out of me," she says.

"That's not my objective. But we need to explore the options."

"The option I'd like to explore is the one where we nail Jack's ass to the wall."

"It may not be that easy," I tell her.

"Day of reckoning," she says.

I give her a nod. A theory is just that. Proving it is something else.

"What are my chances?" she says.

To this point we have never discussed this. We have dealt with the details, the bits and pieces of evidence, the calculations on credibility as to each witness, including Laurel. So far the high point was the coup de grâce delivered to Mrs. Miller in pretrial motions. That evening when I carried the news, Laurel was for an instant, the flicker of an eye, almost giddy. The first time, I think, since she was jailed, that Laurel has entertained seriously the thought that she might actually beat this thing. From the dark pit that is her cell, her kids gone, her life a shambles, it is hard to see any solid ray of hope.

"They've got physical evidence that links you, Jack's testimony, a solid motive in a domestic vendetta, endless circumstances that appear to paint you in the colors of incrimination, your trip to Reno, your visit to the house earlier that night. You want it straight, no sugar?" I ask.

She nods.

"Something less than fifty-fifty.

"Right now they're wounded," I say. "Smarting a little with the loss of Mrs. Miller. An eyewitness who put you at the scene near the time of the murder. That would have been a lock," I tell her. "Still, they're licking their wounds. Not a bad time if we want to talk a deal."

"Is that what you're recommending?"

The lawyer's toughest call. What you can't always say with words. A pregnant pause.

"No. I don't think so. I guess what I'm trying to say is that there are no guarantees." At this moment I am a big sigh.

"And you're not just any client," I tell her. "Not to me. Not to Sarah. Not to your kids. I'd have an awfully large audience waiting for explanations if you go down hard," I say. "Not least of all myself."

"You've done everything you can," she says. "I got myself into this mess."

"Circumstances got you into this mess," I say. "And at this point the only sure way out with your life," I tell her, "might be a deal with the prosecutors."

She mulls this behind the shield of glass. Downcast eyes, for what seems like an eternity. The decision of a lifetime.

"How long would I get?" she says.

"It depends on what they're willing to offer. If I can get them down to second degree, it's fifteen years to life. You might get out in ten."

"What happens to my kids?" she says.

"What happens to them if you're executed?"

"I mean, would Jack take custody?" she says.

We're back to this. My guess is that Jack might end up doing his own stretch in the slammer, once I finish with him here and feds get a glimmer of the way he was trying to play them for sympathy. But I don't tell Laurel this. There's no sense lighting up her day.

"He could," I say. "What difference?"

"I don't want him to raise my children. Besides, ten years is a long time." Suddenly, to Laurel, it's an eternity.

"Your kids would still be around."

"They'd be grown."

"So you'd have grandchildren."

"You really want me to do this?" she says. "Enter a plea?"

"No," I tell her. "What I want is for us to make the right decision."

What I really want, but I don't tell her, is for someone else to make the decision, to take this cup from my lips, to lift the trial from my shoulders.

"You sound like you're afraid to try the case," she says. "Is it that bad?"

"Not if you were anybody else." As the words leave my

lips I see this for what it is: the ultimate admission of a wrung-out lawyer. For more than a decade I've taken the money of a thousand strangers and thrown the dice, always wondering, always worrying, but never looking back. I have dodged my share of bullets. No client has ever died in the little green room. I have known lawyers who have suffered this fate, quivering wrecks, some of whom have spent years seeking absolution in the bottom of a bottle. Harry in a past life.

"It's not the trial that I'm afraid of," I tell her. "It's the result."

"Then I will make the decision for both of us. I want my life back. I want my children back. I don't want any deals. I don't want any plea bargains," she says. "I want to go to trial. I want to plead my case. My decision," she says. "I will live or die with the consequences."

For the moment we are both silent, not running over each other's lines. Then Laurel fills the void.

"She put an awful lot on you," she says.

"Who?"

"Nikki. I know you're doing this for Nikki."

"I'm doing it for all of us."

She makes a face like it's nice of me to say this.

She sits and looks for a long second in silence, then gives me the universal gesture of affection for all those who sit on that side, the flat palm of her hand pressed against the glass that separates us. I match it like we are touching fingers, on my side. And without another word Laurel stands, turns, and is gone.

CHAPTER
20

This morning Harry and I take the courthouse elevator up to four. When the door opens, it's a mob scene. But the lights and microphones are not in our faces. Today the press is doing double duty.

Laurel's trial competes for attention with a circus across the hall, the trial of Louis Cousins, a twenty-seven-year-old whizkid, graduate of Stanford and scion of a wealthy family who is accused of sodomizing and slitting the throats of two teenage girls out in one of the suburbs three years ago.

Cousins has straight blond hair that spends a lot of time covering half of his face, images of Adolf, and eyes that reek of unmitigated evil. His features, while fine, look as if they have been chiseled in Arctic ice, so hard is his demeanor; a face that for its expression could carve the heart out of a passing nun and not look back.

Cousins' trial has become a farm club for shrinks who want to break into the big time of courtroom testimony. This is all paid for by Louis's father, who is leading a sort of psychic safari into his son's past. Each therapist and clinician has a more entertaining notion of Louis's debased and brutal childhood, all of which of course occurred behind the walls of private estates and the tinted windows of chauffeured limos.

After hours of examination, and tests that some might equate to the stirring of entrails in a dish, the high priests of the human mind seem no longer to be in doubt as to what happened, only who did it. This was quickly resolved after a brief consideration of Old Man Cousins' net worth, the source of their fees. It has now been determined that it was one of Louis's nannies who must have debased the boy during his formative years. At least this is what Louis has fished from his repressed memory during hours of psychic handholding and graphic descriptions by his lawyers of death in the gas chamber. His attorneys are now hell-bent for retirement peddling this theory to the jury.

Harry is deeply moved by the compassion of those who heal the human mind. Lately he has asked more than once why Laurel can't come up with her own horrific tales of childhood trauma. Like Harry says, "she could at least sit on the commode for a while and try."

Harry is playing Keenan counsel. In cases involving the death penalty in this state the defendant is entitled to two lawyers: one to handle guilt or innocence—my role—and the other to do what is called the penalty phase, whether if convicted, Laurel should be put to death or be sentenced to life in prison. Harry is therefore on a perpetual search for mitigation, anything that might jerk a tear from the eye of an empaneled juror.

This morning Laurel is brought in without shackles, followed by a matron and another guard, who melt into the background as soon as she is seated at the table with us. This is done each day of the trial, before the jury is allowed into the box, to avoid any implications of guilt that might attach if jurors were to see her constantly in custody, attended by guards.

She is wearing a flowing brown skirt, pleated from the waist, and a white double-breasted blouse, cotton broadcloth with long sleeves, all very plain except for the collar, which is nonexistent and a little severe.

I comment on this.

"A touch from Mary Queen of Scots," she tells me.

Harry, the resident historian, gets into it, that in fact they wore big ruffled collars back then.

"Not when they cut off her head," says Laurel.

Harry considers this for a moment, then concedes the point.

Laurel, it seems, has a refined and sharpened sense of gallows humor.

Still, her dress is tasteful. I have known clients who left to their own devices on the first day of trial would show up looking like the heroine in some potboiling bodice-ripper, blouse tattered by a cat-o'-nine-tails, and tied to a stake like Joan of Arc.

We go over the lineup of probable witnesses for the day.

"First up is Lama," I tell her. "Unless they changed the order."

Cassidy is at work, assembling the bits and pieces of their case.

Word is that Jimmy is particularly angry with me. My treatment of him during pretrial motions. As if this, being the subject of Lama's enmity, is a new experience for me.

I am hearing rumors that Jimmy has stumbled over dirt from the post office bombing, physical evidence involving fingerprints, my own, that federal investigators turned up at the scene. Knowing him as I do, Lama is no doubt puzzled by the fact that the feds are not all over me at this moment like some cheap blanket in a rainstorm. Seeing only a part of the picture, Lama wouldn't know that they've already taken my statement, that in fact they know what I was doing there. I am not anxious to have Jimmy know this, as it would give up a part of our theory surrounding Jack and the Merlows.

"Lieutenant Lama, can you tell the court how the body was discovered?" Cassidy has him on direct.

Lama's on the stand, pursed lips as if the question takes some consideration before responding. I think Jimmy's disappointed. There's only a smattering of press in the front rows. We are not likely to get the full contingent until the Cousins trial is over. Woodruff has allowed the spectacle to be piped outside the courtroom to the cable channel that specializes in notorious trials. But it seems that Jimmy has even lost out on this. While it's true they are taping it, there will be no live broadcast. Without some heavy precedent, some wild advance in the law of severed penises or other legal novelty to boost ratings, Jimmy's testimony is likely to fill the dead air in the middle of the night.

"The victim was found by her husband," he says, "lying in the bathtub of the couple's master bedroom."

"By the victim's husband, you're referring to Mr. Jack Vega?"

"That's correct."

"And about what time was this called in to the police?"

Jimmy looks at his notes. "According to our log sheet at the station, the call was received at exactly zero-forty-three hours."

"And in civilian time?"

"Twelve forty-three in the morning," he says.

"Just before one A.M.?"

"Yes."

"And were you the first officer on the scene?"

"No. A patrol car with two officers was the first to arrive. They were followed by the EMTs—"

"The emergency medical technicians?"

"Yeah. That's right. I got there about—" He reviews his notes. "One-thirty."

"A.M.," says Cassidy.

"Correct."

Cassidy is slow and meticulous, like a mason with bricks, skillful with the mortar, knowing that to build her case everything on these lower courses must be true and level.

"And what did you find when you arrived?"

"The body. The victim was lying on her back in a large bathtub in the master bath. There was some blood in the tub, no evidence of any struggle." He pushes this, a lot of facial ticks and misplaced emphasis. But it's a big point. The state is trying to shut the door on any last-minute ploy for manslaughter, inferences of a battle for the gun, and an accident. They have been moving in this direction from the inception of their case.

"There appeared to be a single gunshot wound under the chin—here." Lama points with a forefinger like a cocked pistol up under the jaw, to one side, a little to the right, close to the throat, showing the path of the bullet up into the head.

"Was the body clothed?"

"No. She was, ahh—" He motions with his hands, groping like he's not sure how to say it. In the buff. Bareass. Jimmy, who no doubt clawed his way out of the womb spitting profanities about darkness and water, is now busy doing the sensitive detective.

"She was in the altogether," he finally says.

"She was naked?" Cassidy looking at him.

Fine. There—a woman has said it.

"Yeah," he says. "Naked."

"Like maybe she was getting ready for a bath?"

"Objection. Leading." I shoot at it while seated, with the eraser end of a pencil.

"Sustained."

Cassidy regroups.

"Did you have any way of determining what the victim was doing just before she was shot?"

"It looked like she was getting ready to take a bath," says Lama.

Oh, good. He got it.

"There was a folded towel on the floor near the bath, and some bath oils on the side."

"You indicated earlier that you found no evidence of a struggle. How did you determine this?"

"A number of things," he says. "It's true that there was a couple of broken bottles on the floor across the room, but quite a distance from where the body was found," he says. "There was no obvious tattooing around the bullet wound.''

Lama's all over the place, mind starting to wander.

''You mean powder burns from the gun?'' Cassidy clarifies.

''Yeah. Powder burns. There was none of those. So we figured the range of fire was some distance, maybe ten, twelve feet, probably while the victim was lying prone in the tub. We believe the bottles were broken when the killer panicked and brushed into them, knocked them off a shelf after the murder.''

''Objection. At this point we have only a dead body—no evidence of murder.''

''Sustained. The reporter will strike the last part of the witness's answer.''

''Lieutenant, could you rephrase your last response?''

''We think the bottles were busted when the perpetrator panicked.'' He spits the *p*'s of each word at me.

''Besides,'' he says, ''the bath towel was on the floor nice and neat, not disturbed or anything like it would have been if there'd been a fight.'' He looks at me like that'll teach you to object.

A cold and calculated shot from a distance is better for their case. It offers the jury some hint of premeditation and deliberation.

''And there was no evidence that the body was moved after the shooting?''

Shameless leading, but I let it go. Lama might put the shooter in another building with a scoped-sight if I push it.

''That's right. From what we could see, she was shot while lying in the tub.''

''Did you find any fingerprints?''

''No. That was real curious,'' he says.

''Why do you say 'curious'?''

'' 'Cuz we dusted real good. And there were places you would expect to find some prints, especially for the victim.''

''And you didn't?''

He shakes his head, lips turned down, an expression from the Old World. ''We didn't even find prints for the victim on the door to the bathroom or on the front of the tub. You'd expect porcelain would hold good prints,'' he says. ''And how's the lady going to get down into the tub without at least touching the outside edge?'' Jimmy looks at Cassidy like this is a riddle, playing it like high drama.

''And what did you conclude from this?''

''That the perpetrator.'' He looks at me. ''That the perpetrator wiped the surfaces clean after he or she,'' he says, ''shot the victim.''

''To avoid detection?'' she says.

''Sure. Why else?''

''In your search of the scene did you find the murder weapon?''

''No.''

''Nothing?''

''No gun.''

''Did you search the entire house?''

''We did.''

''And the area outside?''

''Everything. Real thorough.''

''And you found no murder weapon?''

''No.''

''Did you have occasion to talk to the victim's husband, Mr. Vega, at the scene?''

''I did.''

''And did you ask him if there was a gun in the house? If he or his wife owned one?''

''I did. And I was told that neither he nor his wife had ever owned a gun.''

''What did you conclude from this?''

''That whoever shot Mrs. Vega brought the weapon into the house and left with it when they were finished.''

''So they came prepared to kill?'' she says.

''Objection.''

''Withdrawn,'' she says.

Morgan looks at me a wan smile, like sure, just try to unring it.

"Did you find anything else in the bathroom that morning?"

"Yes. We found a single spent bullet cartridge, nine-millimeter."

Cassidy walks to the evidence cart, studies it for a second, and picks a single plastic bag off the cart.

"May I approach, your honor?"

Woodruff nods.

"Lieutenant, I would ask you to look at the bullet cartridge in this envelope and ask if you can identify it."

He studies it for a second, looks at the notations on the label stuck on the bag. A nine-millimeter looks like any other.

"That's it. That's the cartridge we found in the bathroom. That's my mark on the evidence bag," he says.

"And you bagged this yourself."

"One of the evidence techs," he says. "Under my direct supervision. But I marked the bag—there." He points with a thumbnail.

"I would ask that this bullet be marked as People's Exhibit One," says Cassidy.

"Any objection?" The judge looks at me.

"No, your honor."

"Did you find anything else at the scene?"

"Some fibers," he says.

Cassidy's back to the cart. She returns a second later, handing him another bag.

"Those are the fibers. We found them on the floor near the base of the tub. Again I marked the bag to identify it," says Lama.

This, the fiber evidence, is something new that they have developed, though from reading the lab report I think they are reaching.

Cassidy has this marked for identification without objections. All the little pieces of her case. If she can build on them and show some incriminating link, some relevance connecting these pieces to the defendant and the crime, Cassidy will at the appropriate time try to move them into evidence, like a carefully thought-out chess match, each move calculated for effect.

"Apart from the cartridge and the fibers already identified, did you find anything else that morning?"

"We took into possession a copy of a videotape from a security camera situated on the front porch of the residence."

Cassidy retrieves a videocassette from the cart and approaches the witness. He identifies it from an evidence tag.

"Detective, have you looked at the contents of this tape?"

"I have."

"And can you tell the court what you saw?"

"The tape is calibrated as to date and time, with those elements showing on the top right-hand corner of the picture as it appears on a videoscreen. The tape in question is a special slow-playing tape that lasts up to twelve hours. It's not like the commercial stuff you use at home," he says. "So there's a lotta stuff on it."

He verifies that the tape is dated the day Melanie Vega was killed, but that it stopped for reasons that he does not explain before the time of death.

"We're not interested in everything," says Cassidy. "Just the pertinent parts." What she means is anything that she can use to hang Laurel. "Can you tell the court what you saw on the tape?"

"I'm going to object." I'm on my feet. "The best evidence is the tape itself. Why do we need the witness to characterize it?"

"Your honor, we need to lay a foundation," says Cassidy.

In order to put an item into evidence, it is necessary to lay a proper foundation. In the case of a physical object, this generally means some showing that it is relevant to the issues in dispute in the case. The tape would ordinarily be viewed by the jury at the time that it is admitted into evidence. It is my point that with regard to the tape Morgan has already laid a foundation.

"For that purpose," says Woodruff, "I'll give a little latitude. Do it quickly."

"Lieutenant, if you could just summarize what's on the tape."

"Yes. At eight-seventeen P.M., on the night Melanie Vega was killed, a woman appears on the tape at the door of the victim's residence."

"Can you identify that woman?"

"It was the defendant—Laurel Vega."

With this Lama points at Laurel, sitting next to me. It takes him a second to point straight. That this is out of cadence with his words makes clear that this gesture was planted, something conceived in the mind of Cassidy or one of her assistants as a moment of drama, and badly played by Jimmy.

"You're sure of that?"

"Absolutely."

"Is there any kind of soundtrack on the tape?"

"Unfortunately no," he says.

"Could you tell what the defendant was doing?"

"There was a long and very heated argument—"

"Objection."

"I don't want to be hearing about any arguments on the tape," says Woodruff.

I move to strike the witness's answer, and Woodruff orders it.

"How long did this conversation between the victim and defendant go on?"

Lama looks at his notes. "Four minutes and thirty-three seconds," he says.

"And how did it conclude?"

"The defendant smashed the videocamera with a flowerpot before—"

"Objection, your honor."

Woodruff looks like he's been shot with a cattle prod on

the bench. Bushy eyebrows, all aimed at Cassidy.

"That's all. I don't want to hear another word about the tape," he says. "You want it marked?" Woodruff looks at her. Cassidy's not winning any points with the judge. If we are lucky, we can bank these little moments of enmity toward the opposition, a credit to draw on in a tight moment on a motion or some future fray with Cassidy and her troops.

The clerk does the deed, marking the tape as one of the People's exhibits.

Morgan looks at her notes. She's covered all the critical points with the witness and is starting to reach into areas that are drawing my objections and Woodruff's aggravation.

"That's all for this witness," she says.

"Cross?" says Woodruff.

I stand and approach the witness box, maintaining an appropriate distance, Lama and I locking eyes, a little bit of moisture, pimples of sweat on his upper lip.

"Lieutenant Lama. Is it fair to characterize you as part of the prosecutorial team in this case?"

"I'm a police officer, nothing more, nothing less."

Lama is a lot less, but I won't belabor the point here.

"Isn't it true that on this case you're working with the Deputy District Attorney over there, Ms. Cassidy?"

"That's my job," he says.

"So you're part of her team?"

"If that's what you want to call it," he says.

"You've talked to her about this case—I mean outside the courtroom. Isn't that true?"

"Yes."

"You've shared whatever information you have pertaining to this case with her? You've discussed the testimony that you planned to give here today?"

"Yes."

"In fact, isn't it true that in preparing to testify here today you've gone over your testimony with her in some detail? In fact rehearsed it?"

"We talked about it."

"How many times?" I ask.

"I don't know."

"Two, three?" I play the numbers game.

"I can't remember."

"That many?" I say.

He gives me a look.

"Isn't it true that in preparing to appear here today you rehearsed your testimony with Ms. Cassidy, that you went over it in considerable detail a number of times to ensure that you would get it right?"

Ordinarily I might not press this. But given Jimmy's slamming in pretrial motions, it's a safe bet that Morgan has had Lama closeted with one of the drones from her office for days, more dress rehearsals than a Broadway production.

"We talked a few times." It's all he will say.

"You didn't talk to us, did you?"

"Whadda ya mean?"

"Well, you didn't sit down and talk to the defense attorneys—Mr. Hinds and myself—and tell us precisely what you were going to say here today, did you?"

"I don't have to," he says.

"Exactly," I say. "Because it's your job to convict the defendant, isn't it?"

I'm busy destroying the myth that cops are neutral, simple crime fighters with no ax to grind. The police mind-set in any investigation usually fixes quicker than mercury. Show them a suspect, sometimes with scant evidence, and they point with the relentless force of a compass to a magnet.

"It's my job to solve crimes," he says.

Cape-and-blue-tights time. Lama as the masked avenger.

"Oh—so you have no interest in convicting this defendant?"

"I didn't say that."

"No, you didn't, did you?"

I let the jury savor the point for a moment.

"Can you tell us, Mr. Lama"—somewhere along the way Jimmy's lost his rank. Why cloak him with authority?—"was there an all-points bulletin issued for the arrest of a suspect on the night that Melanie Vega died?"

"Yeah."

"Who issued that APB?"

"I did."

"And who was it issued for?"

"Your client," he says. "Laurel Vega." Having screwed up so badly on the first effort, this time Jimmy doesn't try to point, but merely gestures with his head in the casual direction of our table.

"So you determined fairly early on that Laurel Vega was the principal suspect in the case?"

"That's right."

"How many years of experience do you have investigating crimes?"

"Thirty-two."

"And I guess after all that time you get a pretty good feel for this kind of thing? How to exercise judgment as to when to issue an APB? When to pick up a suspect?"

"Lots of things come with experience," he says.

"And this APB—did it identify the suspect as possibly armed and dangerous?"

"It did."

"This means that police in apprehending the suspect would probably do so with drawn weapons?"

"If they valued their lives," he says.

"Why was that?"

"Because she was dangerous."

"And how did you form all of these opinions so quickly that evening? The opinion that Laurel Vega was the principal suspect and that she was armed and dangerous?"

"The victim had been shot. We didn't find the gun. We had to figure she had it on her."

"Very good, Mr. Lama. But how did you determine that

Laurel Vega was the principal suspect?''

''Well—we had the tape. The security tape,'' he says.

''Oh. You were able to play the tape back that morning at the scene to review it?''

I flip through some pages in my hand, a copy of the police report from that night.

Lama suddenly becomes clairvoyant, sensing where I am headed, eyes like a rabid dog.

''Come to think of it,'' he says, ''we didn't.''

''Didn't what?''

''We didn't view the tape that morning.''

''Why was that?''

''The camera was broken,'' he says.

''And without a functioning camera for this particular equipment, you couldn't actually play the tape back, could you?''

''No,'' he says. ''We couldn't.''

I know this from reading the follow-up investigative reports. The cops weren't able to review the security tape from the house for nearly five hours, until a vendor for the system supplied them with the necessary equipment. By that time the APB had been in effect for nearly four hours.

''So you didn't have the tape at the time the APB issued. So what evidence did you rely on in issuing the bulletin for the arrest of Laurel Vega, the information that she was armed and dangerous?''

''Well . . . her husband,'' he says.

''You mean Jack Vega? Laurel Vega's former husband?''

''That's right.''

''And what did Mr. Vega tell you that caused you to issue the bulletin to arrest Laurel Vega?''

''We asked him if he knew of anyone who might have wanted to kill his wife.''

''And what did he say?''

''He gave us the name of Laurel Vega.''

''Just like that?''

"Well . . . and some other things."

"What things?"

"That Laurel Vega hated the victim. That she was jealous. You know," he says, "the stuff you expect in a divorce."

"Just the usual stuff?" I say.

"Yeah. Pretty much."

"And did Mr. Vega tell you that he actually saw Laurel Vega commit this crime?"

"No. He wasn't home at the time."

"Well, did Mr. Vega tell you that he'd seen Laurel Vega at his home that night?"

"No."

"So what we have here is Mr. Vega's bald allegation, without any evidence to support it, that Laurel Vega hated his wife. Certainly enough to talk to the defendant. To question her," I say. "So the evidence for her arrest must have come when you went to question her?" I say.

"No." He says this through locked jaws, all the sound emanating down onto his chest.

"What?"

"No." Louder so the jury can hear it now.

"I don't understand, then. What evidence did you have for arresting Laurel Vega?"

"We had a dead body," he says.

I look at him, dead center in the box. "Are you telling this court that except for the unsupported suspicions of Jack Vega—bald allegations without any evidence—that you had no basis to issue the all-points bulletin that morning?"

"She had a rug that came from the scene," he says.

"She had a rug that you now claim came from the scene, but you didn't even know that at the time of the APB."

He would jump on the horse of the eyewitness, Mrs. Miller, but that is now excluded evidence. If he mentions it, opens his mouth, any hint, I will have a mistrial in the flash of an eye.

"We found a compact in her purse that belonged to the

victim. Hell, she was in Reno, running from the scene, when they found her.''

"After you arrested her," I tell him. "You found the compact days after you issued the all-points bulletin calling my client armed and dangerous, subjecting her to arrest at the point of loaded pistols. And you had no idea where she was when you issued the APB—did you?''

"At the time she was our best suspect," he says. Righteous indignation on the stand.

"To this day she remains your only suspect because you haven't bothered to look for any others. Isn't that true?''

He looks at me, a tortured expression. Lama would like to answer but doesn't know what to say. If he concedes the point, he's damned; if he says this is not true, I will ask him what other suspects he's pursued, what other leads he's rooted out of the swill of his investigation. We both know the answer to that one.

"All of the evidence points to your client," he says.

"All of the evidence that you've produced," I tell him, "because you haven't bothered to look for any evidence that would exonerate her, that might point to the real killer. Isn't that true?''

I'm busy planting the seeds of my case in the jury box— thoughts of another killer. It's one of the problems with their case. They have backed into probable cause for Laurel's arrest after the fact, finding the compact, and the rug, and Mrs. Miller's crippled identification. At the time of the APB they had none of these. No doubt with half an effort we might have knocked over the initial arrest, though they could have cured any defect in a short time. It was better to leave it alone and use it here to bloody Lama.

"We've been fair and open-minded," he says. "We've conducted a professional investigation."

"You call this professional?''

"I do," he says.

"Is it professional to issue an order to arrest my client based solely on Jack Vega's suspicions?''

He doesn't answer, but looks at me, straightens his tie, then wipes his upper lip with the sleeve of his coat. A better response than I could have hoped for, all in body English.

''I'm waiting for an answer,'' I tell him.

''I gave you one. It was a professional investigation.''

''A moment ago you said that Mr. Vega told you that Laurel Vega hated his new wife. That she was jealous. The stuff you expect in a divorce. Those were your words. What did you mean by that?''

Everything above the shoulders is bobbing and weaving like one of those dogs on a dashboard with its head on a spring, Lama trying to say it without words.

''You know,'' he says.

''No, I don't know. What did you mean?''

''I mean a bad divorce. The two women didn't like each other.''

''And you know about this stuff?''

''Thirty years in law enforcement, you know a lot about a lot of things.''

''I suppose you handled a lot of domestic calls over the years, back in your squad car days?'' I say.

''My share,'' he says.

''Then you know about women in divorces?'' I ask him.

''You bet. Like to scratch your eyes out,'' he says.

With the gender factor of this jury, I can hear Cassidy sucking air at the table, Jimmy about to step in it.

''So women can be violent in a divorce?'' I say.

Suddenly he sees where I'm going, leading him to the pit of political heresy, a reversal of the doctrine that women are the victims in domestic violence. Jimmy's eyes visit the jury box and come back wary.

''Men do it too,'' he says. ''They smack 'em around sometimes . . . the ladies,'' he says. ''So we'd have to step in and stop it.'' Jimmy to the rescue.

"Ah, so it can be violent all the way around?" I say.

"Sure. Absolutely," he says.

"Well, did it ever occur to you that Mr. Vega might have had his own reasons for wanting to shower suspicion on his former wife?"

"What do you mean?"

"I mean it's a bad divorce, one involving a lot of bitterness. Did it ever occur to you that Mr. Vega might have had his own reasons to shower hostility on his former wife? To make accusations against her without evidence? That would be a natural thing in a bad divorce—wouldn't it?"

"We had no reason to hold suspicions that he might be misleading us," he says.

"But you were willing enough to form every kind of suspicion against his former wife. To the point of branding her a murderer?"

"There was evidence," he says.

"All of which I contend is suspect, and all of which I would remind you was acquired after the fact of her arrest. What else did Mr. Vega tell you that night?"

"He was upset. We didn't want to press him," he says.

"You didn't want to press him! *You didn't want to press him!*" I do this on an uptilt with my voice, gaining an octave, looking at him with incredulous eyes.

"I see. So it was easier to arrest my client, to issue an all-points bulletin calling her armed and dangerous, to subject her to the hazards of deadly force, arrest under the pointed guns of nervous officers—it was easier to do this than it was to investigate the facts, to find out exactly what lay behind Jack Vega's accusations against his former wife?"

"In hindsight," he says, "we probably would have done it differently."

With this I can see Cassidy cringe.

"I'll bet you would have," I say.

The first rule of cross. Once he steps in it, leave him there. From the beginning I have suspected that there was something else that motivated Laurel's arrest, something that caused Lama to fall into his own pit of seething vipers on this thing: his hatred of me and his early acquired knowledge that Laurel was, after all, my kin.

CHAPTER
21

In the afternoon, Morgan Cassidy is licking her wounds. Lama has left her with a deficit: his ham-handed acquiescence in the notion that he arrested Laurel without sufficient evidence. Cassidy is now left to wonder whether Jimmy's words might become the capstone of a later appeal should Laurel be convicted.

Lama's testimony has painted a clear image in the jury's mind of a slovenly investigation, of cops not interested in the details, not willing to sift for facts, on a myopic crusade to convict Laurel before there was any real evidence of her guilt.

In a way I view Cassidy as more dangerous because of this; her contortions in trial offer up all the anxiety of tracking a wounded tiger in the bush.

Colin Demming is everything Jimmy Lama is not. He is young, good-looking, articulate, and bright. While civies are usually worn to court, today the officer wears the uniform of the Reno Police Department. Demming is a patrolman in that force, and the man who initially took Laurel into custody at the laundromat on Virginia Street.

Ordinarily I would expect Cassidy to put Demming on the stand, extract what she needs from him, and get him down quickly. But Morgan has found another line of attack, and Demming is the perfect weapon: a cop not connected with an inept investigation.

Cassidy takes her time going over the details of the arrest, how Demming and the other officers were called to the laundromat when a woman spotted Laurel's picture in a paper and called dispatch. How Demming checked for a warrant and found one in Laurel's name. It was issued based on the eyewitness testimony of Mrs. Miller and her review of the single picture shown to her by Lama the night of the murder. I have now discovered where this came from. Laurel tells me that Jack pilfered it from some of Danny's personal belongings, items left by the kid at Jack's house on one of his visits. This was apparently a source of considerable friction between Danny and his father—that the boy's picture of his mother had been used to launch a manhunt for her.

Morgan asks Demming what happened after the cops all assembled at the laundromat.

"Two other units arrived, backup. One of them covered the rear of the building, while I and three other officers went in the front."

"What did you find inside?"

"We observed a woman, at one of the commercial laundry units near the back. There were several other patrons. We asked them to step outside."

"So the suspect didn't see you when you entered the premises?"

"No. She was turned around when we entered. There was a lot of noise from the equipment—washers and dryers. I approached her and had to tap her on the shoulder before she noticed that I was standing there. I told her not to move. To place her hands against the laundry unit, to step back with her feet and to spread them wide. Then I asked her for some identification. She said she'd have to get her purse. I told her to stay where she was and one of the other officers got it."

"Where was her purse?"

"It was on a chair a few feet away."

"Did you obtain identification for the suspect?"

"Yes. We found a wallet inside the purse with a driver's

license. It identified the suspect as Laurel Jane Vega, the same name as that on the warrant.''

"And do you see that woman in court here today?"

"Yes. She's sitting right there." He points to Laurel in the chair next to me.

"Your honor, we'd like the record to reflect that the witness has identified the defendant, Laurel Vega."

"So ordered," says Woodruff.

"Did you then take Laurel Vega into custody?"

"We did. We read her her rights and handcuffed her."

"Now, during this time, as you confronted the defendant, while you were reading her rights and cuffing her, did she say anything to you? Make any statement?"

"Yes. She wanted to know how we found her."

"What was her exact statement? Do you recall?"

"I made a note of it," he says. He refers to a copy of the arrest report. " 'How did you guys find me?' That's what she said."

" 'How did you guys find me?' " Cassidy repeats this slowly, standing, facing the jury square-on. "And what did you tell her?"

"We told her she could talk to a lawyer if she had any questions."

"Officer, I've asked you to bring some documents with you to court today. Do you have them?"

"I do." He reaches inside a folder and pulls out a sheaf of papers. He hands several to Cassidy. She pages through them, hands a set to the clerk, who passes them to the judge, then sashays by our table and drops a set unceremoniously in front of me.

"I'm referring to the form that's entitled 'Prisoner's Inventory.' Do you find that one?"

"Yes."

"Can you tell the court what this form is?"

"This is a standard form that is completed at the booking station in our department whenever an arrest is made. It's used to inventory the items found in the possession of the person who is taken into custody and booked. The items are held, sealed in an envelope, and initialed by the prisoner to be returned if they make bail or whenever they're released.''

"And the particular form we have here?"

"It's for the suspect in this case, Laurel Vega."

"I take it that this was prepared at the time she was booked in Reno."

"Yes."

"Who completed this form, officer?"

"As the arresting officer, I did." He points to his initials at the bottom of the form.

"A lot of small personal items," says Cassidy. She's reading from the form. " 'Handkerchief, car keys, lipstick.' Where were these items found?"

"Those were the contents of the defendant's purse," he says. He points to a notation on the form which verifies this.

"I call your attention to item number eleven on the inventory sheet: 'Woman's gold compact with initials M.L.H.' Do you see that?"

"Yes."

"Was that one of the items found in the purse?"

"It was."

Cassidy retreats to the evidence cart, fishes for a second through a couple of paper bags, and a moment later is back with an object in her hand.

"May I approach the witness, your honor?"

Woodruff snorts, gives a little nod.

"Officer Demming, I ask you to look at this compact and tell me if you've ever seen it before."

He turns it over in his hand, examines it closely, then looks up at Morgan.

"It's the compact I found in the defendant's purse at the time of her arrest."

"The one marked as item eleven on this sheet?"

"Yes. You can see the initials right here." He points.

"Thank you." Cassidy wants it identified as People's Exhibit next in order.

I have no objection. She will wait until Jack identifies it as belonging to Melanie, something stolen on the night of the murder, and then move it into evidence, one of the crowning pieces of her case, leaving us to answer the question of how it came to be found in Laurel's purse three days later when she was arrested in Reno.

"One more item," she says. She's looking for it on the list.

"Try number seventeen," I say.

Morgan looks at me, a condescending smile, as if to say, How do you know what I'm looking for?

On this stuff she is very methodical. The surprises will come later and from left field. Knowing Cassidy, I can only try to brace myself.

"Sure enough," she says. "Officer Demming, I call your attention to item seventeen on the list: 'One decorative three-by-five-foot rug.' Do you see it?"

"Yes."

"Where was this found?"

"It was at the laundromat, in her possession, actually being laundered at the time we made the arrest."

While he's talking, Cassidy's moved to the evidence cart. The rug is no problem to find, it is rolled and tied with twine, an intricate design in blue thread woven through it. She asks the bailiff to give her a hand. He picks the rug up and carries it over to the witness box.

"Officer Demming, can you identify the carpet that the bailiff is now showing you?"

He looks at it, checks a tag that's been affixed to one corner.

"Yes. That's the rug that we found in the defendant's possession when we took her into custody. The one she was laundering."

All the little pieces lining up in Morgan's case. Whatever ground Lama has lost, Demming has more than made up. Cassidy has visions of Jack on the stand, identifying the rug as part of the murder scene that night, confirmation that Laurel was there. How else could she have acquired it?

"Let's get into the question of the laundry for a moment," says Cassidy. "You say that the defendant was washing this rug. Was this in an ordinary washing machine?"

"No. It was a large commercial unit of some kind. The manager told me that it was one of the last ones left in the city. It uses chemical dry-cleaning solvents to clean woolen goods, other fabrics that you can't clean in soap and water."

"So this would be pretty caustic stuff, these chemicals?"

"Objection," I'm intoning to Woodruff, who seems like he's dozing on the bench. His eyes suddenly open.

"Unless the officer has a degree in chemical engineering that we haven't heard about, the question calls for speculation."

"I beg to differ," says Cassidy. "This goes to the appearance of the chemicals as well as the defendant when she was using them."

I get a quiver down deep inside. She's nibbling around the edges of that which is verboten, the inference that Laurel was busy destroying evidence, though her question is just inside the foul pole for the moment.

"Maybe counsel could clarify the question," says Woodruff.

Morgan makes a face, like "if I have to, fine."

"Could you smell these chemicals, officer?"

"You bet."

"And what did they smell like?"

"The vapors were very strong," he says. "They burned your nose and left a few of us coughing for a couple of minutes until we could get out of there, into the fresh air."

"Was the machine open at the time that you confronted the defendant?"

"No."

"Then I don't understand. How did the vapors escape?"

"The defendant apparently had opened the machine during

one of its cycles and had managed to get her hands into the solvent.''

''Were you concerned about this?''

''Enough to ask the manager what the stuff was.''

''What did she say?''

''Objection. Hearsay.''

''Sustained.''

''Well, let me ask you. Did you have occasion to look at the defendant's hands?''

''Oh, yes.''

''And what did they look like?''

''A lot of red blotches,'' he says. ''Chemical burns, all the way up onto her forearms.''

''Did you ask her about this?''

''Yes. She said it was an accident.''

''Accident?'' says Cassidy. ''Pretty clumsy, wouldn't you say? Pretty convenient accident?''

''Objection—calls for speculation.''

''Sustained.''

''Officer, do you know anything about gunpowder-residue tests?''

''I'm going to object to this whole line of inquiry, your honor. The witness is not a forensics expert. He's not been qualified.''

''Good point,'' says Woodruff.

''He doesn't have to be a qualified expert to answer whether his department attempted to conduct any powder-residue tests on the defendant's hands after her arrest.''

Woodruff gives it the smell test, a twitching nose. ''That's all you want to ask him?''

''That's it, your honor.''

''Go ahead,'' says the judge.

''Officer Demming—do you know whether your department attempted to conduct gunpowder-residue tests on the hands of the defendant after her arrest?''

''I do not.''

"Then you wouldn't know whether such tests were possible given the chemical contamination of the defendant's hands?"

"Objection!" I'm on my feet, shouting at the bench.

"That's it," says Woodruff. "Not another word," he says. "The question will be stricken from the record. The jurors are instructed to disregard the last question of the prosecutor. Ms. Cassidy, I want to see you in chambers with Mr. Madriani as soon as we are finished with this witness."

"Yes, your honor."

"Nothing further of the witness," she says. Cassidy takes her seat, declining to engage Woodruff's eyes as they bore a hole through her forehead.

I am steaming down deep, under the collar, but I try not to show this. One of the biggest mistakes you can make on cross: unleashing your venom on a witness who will at least give the appearance of neutrality.

"Officer Demming." I smile at him, big and broad, count to ten. "Thank you for coming all the way down here," I tell him.

"Part of the job," he says. He looks at me with stern eyes. He knows I am the devil.

"I have just a few questions by way of clarification."

He nods like he understands, though his expression is something you might reserve for a trip to the dentist.

"You say that when you received the call to respond to the laundromat that you checked for a warrant, and that you were informed that one had been issued?"

"That's right."

"You were also told that the suspect could be armed. Is that correct?"

"It is."

"And when you took the defendant into custody, did you find a weapon in her possession?"

"No."

"No weapon concealed on her body?"

"No."

"No gun in her purse?"

"If we'd found a gun, it would have been listed on the inventory sheet. Did you see one?"

Testy.

"So you didn't find one?"

"That's what I said."

I could push him further, ask him if he thought this was strange, no gun, after being warned that Laurel might be armed and dangerous. But such questions with an obviously hostile witness have a way of imploding. Demming might speculate that if she had a gun, she could have dumped it somewhere, planting the damaging specter in the minds of jurors.

I leave this alone.

"When you approached the defendant did she put up any kind of resistance? Did she struggle with you?"

"No."

I don't belabor the point that she probably had a dozen handguns pointed at her at the time. Cassidy has wisely stayed away from this since Lama's testimony, and it does not serve my own ends at this moment.

"Other than the single statement by the defendant that you alluded to earlier, did the defendant say anything else when you took her into custody?"

He thinks for a moment. If he tries to say it again, I will cut him off.

"No. Not that I can remember."

"She made no confession?"

"No."

"She didn't say 'I did it'?"

"No."

"She didn't try to run?"

"That would have been difficult," he says.

"But she didn't try?"

"No."

"Officer Demming, you say you found the carpet belonging to Laurel Vega in a commercial laundry unit. Is that correct?"

"Yes."

"Now, obviously, when you approached the defendant in the laundromat your first concern was not the contents of what was in the laundry, was it?"

"I don't understand the question."

"I mean, you had a dangerous suspect on your hands here. Someone you were told was armed and dangerous. Isn't that correct?"

"Yes."

"Well, you were sort of preoccupied watching her, weren't you? A little too busy to be noticing what was tumbling in the laundry unit?"

"That's true," he says.

"So how did you find out that the rug inside the unit belonged to the defendant?"

"She told us."

"She *told* you?" I make a big point of this, a lot of emphasis in the voice.

"Yes. That's right."

"So she wasn't trying to conceal her possession of this item from you?"

"No."

"She volunteered the information that the rug was hers?"

"That's correct."

The point is clear. If the rug is incriminating evidence linking her to the murder of Melanie Vega, why would Laurel tell the cops it was hers? Why not just leave it—walk away? Tell the cops that whatever was in that unit belonged to somebody else?

In Demming there is a little bit of the old adage that the worst witness can always give even the darkest cloud in your case some tint of a silver lining.

"That's all I have for this witness," I say.

Demming collects his papers and starts to get up.

"Oh. One more question, officer." I'm halfway back to the counsel table when I turn.

"About Mrs. Vega's hands. You said that when you took her into custody they were inflamed, irritated. I think your words were"—I look at my notes—" 'A lot of red blotches. Chemical burns, all the way up onto her forearms.'

"This would be pretty painful, I would imagine?"

"No doubt," he says.

"Still," I say, "this didn't stop you from using metal cuffs, and cuffing both of her hands up behind her back before pushing her into your squad car—did it?"

He looks at me. "Standard procedure," he says. "We're required to—"

"That's all for this witness." I leave him standing there, offering the only excuse he can to the jury—a plaintive look.

Since we are between witnesses, we don't retire all the way into the judge's chambers, but huddle in a narrow hallway out of earshot of the jury, and off the record. Harry and I, Woodruff and Cassidy, stand in the little hallway leading to the judge's office, in semidarkness. Lama has tried to edge his way in as the representative of the people, as best he can, but he is left dangling with his ass-end halfway in the courtroom, trying to look over the shoulder of the taller Cassidy.

Woodruff is clearly kindling some smoldering hostility. He looks at Morgan.

"I've had all of this I'm going to take," he says. "Maybe I look the fool to you," he says.

"I don't know what you're talking about," says Cassidy innocently.

"I'm talking about matters that I ruled on in pretrial motions. Do you remember? Correct me if I'm wrong, but we had a conversation about inferences and evidence being destroyed, and you were told that comments on such matters would be off-bounds. Do you remember now?" he says.

"Certainly I do," she says.

"Then what the hell was that all about?"

Cassidy gives him arching eyebrows, a look as if she's not

sure what he's talking about. This is enough to ignite a flame under the judge.

"You know very well what I'm talking about," he snaps. "That crap out there about gunshot residue," he says. "I gave you latitude for one narrow inquiry and you abused it. You want to be joining Mr. Madriani's client in jail, just keep it up," he says.

I can tell by the look that Harry finds this particularly pleasing. If there were rocking loge seats, he would go for popcorn.

"I keep a little score sheet up on the bench," Woodruff tells her. "Try me one more time," he says, "and a little mark goes down by your name. For the first one I'll fine you. Collect two of them and when this trial is over I'll want you back here with your toothbrush. Do I make myself clear?"

"Your honor. The jury has to be allowed to hear the evidence, to form its own—"

"Do I make myself *clear?*" Woodruff booms in the little hallway. I know it can be heard out into the courtroom.

Harry is veritably itching, hoping, praying, that she will say just one more word.

"Yes, your honor."

The wrong ones.

"Good." Woodruff pushes past her and leaves us all standing in the dark, looking at one another, Cassidy rolling her eyes, like what a bastard, but she's playing to the wrong audience.

Jenny Lang is a problem for us. We thought she was chaff on the state's witness list, several dozen false targets that the prosecution will always throw out, hoping that you waste your time investigating, chasing a name they have no intention of actually calling.

I look at Harry. He gives me a shrug, like let's hope it's nothing.

Lang is a friend of Laurel's from a past life. A woman who shared her circle six years ago when their children attended the same private school and Laurel was married to Jack. Since then their paths have diverged. Lang works as a bookkeeper for a lobbying group downtown. She and Laurel do lunch on a rare occasion, the last time about eight months ago.

Cassidy has supplied no statement reduced to writing summarizing Lang's testimony, and when Harry and I grilled Laurel as to why Lang's name showed up on Morgan's list of witnesses, Laurel didn't have a clue. We figured she had to be a loss leader. We were wrong.

Today Lang is dressed in a suit, patterns of black and white with a dark cravat at the neck, and high heels, what the busy businesswoman wears on the job. Lang might stand five-foot-three and tip a hundred pounds on the scale, with salt-and-pepper hair cut short off the shoulders.

As she turns to take the oath, Harry and I are scrambling trying to figure where and how she fits in their case. She swings her purse from the strap off her shoulder, holding it in one hand while she raises the other and swears to tell the truth. If there is a sense of foreboding in all of this, it comes from the obvious manner in which Lang avoids eye contact with Laurel.

"Please state your name for the record?"

"Jenny Lang."

"Your full legal name?"

"Jennifer Ann Lang." She is a feeble wreck on the stand, not happy to be here. This hangs like a sign about her neck, like an invitation to a mugging.

Morgan has positioned herself in a direct line between the witness and Laurel, feet spread wide, hands on her hips, forming an impenetrable barrier between the two women.

"Ms. Lang. Do you know the defendant, Laurel Vega?"

"Yes. We were, we are friends," she says.

"Can you tell the court how long you've known the defendant?"

"Gee. It's been—I don't know." She thinks for a moment.

"At least eight years, on and off," she says. "Our children went to school together."

"When's the last time you saw each other, before today?"

"Perhaps six months," she says. She tries to see around, to find Laurel for some confirmation of this, but is barred by Cassidy, who is now doing her own rendition of the Great Wall of China.

"And what was the occasion of that last meeting?"

"A luncheon date," she says.

"Do you recall the location of that meeting?" All the little details of her memory so that the jury will take with credence whatever damage it is that Lang is intended to inflict here.

"It was at Sabrina's. A restaurant on the Mall. We used to meet there quite often."

There's a lot of nervous posturing here by the witness, aimless smiles at the judge, at Cassidy, at no one in particular. Jennifer Lang seems to know where Cassidy is headed, and instinct tells me she is not particularly anxious to get there.

"Let me take you back to June of last year, Ms. Lang, and ask you if you remember a conversation with another woman, a Ms. Ann Edlin, who worked in your office?"

"I remember Ann."

Suddenly Laurel grips my thigh under the table and leans into my ear. "Ann Edlin," she whispers. "She's on Jack's staff." In hushed tones Laurel tells me that this is trouble. The small world that is the Capitol.

"And do you remember during a conversation relating certain things to Ms. Edlin, things that had been conveyed to you during your earlier luncheon meeting by the defendant, Laurel Vega?"

Jennifer Lang is looking up at the ceiling, her chin quivering, head starting to sway. I think maybe there are tears beginning to well in her eyes.

"But you said—"

"Do you remember . . . ?"

"Yes. I remember talking to Ann."

"Ms. Edlin?"

"Yes."

"And do you remember telling her about matters involving the defendant's marriage, information given to you by Laurel Vega over lunch?"

Lang bites her lower lip like she could chew it off. "I thought we weren't going to have to get into all of this," she whines.

"Just answer the question," says Cassidy. "Do you remember—"

"Yes."

"Let me finish the question. Do you remember telling Ann Edlin about matters involving the defendant's marriage— things related to you by Laurel Vega over lunch?"

"Yes." Lang is upset. It is clear that some deception is being played out by Morgan. She is famous for little agreements, inducements to get a witness to testify, that suddenly go sour when the witness is on the stand. In Cassidy's book this saves time and money that might ordinarily be spent preparing and serving subpoenas.

"Can you tell the court what it was that you and Laurel Vega talked about that day over lunch?"

Lang doesn't have a choice. Cassidy knows what was said, because she has a witness, unless Lang wants to backtrack and claim that she embellished on the earlier conversation when she repeated it to Edlin. The witness, caught in a trap of her own making.

"We talked a lot about a lot of things," she says.

"Like what?"

"Like our kids."

"What else?"

What is happening is clear. Jennifer Lang has fallen into the pit of shifting loyalties. The Capitol employment market is not unlike the human auction blocks of the antebellum South. The only difference is that careers are bought and sold instead of people. This is a place where allegiances shift faster than most of us change our underwear. In such a setting there is no such thing as a friend, at least not an enduring one. Ann Edlin, it seems, quickly found the currency of advancement under the golden dome, a few closely held confidences whispered into the ear of her new boss, Jack Vega.

"We talked about the divorce," says Lang.

"That would be Laurel Vega's divorce from her husband?"

"Right." Lang is seething as she looks at Cassidy, a mix between anger and fear.

"And what did Laurel Vega tell you about that divorce?"

"She said it was becoming particularly difficult because of the children. You should understand—she was very distraught at the time." Lang is trying to sugarcoat it.

"And why was the divorce becoming difficult?"

"Because of the custody issue."

"The children?" prods Cassidy.

Lang nods.

"You have to answer so that the court reporter can *hear* you."

"Yes."

Laurel seems to offer up psychic absolution to her friend at this moment, sitting forward in her chair, an idyllic smile on her face, though she cannot see Lang. Laurel's is a hopeful expression, as if to say, "If the truth will out, I have nothing to fear." Such is the naiveté that seems to run like a disease through Nikki's family and has afflicted Laurel at this moment.

"This was particularly bitter, this custody battle?" says Cassidy.

"You bet. Her husband was being a real prick," she says.

Woodruff looks at her, a wrinkled brow.

"Sorry, your honor. I could say it in other ways, but it would lose something in the translation."

"So Laurel blamed her former husband for this? The custody thing?"

"You bet."

"Did she blame anybody else?"

Cassidy bears down now, going for the jugular. Lang looks at her from the box. She would like to say no, but she has to worry. The prosecutor has clearly talked to Edlin.

"In part she blamed someone else," she says.

"What do you mean in part? Who else *was* there? She didn't blame the children?"

"No. The children wanted to stay with their mother."

"At least that's what she told you?"

"Yes."

"Well, then, who else was there to blame?" Cassidy has her back to me at this moment, but I can image the simpering little grin as she narrows the field.

"His new wife," says Lang.

"Melanie Vega. The victim," she says.

"Yes."

Cassidy pauses for a moment, and for the first time she moves, toward the jury box, facing them square on, like looky what I brought you.

Lang at this moment does not look at Laurel, but stares off, toward the ceiling and the back of the courtroom.

"Tell the court," says Cassidy. "Why did she blame Melanie Vega for her problems in the custody case? Wasn't it Jack, her former husband, who was initiating those proceedings?"

"I think she was very upset. I don't think she knew what she was saying."

"That's not what I asked you," Morgan turns and snaps.

Lang shrinks an inch in the chair.

"Why did she blame Melanie Vega?"

A long sigh from Jennifer Lang, like a body giving up the ghost. Then she says: "Laurel said that Jack would never have gone after the kids if Melanie hadn't put him up to it."

"So she didn't blame Jack, she blamed Melanie?"

"She blamed both of them."

Lang's face is twisted up, a pitch for absolution from the

stand, now aimed directly at Laurel, in which the return is a generous smile. I'm driving my knee into Laurel's thigh to keep her from mouthing words of reassuring friendship to the witness, little encouragements like "It's all right" or "I understand." Knowing Laurel, she will be uttering these when they strap her into the chair in the little green room.

"What else did she tell you?"

"Oh. This is so hard," says Lang.

"Tell the court what she said." Cassidy is now moving on the witness box, closing the distance. I could object, but it would only draw more attention.

"She said Melanie wanted the kids—to spite her. To destroy what was left of her family," says Lang. Each time she speaks it is a spike in our case, fuel to feed their theories of a motive.

"What else?" says Cassidy.

Enough, I think.

Jennifer is starting to break on the stand, tears coming with more frequency, a handkerchief out of her purse.

I could ask for time, to allow the witness to compose herself, but it would only serve to draw this out, lend more drama. What Morgan wants. Instead I am left at the table, feigning expressions of boredom and disinterest. Unfortunately, at this moment, the jury seems riveted.

"What else did she tell you?" says Cassidy.

"She told me—"

"In her own words if you can," Cassidy cuts her off.

Lang regroups, looking off at the middle distance. "She told me—she told me that there were times when she could have killed the bitch."

This is what Morgan has been searching for, the gemstone in this load of swill.

At this moment there's a rustle in the courtroom, one of those seminal moments in a trial where there is a palpable shift in momentum. Morgan senses this and turns the blade in the wound one last time, feeling for that mortal penetration.

"And who was she referring to? Who was the person Laurel Vega was referring to as the bitch?"

A lot of shrugging of shoulders, movement in the box, Lang like some unfortunate fish hooked through the gill.

"Wasn't it Melanie Vega that she was talking about?"

"Yes." An explosion of tears from Lang. "I didn't want to," she says. Imploring looks at Laurel, all the worse for our cause. Not likely that this is a lie, some fabrication concocted by an enemy. It is the stuff of which truth is made in the eyes of a jury.

"That's all for this witness," announces Cassidy.

"Under the circumstances, we should give the witness time," says Woodruff. "Can you go on or would you like a recess?"

Lang motions with her hand that she would rather go on, to finish this now.

"Cross," says Woodruff.

"Ms. Lang, just a couple of questions," I say. "When you heard these words from Laurel, did it strike you that she was serious, that she actually intended to kill Melanie Vega?"

"Objection—calls for speculation on the part of the witness."

"Sustained."

Still, the seed is planted.

"Let me ask you," I say, "in your life, during a moment of extreme frustration or pain, have you ever said to your children, your husband, to a friend, that there are times when you could kill someone?"

"Sure," she says. Lang sees where I am going, anxious to help.

"And when you made such statements, were you serious?"

"No."

"So it was a figure of speech, nothing more?"

"That's true," she says.

"Let me ask you. Did you call the police to alert them when Laurel Vega told you that she could kill Melanie Vega?"

"No," she says.

"And why not?"

I can see Cassidy cringing at the table. "Objection, calls for speculation."

"No, no. I'm not asking the witness to speculate about the defendant's state of mind, but to comment on her own. Why she didn't call the police."

The many ways to slice up evidence.

"Overruled."

"Why didn't you call the police and tell them about this comment on the part of Laurel Vega?"

"Because I didn't think she was serious."

"Exactly," I say. "You viewed it for what it was, a figure of speech and nothing more, isn't that true?"

"Absolutely," she says. A smile on Jennifer's Lang's face, redemption at last.

"That's all I have for this witness."

"Very well, you're excused," says Woodruff.

Lang rises from the stand. She tries to take Laurel's hand at the table, some consolation, a show of support, but I am blocking her way, ushering her through the railing, out of the courtroom. Each move by Lang at this moment, grasping hands of friendship extended to Laurel, is like a pygmy shooting blow darts into the side of our case. It is not possible to assess what damage has been done here, but the fact remains that unlike the subjects in other figures of speech, Melanie Vega is dead. Clearly *someone* wanted to kill the bitch.

CHAPTER
22

It is perhaps the most singular and disturbing part of our case to this point that the one piece of evidence Laurel does not dispute is the testimony of Jennifer Lang. In the hallway to the holding cell after today's session, Laurel apologized for not warning me. She had forgotten the remark made to Lang over lunch so many months before. Idle chatter, she called it. The stuff of a bitter divorce.

All of this makes me wonder if she has said such things to others, whether Harry and I should brace ourselves. I have visions of a procession, Laurel's acquaintances marched to the stand by Cassidy in a line reminiscent of the rush to the Klondike. Hopefully, the damage, which at this point is difficult to assess, is done.

Tonight I am busy getting Sarah ready for bed when the phone rings.

"Hello." The receiver in one hand, I'm trying to untie a knot in Sarah's shoe with the other.

"Hi." The voice on the other end is distant, something from another planet, and for an instant I do not recognize it.

Then I say: "Danny?"

Sarah's eyes grow wide. "Oh, let me talk to him." She makes a swipe for the phone, but misses.

"Later," I tell her.

"Did I call at a bad time?" he asks.

"No. No. Not at all," I tell him. I suppress the urge to ask the one question that I cannot: "Where are you?"

"How's Mom doing? We don't get much news back here, and I'm afraid to write," he says.

It is clear that he and Laurel have discussed this, writing, and that she has cautioned him not to. A return address on an envelope, a postmark, and Jack would be all over her for conspiring to violate the court's order of temporary custody. Letters to the jail are scanned and monitored in a dozen different ways.

"She's doing as well as can be expected, under the circumstances," I tell him.

"Will she be out pretty soon?" he asks.

"We all hope so," I tell him. "We have a ways to go." I don't talk about the downside; what if she's convicted. But I can tell by the silence at the other end that this thought is now being processed in Danny's mind.

"I wanted to call her," he says. "At the jail, I mean. But I'm not supposed to. Mom told me they listen in."

I don't say anything, but issue a few grunts on the phone. I can't participate in this and take the stand if I am called again to testify in the custody case. I must be able to say truthfully that I didn't tell him what to do, that I have no idea where he is.

"Is Dad looking for us?"

"Turning over every rock," I tell him.

He laughs a little, nothing sinister, but amused, that perhaps he has finally outwitted his father.

"You won't tell him that I called."

I tell him his father and I no longer share much information or news of any kind. "When we pass in the hall, we don't even say hello," I tell him.

"I'm sorry," he says, like he is in some way responsible for this.

"Not your fault," I tell him.

"Sure," he says. I can sense some awkwardness on the other end, juvenile insecurities.

"Is Mom gonna have to testify?"

"I don't know. We'll cross that bridge later. There's a lot of evidence against her, and it would probably help to answer some things if she took the stand."

"Then it's not going so good?" he says.

"Some days yes, some days no," I tell him. "We're not throwing in the towel just yet."

"I'm really glad you're helping her," he says. "I know Mom is too. She doesn't always say it, but I know she is."

Visions of Harry and me, Don Quixote and Sancho. I warn him that there are no sure things, a lot of evidence yet ahead of us, imponderables to explain. When he pursues for details I tell him that I cannot discuss these.

"Maybe it would really help if I came back?" he says. "What do you think?"

Laurel would kill me. "That's not for me to say. We shouldn't be having this conversation," I tell him.

"Oh. I didn't realize." The sense of Danny retreating from the receiver at the other end.

Before I can say another word, the operator breaks in. "That'll be another ninety-five cents, please."

I hear the ding of coins tripping the meter of the pay phone.

"We'll have to talk quickly," he says. "I'm running out of quarters."

"Are you okay?" I ask him.

"Oh, yeah. Maggie's real good to us."

The first clue that Julie is with him. I don't ask who Maggie is. I don't want to know.

"Is Julie there?"

"Yeah. Right here. You want to talk to her?"

"Just a word," I say.

Her voice comes on the line. "Hello, Uncle Paul."

"Hi, sweetheart. How are you doing?"

"Not so good, I want to come home," she says. I hear a

lot of grousing on the other end, Danny snatching for the phone.

"Get away. I wanna talk." Julie fighting him off.

"Uncle Paul, I don't know what we're doing here. Can you talk to Mom, see if we can come home?" she asks me.

"Just hang tough," I tell her.

"Mom's got enough problems," I hear Danny's voice intoning.

"We're doing everything we can," I tell her. "It'll be over before you know it. Then we'll talk and see what we're going to do."

"What do you mean?" she says. "Like who we're gonna live with?"

It's tough to bullshit teenagers.

"You're going to live with your mother."

"And what if she's convicted?" she says.

"I don't think that's going to happen."

"What if it does?"

"Gimme the phone." Danny trying to grab it.

"Stop it," I tell them, but they can't hear me. Pain in my ear as the receiver slams into something solid on the other end. Danny wins the battle. His voice comes up on the line.

"Don't bother Mom with this. We're fine," he says.

"Speak for yourself," says Julie.

"I wanna talk." Sarah's tugging at my sleeve.

"Just a minute," I tell her.

"Tell Julie not to worry," I tell him.

"Aw, she's a spoiled brat," he says.

"Your mom wouldn't like to hear that," I tell him. "Give her a break. She's younger than you, and she's scared."

"I'm sorry," he says.

"Is there anything you need?" I ask him.

I have no idea what ruse I would employ to get it there without knowing the destination. My first thought is Harry, the doer of all things suspect. Harry would see this as a minor mission of mercy, and Jack's lawyers would never ferret him out. Danny could call him direct.

"No, we're fine," he says. "Is Sarah still there?"

"Yes."

"Can I talk to her?"

I put my daughter on the line.

"Danny, where are you?" she says.

I want to hum and plug both ears at the same time. I am hoping that Sarah won't repeat some place-name in my presence. I'm using both hands to untie the knot in her shoe while she shows me a toothless grin, talking on the phone.

"Where's that?" she says.

"How far away?"

"What are you doing there?" My daughter is a litany of questions.

"Who is Maggie? Is she nice? Why can't you come home?" she says.

There's a moment of silence as he tries to explain in tones that a seven-year-old might understand.

"You know," she says, "everybody's gone. Yeah," she says. "First Mom." Sarah says this as if her mother is off on a trip, like she may be returning any day. There are times when I have wondered if Sarah has really dealt with the death of her mother or simply withdrawn into her own protected world of fantasy.

"Then Auntie Laurel disappeared, and now you guys," she says. "I want to know what's going on. When are you coming back?" she says. She is actually angry, like "give me a break, enough of these adult games."

For the first time it strikes me what all of this has done to Sarah. Every familiar point of contact in her world now gone. And though I am trying to reassemble a part of her life, getting her aunt out from under the cloud of murder, even this makes me an absentee father who is either in court or locked in his office, mulling over papers until the wee hours.

There is a lapse on the phone, Danny talking. She laughs a little, then listens some more.

"There is a lady," she tells Danny. "Her name is Dana. But I don't like her."

With this I look at Sarah.

She's studying me to see the effect. I suspect that this is intended more for me than Danny.

"I didn't say she was bad or anything." Sarah getting defensive. "Just I don't like her."

"That's not a nice thing to say," I tell her.

She makes a face, like the truth seldom is, her ear glued to the phone.

I have allowed Sarah to grieve for Nikki in her own way, and I see this, her attitude toward Dana, as a part of that normal mourning process. I would deal with it, except that I view it as both necessary and harmless. There is no real hostility here, but rather an undercurrent of suspicion on the part of my daughter toward anyone who might be seen as a surrogate for her mother. In this case the only apparent candidate is Dana, for we seem of late to have been thrown together. The circumstances of Laurel's case have seen to that. For my own part it is not an unpleasant experience, this woman of mystical beauty and quick intellect. In the last week we have spent a couple of warm evenings by the fire at my house, after Sarah has gone down, sipping wine and talking until late. The hum of adult voices heard once more in my home. The communion of two lonely souls.

For the last two days she has been in Washington, D.C., business on the impending judgeship. While Sarah tugged at my sleeve with demands that I read to her, Dana and I have spoken each night by phone, long distance.

We have discussed in general terms a possible vacation to tropic climes in the fall, the three of us. Dana has suggested something like Club Med, where they have special programs for children. So we have started to collect literature.

All of this, I suspect, has generated a kind of rivalry rippling just under the surface, little jealousies that a seven-year-old mind lacks the art to conceal.

Suddenly Sarah is finished talking with Danny. In the abrupt way children end all conversations, she hands me the receiver and is off the bed and down the hall.

"Danny?"

He's still there. "Yeah."

"Don't be a stranger," I tell him. "Call whenever you want." I tell him I'll leave word with my secretary at work to break in if he should call. He has the number.

"Is the Vespa okay?" he says.

"It's fine. But I keep finding Sarah out there playing on it, pretending she's taking you for a ride," I tell him. "But she's very careful."

"That's okay. Just don't let her mess with the box on the back, all right? All my stuff's in there." The world coming apart and Danny is worried about "stuff" in the box on the back of his bike.

"It's locked, remember? I assume you have the key."

"Yeah, well, just tell her to be careful."

"I will," I tell him.

"I'm sorry about all of this," his last words to me on the phone. A boy, growing into a man, taking on the burdens of his mother.

"It's not your problem," I tell him. "We'll work it out. Try not to think about it," I say. And we hang up.

CHAPTER
23

Dr. Simon Angelo is the Capital County coroner hired two years ago from a state back east. He holds degrees from three universities and belongs to a score of professional societies. These litter his curriculum vitae, which Morgan Cassidy has just laid before me on the counsel table.

Angelo is mid-forties, though by dress and appearance he looks older. He has a fringe of graying hair that rings his head above the ears like clouds with their tops sheared in the jet stream. He is slight of build, with sharp features, a chin that finishes the face in a rounded point, and deep-set dark eyes that give the appearance of a mind engaged in perpetual deliberations. Simon Angelo is every man's vision of intrigue at the Court of the Medici.

In front of him this morning, balanced on the railing that forms the front of the witness stand, is a square box, something that in the last century might have contained a woman's hat.

I stipulate on his qualifications to testify as an expert, and Cassidy passes out copies of his résumé to filter through the jury box.

Under the framework of a dozen preliminary questions, Angelo re-creates the death scene: Melanie Vega, lying at the bottom of a dry bathtub, her eyes open, pupils fixed and dilated.

Time of death is the first evidentiary bridge he and Cassidy cross. It is a pivot point because of the argument between Laurel and Melanie on the front porch earlier in the evening. Cassidy would no doubt like to push the murder closer to that point in time.

"Our original report placed it between eleven and eleven-thirty P.M.," he says.

Alarms go off. "Revision on the way."

"And do you still consider that to be an accurate estimate?"

He talks about postmortem lividity and loses the jury in a sea of scientific jargon halfway through.

"Could time of death have been earlier?" says Cassidy.

"It's possible," he says. "Lividity can vary from case to case, and the information here was at best sketchy." What he means is that it was based on observations by the EMTs (Emergency Medical Technicians) before Angelo arrived on the scene.

"So fixing time of death is not an exact science?" she says.

Angelo gives her a benign smile, something well planned.

"Not at all," he says.

They are laying the groundwork for some major wiggle room. Before our pretrial motions, when Cassidy had Mrs. Miller to identify Laurel at the house near the eleven-thirty benchmark that appeared in the coroner's report, the state was more than willing to live with their estimate as to the time of death. Now they would like to fudge a bit. Jurors might wonder why, if Laurel was so intent on killing Melanie, would she argue and then wait for three hours to carry out the deed?

"Is it possible that the death could have occurred as early as eight-thirty?" says Cassidy.

This is less than ten minutes after the two women argued on the porch, and three hours earlier than their original time estimate.

Angelo is a million pained expressions on the stand, the revisionist at work. He tells the court there are factors in this case that are unusual. Whether the body was wet or dry at the time of the crime. This could affect the cooling rate which normally goes into the equation, the fact that eye fluids—another measure of the time of death—were damaged by the fatal bullet. By the time he finishes he has thoroughly discredited his own earlier estimate.

"Upon reflection," he says, "I suppose it is possible that death could have occurred as early as eight-thirty," he tells her.

"Thank you, Doctor."

Indeed. It is why a court of law is not the place for unmasking truth. The two of them have now rewritten the initial coroner's report to conform more closely to the evidence on Cassidy's plate after our pretrial motions.

Laurel leans into my ear, sensing that momentum on an item of import has shifted, asking me the significance. I wave her off. Things are moving too quickly.

"Doctor, can you tell us the cause of death?"

"Death was caused by a single gunshot wound to the head."

"Can you be more specific, describe the wound?" she says.

"If I may, your honor?" Angelo is pointing to the square box in front of him on the railing.

Woodruff nods.

Angelo lifts the lid and pulls a human skull from the box. There are a few gasps, and a lot of murmuring in the courtroom, shifting weight and conversation in the press rows behind us. Laurel grips my leg hard under the table. Then I realize what all the commotion is about. I lean into her ear.

"It's not real," I tell her. "It's only a model."

Angelo has fashioned a plastic life-sized model of the human skull, into which he has drilled a hole approximating the path of the bullet, with parts of brain, bone, and other organs that can be removed. He offers this to me for examination before he testifies.

I rise from the table and take it. It looks identical in every respect to the human form that inspired it. I take it and hold it in my hand, turning it upside down, peering into its cavities and crevices. There are structures inside, visible to the eye, soft tissue that has been re-created and fastened to bone, the tongue and palate with neat holes bored through each, shattered bone I can see, through one eye socket. I would bounce the thing like a basketball if I could, to demonstrate for the jury that there is nothing sacred in this. It is not real.

We talk about what it is made of, resins and polymers.

"Is it identical in every respect to the skull of the deceased?" I ask.

Angelo makes a face. "As close as I could make it without severing the head, removing all the tissue, and making a death-mask mold," he says.

Leave it to me to suggest this. I glance at the jury. They are not happy at this moment. A lot of grim looks in my direction, although three minutes ago I would venture that some of them actually thought this was the severed head of Melanie Vega.

I pass on it for purposes of demonstration, and Angelo drifts into his narrative, explaining the fatal wound to the jury, holding the head like Señor Wences in one hand and a pointer in the other.

"The bullet entered the soft tissue under the angle of the mandible—that's the lower part of the jawbone," says Angelo. "Just to left of the midline. Here." Angelo points to the hole clearly evident under the chin. "It then proceeded in an upward and posterior direction toward the rear of the skull, passing through the sublingual gland, which is just under the tongue, piercing the tongue and the posterior tip of the soft palate."

I can see several of the jurors swallowing hard, a sensation like ice cream glued to the roof of their mouth.

"It then passed through the paranasal sinus cavities, impacted and fractured the sphenoid bone, which forms the floor of the brain pan. Here," he says. "The bullet splintered bone fragments, some of which became embedded in several areas of the brain. The bullet finally came to rest in the left temporal lobe. Here.'' He points one more time.

"Doctor, can you describe the position—whether Melanie Vega was sitting or standing at the time she was shot?''

"According to all of the evidence, we believe that at the time she was shot the victim was lying on her back, reclining on a slant of about forty-five degrees, against the back contour of the tub. Her head was tilted back, lying against the back edge of the tub.'' He holds the back of the skull in the open palm of his hand, the empty eye sockets facing up, toward the ceiling. "About in this position,'' he says.

He rotates the skull in his hand until the crown of the head is facing the far end of the jury box, and the feet, if they were attached, would be off in the direction of our table.

"The fatal bullet was fired from off in about that direction,'' he says. Angelo points with an outstretched arm directly at Laurel. Everything calculated for effect.

"I would estimate the range of fire to be about four to six feet.''

The picture they are painting is clear, a cold and calculating shot while Melanie Vega lay resting in the tub—a veritable execution.

"The angle of fire would be roughly from this direction.'' Angelo brings the steel rod in on a slow line of flight with one hand, toward the skull resting in the other, until it passes between the curving bone of the mandible forming the chin and engages the structures of tissue. He finds the hole pre-drilled in these, and forces the rod past a few obstructions. You can hear the braiding of plastic as the rough steel pushes its way in. A few grimaces in the jury box. He jams the rod into the head, six inches or more, until it becomes lodged, leaving several inches protruding from under the chin at the base of the skull, tracing the line of fire.

I look, and all eyes are on him. The jurors are mesmerized by the clinical brutality of this, as if Angelo has just committed a second act of mayhem on the victim, retracing what the state says my client has done. One of the women, a divorcée I had fought to keep on the panel, is now looking at Laurel with eyes of wonder, how one woman could do this to another.

It seems Laurel herself is looking a little green.

"Could you tell us, Doctor, did this wound cause instantaneous death?" says Cassidy.

"If not instantaneous, the victim died within a very short period of time. Minutes," says Angelo. "There was massive brain damage," he says. "Not only from the bullet but from numerous bone fragments that invaded the brain tissue."

He puts the plastic skull on the railing that forms the front of the jury box, where it rests like some wicked hologram, a head without a body.

Cassidy takes Angelo through some pictures, stills taken at the scene. The doctor identifies these, and after some objection and argument the court settles on five tasteful prints that it says should not enflame the emotions of the jury. These are put into evidence and begin to filter through the jury box. With each passing hand, as the prints make their way, there are eyes darting, quick stolen glimpses of Laurel.

Cassidy asks Angelo about the bullet retrieved from the wound. He describes it as a three-eighty or a nine-millimeter, he's not exactly sure. But when Cassidy shows him a lead bullet in a plastic bag, he identifies it as the one taken from the head of Melanie Vega the morning of the autopsy, pried from her brain with gloved fingers so as not to scar it for possible ballistics comparisons should they later find the weapon.

Next, Cassidy bores in on the evidence Angelo used to determine the range of fire. This is critical to their case. She wants to avoid any hint that there could have been a struggle for the gun, some unintended mishap, or evidence of some lesser crime than capital murder.

Angelo confirms that without the murder weapon it was difficult for ballistics to perform the usual firing tests.

"There was no 'tattooing' around the wound," says Angelo. "But we did detect nitrates, evidence of gunpowder residue, on the upper part of the body. The limited amount of nitrates, and their pattern, some of it deposited in a spreading pattern around the level of the nipples on each breast, would indicate to me a range of fire of between four to six feet.''

Cassidy gets him to explain that tattooing is caused by unexploded grains of gunpowder expelled from the barrel under high pressure. At close range these will impregnate the skin, leaving the equivalent of a tattoo on the skin around the wound. The closer the range, the tighter the pattern.

''Would the lack of tattooing, the probable distance involved in this shot—which you estimate to be between four to six feet—rule out any struggle for the gun?''

''I would think so. If the victim were actually close enough to reach for the gun at the time it was fired, I would expect to see some tattooing on the body somewhere.''

''Besides the absence of tattooing, in your examination of the wound did you find anything else that was in your view peculiar?''

''Yes. I discovered microscopic pieces of metal in the tissues immediately inside the entrance wound.''

''Do you have any opinion as to what caused these?''

''No. Metallurgic reports indicate that the substance in these fragments is composed of a low-quality, low-carbon steel, minute shavings. Since this is not a steel-jacketed bullet, they could not have come from the bullet itself.''

''Then where did they come from?''

''It's hard to say,'' says Angelo. ''My best guess is from the barrel of the gun itself. Some defect,'' he says.

This is clearly lame. Soft lead does not cut case-hardened steel. Still they leave it at that.

Cassidy then turns her attention to the unborn child, the fact that Melanie Vega was pregnant at the time of her death. It is clear that she would end on a high point. In this case emotion.

''Was there any way to tell the gender of this child?''

''It was male.''

"Doctor, can you tell us how far along fetal development was at the time of death?"

"From all indications it was in the early stages of the second trimester. I would say about four months," he says.

"And can you tell us the cause of death for this unborn child?"

"Asphyxiation," he says.

"Please explain?"

"A fetus in the womb has no independent source of sustenance other than from the mother through the umbilical cord. This carries not only nutrition, but oxygenated blood, which keeps the child alive. If the mother dies, her heart ceases to pump blood, and the child's oxygen supply is cut off. Unless the child can sustain life outside of the womb and is removed within minutes, it will suffocate."

"It must have been an agonizing death," she says.

"Objection!" I'm on my feet.

"Is that a question for the witness?" says Woodruff.

"Yes, it is, your honor." Cassidy scrambles to cover up.

"Do you have a medical opinion, Doctor, would this be an agonizing form of death for the unborn child?"

"There are no solid medical studies," he says. "We are not sure how much pain a fetus at that stage of development feels."

I can think of a score of organizations who would be happy to supply him with literature.

There is a hush of voices in the audience, as if there is some serious division of views on this. Several jurors shake their heads. The only one, it seems, who doesn't have an opinion is Laurel. She seems to sit, utterly dazed by the evidence of a dead child. Though we have discussed this several times, the effect on Laurel is always the same: to deliver her into a world of her own.

"Doctor, is there any way to medically ascertain whether the child was potentially viable at the time of the mother's death?"

"Potential viability" as used here means that if left undisturbed, if the mother had not been killed, the fetus would have had every chance of surviving to term, to being delivered healthy and alive.

"It would be my considered medical opinion that this unborn child, the fetus carried by Melanie Vega, suffered from no deformities, no congenital defects or abnormalities that might have prevented a normal birth. For this reason it must be considered potentially viable," he says.

If this stands uncontested, Cassidy will be entitled to a jury instruction at the appropriate time regarding multiple murder—and invoking the death penalty.

When I look over, Morgan is scavenging one more time through the evidence cart, a large manila envelope from which she pulls what appear to be several large color photographs, hues of red and cyanotic blue.

I'm on my feet. "Your honor, if Ms. Cassidy has what I think she has, I'm going to request a recess and a conference in chambers."

"What is it you have there?" says Woodruff.

"Some pictures, your honor." She hands them up to the judge, three color glossies from what I can see, eight-by-ten.

The glasses propped on the end of Woodruff's nose nearly drop off on the bench as he gets a gander.

"We'd better talk," he says.

We're in chambers, Cassidy, Harry, the judge, the court reporter, and myself, all talking at once.

"There's no conceivable reason these shouldn't come in," says Cassidy.

"There's every conceivable reason." I walk on her line.

"Your honor, highly prejudicial," says Harry.

"These are awful." Even Woodruff is on her case.

"Well, excuse me, your honor, but removing a dead unborn child from the womb of its murdered mother can be a little messy." Cassidy leaning on the prerogatives of womanhood, trying to cow the judge. "The next time we'll ask the M.E. to wash it off first, before they shoot pictures."

"That's not what I meant and you know it." This has Woodruff backpedaling, wondering no doubt what women who vote might think of his comment and whether Morgan might carry the message.

"The child is dead," she says. "These pictures evidence that fact. It is a multiple murder and the state is entitled to produce the evidence."

"She has a point," says Woodruff.

"The medical examiner has already testified," I say. "There's no question that the child is dead. The state already has ample evidence. The question here," I tell him, "is whether the pictures are prejudicial. There's no question, they are highly inflammatory."

"What about that?" says Woodruff. He is rubbernecking now, like a zealot at a Ping-Pong tournament, playing for time, looking for some winning point, a backhand smash upon which to hang his decision.

"Fine," she says. "We concede we don't need all three photographs. One will do," she says. "Surely one of these must be acceptable to the court. Under the law, there is a homicide here, and we are entitled to produce the evidence."

Woodruff looks at the photos again. He puts one aside quickly and studies the other two, waffling motions with his head, wavering judgment written in his eyes.

Abstract arguments of unborn death I can deal with. Pictures of an embryonic infant, smaller than the palm of my hand, its oxygen-starved body turned the cyanotic blue of a night sky, is another matter. Confronted with such evidence, jurors become myopic. A terrible crime has been committed—not just an adult who could deal in the world, whose conduct may well have brought her own demise, but an innocent, an unborn infant. On such evidence juries are expected to act. They are not likely to be deterred by theories of another killer from whom they cannot exact justice. If these pictures come in, any one of them, the prosecution has become a locomotive moving on a single track, and Laurel Vega is tied to it.

Woodruff has a hand in the air, about to slap one of the pictures on the desk like a trump card in bridge.

"We will stipulate." I speak before Woodruff can drop his hand.

He looks at me. "Stipulate to what?" he says.

"We'll stipulate to the elements of multiple murder. In return the state puts on no more evidence regarding the unborn child, nothing until closing argument," I say.

Harry's pulling on my arm—"Ullbay itshay"—talking pig Latin in my ear.

I pull away from him.

"The prosecution insists that the photographs are necessary to establish the elements of multiple murder. We will concede that multiple murder has occurred here. Not that my client did it, but that whoever did is guilty of multiple murder."

"Do you understand what you're offering?" says Woodruff. "Once entered into, you can't withdraw it. Giving up all right of appeal on the point later. If she's convicted you're conceding special circumstances, grounds for a capital sentence."

Harry's in my ear. "He's right," he says. "If she goes down, there's no room to wiggle."

I look at him. "If the pictures come in, she goes down," I say. "And then we have to look at them again in the penalty phase. What do we do then?" I ask him.

This, the limited options open to us, saps the wind from Harry's sails.

The only one who seems to take much joy in all of this is Morgan. This is classic Cassidy: confront the court with the repelling images of unborn death, work the judge on all the angles political and legal, and then watch us scramble to make concessions.

"The pictures," I tell Harry, "are all poison. If we have to swallow—"

I look at Woodruff. He gives me a judicial shrug, like fairness compels him to give her one of the photos.

"Then the only question," I tell Harry, "is whether we swallow it now or later."

"We need to confer, your honor." The fight has gone out of Harry, but he's still trying to get me out of the room to talk.

"Either a stipulation or one of the photographs," says Cassidy. "One or the other. Make up your mind."

"Do you want to talk to your client?" says Woodruff. "It's a big point. I think maybe you should talk to her."

Cassidy makes a face of exasperation.

From the glazed look in Laurel's eyes when confronted with the cold evidence of the dead child, questions of a stipulation on points of law at this moment would be the most obtuse of abstractions. I am not likely to penetrate her shell of pain.

"A lawyer's call," I say. "A question of strategy," I tell Woodruff.

He makes a face, conceding the point. "Then what will it be?"

"The stipulation," I tell him. "What else?"

"You got it. The pictures are excluded," he says. "And I don't want to hear anything more about the unborn fetus until closing argument. Is that understood?" He's looking at Cassidy. Woodruff knows what we have given up. He is going to make sure that we get every inch in return.

"We should have the right on redirect with this witness, Dr. Angelo," she says. "To the extent the defense raises the issue on cross."

"For what purpose? You've got your evidence. The elements are proven by the stipulation," says Woodruff.

"If the defense opens the issue—"

"Read my lips, counsel. Not a single w–o–r–d or I will declare a mistrial. Do I make myself clear?"

Cassidy gives him a sick grin. "You won't hear it from me," she says.

"Just so we're clear." At this moment Cassidy is staring into the brushy eyebrows of death. There is not a doubt in my mind that if she crosses him on this point, Austin Woodruff will draw and quarter her.

We huddle over the table to craft the language of a penned stipulation, something that Woodruff can read from the bench into the record.

Harry doesn't have the heart for this. He wanders off, out of chambers, to talk to Laurel.

I've got Angelo on the stand, staring at his beady little eyes in the box.

I have told Laurel what I have done, the stipulation. She seems to accept this with equanimity.

Woodruff has read the stipulation to the jury, a lot of bobbing heads and wondrous looks like they don't know exactly what to make of all this lawyer talk. But the consensus, if I am at all literate in idioms of body language, is that it was not good for the defense.

Angelo has done our case immense damage and he knows it. At this moment he is wary, though he has no reason. It is the first rule of cross-examination: if you can't score, don't wade in.

"I have only a few questions," I tell him. "Points of clarification. Doctor, you testified at length regarding powder residue, the lack of tattooing on the body."

He nods at me.

"Did you bag the hands of the victim at the scene before moving the body?"

"I did."

"Can you explain to the jury why this is done?"

"It's a usual procedure," he says. "Paper bags are placed over the hands and tied or taped at the wrists to ensure that any microscopic evidence under the nails is not lost. It also protects the hands from becoming contaminated by fibers or other trace evidence during transportation."

"Did you check the victim's hands for such evidence during the course of your examination of the body?"

"I did."

"And did you find anything?"

"Nothing of any consequence. The underside of the fingernails were clean. No fibers or tissue. No hair samples. Nothing that might have indicated a scuffle or struggle by the victim prior to death."

"Did you examine the hands for gunpowder residue?"

He gives me a considered look. "No."

"Why not?"

"There didn't seem to be any point. We determined the range of fire to be too far away to have deposited any substantial amounts of residue. And what was the point? She hadn't shot herself. The gun wasn't in her hand."

"You didn't think it was important to determine if she had grabbed the gun, struggled with her assailant?"

"No. I've already testified that wasn't possible."

"You're sure about that?"

"Absolutely," he says.

I nod and leave it.

"Let me ask you, did you ever resolve in your own mind the caliber of the bullet?"

"It's difficult," he says. "Some calibers are very close. Looking at the bullet alone, you can't always be sure."

"I understand. But have you resolved the question as you sit here now?"

"I think ballistics has clearly indicated," he says. He looks in his notes. "Nine-millimeter," he says.

"And you concur with that?"

"I would defer to them on such questions," he says.

"Have you dealt with such bullet wounds before? Nine-millimeter?"

"Many times. It's a common caliber in street crimes."

"Then you're familiar with the type of wound a nine-millimeter bullet can make?"

"Yes."

"The kind of damage it can inflict?"

"At close range it can be very destructive, quite deadly."

"Would you say that the normal nine-millimeter round has good penetrating power? Have you ever seen a nine-millimeter wound that has passed completely through a body?"

"I have seen such wounds."

"Even when the round strikes bone?"

"On occasion, depending on the size of the bone, the girth of the body, it could pass through."

"You say that the shot that killed Melanie Vega was fired a distance of only four to six feet before it struck the victim, and yet it lodged in the midpoint of her brain. Can you explain that?"

"Very few people can explain the course of a bullet. There are too many variables. The powder charge, the weight and substance of the bullet, the density of objects it strikes on its path. Any one of these can account for variations in the depth of penetration."

"So if a bullet passed through an object, it might slow it down?"

"Depending on the object. Of course."

"Let's talk a little about the unexplained fragments of metal in the wound. You testified that you found small specks of metal—steel, I think you said?"

"Low-quality, low-carbon steel. Yes. There were I believe four or five of these."

"Did you conduct any kind of microscopic examination of these before submitting them to metallurgy for testing?"

"Yes."

"What did they look like?"

"Shavings. Like little twisted metal threads."

"And you have no idea what they are?"

"As I said at first, I thought they were shavings of lead, from the bullet. Apparently that was not the case."

"Would you defer to Ballistics on this?"

"Sure. If they know what they are."

"Doctor, let me ask you, how did you first discover that the victim was pregnant?"

"During the course of a complete autopsy it's general procedure to enter the abdominal cavity—"

"Then it wasn't obvious to you from external examination that Melanie Vega was pregnant?"

"No. She made extraordinary efforts to keep her weight down."

"Isn't it strange that no one told you?"

"What do you mean?" he says.

"I mean, this is a woman, four months pregnant, and her husband never told you?"

"I never talked to Mr. Vega."

"But there was no record of such a disclosure by Mr. Vega in the investigative reports, as part of his interview on the evening of the murder? You read those reports, did you not?"

"Yes, I did."

"And there was no disclosure in the reports, was there?"

"No. Not that I recall."

"Don't you consider this unusual, doctor? I mean, a distraught husband, his wife murdered, talking to the police, and he doesn't think to tell them about this double tragedy?"

"Objection. Calls for speculation."

"It calls for expert opinion," I say. "The doctor has performed thousands of autopsies, read thousands of police reports in connection with those autopsies. I'm asking him if as an expert in the field he does not find the failure to disclose such information on the part of a distraught husband to be peculiar."

"I'll allow the question," says Woodruff. "With reference only to your realm of experience, Doctor?"

"A little peculiar, perhaps," he says. "But I suppose the man was quite upset."

"Hmm." I do a little pirouette in front of the witness box,

so that as I speak I am looking away from the witness and toward the prosecution's table.

Harry and I have come up empty on the semen from the sheets of Melanie's bed. The laboratory which examined these for us was unable to complete DNA testing. The dried semen was too old for a valid sampling. So we have finally come to the moment of confrontation. I can no longer conceal my hand.

"Doctor. As part of your examination did you by any chance determine the paternity of the unborn child?"

Cassidy's eyes flash and she grits her teeth. I have crossed the Rubicon, the first overt assault on Jack, the outlines of my defense now seeping through the fog.

Cassidy whispers into Lama's ear. I suspect the same instruction I gave Harry this morning, a subpoena to take blood from Jack Vega. By the time we are finished Jack will have more holes than a pincushion.

There's a stirring in the press rows. Notwithstanding admonitions by the court, it will not take long for this inquiry to filter back to Vega. As a witness he is sequestered outside, where our process server will no doubt find him this afternoon, ministrations with sharp needles to follow.

"It's a simple question, doctor. Did you determine the paternity of the child?"

"To what purpose?" he says.

"Yes or no?"

"No," he says. "There was no reason."

Angelo may not think so, but as I look at them in the box, the question of this child's origin is not lost on the jury.

CHAPTER
24

This morning as the jury files into the courtroom, Dr. Angelo's plastic skull of Melanie Vega rests on the top shelf of the evidence cart, its head pinioned by the steel rod which protrudes over the front edge of the cart, empty eye sockets engaging each juror as they take their seats. Cassidy has no doubt arranged this grim greeting; Melanie's plastic proxy silently asserting its own brief for justice.

Laurel seems gripped by this as she sits next to me, flanked by Harry on the other side; a gruesome visage, she seems to falter just a bit.

As Cassidy arrives in the courtroom, she goes through the same exercise she has performed each day for the past week. Dressed to kill, no pun intended, in a designer suit, she wears a pair of white running shoes. In full view of the jury she opens a paper bag and pulls her leather pumps with two-inch heels. She changes into these at the counsel table. This is a message to the jury that she is no Mercedes-minded lawyer, but just one of the folks, a working stiff like them.

This has several of the women looking, silently taking note. The subtle messages that influence.

As she tries her case, Cassidy is methodical in the way that Sherman was on his march to the sea. She leaves in her wake a scorched landscape of twisted testimony and half-told truths.

If there is a single piece of physical evidence she suspects might give us comfort, she will torture it until any effort to explain its relevance is lost on the jury.

Yesterday Morgan brought on a fibers expert who identified the bits of fluff from Melanie's bathroom floor. She goaded the witness until he finally identified the fibers as similar in all respects to carpet fibers taken from the rug found in Laurel's possession at the time of arrest.

All during this Laurel was protesting in my ear that the carpet taken in Reno was hers, from her own apartment.

This seemed to be borne out by the witness's later testimony. Three minutes later, under cross, I got him to concede that the fibers were as common as grains of sand on a beach, sold by a score of manufacturers and found in half the homes of America. The witness readily conceded that he could not state with scientific certainty that the fibers in the evidence bag came from Laurel's rug. I could tell that by the time he left the stand the man was wondering why Cassidy had called him at all. But then she leaves no stone unturned. After all, the other side can always stumble.

For Morgan it was just one more reach, but no ring, so this morning we do ballistics.

Nico Perone is the resident ballistics expert. Short, balding, and with a gut that hangs over his belt like Santa's toy bag. As a witness he does not make a good appearance. If you were selling scandal on a national scale and Nico had a corner on the market, you would not race to put him on the tube's morning talk-show circuit. The man's respiration is elevated by the two-step climb into the witness box. Perone could work up a good sweat in January on a stroll in the Arctic. As for his dress, Nico wears part of this morning's breakfast and what looks like last evening's dinner on his tie.

In the battle of cops against criminals, he is a partisan and a front-line fighter, a friend and follower of Jimmy Lama's. There is nothing objective about Perone's science. I have seen him slip and stumble in a few cases, usually into pits of his own making, stretching the evidence to fit the crime.

This morning he is on the stand, ready to swim in his own perspiration. The sleeve ends of his coat are already dripping from where they have mopped his head, and Cassidy, the friendly one, has merely asked him his name.

They cut through the preliminaries, the courses Nico has taken at the FBI Crime Lab in Washington and other places that qualify him as a witness. Morgan shows him the bullet in the little bag, and he identifies it as the one he examined and upon which he rendered a report in connection with Melanie's murder.

"Mr. Perone, what can you tell us about the characteristics of this bullet? Its caliber and weight?"

"Nine-millimeter, Luger," he says.

"Is that a make?"

"Style," says Nico. "Some people call it a parabellum. First introduced for use in the Luger automatic pistol in the early part of the century," he says. "That one weighed in at a hundred and twelve grains. I'd be willing to bet, however, that it was a hundred and fifteen when it was made."

"Is that a professional opinion?"

"Yeah. 'Cuz they don't make it in a hundred-and-twelve-grain weight," he says.

There's a few smiles in the jury box.

"I'd take book," he says. "The rest of that bullet got itself lost somewhere inside the victim," he tells her.

"You mean fragments that dislodged?" says Cassidy.

"Yeah."

Watching them work together, Nico and Morgan, is an experiment in chemistry. Nico has never come across as professional. He has all the polish of a cast-off pair of shoes on the feet of some vagrant.

"Besides its caliber, can you tell the jury what kind of bullet this is, what it's made of?" she says.

"A lead alloy," he tells her. "That's what is known as a lead hollow-point. That particular kind of bullet comes in three types," he says, "lead hollow-point, lead with a partial steel jacket, and a fully jacketed round. A jacket means the lead in the bullet is either partially or fully covered in a steel outer casing," he says.

"What's the difference in performance?" says Cassidy.

"Lead and partial-jacket have a tendency to jam, but they got more stopping power. Full jacket works smoothly through the action of the firearm, don't jam as much, but it don't spread either. Less stopping power. The lead, when it hits something hard, tends to spread. You can see on this one we got a little mushroom." Nico's holding the bag with the bullet in his hand now.

"A mushroom?" says Cassidy.

"Yeah. You can see where the bullet hit something, probably bone, and ballooned out at the tip." He points with his thumbnail.

"See? Right there," he says.

"And this would cause more damage?"

"You bet. If a bullet spreads, it transfers more kinetic energy to the target. That causes more damage. What shooters call stopping power."

"Would you consider this a pretty deadly round?"

"Sure. At close range it's real effective. What many police agencies use today, though most of their bullets are jacketed."

"So in your professional opinion the bullet in this bag has more stopping power than bullets used in standard-issue police weapons of the same caliber?"

"Oh, yeah. Whoever used this one was looking to do a number," he says.

"Objection."

"Sustained. Just answer the questions," says Woodruff.

Cassidy moves away for a moment to regroup. This gives Nico a chance to wet his coatsleeve to the elbow.

"Let me ask you, Mr. Perone, did you have occasion to perform any kind of microscopic examination of the bullet in that bag?"

"I did."

"And what did you find?"

"The lands and grooves, the marks left on the bullet from the barrel of the firearm, indicated a right-hand twist. Pretty common for many types of manufactured handguns."

"Anything else?"

"Yeah. There was something wrong with the gun. Besides the lands and grooves, there were little ridges cut in the sides of the bullet, some kind of a defect in the bore of the weapon."

"Could you tell what caused this?"

He makes a face and shakes his head. "If I had to guess—"

"No guessing. Your professional opinion," she says.

"Sure. My professional opinion. I would guess maybe some oxidation in the barrel. Little pits of rust," he says. "Sometimes these cause little microscopic ridges that drag on the bullet as it runs down the barrel."

Cassidy's giving him slow nods on all of this. Her task here is not to score any particular points. A bullet is a bullet. This particular one happened to kill Melanie Vega.

Instead Morgan's role is to account for any anomalies in the evidence, to raise any possible inconsistencies before we can, and to resolve them as nothing unusual, to steal any wind we might try to use to puff up the sails of our case, to prevent us from making our own theory of what happened seem more plausible than hers.

She moves to the evidence cart and comes back with another little bag, this one containing the brass cartridge found on the floor at the scene.

"Mr. Perone, I would ask you to look at the bullet casing in this bag and ask if you've had an opportunity to examine it."

He turns the bag over, studies it for a moment.

"Yeah. I have."

"Can you tell us what caliber it is?"

"It's a nine-millimeter Luger."

''The same as the bullet in the other bag?''

''That's right.''

''Is there any way that you can tell whether this bullet and this cartridge were at one time part of the same loaded or complete bullet?''

''Very difficult,'' he says. ''Particularly with a nine-millimeter parabellum. Because they don't generally crimp the round when they load 'em.''

''What do you mean by 'crimp the round'?''

''When you load a cartridge, the last step in the process is called seating the bullet. This can be done manually, with a loading press, or by a machine in a plant. Either way, when the bullet is seated, the die, the part that presses it into the cartridge casing, either crimps the edge of the casing a little around the bullet to hold it or it doesn't. On the nine-millimeter most dies don't crimp.''

''Why is that significant?''

''If the casing is crimped, it's difficult, but there's a chance that you can match up irregularities around the mouth of the casing with impressions left on the bullet where it's crimped. If it ain't crimped you can forget it.''

''And this one?''

''You can forget it.''

''So there's no way you can tell us whether this bullet and this cartridge were part of the same complete unfired bullet at one point?''

''I can't.''

''Let's turn our attention to the cartridge casing,'' she says. ''Is there anything you can tell us about this casing?''

''It's a reload,'' he says.

''What does that mean?''

''It means the cartridge has been fired and reloaded—in the case of that one, many times.''

''How can you tell this?''

''Tool marks on the rim for one thing. A semiautomatic pistol—that bullet is generally fired from a semiautomatic—

discharges the casing after it's fired. It ejects it from an ejection port, an opening in the side or the top of the firearm. To do that, an ejector has to grip the rim of the empty cartridge and pull it out of the chamber. This leaves little tool marks on the rim.''

"How many tool marks did you find on the cartridge in question?"

"At least eight that I could identify."

"Would this mean that the bullet was reloaded at least eight times?"

"Not necessarily. Some of them could have been caused by whackin' off."

Cassidy looks at him like maybe she hasn't heard him right. Harry starts to snigger. Cassidy shoots him a glance, and Hinds coughs to cover up.

"Manual ejection," he says. "You put the bullet in the magazine, maybe with others, and then manually you work the bolt or the return back and forth, seating the bullets in the chamber and ejecting them one at time, without firing. Sometimes people do this to make sure a gun won't jam when they go to fire it. In the trade, some people call it whackin' off."

"No need to explain," she tells him.

Knowing Nico, he might show the jury.

"But how do you know that all the tool marks on this casing weren't caused by manual ejection?"

"Because there's other marks that tell us it's a reload."

"What kind of marks?"

"There's stress and metal fatigue that you can see under a microscope, and what we call sizing marks, along the side of the cartridge. Bullet casings are usually made of brass or some other soft metal. They tend to expand when fired. Once they're ejected, you ain't gonna get 'em back into the chamber of the weapon unless you first put 'em in a sizing die and press them back down to size. When you do this, to reload the round, it leaves stress marks on the cartridge. Also, the end of the casing, the part that hits up against the breechblock, will start to show wear after it's been fired a few times. On this one you can barely read the word *Luger*."

"What does that tell you, Mr. Perone?"

"That tells me that the casing in your hand has been fired more times than some pimp's pecker," he says.

Perone is Harry's kind of witness.

"Wonderful." A pained look from Morgan, like "see what the state gives me to work with."

"Let's keep it on a professional plane," says Woodruff.

"Sorry, your honor." Nico gives the judge a grin.

"Assuming someone didn't have the equipment to reload this type of ammunition, is it possible for a man or woman to obtain this kind of reloaded ammunition?"

"Sure. You can get it at any shooting range. Some gun shops sell reloads. You can pick it up at gun shows by the bushel. A million places," he says.

This is the critical point that Cassidy is making with this witness—that anybody, including Laurel, could have obtained the bullet that killed Melanie Vega.

"So there's no way to tell where this ammunition might have come from?"

"Not really."

"Let me ask you, is there any way to tell what kind of gun this bullet was fired from?"

"We know that at one time or another it was fired from at least four different firearms. Tool marks, ejection marks, will sometimes give you a clue as to the make of gun. In this case there's too many marks, some over others. There's no way with a bullet that has seen that much wear."

"So you couldn't tell us the make or model of the weapon used to kill Melanie Vega?"

"No."

"If the gun were found, would it be possible to do a comparison to match the bullet to the firearm?"

"Oh, sure. There's enough of the bullet there. But we'd have to have the gun. Then we could try and do a match."

Cassidy doing a lot of nodding, the message clear, of course they have no gun because the killer got rid of it.

"Mr. Perone, have you ever performed gunpowder-residue tests?"

"Yes."

"Can you explain to the jury what such tests are designed to do?"

The hair on my neck starts to rise.

"GSR is used to determine if nitrates or other residues from the discharge of a firearm have deposited themselves on the hands, face, or clothing of a suspect. The residues can be chemically collected and removed for testing."

"And let me ask you—did your office try to perform gun-powder-residue tests on the defendant, Laurel Vega, immediately following her arrest and removal to Capital County?"

"Your honor, may we approach?" I'm on my feet.

Woodruff waves us on, a sidebar to the other side of the bench, away from the witness.

"What are you getting into, Ms. Cassidy? Remember we talked about inferences," says the judge.

There's a lot of whispering at the bench, hands shading the side of mouths.

"I haven't said a thing about what happened to her hands," says Morgan.

"But you're getting pretty close," I say.

"Your honor, we should have the right to ask the witness whether he was able to do GSR, and if not, why," she says. "Nothing more. Just that."

"Oh, sure," I say. "The defendant slopped her hands in solvents. Now, we don't mean to infer anything by this, but it sure as hell screwed up our gunpowder tests. Sure, just let the jury form its own conclusions."

"Isn't that what it's all about?" She looks at me and smiles.

"I'm inclined," says Woodruff, "to let her ask. But keep it short and narrow," he says.

I'm rolling my eyes.

We're back to the tables.

"Did your office try to perform gunpowder-residue tests on the defendant, Laurel Vega, immediately following her arrest and removal to Capital County?"

"Yes."

"And were you able to do so?"

"No."

"Can you tell the court why not?"

"The defendant's hands had been chemically burned. Some laundry solvents had gotten all over them. Under the circumstances they were contaminated and GSR tests weren't possible."

"These chemicals would interfere with the tests—is that right? Make it impossible to detect gunpowder residue?"

"Yes."

"Why is that?"

"Ms. Cassidy, you're treading," says Woodruff.

She looks at him. "I'll withdraw the question," she says. "I have nothing more for this witness."

I'm champing at the bit when I get to my feet.

"Mr. Perone, let me ask you—you say that GSR tests are generally used to detect gunpowder residue from the clothing, hands, and face of a suspect. Is that right?"

He makes a face. "Yeah. More or less," he says.

"Well, are they or aren't they?"

"Yeah. They are."

"Did you perform GSR tests on Laurel Vega's clothing after her arrest?"

"Yeah."

"And did you find any gunpowder residue, any evidence on her clothing that she had recently fired a firearm?"

"Objection. Exceeds the scope of direct," says Cassidy. "Your honor, I limited my questions to the defendant's hands."

"She questioned the witness about gunpowder residue," I say. "She opened the issue."

Morgan's getting into it with Woodruff, telling the judge that if I want to get into other areas I can call the witness in my own case-in-chief.

"Overruled," says Woodruff. "The witness will answer the question." A lesson to Cassidy, one walk too many on the wild side with Chuckles.

"Mr. Perone, did you find evidence of gunpowder residue on Laurel Vega's clothing immediately following her arrest?"

"No."

"After her arrest did you examine the area around the defendant's face and neck for evidence of gunpowder residue?"

"Uh-huh."

"I didn't hear you," I say.

"Yeah."

"And did you find any gunpowder residue on her face and neck indicating that she might have recently discharged a firearm?"

"No. But it had been a few days since the shooting to the point of arrest. She probably showered or bathed."

I look at Cassidy. She is steaming at the table, looking at Woodruff, optic slits that could kill.

"Mr. Perone, I call your attention to the little marks on the bullet. I think the district attorney referred to them as little ridges. Do you remember these?"

"Yeah."

"You said that you weren't sure how these were caused, but that it might have been the result of rust in the barrel of the firearm, is that correct?"

"One theory," he says. "Unless you got a better one."

"I'm not here to answer questions," I say. "You are."

Nico wipes some more sweat from his brow.

"Let me ask you, are you aware of small fragments of metal found in the fatal wound of the deceased, Melanie Vega?"

"Objection," says Cassidy. "Exceeds the scope of direct."

"I'm working on the little ridges, your honor. I think I can demonstrate a connection."

"If you can," says Woodruff, "subject to a motion to strike. Keep it short," he says.

"Did you ever see a report regarding these metal fragments, Mr. Perone? The ones found in the victim?"

"Yeah."

"Were the fragments sent to your office for analysis?"

"Metallurgy," he says. "They consulted with us."

"And did you have an opinion as to the origins of these fragments?"

He makes a face. "Low-quality steel," he says. "Bullet could have passed through something."

"Where?" I say. "The victim was completely unclothed at the time she was shot. The bullet wasn't fired from outside, through a screen, was it?"

"Not that I know of."

"Nothing was found at the scene with a bullet hole in it. Did you find a metal object that was shot up?"

"No."

"Well, then, where did these metal fragments come from?"

"Your guess is as good as mine," he says.

"You're the expert," I tell him.

"They don't give out crystal balls at the FBI ballistics lab," he says. "You guys got the corner on those." Nico does a gesture with one hand to his crotch, grabbing, something from Michael Jackson. This is all down below the railing of the witness box, where the jury can't see it. When pushed on the stand, Nico will show you his credentials—a charter member of fuck-the-lawyers club.

"So you think it was something that the bullet passed through on its way to the target that caused these metal fragments to be deposited in the wound?"

"Been known to happen," he says.

"These, the fragments, are described as microscopic threads of low-carbon steel?"

"That's what they say," says Perone.

"Metallurgy?"

"Yeah."

I take a little walk in front of the witness stand—some posturing for effect.

"As a ballistics expert, is it safe to say that you come into contact with a good many assorted items besides guns and bullets?"

"Like what?" he says.

"Like explosive devices, silencers, Taser weapons that fire projectiles?"

"We see some of those."

"So you have pretty broad expertise?"

"You could say that," he says.

"You can't generally buy this stuff? I mean, a good time-delay bomb or something detonated by remote control?" I say. "Still, some people make them, don't they?"

"Yeah, sure," he says. "You can buy how-to books, get articles in the *Soldier of Fortune* press. If you're good with your hands," he says, "and you don't splatter yourself all over the ceiling, you might make a bomb that works."

"Your honor." Cassidy's out of her chair. "Unless I've missed something, the victim wasn't killed by a bomb."

"If you could bear with me, your honor."

Woodruff motions with his hands, like hurry up.

"So all this stuff—bombs and silencers—can be handmade if you have some skill and know what you're doing?"

"Sure."

"For example, if somebody came up to you and asked you how to make a silencer, what would you tell them?"

"For starters that possession's illegal," he says.

"Of course. But just as an example, if you wanted to, you could tell them how to make one, couldn't you?"

"Sure."

"How?"

"Right here?" he says.

"Why not? The information's not illegal, is it?"

"No."

I motion for him to go on.

"You get two pieces of metal tubing," he says. "One quite a bit larger in diameter than the other. You drill a lot of holes in the smaller tube, like Swiss cheese," he says. "Then you put the smaller tube inside of the bigger one. You gotta leave an air pocket between 'em. You find some way to fasten the two pieces of tube together, usually some kind of a flange. The inside tube has to be just a little bigger than the bore on the barrel of the firearm. You figure a way to fasten it to the end of the barrel. Usually threaded."

"That's it?"

"You'd want to pack some kind of material to deaden the sound. Put something into the air space between the two tubes," he says.

"Like what?"

He makes a face. "Something that wouldn't burn if it got hot. In the old days, the wise guys in New York and Chicago, some of 'em used little sheets of asbestos, rolled up," he says. "Guess if they did much business, their lungs went to shit." He laughs, all alone.

Nico gives Woodruff a nervous grin. "Sorry, your honor. My language. But I guess you could say poetic justice," he says.

"So what do they use today? To deaden the sound?" I ask him.

"Whatever won't burn. Steel woo—" He stops before the words clear his lips.

"Yes?"

"Steel wool. Some people use steel wool," he says. The look in Perone's eyes at this moment is perhaps the most I will receive by way of a fee in this case.

"And when you pack that steel wool, pieces would work their way through the little holes of the inside tube, wouldn't they?"

Nico's nodding his head like he's in a daze.

"Wouldn't they?"

"They could," he says.

"So that a bullet traveling down that tube might pick up tiny threads, small fragments of low-quality steel, steel wool," I say. "And the bullet might carry these, might deposit them in a wound. Isn't that right?" I say.

By now Perone is no longer responding to my questions. Instead he is looking at Cassidy, wondering what degree of wrath he will receive when she gets him outside of the courtroom. He has delivered to her doorstep, packaged and ticking, the one thing any good trial lawyer hates, surprise.

"The steel wool of a silencer might leave little unexplained grooves and ridges in the lead of a soft, unjacketed bullet? Isn't that right, Mr. Perone?"

He's nodding—grudging concessions from the stand.

"Answer the question," I say.

"Yeah," he says. "It's possible."

"A silencer would answer a lot of questions," I say. "Wouldn't it? Like why there was so little soot or gunshot residue on the victim. Why there was no tattooing on the body."

Much of this would have been filtered by the silencer, and Nico knows it.

"It might," he says.

"It would also explain why no one heard the shot that killed Melanie Vega, wouldn't it?"

He looks at me, stone-cold eyes.

"A possibility," he says.

"That's all I have for this witness."

As I turn for the table it is with some sense of satisfaction. All of this leaves the prosecution to make a considerable reach if it is going to sell the theory that Laurel pulled the trigger. She must either run in circles of intrigue that rival James Bond or they must have the jury buy into notions that my sister-in-law is the modern merger of Henry Ford and Annie Oakley, a woman who not only loads her own ammunition, but is master of the tool and die, somebody capable of fashioning to tight tolerances a silencer for a semi-automatic handgun—the things that can stretch credulity in a trial.

CHAPTER
25

This afternoon the courtroom is cloaked in the muted light of flickering images from a large television monitor, rolled out in front of the jury panel, the overhead lights turned low.

Harry and I, Cassidy and Lama, jockey for location at each end of the jury box to see the screen. Laurel has moved from the counsel table and is shadowed in the courtroom by a matron who hovers a few feet behind her with each step that she takes. The judge is off the bench, white hair, brushy eyebrows, and flowing robes, a phantom in one dark corner of the room.

On the screen are the florid images of Laurel captured on color videotape, charging across a crowded corridor in this same building, seven months ago, two floors below where we now stand, to lash out with her purse like a leaded sap. It crashes on Jack's shoulder, skimming an inch past Melanie's face, sending the purses of both women crashing to the floor, their contents scattered.

Cassidy asks that the tape be shown again. This time it is rewound further back. In her headlong charge, Laurel knocks down an old man who had the misfortune to wander into the path of fury. Laurel does not even break stride. The unmistakable explosion of her rage, tracking on Melanie like a heat-seeking missile. For lawyers attempting to make out a motive for murder, it is the pictorial equivalent of a million words.

Caught dead center on the screen, Laurel's face is flushed,

filled with fury, and while the video images afford no sound, angry words can be read on her lips, threats being spit like toxin from a cobra.

It takes three people to ultimately block her way. I am one of these. The broken strap of Laurel's handbag is outstretched in her hands at Melanie Vega's throat as I haul Laurel away. Melanie's purse is on the floor, and as I struggle with Laurel, the camera catches me roller-skating on a cylinder of lipstick. So much for grace.

Cassidy has these images played back a third time for the jury just in case they missed some part of it, this last rendition in slow motion so that they can fully appreciate the choreography of this rage.

Then the monitor on its cart is rolled to one side.

Lama is puffed up with himself. It was Jimmy who found the tape and brought it to Cassidy, ferreted it out, information from the courthouse groupies who told him about the brawl.

As the lights come back up, Morgan has a witness on the stand. He is midway through his testimony, having been interrupted only long enough to show the video. George Ranklin, the bailiff who was outside of Department Fourteen the day of the altercation, has laid the foundation for introduction of the tape. Lama spent ten minutes outside the courtroom prepping him.

Morgan quickly gets Ranklin to testify that he was close enough during the courthouse incident to hear angry words spoken by Laurel.

"Officer, can you tell us, as you sit here today do you recall what it was exactly that Laurel Vega said during the attack on the victim?"

"I heard her say, 'I'll kill the bitch.' "

It is one of those seminal moments in a trial, an alleged perpetrator spouting prophesies, the kind of statement which after an act of murder makes little hairs stand out on the neck of those who hear them. Several of the jurors now take a moment to study Laurel.

At this moment, when she is the object of their interest, Laurel is in my ear, an ardent plea that this is not true.

"You were there," she says. "You heard it. You know I didn't say that."

The "b" word is evident on the tape; the rest of it I think is some artful suggestion by Lama. I have no such recollection of any death threat, though in private moments, in the confidence of the jailhouse cubicle, Laurel has said as much to me, that if someone else had not acted first, she could indeed have killed Melanie.

"Were those the defendant's exact words?" says Cassidy.

Ranklin makes a face. " 'Let me kill the bitch,' or 'I'll kill the bitch,' something like that," he says. "It was a long time ago in a crowded room with a lot of noise."

Morgan strides toward the jury. " 'Let me kill the bitch,' " and she looks at Ranklin purposefully—"or 'I'll kill the bitch.' " She repeats the witness's words while Lama emits glazed expressions of malicious pleasure from the counsel table.

"That's what I remember," says Ranklin.

"And when did she say this?"

"While she was being restrained," he says. "Immediately after she attempted to strike the victim."

"Who was doing the restraining?"

"I recall that it took a couple of gentlemen," he says. "Her lawyer, over there." He points to me. "And one or two others."

"But you have no doubt that those were her words: 'Let me kill the bitch,' or 'I'll kill the bitch'?" Given the chance, Cassidy would carve these words over the judge's chair, just under the state seal and its motto of "Eureka."

"That's what I heard."

"Officer, do you recall reading about the murder of Melanie Vega in the press?"

"Sure," he says. "It was big news. Of particular attention to those of us who worked in the courthouse, because we were seeing the Vegas every day in court during the custody case,'' he says.

"And you remember that this altercation—the attack by the defendant on Melanie Vega—as having occurred on the afternoon of the same day that Melanie Vega was murdered, is that correct?''

"Yes. There was a lot of talk about it in the courthouse the next day.''

"Talk by who?''

"The people who worked there, who'd heard about the ruckus between the two women.''

"So would you say there was a general perception on the part of people who had followed the custody case that there was bad blood between the two women?''

"Objection. Calls for speculation.''

"Withdrawn,'' says Cassidy.

"Did you have occasion to watch any portions of the Vega custody case while you were on duty?''

"I saw some of it,'' says Ranklin. "A few hours.''

"And from your own personal observations, was it your impression that there was a general sense of animosity harbored by the defendant, Laurel Vega, toward Melanie Vega?''

Ranklin laughs. "It comes with the turf. A bitter divorce. Disagreement over custody. Sure. There was bad blood,'' he says. "It was obvious to anybody who watched.''

"Thank you, Officer. The witness is yours,'' says Cassidy. She takes her seat next to Lama, who as he looks at me is the picture of satisfaction.

Ranklin is in his mid-twenties, a fixture in the courthouse for the last five years. He has bounced between assignments in a couple of departments. I have seen him a hundred times in the elevators, nodded to him, and said hello. He is a friendly soul, a strapping kid, well over six feet, an advantage for security in a courthouse setting, the ability to intimidate without resort to a weapon.

Ranklin is a bit of cipher to me, so I probe carefully around the edges, not anxious to cause any irritation. I paint him quickly into the posture of the neutral law-enforcement officer that he is, just doing his job. It is how the jury will no doubt see him. I want them to know that I am looking through the same-colored prism that they are using. Perspective is everything.

"In your position with the court you must observe a lot of trials? You spend more time in this place than I do."

He agrees, and laughs a little. This sands some of the edge off any anxiety. Many young defense lawyers have learned through sorry experience that you can do your case no end of damage by leveling a broadside on a detached and neutral cop.

"I suppose you would develop a keen sense for reading witnesses on the stand? A well-tuned ear for hostility?"

He concedes that this is something one picks up.

"Did you actually have occasion to hear or see any of the testimony of the defendant, Laurel Vega, when she appeared in the custody case?"

He says that he did not, that he was in another department at the time.

"So other than the brief encounter out in the hallway you never had an opportunity to personally observe any statements by the defendant as they might have reflected on her feelings toward the victim?"

"That's true," he says.

If he saw parts of the custody case, and formed opinions of bad blood between the two women, there is only one other possibility. Ranklin must have listened to Melanie Vega harangue Laurel from the stand. While this might reflect more on Melanie's hostility toward Laurel, it is still Melanie who is dead. That I might be able to show that she inspired her own demise still serves to flesh out a neat motive. So I leave it alone.

"Officer Ranklin, let me ask you, are you absolutely certain that outside of the courtroom that day you heard Laurel Vega say she wanted to kill Melanie Vega, that she actually used the word 'kill'?''

''That's what I heard.''

''Are you certain that she might not have used the word 'bitch,' and said something else?''

''No. She called her a bitch and said she wanted to kill her.''

Lama has done his homework on this one—Mr. Persuasion. Ask me what I heard in a conversation, even an angry one, seven months ago and I would be lucky if I could remember the participants, much less the words that were used.

''Officer, did you have to make any efforts to restrain the defendant as a result of what we have just observed on the videotape?''

''No. You were doing a pretty good job of that as I recall,'' he says.

''So the defendant did not persist in her attempts to reach Melanie Vega?''

''I don't know that I would go that far.''

Ranklin insists that he heard a death threat, so my job is to live with the words but to diminish their import. I try another tack.

''Would you characterize the event as a quick flash of anger that seemed to pass in a couple of seconds?''

He mulls this over, makes a face. ''I guess you could call it that,'' he says. Finally a concession.

''And you didn't actually have to step in between the two women to break it up, did you?''

''No.''

''In your capacity performing court duties, have you ever had to physically restrain parties or members of the public during a trial or other proceedings?''

''Several times,'' he says.

''And have you ever heard threats being uttered by people during such heated moments?''

''It's not uncommon,'' he says.

''Death threats?'' I say.

''Yes.''

''And isn't it your experience that in most cases those threats are in fact idle? That they are not carried out? Isn't that what occurs in most cases, people making foolish statements they don't mean in the heat of an argument?''

This is something readily in the experience of every juror. There is only one credible answer and Ranklin knows it.

''That's true,'' he says.

''And at the time that you say you heard the defendant make such a threat against Melanie Vega, was there anything peculiar about it that would cause you to think the words were anything other than idle words of anger?''

Ranklin is in a box on this. If he says there was, it begs the question, ''Then why, Officer, did you not take her into custody?''

''No,'' he says.

''So you believed it was an idle threat?''

''Yes.''

''And in fact, as you sit here today, knowing all the things that you know about this case, based solely on your personal knowledge of the facts as you know them, you cannot tell the jury that the words uttered that day by Laurel Vega were in fact anything but an idle threat, isn't that true, Officer?''

''I suppose,'' he says. Ranklin is more grudging on this, not sure exactly what he is giving up.

''You don't have any personal knowledge that Laurel Vega actually killed Melanie Vega, do you?'' I clarify it for him.

''Oh. No,'' he says, happier with the inference this conveys.

''And you didn't bring any charges against either woman as a result of the events you witnessed in the corridor, did you, Officer?''

''Well . . . no.''

''Why not?''

''It was a judgment call,'' he says.

"It was over as quickly as it started? Nobody was hurt?" I say.

"That's right."

I leave it alone. Push some more and he may tell me that in fact it was a mistake in judgment, that on reflection he should have taken Laurel into custody. The subtle suggestion will not be lost on the jury—that if he had, a murder might have been prevented.

"Fine. Let's talk about what happened after this altercation was over. Do you remember what you said to me at the scene?"

Ranklin makes a face. Looks at me. "Can't say that I do."

"Do you remember suggesting something to me?"

He thinks for a moment. Draws a blank. "No."

On cross I can lead. I make the most of it and end up testifying.

"Don't you remember telling me that I might want to take my client to the lawyers' conference area so that she could compose herself?"

Cassidy's about to rise and object.

"Oh, yeah. I remember that."

"Before we left, before I took the defendant and left the corridor, do you recall what happened?"

"It's been a long time," he says.

Not so long, however, that he doesn't remember a death threat that never took place.

"Do you remember picking up a woman's purse from the floor? People helping to gather the items that had fallen and been kicked around on the floor?"

"Oh, that," he says. "I remember a handkerchief. I tried to give it to one of them, but she said it didn't belong to her."

"That's right," I say. "Maybe we could take another look at the tape, Officer."

I ask Woodruff's bailiff to roll out the monitor and hit the lights. Ranklin comes off the stand so he can see better. The judge comes down from the bench. The bailiff starts to rewind the tape, and I stop him.

"Pick it up from right there," I tell him.

"But the altercation's back further," he says.

"That's all right. Run it from there."

Woodruff's bailiff makes a face, like "it's your show." When the picture comes up, we are all gathered in a tight cluster in the center of the courthouse corridor, Laurel and Melanie, Jack between them, and myself tugging on Laurel's arm. Ranklin is holding the hanky that Melanie has just rejected. Somebody hands him the purse with the broken strap, and he puts the handkerchief in it.

"There's the handkerchief," he says.

"I see it."

People are passing items to Ranklin. He's not looking, but taking them in his hands, talking to me, eyeing Laurel and dropping the items into the purse. A couple of seconds later he hands this to Laurel and we turn and walk away.

"Could you rewind it and then play it back in slow motion?"

"Whatever." The bailiff punches buttons on the remote. He starts to play forward. Melanie brushing the handkerchief off Jack's pants. Ranklin picking it up. Somebody handing him the purse.

"Go slow."

"There—I think she just called her a bitch." Ranklin's trying to read lips. "Can't make out the rest," he says.

"Stop. Right there. Back it up a few frames," I tell the bailiff.

He plays it back and puts it in freeze-frame.

"Officer Ranklin—what is that in your right hand?"

He strains to look. "Something somebody handed me off the floor," he says. "From one of the purses."

"Can you tell me what it is?" I ask.

Only Ranklin would not comprehend the significance of this, because he's been sequestered outside of the courtroom, as a witness, told not to read any accounts of the trial.

"It looks like a woman's gold compact," he says.

The expression on Jimmy Lama's face is worth a year's income. It is the sick image of defeat pumped from the stomach of victory. Lama's eyes are wide with denial, his palms upturned, offering gestures of bewilderment to Cassidy.

On the screen is an image worth a thousand explanations and lame accountings—the bailiff handing Laurel her purse, and in it, Melanie Vega's gold compact.

CHAPTER
26

This afternoon it is nearly five when I get back to the office. There are messages, a pile of pink slips littering my desk.

I do telephone triage, and a phone message from Clem Olsen comes up on top. I dial and I get the Wolfman. He has some information, the print from Kathy Merlow's tube of paint which I gave him at the reunion. But as usual Clem doesn't want to talk on the phone.

The Brass Ring is one of those haunts of cops and lawyers, a block from the courthouse. It is to the legal profession what Geneva is to the U.N.—a place where warring sides can sit and talk. When I arrive there are maybe a dozen people inside, a few cops, a small cluster of deputy D.A.s at the bar, with a couple of public defenders exchanging stories of courthouse comedy and lore, slapping a dice cup for drinks.

Little snippets of the points I scored this afternoon in Laurel's case have filtered here among those who follow such things. One of the P.D.s reaches out and slaps my back as I walk by, offers a good word, and encouragement to stick my pike further into the belly of the beast tomorrow.

In the chess match that is a trial, Morgan Cassidy has traded a knight for one of our pawns. In return for some veiled and foggy threats of death, she has now lost one of two pieces of hard physical evidence purporting to link Laurel to the scene of the crime: Melanie's gold compact. The other, the bathroom rug, relies solely on Jack's testimony for its proof—his word against Laurel's that the rug was in Melanie's bathroom the night of the murder.

Cassidy's case begins to look more problematic with each passing day, and a few things become clear. Jimmy Lama's early investigation is what is steering their theory, and I am beginning to get the feeling that Lama is taking Morgan for a ride. I think Jimmy's chronic myopia has settled like the Black Plague over them. It is a matter of Lama immersed in a vendetta.

It takes all my faculty for fantasy to imagine Lama's passion to nail Laurel once he found out that I was related. For Jimmy this could only have fallen under the category of a magnificent obsession. As a cop assessing evidence, it has glazed his powers of perception. Once Lama knew of the relation between Laurel and me, there was only one suspect, one theory. Cassidy is now faced with hard facts which do not square with their early assumptions. All the ways a theory can go sour on you.

I would pay for status as a fly on their wall to hear the dressing-down Cassidy will give him for failing to review the courthouse tape to its end. If there is anything to aversion therapy, Lama will never leave a theater again before the credits finish rolling and the screen goes dark.

The dice cup is being slammed on the bar, a bang and the roar of voices as one of them is stuck with a round of drinks. As I look up I see Clem coming through the door. He swings between some tables, shakes a few hands, a couple of cops off the day shift. I hear the Wolfman, gravel in his throat, then bits and pieces of some off-color joke in a Mexican dialect, followed by a lot of laughter. This is Clem the politician. Next week he may be working Community Relations and telling these same guys that positive racial attitudes all start at home with an open mind and a clear conscience. Clem is the only man I know who could sit through five days of sexual sensitivity training and cop a feel from the female instructor as his graduation prize.

"Sorry to keep you waiting," he says. "Hope you haven't been here long."

I wave this off, and gesture to the seat on the other side of the table.

I don't get the Wolfman routine this afternoon. Instead Clem is looking over his shoulder, worried what his friends might think if they see him consorting with the enemy in the midst of trial. He tells me I am too hot at the moment for the normal social chitchat of this place. Lama, he says, wants a pound of flesh, and while merchants in Venice might settle for my heart, according to Clem, Jimmy wants to start at the soft underside of my genitals.

"What did you do to get him so pissed off?" he asks. "Ranting and raving all over the office," he tells me. "Jimmy has trouble deciding whose name to take in vain, yours, or as he puts it, 'that cunt' they forced him to work with."

Clem looks at me. "Who's trying the case?" he says.

"Morgan Cassidy," I tell him.

"Oh." Nothing more, like maybe Clem concurs in Lama's initial assessment.

Clem wants to go for one of the back booths, where we can talk in private. Not be disturbed, as he says.

We do it. The waitress comes up. Clem orders a boiler-maker. I do grapefruit juice.

"On the wagon?" he says.

I have to pick up Sarah from the baby-sitter's in a few minutes. I tell him this and he nods like he understands. Since Nikki's death I have a heightened sense of responsibility for my daughter, and a whole new appreciation for single parents. I have often wondered about the things that stick in a kid's mind as they grow older and realize that there is a darker seam to life, that the smell that always seemed to float about Dad's head like an ether was not Aqua Velva after all.

"Did you hear about Louis Cousins?" he says.

Cousins, the kid on trial across the hall from us, was convicted on two counts of first-degree murder a week ago.

I shake my head.

"Jury came back an hour ago." Clem extends his arm straight out in a fist, then turns it over and does a thumbs-down gesture like Caesar. "Death," he says.

I cannot say that I am surprised by this. Psychological defenses rooted in allegations of childhood abuses have been trotted out all too often of late, and overexposed in the press. Like knock-off Colonials in a housing tract, they are losing their impact.

The implication for us, however, is that the press will now be free. We will be garnering a larger share of the attention, which I could just as well do without.

Clem's in no hurry. I think he figures I'm good for a dozen drinks. I will buy him a gift certificate at the bar and let him carouse with his friends.

"What did you find out?" I ask him.

"Nothing on the picture," he says. "Struck out on all counts." Clem is talking about the photo given to me by Dana of the man known as Lyle Simmons, who if she is right was the triggerman seen with Jack in the bar across the river—the courier who delivered the bomb to the post office—and the guy who took out the Merlows. I would have figured, being that busy, he would have had a record to rival Capone.

"We checked all the aliases," he says. "Without prints . . ." He makes a face like dream on. "Which brings us to the other matter."

He's talking about the fingerprint of Kathy Merlow from the tube of paint I palmed off the grass during our encounter in Hawaii.

"Took almost an hour on the computer." This doesn't sound like much, but on the high-speed automated system of scanning an hour is a lifetime. "We got a hit," he says.

Clem pulls a slip of paper from his pocket. "One Carla

Leopold, born Paterson, New Jersey, August twenty-six, nineteen and—''

''Save the background, let's cut to the chase,'' I tell him.

''This is the good part,'' he says. ''Honors graduate, Columbia, degree in accountancy.''

''You sure we're talking about the same woman?''

He gives me a big grin. ''Employed by one of the large accounting firms in New York City, five years' experience. Next employer Regal International Trading Consortium, corporate accountant and bookkeeper. Employed two years.''

''Where is this leading us?'' I ask him.

''Bear with me,'' he says. ''Regal is one of the new line of trading and investment houses. They make their money the new and improved way.''

''How's that?''

''They launder it,'' says Clem.

He sits looking at me, big round eyes across the table, like ''how's them apples?''

The waitress arrives with our drinks. Clem starts slurping the foam off his iced mug. I give the woman payment and a tip and she leaves us.

''Word is you got narco-dollars, Regal International will buy you a piece of the rock,'' says Clem. ''They do Rumpelstiltskin and his straw routine one better. They turn white shit that goes up somebody else's nose into tax-free no-load muni bonds. Or at least they did until two years ago.''

''What happened?''

He takes a drink of draft, knowing he has my attention now.

''IRS and Justice came down around their ears. Full-court press. Indicted all the principals. Tried to get them to roll over on their clients. On the theory that you always follow the money, they called in your girl Carla.''

I'm giving him funny faces, not exactly tracking on where he's headed.

''Seems with the heat on, her former employers had funny notions about downsizing. Layoffs were done off a barge, after a cement facial, somewhere up the Hudson. Two of her co-horts, other bean-counters, went the way of the disappeared,'' he says. ''Ms. Leopold suddenly realized her career options were being limited. She agreed to testify in return for some kind of a deal. She copped a plea, mail fraud, conspiracy, and racketeering, multiple counts. That's how her prints showed up in the computer,'' he says. ''In return she was supposed to get sanctuary.''

''Supposed to?'' I say.

''She never got the benefit of the bargain.''

''What do you mean?''

''I mean she'd be thirty-three if she was still alive.''

Clem knows about her death. I am wondering how.

''An auto accident on the Jersey Turnpike in the middle of a blizzard,'' says Clem. ''A year ago last November.''

With this I am sitting bolt upright. I nearly choke on grape-fruit juice as the acid singes my throat.

''Body burned beyond recognition. Car went up like a fuck-ing buzz-bomb. Word is, it may have been an o.c. hit.'' Clem's jargon for the underbelly of life—organized crime.

He is asking me where I got the fingerprint on the paint tube. According to Clem, the guy who ran the check on the computer for him at State Justice is now curious.

I dodge this with a lot of verbal feints and weaves, and finally distract him with a question.

''Are you sure about the print, couldn't be a mistake?'' I say.

''No way. Positive make,'' he tells me. ''Matches on more than a dozen points of comparison. Little ridges that don't lie.''

Clem's still waiting for an answer about where I got the print. He may have to wait until hell freezes.

At this moment I am certain that my face is a mask of glazed expressions as I conjure the enigma that was Kathy Merlow, and a whole new universe of unanswered questions.

• • •

I see apparitions, the chalked and powdery complexion of death, visions of Nikki as I saw her alone on that last day to press the wedding band on her finger for the final time, alone among the tubes and tanks and other instruments of horror in the back rooms of the funeral parlor. Visions of Nikki laid out in white satin. It is an image I relive with regularity, though now it is invaded by other, more disturbing pictures. The synapses of the brain trying to sort sense from confusion. Another face, images of fiery death, and Kathy Merlow. Somehow these two, Nikki and Merlow, have become snarled in my mind, as I am restrained, caught up, lathered in sweat. Flames, and a tangle of twisted metal on some unrecognized roadway. Blood on matted bedsheets, the palm trees of Hana, and a pitched ringing, relentless, insistent in my ears. Images give way to sound, Nikki and Kathy Merlow, faces fade as my brain finally sorts fact from phantasm. I roll over, untangle myself from the sheets of my bed, and pull the receiver from the phone. The ringing stops. Nightmares that pass for slumber.

I swing my legs and sit up in soaked bedsheets.

"Hello—Paul?" A voice, a million miles away, like something through a tube, familiar. It is Harry.

"What the hell time is it?" I say.

"Five-thirty," he tells me. "Sorry to get you out of bed."

"It's all right. I wasn't sleeping well. What is it?" I'm wiping perspiration from my forehead, sleep from my eyes.

"Have you seen the morning paper?" he says.

"No. Why?"

"I think you better take a look. And do yourself a favor," he says. "Sit down before you open it."

"What's wrong?"

"Somebody has inserted a blade, at the sixth cervical vertebra, about eight inches in."

"To who?" I ask.

"To you, my friend. Second lead, page one, above the

fold,'' he tells me. '' 'Local Defense Attorney Linked to Postal Bombing.' ''

''Oh, shit.'' I sit, still trying to chase visions of dread from my sleep-ravaged brain. My mind at this moment begins to swim, struggling to sort the real fears from the imagined.

''I don't get it,'' I say. ''The feds already questioned me.''

''It doesn't say anything about that. Just that your finger-prints were found all over the place after the bombing, and that certain employees saw you talking to the dead postal worker moments before the blast. Somebody's doing a num-ber,'' he says.

''I think you better get yourself together. I'll meet you at the office.'' Harry hangs up.

I start to forage for clothes, my mind racing to assess the damage that this will do to Laurel's case, a trial in midstream, scandal affecting her lawyer.

Then I pick up the phone and dial Mrs. Bailey. I will need coverage with Sarah. I am abusing the old lady's good nature, but as always she is there for my daughter, more than I can say for myself. She will be over in ten minutes.

I'm in my underwear, buttoning up my pants, when I dial again. This time it is a groggy feline voice at the other end, something sultry from sleep.

''Hello. It's Paul. I need some help,'' I tell her.

''What is it?''

''Somebody's tagged me with the bombing. In this morn-ing's paper.''

''What. Who would—''

''I don't have time to talk. I need your help. There's a judge who's going to be taking a long hard look at me this morning. An explanation from some authoritative source could go a long way,'' I tell her.

''I don't understand,'' she says.

''Neither do I.''

Silence on the other end. "Sure. Whatever I can do. Where can I meet you?" asks Dana.

We set a time, the county courthouse, and I hang up.

For nearly two hours we assess damage while walking the floor at the office, Harry and I. As the arching light of dawn turns to day, I can see the incandescent lights as they dim on the Capitol dome five blocks away.

We reread the story, first silently, then out loud to each other, looking for nuances we may have missed. We explore the possible sources. Harry is thinking Jack. By now he would have gotten word that he is the centerpiece of my case. He is well connected with the press. But Harry hasn't told me how Jack would get the information that my prints were found at the scene, with the wraps thrown around a pending investigation.

The staff reporter on the byline is not a name I have heard before. It is the stuff of which scandal is made. Attributions to "highly placed but unnamed sources close to the investigation." It does not say, in so many words, that I am a suspect, but in the interests of a good story buries me in a mud slide of inference and innuendo. If this were the Inquisition, they would be pouring hot lead in my ear by morning as a means of leading me to the Lord and coaxing my confession.

What makes this most baffling is that I have come clean with the FBI, hours of questioning behind closed doors. They know precisely what I was doing talking with Marcie Reed. All I can figure is some enterprising reporter who got his hands on only half of the story.

The problem as we see it, and Harry sums it up quickly, is that the jurors in Laurel's case are not shielded from this news. It would not be covered by the court's gag order, there being no obvious link between the bombing and Melanie's murder. Left as it is, the jury, seeing my name coupled with the events at the post office, would not be believing much that I say in

Laurel's defense, the case of one felon pleading the cause of another.

"He can't mask it, but maybe he can take the tinge off. An instruction to the jury." Harry's talking about Judge Woodruff. We have called four times in the last hour. He's not yet in chambers, though by now he has no doubt read his morning paper.

"It's probably just a one-day story," I say. "By tomorrow it'll be old news, off the front page, explained and corrected."

"You sound like the fucking founding fathers," says Harry. "An innocent's notion of the First Amendment," he tells me.

This from a man who spends his life reading the newspaper.

"Hang on to your nuts," he says. "They don't call it the press for nothing."

"They got the facts wrong. They'll fix it," I say.

"Like the man said, fifteen minutes of fame," says Harry. "You get yours by flashlight up the kazoo."

I tell him to relax. I try the judge on the phone. Now the clerk's not answering. We can't wait any longer, so we decide to walk the few blocks to the courthouse. We can die of anxiety there as well as here. Besides, by now Dana should be on her way over.

We drop down the elevator in the building. I step out and get my first glimpse of them. A van with a dish on top parked out front. Then two more down the block. I wonder if maybe there's a fire in one of the high-rises. Then, as I step out onto the street, I get a microphone in the face.

"Mr. Madriani, what can you tell us about the bombing?"

Another guy with a pen and pad. "Are you being charged? Are you talking to authorities?"

"How long have you been under investigation?"

Harry is looking at me. "Holy shit."

We grab the doors, step back inside, close them, and turn the lock. We're getting a lot of glare from the strobes on the cameras bouncing off the glass of the door. A horde is now moving in.

One of the more enterprising souls is pulling on the handles, rattling the heavy door in its frame.

Harry's got my elbow, dragging me toward a door down the hall. The way to the garage. We get in his car, and coming up the ramp to the street there is another throng.

"I should have put you in the fucking trunk," he says. "Hang on."

He nearly runs some guy down who is so burdened with batteries and lights he cannot move.

"So much for a one-day story," he says. "Any more theories?"

I look back over my shoulder out the rear window, and a few of them are running for their cars. A woman reporter with her camera crew is hoofing it down the street, figuring I am due in court and it's only three blocks.

Harry asks me what I think Dana will do about all this.

"I'm hoping she'll vouch for me with Woodruff. Tell him what happened, that I was merely interviewing a client. That I'm not a suspect."

"You've been bitten by the love bug," he says. "She is probably the leaker."

When I look over at him I see a lot of wrinkles and furrows, advice to the lovelorn from Harry. He is talking about Dana like he suspects she has lifted her leg, making me the leakee.

"Why would she? She has nothing to gain."

"Birds of a feather," he says.

"You mean Cassidy?"

"I mean estrogen's thicker than water," he says. "There are some of them who get off just tubing some poor slob." The "them" Harry is talking about is the other half of humanity, the vast fairer sex. "Maybe you didn't scratch the right itch the last time you got it on." Harry's getting personal now. "I warned you," he says. "Two female prosecutors."

Harry thinks the enmity in the workplace toward males is something genetic, like the encoding on the X chromosome, that there will be no peace until women are sent home. He's still blinking, wondering how a gender that makes up more than half of the species acquired all the perks of minority status and got its head under the tent of affirmative action.

"There are rules in this stuff, like the canon of ethics," he says. "We all know the first one: 'Thou shalt not dip thy quill in the company ink.' "

I remind him that Dana doesn't work for us.

The second, he says: " 'Beware of false prosecutors who come to you in the night in sheep's clothing or slinky garb, for they are ravening wolves,' " he says. To Harry there is little that is sacred.

I give him a smile but don't say anything.

"Sure, laugh," he says. "But it ain't me running down the street who's being chased by Tabloid Mary," he says. "It's your ass that's in the flames. Burnt offerings to the god of yellow journalism," says Harry.

In the distance a half block away I can hear some asshole shouting, "There he is!" The patter of feet, heels on concrete, like a stampede of hookers ahead of the paddy wagon.

We're making for the sanctuary of court, across the intersection between the parking lot and the courthouse, against a light that says DON'T WALK. We are nearly hit by a car. We run up the ramp to the back door.

It takes us a couple of minutes to negotiate the metal detector. It is here that the first camera crew catches us. Harry is panting, out of breath, busy putting his belt with its metal buckle back through the loops in his pants. Pictures at five. We move away. They try to follow. The guard is pointing to the conveyor belt and telling them to unstrap for inspection.

Harry turns around and gives them the finger. Their lights still on, film still whirring. "See you assholes upstairs," he says. "And leave the fucking cameras and mikes outside, in the hall," he tells them. Harry Hinds on public relations.

He sees the look on my face. "Don't worry," he says. "They gotta bleep out all the bad stuff." Harry's never heard of lip-reading.

We look like two brush salesmen toting sample cases as we finally make it to the elevator. Harry's is filled with exhibits and pieces of evidence for our case. My own has lined-out questions for examination, in the case of today, for Jack Vega, who is due up in the state's case—if I am not suspended from the practice before then.

When we arrive at the clerk's station behind the courtroom, Dana is already inside with Woodruff. The clerk knocks on the door and we are told to wait a couple of minutes. Morgan Cassidy has been summoned by the judge and is on her way. Woodruff apparently is concerned by appearances of ex parte communications. He doesn't want one of the lawyers inside behind closed doors without opposing counsel being present.

Two minutes later Cassidy breezes into the office, followed by Jimmy Lama. She walks past us like we are not there, nothing but an imperious look. Lama's expression is dour, like maybe he's not looking forward to this meeting.

The clerk opens the door and we all press into chambers. Woodruff is seated behind a large mahogany desk. Dana has one of the two stuffed club chairs across from him. Her briefcase is in her lap.

"Your honor, if I could explain." I don't waste any time. "I take it you've seen the morning paper?"

Woodruff has his hand up. "I've seen it and I've talked to Ms. Colby. She's already told me what happened," he says. "An inaccurate news story," he says. "Right now I'm more concerned about how it got in the paper." He means whether there is some ulterior motive for this, and whether it takes its inspiration from the trial.

Woodruff may have the bushy eyebrows and the genteel twinkle of Walter Cronkite, but this morning he is a mean face, all of it aimed at Morgan Cassidy. There has been no love lost between her and the judge.

"What can you tell us about this, Ms. Cassidy?"

"Not a thing, your honor. You don't think—"

"Well, it didn't come from our shop," says Dana.

Cassidy gives her a look to kill.

Harry's smiling. The other side of the gender conspiracy—a catfight.

"How about your people?" Dana's looking at Jimmy Lama.

His Adam's apple comes halfway up, and then does a jack-knife. A lot of nervous eyeing of the judge. "No," he says. "Absolutely not."

"I don't understand," I say. "I thought the postal investigation was a federal affair?"

"We called in the local bomb squad, and forensic support," says Dana.

"Maybe we should get whoever headed it up over here," says Woodruff.

"No need. They're here already," says Dana. "Lieutenant Lama was local liaison."

With this Jimmy is seven shades of purple, a lot of fidgeting and nervous glances, more than a few of them in my direction. Lama on the carpet. Woodruff demanding answers. Who had access to information? The fingerprint reports?

"It didn't come from our side," says Jimmy. Absolute denials which he undercuts a moment later with assurances that he'll check it out and get back to the judge.

"By this afternoon," says Woodruff.

"You got it," says Lama.

"What?"

"Your honor," says Jimmy.

Woodruff gives him a look that says, "That's better."

Lama's muttering to Cassidy. Denials sputtering like they are out of gas. "Our people wouldn't do this."

All of them except one, and I am looking at him right now. There is no longer any mystery in my mind as to the source of this news story. Humiliation over the courthouse tape, the loss of the compact as evidence was the last straw. This is classic Lama, time-honored techniques designed to screw one's opponent. To Jimmy life is one large board game of getting even.

Something tells me there is no way Woodruff will ever prove Lama was involved. He would have more layers of insulation on this than the average Eskimo. A dozen people between himself and the reporter, his name or fingerprints on nothing. Under the circumstances the court cannot call the reporter who wrote the story onto the carpet and demand to know his sources. Ostensibly Woodruff has no jurisdiction. The information in the article does not relate to evidence in our case. It is all tangential, intended only to cripple me as counsel. In this Lama has been deft.

Woodruff wrings his hands over the desk, making noises about a mistrial. At this moment, given the holes we have punched in their case, this would be a gift-wrapped package to Cassidy. She now knows our theory of defense. She could shore it up and try the case again.

The judge says he will poll the jury to see how many have read the article, what effect it has had. In the meantime he will craft an instruction. He orders Lama to return after today's session to report progress on this, his inquiries regarding the story. Jimmy is bowing and scraping. Your typical toady in the face of authority, Lama is vowing to get to the bottom of it.

By five o'clock he'll be back with iron-clad assurances that nobody in the department was involved, and Woodruff will be left as I am, to harbor empty suspicions without proof.

Lama and Cassidy head out to the courtroom to prepare for the day's session. Harry follows them. Dana and I huddle in the hallway just beyond the clerk's station.

"That bitch," she says. I am struck by her language. This is an anger I have not seen in Dana before. Her face is flushed, her hands shaking. She is looking at the wall behind me at this moment, not engaging my eyes. The expletive uttered as if she were talking to herself. As if I were not present.

"She's spent months trying to derail the appointment," she

says. Dana's talking about her judicial aspirations. Her wrath, it seems, is predicated on something more than her personal loyalty to me. Cassidy in her denials to the court has in her own inimitable way implied that if it was not the local authorities whose indiscretions led to the embarrassing news article, then there is only one other possibility—it had to be Dana or some of her people. She does not take kindly to being played the stooge.

"Fine. That's the way they want it," she says, "we'll give it to them in spades. A little leveling of the playing field," she tells me. "When do they swear Jack?" she asks.

"This morning," I tell her. "He's first up."

"Then he's fair game anytime after that?"

I nod.

"You'll have unsealed indictments and public records of conviction, certified copies by noon," she says. "I'll see to it that a courier delivers them."

I thank her for standing up for me, explaining to Woodruff.

"All in a day's work," she says. But now she tells me there is bad news. Things are not going well in their search for the witness who saw Jack with the man they know as Lyle Simmons in the bar across the river. The guy has completely dropped from sight.

"Your people haven't stopped looking?" I say.

"No. But I don't want to mislead you either. The man hasn't been seen in more than two months. He has strong inducements to stay lost. The unrelated criminal charges," she says. "If we do find him, it may not be in time."

"The man's a linchpin in my case," I tell her.

"You can make a case on Jack without him. He's dirty," she says. "You know it wasn't his child. The guy was burning with jealousy. He used the death of his wife to try and cut a deal on his sentence. There will be letters to that effect in the file," she says. "You can draw and quarter him."

"I wish you were on the jury," I tell her.

"Their case is hemorrhaging faster than a peptic ulcer,"

she says. "The compact which no longer ties your client to the scene, a silencer, all the signs of a hired job. And Mr. Vega with a motive. Sounds like that's where it's at," she says.

"It would be that much stronger with a triggerman."

"You want it all," she says. "We'll try. But you shouldn't count on it." The way she says this makes me think I am being told to make other arrangements, something short of the best evidence. I begin to wonder if this witness of theirs is not dead.

"Are you free tonight?" she asks.

"Except for fatherhood," I tell her. "Dinner my place?"

She tells me she will bring the wine.

"Say seven," I say.

She smiles. Then a warm and wet peck on the cheek in the dark corridor.

As she turns on her heels and heads down the hall, I see Harry, sitting in a chair in the clerk's station, taking this all in, his face an etching of paternal disapproval, like some patriarch whose eldest son has just run off with the village trollop.

CHAPTER
27

He is the centerpiece of the state's case—the grieving widower. Jack is at the front of the courtroom, some last-minute words with Cassidy. Vega as usual is up on his toes, prancing in place like some kid about to wet his pants. He's been escorted to the stand by Jimmy and one of the minions, who act like two cruisers pushing reporters away.

Vega wears a suit the price of which could support a family for a year, a silk tie and a matching kerchief in the breast pocket, maroon, Jack's standard color.

As he talks he cannot keep his gaze off me, darting little slits, sallow cheeks and lips stretched white with tension. I am assembling papers at the counsel table, but I refuse to divert my eyes from him. Jack and I play a game of ocular chicken.

Vega's is a face not so much of determination as pure meanness. I have seen him turn this on witnesses in legislative committee before unleashing his wrath, usually in defense of some protected interest which has lavished its largess to sweeten Jack's judgment. Vega is merciless on those without influence, volunteers for consumer groups, or students with a brief for the environment. Under Jack's rules those without money have no business living in a democracy.

This morning I go back to meet Laurel in the holding cells, a few words of caution before she is led out into the courtroom.

When I see her inside the cell she is putting the final touches on her hair with a brush. It seems she has taken more interest in her personal appearance now that the kids are out of the way, to her view, safe and out of the clutches of Jack.

I tell her that he is outside ready to take the stand, that the jury will be watching her for each telltale sign of a response to everything he says.

"Anything, a twitch of the nose, a pained expression, and they can read into it. It's vital that you hold your emotions. There is no telling what he will say."

This is shorthand for the obvious, that of all the witnesses Jack is the one most likely to embellish on the evidence, to take liberty with the facts where he can.

"You don't think he would lie?" She gives me a stark expression.

For an instant, the very fact that she could ask this with a straight face catches me off guard. Then little cracks in her demeanor, wrinkles around the mouth, and the dam breaks. We both laugh.

"It is a possibility," I tell her.

"No. Rain tomorrow is a possibility," she says. "That Jack would lie when the truth will do just as well, that's more like the law of gravity," she says.

"Just be natural. Be yourself," I tell her.

"If I were being natural I would knee him in the nuts and scratch his eyes out," she says.

"I take it back. Don't be yourself."

"Sorry to be difficult," she says.

I don't want to place Laurel in an emotional straitjacket. If Jack tells a whopper, the jury will expect some normal reaction of denial. What I don't want are histrionics at the table.

"High emotion," I tell her, "is the stuff of which murder is made. Show them a temper, a flash of anger, and it is easier for them to see you with a gun in your hand."

"I understand," she says. "I can call him a liar, just not a fucking liar."

"Something like that," I say.

We gather ourselves. She takes my hand and squeezes it, and together we head out, Laurel, I, the sheriff's guard, and a female matron, toward the courtroom.

There are extra rows of press here today, the overflow from Louis Cousins' case, as well as some of the capital press corps, all with sharpened pencils. There is an electricity in the air. It is the smell of news when crime is injected under pressure into the political class and ignited by a spark. Like the stench of ozone after lightning.

We take a seat at the counsel table. Some guy with a notepad comes up and starts to ask questions of me over the bar railing—what I think Vega will say on the stand. I tell him to watch and see.

Then he starts talking about the post office bombing and my fingerprints. As soon as this happens three more join him, and when I turn around there is a small crowd. I tell them I have no comment but they persist.

Woodruff's bailiff wanders over.

"Either take your seats or we'll be giving them to people waiting outside in the hallway." Suddenly there are bodies racing in a dozen directions like the last land rush.

As the jury is led in, I can tell that the bombing story has taken its toll. The usual drifting of gazes about the room is absent. This morning all eyes are riveted on me, murmurs between a few of them like perhaps they are surprised I am here and not in shackles.

Woodruff takes the bench. Cassidy directs Vega to a chair inside the railing, where she holds him for the moment.

"Before we start today," says Woodruff, "there is some business I must get out of the way."

He immediately talks about the news article, the letter bomb, and my fingerprints at the scene. He polls the jury as to effect. Three of them say they have never seen the piece, nor heard any reports in the media. Some people live on Mars. The others concede that they have seen it, and to varying degrees were curious. One juror, a man in the second row, says if there is smoke there must be fire. According to this guy I should not be trying the case if there is even a hint of suspicion. He is immediately excused by Woodruff and replaced on the jury by one of the alternates. This brings a lot of sober expressions from the others. Any further polling at this point would be an idle exercise. They will not be volunteering their private thoughts.

Then, in wooden tones the judge reads them a carefully crafted instruction that they are not to consider any of this in judging the evidence of this case. He nibbles around the edges of exoneration, that I have cooperated fully with authorities, that I am not at this time and have not been a suspect in the bombing, that inferences to this end in the article are inaccurate.

I can hear the scratching of pencils in the press rows behind me. Then, as abruptly as he started, he brings it to a close. I can sense that there are a dozen hands that would go up like skyrockets if this were a press conference. Cassidy and Lama sense this too; there is a wicked grin on Jimmy's face. Enough latitude for more speculation in tomorrow morning's newspaper.

"Call your next witness." Woodruff looking at Cassidy.

"Mr. Jack Vega."

Jack takes the stand and is sworn.

When he identifies himself for the record it is with his legislative title as a member of the Assembly. He wears this like a badge of honor, oblivious to the fact that in opinion polls on the issue of integrity it places him well beneath those who go door-to-door peddling aluminum siding, and only a halfnotch above the lawyers who are about to question him.

"Do you know the defendant, Laurel Vega?" asks Cassidy.

"I do. We were married for some years, until divorced," he says.

"And do you have children by the defendant?"

"Two," he says. "A boy and a girl, thirteen and fifteen,

though I haven't seen them for nearly a month."

"Who has legal custody of these children at the present time?"

I am getting uneasy feelings about where this line is taking us.

"I do."

"But you have no idea where they are?"

"No."

"Your honor. I am going to object on grounds of relevance. Where is this taking us?"

Without hesitation Cassidy says, "Into the issue of motive, your honor."

"Overruled. Continue," he says.

"When was the last time you saw your children?"

"It was twenty-eight days ago," says Jack. "My daughter told me she was going to stay overnight with a friend."

"And your son?"

"He'd left the house, though he hadn't told me where he was going. I found out later that he went to see his mother at the county jail."

"The defendant, Laurel Vega?" says Cassidy.

"Right," he says.

"And that was the last time you saw either child?"

"Right."

"Have you reported them missing to the police?"

"For what good it would do," he says. "She knows where they are and won't tell."

"Objection." I'm on my feet. "Move to strike."

Woodruff orders the comment stricken from the record and tells the jury to disregard it. But the seed is planted.

"They're treating it as a civil domestic matter," says Jack.

"What does that mean?"

"Objection. Calls for speculation."

"Sustained."

"Mr. Vega, were you involved in a battle with the defendant over legal custody of your children?"

"I was. She made it very bitter," he says. "And then she blamed it all on my wife, Melanie."

"Objection, your honor."

Woodruff is getting angry with Vega. "Sir, do you know what a question is?"

"Sure," says Jack.

"Then just answer the questions and keep the commentary to yourself. Do I make myself clear?"

Jack forgets that he is not in the Legislature, the forum of political princes who float on an ether of arrogance without rules of conduct or evidence. He is not used to such treatment. He doesn't answer Woodruff, but instead gives him a curt nod.

"Yes or no for the record," says Woodruff. The road to contempt if Jack keeps it up.

"I understand," says Vega.

"Do you recall during this custody battle a physical assault made by the defendant, Laurel Vega, on the deceased Melanie Vega?" says Cassidy.

"I remember it very well," he says. "She." He points to Laurel. "She hit her, Melanie, very hard with a heavy purse. My wife complained to me later about a bruise and a sore arm as a result."

"And do you remember threats being uttered against Melanie Vega by the defendant at the time of this attack?"

"You bet," he says. Jack can hardly contain himself in the box. Given a platform, he would be doing some hefty table dancing at this moment.

"She said she wanted to kill Melanie."

"Those were her words?"

"No. She said she wanted to 'kill the bitch.' " As Jack says this he looks at Laurel and me, fire in his eyes. He has been suppressing this venom for months. Now it spills like some oozing toxic gel over the witness box.

They embellish this around the edges, a few more pithy quotes all attributed to Laurel, who by now, if you could defame the dead, would be standing trial for slander. Jack should be writing headlines for the tabloids. Then Cassidy has him identify the rug from the evidence cart. Jack is adamant that this scrap of carpet was located in the master bath of his home the night Melanie was murdered. The only way Laurel could have gotten it, according to Jack, is if she had been present in the home that night.

Morgan then takes him on a blistering cruise of several conversations, most of which I suspect never took place. These are supposedly private encounters between him and Laurel during periods of visitation when she would come by the house to deliver or pick up the kids. To listen to Jack, these were angry tirades issued by Laurel, none of which were provoked by either him or Melanie.

Through most of this, tight-lipped and tense, Laurel is restraining herself, protesting only quietly in my ear. Then at one point she says, ''He's a fucking liar.'' Almost loud enough for Woodruff to hear.

When I look over she is not smiling.

During one of these encounters, according to Jack, there was a particularly ugly conversation during which Laurel said she wished the two of them, he and Melanie, were dead.

''I suppose half a loaf is better than none,'' she whispers through a cupped hand in my ear.

Cassidy, I think, hears it, though the jury does not.

When I look at Laurel there is a willful gleam in her eye. It is the reason I worry about putting her on the stand.

''Laurel was always jealous and angry, particularly at Melanie,'' says Jack. ''She couldn't deal with younger women,'' he says.

''Maybe if you'd screwed fewer of them during our marriage my outlook would have been different.''

Several of the women on the jury giggle.

Woodruff slams the gavel on this and points it at Laurel. ''Madam—you can be bound and gagged in that chair,'' he says. ''Counsel, control your client,'' he tells me.

I apologize for her conduct. I'm telling her to cool it, in tones that the court can hear.

"Go on," says the judge.

Cassidy saves the emotional blast for last, the story of how Jack came home and found his young wife dead, shot through the head in the bath. Jack relates all of this in morbid detail, and actually produces a tear, a single lonely bead running down one cheek for the jury to see.

All the while Laurel has one hand on top of the table, rubbing two fingers together in an obvious gesture, the world's tiniest violin.

I move as quickly as I can to cover her hand, but Cassidy sees this and complains.

"A nervous tic," says Laurel.

"Your honor, she's sending signals to the jury," says Cassidy. "Commenting on the evidence."

"I can't help it," says Laurel. "It's a nervous condition I have whenever the sonofabitch lies."

"That's it," says Woodruff. "Counsel to the bench. And you, madam. You shut your mouth. Do you understand?"

We go up and Woodruff makes a show of fairness, but most of the hunks taken are out of my ass. He tells me if I cannot control her he will do it, and the picture for the jury will not be pleasant.

We go back out and Cassidy picks up again with Jack. Vega tells the court that he lost not only a wife but a child.

"Mr. Vega," says Cassidy, "can you tell the court when it was that you first learned that Melanie was pregnant?"

On this Jack weaves a yarn that it was Melanie who first told him, that they were looking forward to the new child, a melding of his existing family, the older children with the new. He tells the jury that they had taken no precautions, that Melanie was not on the pill.

I am incredulous. He says nothing about his own vasectomy. At this moment it hits me. Jack has told Morgan nothing about this. Vega, the ultimate deceiver, has laid her bare on the biggest element of our case, Jack's jealousies, the motive for murder, that somebody else had fathered his wife's child.

It is on this plateau of martyrdom that Morgan leaves Jack, turning him over to me on cross.

For a long moment, one of those watersheds, a dramatic pause at trial, Jack and I study each other with wary eyes as I approach the witness box. I make a face for the jury to see, like I accept only a small portion of his testimony as gospel. In dealing with Jack, the order of evidence is critical. My task is clear: to dismantle his character a stick at a time and then hammer on the joint themes of motive and opportunity.

"Mr. Vega. We know each other, don't we?"

He looks at me but does not answer, uncertain whether I am referring to kinship, or perhaps the fact that I know him by character.

"I mean to say that we were once related by marriage. Is that not so?"

"Yes," he says. He tells the court that he once considered me a friend. His use of the past tense is not lost on the jury.

I want to get this before them early so Jack cannot use it later, inferences that I bear personal animus toward him based solely on the sorry family experiences between him and Laurel. Jack would use this like a shield, as if I am beating on him in some personal vendetta.

Then I ease into it, reading one of his statements to the police the night of the murder, when he told them he never owned a gun. He insists that he does not. I remind him about the chrome-plated collector's item, the nine-millimeter pistol given to him by some lobbyist to toughen his stance against a gun-control bill, years before.

Darting eyes in the box, he decides to tough this out, my word against his.

"I, ah—I have no recollection of that," he says. It is classic Jack. No denial, just a weak memory.

The paper blizzard starts. I hand copies to Cassidy and the court clerk for use by the judge.

"Mr. Vega, do you recognize this document?" I hand him a copy. He pulls a pair of cheaters from his pocket and reads.

"Looks familiar," he says.

"It should," I say. "Is that your signature at the bottom of the last page?"

He looks. "Yes," he says.

"Is this not the property-settlement agreement you signed with the defendant, Laurel Vega, at the time of your divorce?"

Then it dawns on him. "I remember now," he says. "There was a gun. Long time ago. I'd forgotten," he says.

"Would you look at page twelve, item eighty-seven?"

"I've already said I remember about the gun."

"Fine. Now look for the item."

A lot of anger in his eyes, Jack flips through the pages and finds it.

"Could you read that one item?"

"Fine, for what it's worth," he says. "To the Petitioner, one chrome-plated nine-millimeter semiautomatic pistol in walnut box," he says. "There. I already told you about it."

"But you didn't tell the police about it the night of the murder. Why not?"

"For the obvious reason that I forgot."

"What happened to the gun, Mr. Vega?"

"I, ah . . . I don't know," he says. "I don't remember."

I am convinced that this is not the murder weapon. Jack may be a fool, but he is not demented. He would never use a gun that could be traced back to himself, not when it is so easy to get another weapon and somebody else to pull the trigger. What this does, however, is to set a pattern for the jury, of Vega's convenient memory.

"So it wasn't true what you told the police the night of the murder," I say. "That you never owned a gun?"

"People forget things," he says. "How am I supposed to remember everything I owned all of my life?"

"Do you often have trouble with your memory?" I say. It is a stinging question, but not subject to objection.

He doesn't answer, but gives me a look, something that might turn the more timid to stone.

"Well, then, let me ask you this," I say. "Do you consider the listing of items in this document, the property-settlement agreement signed by yourself and the defendant, to be a more accurate reflection of physical possessions, yours and the defendant's, than your memory?" I say.

"That's why people usually write things down, isn't it?" he says. "Because they tend to *forget.*"

He puts all the emphasis on the last word, like this should be obvious to any idiot.

"Precisely," I say.

He tries to hand the document back to me.

"Not quite yet," I say. "Would you turn to page four, item twenty-six?"

He flips pages.

"Please read it aloud to the court?"

He scans it first, then looks at me, an expression like some doe about to be nailed by a train.

"Read it," I say, my tone stiffening.

"To Respondent—" He stops reading and silently absorbs this.

"Fine. With the court's permission I'll read it. 'To the Respondent, one handcrafted white woven bath rug, with geometric floral design, label "by Gerri." ' "

"But she didn't get it," he says. "I did." Jack's coming out of the chair.

"Did you sign this agreement?"

"Yes," he says.

"And who was the Respondent in your divorce?" I ask him.

He's seemingly baffled, wondering how this could have happened. The gun is one thing. He doesn't answer the question.

"You were the Petitioner. Isn't it a fact that the bathroom rug with the label 'by Gerri' belonged to your former wife, to Laurel Vega? Isn't it a fact, sir, that it went to her as part of the property-settlement agreement following your divorce?''

A lot of shrugging shoulders. Jack looking at the print on the page like if he studies it long enough it might disappear.

I retreat to the evidence cart and grab the rug, approach the witness box, and flip the back of the carpet, sticking it six inches under Jack's nose.

"Tell the jury what that label says," I tell him. "Read it to the jury."

When he looks up at me, the cheaters have slid halfway down his nose.

"What does it say?"

'' 'By Gerri,' '' he says.

"Thank you."

I leave the rug balanced in front of him on the railing, like an albatross around his neck, and turn. When I do, I see Cassidy looking at me, wondering how they could have missed this. I cannot blame them. I would never have found it myself, except for my recollections about Jack's antics with the gun, and Laurel's admonition the day I met with her in the jail, that Vega had raised such a stink about the pistol, demanding that his claim be embedded in the settlement agreement. When I got to reading, one item led to another. What Jack must be thinking at this moment—the things we do that bite us in the butt.

There is now a major cloud hovering over the last piece of physical evidence linking Laurel to Melanie's murder. And while Jack is still insisting that the rug was in his house the night she was killed, he has no clever explanation for its appearance under Laurel's column in the property-settlement agreement.

This afternoon Harry drinks his lunch in celebration of this, two Manhattans and a Long Island Tea. His nose is redder than Rudolph's by the time we return to court, where a courier is waiting for me with a large box. True to her word, Dana has delivered Jack into our arms, not with a kiss, but a kick.

We retire to one of the rooms back of the court, where Harry and I examine this stuff privately. It is gold; certified copies of the grand jury indictment and record of conviction, Jack's plea to the federal district court on multiple counts of political corruption. Dana has even provided copies for Woodruff and opposing counsel, with a note that the press will be alerted to the conviction at two this afternoon. Jack can expect a crowd on his way out, boom mikes in the face and bright lights.

This afternoon Harry is ready to subpoena Vega's bank records, personal and legislative, a legal copy service is waiting for him to telephone with the word. If Jack hired somebody to do the deed, as Dana suspects, there should be some large cash withdrawal in the period just before and possibly just after Melanie's murder. When it comes to money, Vega is a prudent man. He would want to work on the installment plan.

This afternoon I go to work on a theme that will become central to our case, that Jack has every reason in the world for incriminating Laurel in this case. I ask him if he is sorry to see his former wife, the mother of his children here, at the defense table charged with murder.

In the tempered terms of a statesman he calls it "a tragedy."

We review Lama's earlier testimony that it was Jack who immediately fingered Laurel without a shred of hard evidence the night of the murder.

"They asked me if I knew anyone who might want to kill my wife," he says. "She'd made death threats. What was I supposed to say?" Jack has spent the noon hour having his ass kicked by Cassidy. He is now doing better, and he knows it.

"When did you take legal custody of the children?" I ask.

He gives me a date.

"Then it was after the arrest of their mother for murder that you finally got what you wanted?"

"She was no longer available to care for them. What else was there to do?"

"She wasn't available because she was in jail, based largely on your accusations."

"That she made death threats against Melanie," he says.

"And the assertion that the bathroom carpet found in her possession was from your house." This is not a question, but he answers it.

"It was not an assertion. It was the truth," he says.

"Based solely on your word," I tell him. "And the fact remains, you got the children and she went to jail. I suppose that's one way to end a bitter custody battle."

"What's that supposed to mean?" he says.

"What do *you* think it means?" Better from his mouth than mine.

"If you're trying to imply that I falsely accused her, you're wrong. Worse," he says, "you're a liar."

"So you wouldn't do anything like that? You would never knowingly deceive the authorities in their investigation of the case?"

"No," he says. Jack puts up a wholly indignant look, the pious and trusted public official.

"You just forgot about the gun?"

"That's what I said."

"Let's talk about how you found out your wife was pregnant. You told the court in earlier testimony that your wife told you about this. Is that correct?"

He looks at me. "To the best of my recollection." More faulty memory.

"To the best of your recollection?" I smile broadly and turn toward the jury. "This is your wife telling you that she was about to have your child. Surely you would remember something like that?"

"Yes," he says. "I remember it."

"And when was this, approximately?"

He thinks for a moment.

"Late last summer sometime."

"Can't you be more specific?"

"I think it was August or September. I can't be sure."

"And where did she tell you this? What were you doing?"

"I can't remember. I think it was in the living room. I was probably reading."

"You can't remember what you were doing? This news must have made a real impression on you," I say.

He looks at me. If Jack had something in his hand at this moment he would throw it.

"Mr. Vega, do you remember receiving a telephone call on October tenth from a Dr. John Phillips, your wife's obstetrician, when she was out of the house?"

It is a thick look I get from him, a flicker of eyelids questioning how could I know that.

"Do you remember being told at that time by Dr. Phillips that Melanie was pregnant?" As I say this I am holding telephone records in my hand, the familiar forms by the local carrier in this area with red lettering across the top that I am perusing. Jack cannot miss this. What he doesn't know is that these are mine from my house, not his or the physician's.

He considers for a moment. Wipes a bead of sweat off his upper lip. "I might have," he says.

"You might have talked to Dr. Phillips?"

"Yes."

"And he told you about the pregnancy, didn't he?" Telephone records might show a call was made. They wouldn't tell me the content of the conversation. For this, either the doctor has talked, or I have information from the tap on his phone. Jack knew the feds had tapped. Either way there are risks in lying.

"You've been prying into a lot of personal things," he says.

"Your honor, I would ask that the witness be instructed to answer the question."

x Before Woodruff can speak. "He might have," says Jack.

"The doctor told you about the pregnancy, did he not?"

"The doctor, Melanie. What difference?" he says.

Jack still doesn't see where I'm coming from.

"I'm going to ask you one more time. What did the doctor tell you?"

"Something about a test," he says.

"A pregnancy test?"

"Yes."

"What about it?"

"That the test was positive," he says.

"Meaning?"

"That Melanie was pregnant."

"So this was on October tenth?"

"If you say so," he says. "I don't know the date."

"Would you like to look at the medical records?" I ask. "The doctor made a notation of the conversation." I turn to the table to get them. These we have subpoenaed from the physician.

"I'll take your word for it," he says.

"Well, then, I ask you, how could Melanie have told you that she was pregnant as early as August or September if she wasn't tested until October and the results delivered on October tenth?"

A lot of faces from Jack, mostly pained expressions. He could have a million answers for this, that women know these things before they are tested, that she wasn't tested until later in the pregnancy, that he was wrong about when Melanie told him. But he doesn't come up with any of these. Instead he backpedals and trips over his own lie.

"I thought it was Melanie who first told me. Maybe I was wrong," he says. "Maybe I heard it from the doctor first. I don't know what difference it makes."

The problem here is that Jack can't be sure what the physician has told me, if anything. Vega can't recall whether he made admissions at the time of the telephone conversation that this was the first he was hearing of the pregnancy. I could show him the transcript of his tapped phone to assure him that, while as Dana said, "you could hear a pin drop," Jack did not actually say anything. But it's too late. It is the problem that when you litter the landscape with too many lies you forget where the truth is.

Vega simply attributes this once more to a faulty memory. Only this time the jury is looking with more than a few arched eyebrows.

"So from what you can remember now you did not hear about the baby for the first time from Melanie, but from the physician, and this was roughly three weeks before your wife's death?"

"I don't know." Jack's ultimate refuge when cornered.

"Did you ever talk to your wife about the pregnancy?"

"Sure we talked about it. What the hell," he says. "What? You think we wouldn't discuss something like this?"

"I don't know. Did you?"

"Absolutely," he says.

"When? Where?"

"Several times," he says. "Lots of places. We were very happy about the child."

"You wanted this baby?"

"Absolutely." Jack is absolute about everything except the details.

"Quite a feat, wasn't it?"

"What do you mean?" he says.

"Your child must have been one of the miracles of modern medicine."

"How's that?"

"Isn't it true, Mr. Vega, that twelve years ago you underwent minor surgery, a procedure carried out in your doctor's office, a vasectomy?"

Jack suddenly swallows his Adam's apple, three or four heaving bobs. "Whatya—"

"As a result of this procedure is it not a fact that you were incapable of fathering a child during your marriage to the victim, Melanie Vega?"

"What are you talking about?"

"Isn't it a fact, Mr. Vega, that the unborn child who died in your wife's womb was fathered by someone else?"

"No," he says. "That's not true."

"Should I get your medical records? I have them right here."

"No. I had the vasectomy," he says. "But the child was mine."

"How is that possible?"

"I don't know. I'm not a doctor. But sometimes things happen. I just figured it didn't take."

"You figured it didn't take?"

It is the key to our case, the crowning blow, the fact that the child is not Jack's, that he has known this from the inception and now lies about it bold-faced before the jury, the motive for murder.

"Mr. Vega, isn't it a fact that you didn't discuss this child at all with your wife? That she kept the pregnancy a secret? That she went to her death believing you knew nothing about it? Isn't it a fact that she tried to conceal it from you because she was having an affair with another man, and that you found out about this?"

"That's not true," he says.

"She didn't know about the call from her physician, did she? The one you intercepted."

"I don't know."

"You didn't tell her though, did you?"

"No. I forgot." The same old saw.

"Isn't it a fact that your wife had another lover?"

He sits staring at me in the box, wordless.

"Isn't it true that she had another lover and that you found out? Who was it, Mr. Vega? Who was it that got your wife pregnant? Who?" I say. "Who . . . ?"

"Enough." When the word comes it is screamed at me from behind, a female voice, anguished and broken. I turn, and it is Laurel. Standing at the counsel table, tears lining her face.

"Enough," she says.

Harry has a hand on her arm, trying to get her to sit, a stunned expression on his face like she erupted without warning.

Even Woodruff is dumbfounded, palming the handle of his gavel but not striking the bench.

A matron moves in behind, putting two hands on Laurel's shoulders, a signal for her to sit, evidence in the eyes of the jury that she is not free to move about as she wishes.

"Enough about the child," Laurel says, and with that she slumps back into her chair.

I look, and the jury is mesmerized. All eyes on Laurel.

Almost in a daze I say: "Your honor, could we take a brief recess?"

We regroup back near the holding cells, and I tell her that this is not good. Her conduct has injected a whole new element into our case. What the jury thinks of this I have no way of knowing.

I cannot read them as to Laurel's emotive appeal, whether they might see this as an admission that she had something to do with the murder, or was merely taking pity on Jack.

What she tells me is that she could no longer deal with the matter of the child, my picking away further at questions regarding this dead infant and its origins.

"Everybody is talking about it like it was a thing. An event and nothing more," she says. "It wasn't. It was a living breathing human being. A baby," she says. "A little baby. Its life snuffed out before it had a chance." Laurel, the good mother. It is the most troubling aspect of the case to her, that an innocent child has been killed.

She apologizes, but says she simply cannot deal with the dead infant.

I tell her that I will stay clear of it. My hand in the air, two fingers like a scout. The point is now made, I tell her.

It is all I can do given her explosive attitude on the subject.

One more outburst and there is no telling what could happen to our case.

"Nothing further will be said by me about this child until my closing argument," I tell her. "Then I will have to talk about it. But I will do it briefly and discreetly."

She nods as if she understands.

"Are you all right?" I ask.

"Yes."

I take her by the arm and we head back out. When we get to the courtroom, Cassidy turns a wicked gaze on Laurel. Lama actually grins. She has given them something they have not been able to make from their own case, the whiff of suspicion, the suggestion that Laurel is now gored by conscience, that she cannot deal with the unintended consequences of her own violent act.

I can tell by the look in Morgan's eye that we have not heard the last of this dead child. I shudder to think what might happen if I am forced to put Laurel on the stand.

Woodruff comes out. The bailiff calls the court to order, and Jack heads back into the box. The judge tells me to proceed.

"Mr. Vega, how long have you been a member of the Legislature?"

"What does that have to do with anything?" he says.

"Just answer the question."

"Twelve years," he says.

"You're not planning on running for reelection, are you?"

"No. I'm retiring," he says.

I look to Harry and he lifts the top off the box.

"Retirement?" I say.

"Yes."

"I've heard some of them called 'country clubs,' but I've never heard the people who are sent there called retirees," I say.

He's looking at me, not saying a word. But from the expression I know that Jack is the only other person in the room at the moment who knows what I am talking about. For the first time today we are speaking the same language. His face like a stone idol, struck by a lightning bolt. He's looking now at the box. I can only imagine what is running through his mind. For Jack, an out-of-body experience.

"I'm going to object to this." Morgan is out of her chair, about to step on a land mine. "The question of Mr. Vega's future plans is irrelevant. If counsel has a question, he should ask it, and stop badgering the witness with inane comments," she says.

"Then I will," I say. "Mr. Vega, is it not a fact that you have entered a plea of guilty to multiple felony counts, violations of federal law relating to political corruption?"

There is a swell of movement, like an undulating wave through the press rows, an audible gasp from the audience, the kind of revelation that comes in a courtroom once in a blue moon. A reporter in the second row actually says "Holy shit," loud enough for Woodruff to hear it but ignore. One guy near the center aisle turns, pad in hand, and with a finger in the air circles his hand in a quick motion, like the signal to start engines. I can see cameras and lights outside through the glass slit in the courtroom door, revving up—part of the media ride that Jack will be taking.

He still hasn't answered my question.

"I . . ." Cassidy breaks off before she starts her sentence. Heated whispers in Lama's ear. Jimmy is all shrugs, like a cheap stuffed doll that's been repeatedly kicked in the ass. He doesn't have a clue.

"Your honor, I'm going to object to this . . . to this line of questioning. We've . . . We've received no notice of any of this."

"Nonetheless, it is true, is it not?" I'm bearing down on Vega.

Woodruff holds up a hand. "The witness will not answer. There's an objection pending."

"Your honor, we have certified copies both of the indict-

ment and the record of conviction. We are not responsible for
the state's lack of knowledge in this area. We are not required
to share the fruits of our own investigation with them.

"I would point out that Mr. Vega is the state's witness. We
did not call him. These convictions go to his qualifications to
testify. If he chose not to disclose this disability to the state,
that's their problem. They should take it up with him."

"But, your honor," says Cassidy.

"He's got a point," says Woodruff. "You called the witness."

"But the conviction wasn't public record."

"First maybe we should find out if there was a conviction."
Woodruff motions for the papers, to examine them.

I hand a set of the documents up to the bench, and Woodruff
scans them. Another goes to Cassidy, who quickly sits and
pores over them with Lama, a lot of grim looks.

All the while Jack sits in the box, turning various shades of
gray. A couple of times Woodruff consults with him quietly
over the edge of the bench and receives sober nods from Jack.

"It appears these are authentic," says Woodruff. "Certified
copies," he says. "Subject to a later motion to strike, I will
allow counsel to explore the question," he says.

Cassidy's still protesting. "Unfair surprise," she says.
"We've been sandbagged by federal authorities," she tells
Woodruff. At one point she actually mentions Dana by name,
in the same way one might spit out another four-letter word.

It is all to no avail. Woodruff says her objections are noted
and tells her to sit down.

I hand a set of the documents to Jack, the only player who
hasn't seen them, and I ask him if in fact they do not accurately reflect the convictions entered in his name in the federal
court.

He starts to whine about his deal. "They weren't supposed
to release any of this until the end of the trial," he says. "We
had an arrangement," he tells Woodruff. He's ignoring me
like I'm not here, making his appeal to the black robes.

"Take it up with the federal court," says Woodruff. Jack is pitched back into the dark pit with me.

"Mr. Vega, I ask you one more time. Do these documents accurately reflect your convictions under various pleas of guilty to felony charges in the federal court?"

"I suppose," he says. "I'm not a lawyer." Like the iron statues of Lenin, you can hear the thud, the sick leaden sound. Jack the upright legislator has just toppled.

With this there's a swell of murmuring in the front rows. Pencils worked to a dull point. A couple of the electronic folks head out to strike postures and make news in front of their cameras.

The final blow. I reach into the packet of documents and pull out a sheaf of stapled pages, four in all. It is a sentencing brief prepared by Jack's lawyers. I call the court's attention to the document, and a minute later we are all singing from the same sheet. I ask Jack to read it. When he is finished I wade in.

"Did your lawyers prepare this?" I ask him.

"Yeah."

"Then you advanced this argument to the federal court. That because your wife was murdered you made a hardship appeal for straight probation on the federal charges. No prison time," I say. "Is that right?"

"The kids needed a father," he says. "She was in jail." He's pointing to Laurel.

"Yes, based almost entirely on your allegations," I say. "There are some who might suggest that you should have been there instead." I'm talking about jail.

"I didn't commit murder," he says.

"And neither did my client. And you know it," I tell him.

He doesn't respond to this. The best answer I could have hoped for.

"The fact remains," I say, "that while your wife was dead and your former wife was in jail awaiting trial on charges of murder, that the only one who actually seems to have benefited from this sorry state of affairs was you. Isn't that so?''

"How did I benefit?" he asks.

"Your wife had a lover. You were jealous. She got pregnant. So you killed her, framed your former spouse, and used the tragedy to ease your own sentence on criminal charges. Masterful," I tell him. "Brilliant. It almost worked."

"That's bullshit," he says.

"What one could expect from a man who has survived by his wits in the Legislature for two decades." I speak like this is some den of thieves, a rabbit warren for breeding organized crime, which Jack has now confirmed by his own conduct. What the public suspects, what we both know, that there is a litany of further indictments in the offing. With any luck these will be breaking during our case-in-chief.

He repeats the denial, Jack's stock-in-trade: "Bullshit. This is bullshit."

Woodruff seems to give him license here, realizing that the witness is at a loss for words, that in defense he should be allowed his best form of expression. It has its effect on the jury, and Jack slowly realizes this.

"I lost my wife." He sits up straight in the chair, finds the last scrap of dignity, and stares me in the eye.

"And you found the silver lining in that adversity, didn't you?" I wave the sentencing brief in my hand for him to see.

It is a question that requires no response. The answer lies in Vega's weary eyes as he surveys the media, knowing what is in store. It is a classic case, Jack digging himself a hole by his convenient memory. It started with the gun, a throwaway issue in this case, that he could easily have disclosed to the cops. But to Jack there was more intrigue in concealment. The adventure of deception has made up the better part of his life. This first slipup tainted him as to the second, the rug and its true ownership. If Jack had been a standup guy on the pistol and told the cops about it, his word might have carried more weight as against the black-and-white terms of the settlement agreement.

As it is, this all now devolves in a common theme about Jack's neck, that nothing he says can be believed, that here sits a man who is a stranger to the truth. It is a portrait now stretched and displayed in the chipped and frayed frame of political corruption, an image that could be properly hung only in a rogues' gallery.

CHAPTER
28

This morning I'm in the office going over some last-minute details before heading for court when the com-line on my phone buzzes.

"Yes."

"Your nephew is here to see you."

"Who?"

"Danny Vega," she says.

"Here?"

"Yes. Shall I send him in?"

The shock of my life. "Go ahead," I say.

A minute later shadows on the translucent glass of the door, and Danny ambles into my office. He's lost some weight and looks like he hasn't shaved the light peach fuzz from his chin in a few days. His clothes have the look of travel, a wrinkled shirt and jeans with tailored fraying around the knees that could use a washing, dark athletic shoes like combat boots, and no socks.

"Uncle Paul," he says. It's always the same with Danny. He will be calling me Uncle Paul when he is thirty-five and I am walking with a crutch. A shy grin. He holds out his hand for me to shake.

"What are you doing here?" I'm standing over my desk, gripping his hand. I don't mean to be inhospitable, but Danny's timing has always left something to be desired. He was safely ensconced a half continent away for the duration, and neither I nor his mother need this distraction at the moment.

"I was worried about Mom," he says. "Thought maybe she could use some support."

"Where's Julie?" I ask.

"She's fine. She's back there," he tells me. We are still playing cryptic games as to where precisely this is. "I came out on the bus," he says. "Maggie knows. I just couldn't stay there anymore. I had to see how Mom was doing."

"She's fine," I tell him. "I have a feeling she's going to be pretty upset when she finds out you're back here."

"Yeah. Well . . ." He shrugs a little, like "maybe she asked for too much."

"I saw the morning paper," he says. "The news about Dad."

He could not miss this. Every paper in the state is carrying it on the front page: LONGTIME LEGISLATOR CONVICTED OF CORRUPTION.

As much as Danny does not get on with his father, he takes no pleasure in Jack's misfortune. He asks me if it's really true. I tell him that it is, and Danny floors me with his perception.

"I guess I always knew that someday he'd get in trouble," he says. "What will happen to him?" he asks.

I shake my head, like I haven't a clue.

"Will he go to jail too?"

"I don't know," I tell him. "That's up to the judge."

"But it helped Mom's case?" he says. "I mean the information about him." In the tradeoffs of life Danny can live with this, his father's conviction, if it helps Laurel.

"It helped," I say. How can I tell the boy that I'm trying to put the ring of murder around his father's neck?

"Things are going well for your mother at the moment." I leave it at that and change the subject before he can pursue further. "You can't stay here," I tell him.

"Why not?"

"The court in the custody case has an outstanding order," I say.

"Have I done something wrong?"

"No, but your dad has custody."

Danny was thinking that maybe the news in the paper changed all that. I assure him that it did not. If his father is sentenced to time in prison, and Laurel is still in jail, Danny and Julie will become wards of the court. If that happens I will wade in and try for custody.

"I'll stay at Mom's apartment," he says. "Nobody will look there." It's like he's already figured this out.

What can I say? "Why don't you go now. And clean up. I'll have some food sent over. Groceries," I tell him. Harry knows a woman who can take care of this. "Do you have clean clothes over there?"

He nods. "But I wanna know everything that's happening," he says, "in Mom's case."

"I don't have time right now. I'll call you. We can talk later," I tell him. "Dinner at my place tonight. You can get the Vespa then." This has been in my garage since Danny left Capital City.

"I've already got it," he says. "Stopped by on the way over here. Hope you don't mind?" he says.

"Why should I mind? Clean up and get some rest," I tell him. "You look tired." The boy has rings of unrequited sleep under his eyes.

"Sure," he says. He turns to leave.

"And Danny—don't go near the jail." Like a seer I know what's running through his mind—a visit to his mom. "They'll nail you as soon as you sign in," I tell him. "You'll be living with your dad again."

I see this register in his eyes, the admission that this is probably where he was headed. He nods, and like that he is gone.

• • •

Cassidy cannot rest her case on the sour note that was Jack's testimony and the hair-raising revelation of his criminal convictions.

Today Dana is just outside the courtroom, waiting to see what happens. As a name I had placed on my witness list, chaff for Cassidy to mull over, she cannot enter. I think her proximity here is a bad idea and have told her so. On the way in Cassidy was giving her looks to kill. Morgan knows where the information to destroy Jack came from, and Dana by her mere presence here is now rubbing salt into the open wound. This is payback, I think, for Morgan's earlier attempts to interfere in Dana's judicial aspirations, Cassidy's efforts to turn the Queen's Bench against Dana, and Lama's shot at shifting blame for the news leaks on the bombing to Dana and her people. All of these efforts have failed, but Dana is not one to forget.

From the inception I have wondered how much of Dana's help in our case has been inspired by her belief that Laurel is innocent, by her affection for me, and how much by her increasing enmity toward Cassidy.

As for Jack, he is nowhere to be seen today. Vega is ducking the horde of media, which I am told are camped like vandals at his condo. I have visions of fiery torches dripping tallow in the night, their holders demanding that Jack come out and talk. Now that his conviction is public, sentencing in Jack's case has been scheduled for a week from today. Harry is offering odds that he will do time. Federal judges, says Harry, do not like to be used, and Vega's efforts at sympathy using Melanie's murder has the odor of exploitation about it.

While there is no question but that Jack's testimony was originally intended to conclude the state's case, this morning when court is called to order, Cassidy tells Woodruff that they are putting up one last witness.

She asks leave of court to recall Simon Angelo, the county coroner.

"Is there objection?" says Woodruff. He looks at me.

I confer with Harry, who gives me one of his patented shrugs. Harry is certain that they are back-filling, some window-dressing so they can give the illusion that they are ending on a high note. Angelo is a safe witness, somebody Morgan can control, who is not likely to do more damage to their case.

I am nervous about this. If Cassidy wants something more from Angelo, there are only two possibilities: she forgot to cover some item with him originally or his testimony is intended to shore up some major hole we have ripped in their case.

I put up an argument. "Your honor, if the state wants to recall the witness, it should do so on rebuttal after we've presented our own case."

Cassidy argues for some latitude, some equitable setoff for being sandbagged, the surprise on Jack's conviction. This strikes a sympathetic chord with Woodruff. He asks her how long Angelo's testimony will take.

"Ten minutes," she says.

"I'm inclined to allow it," he tells me, and gestures toward Cassidy to call the witness.

Angelo takes the stand and is reminded that he is still under oath.

It is when Morgan begins anew the task of qualifying him as an expert that little shivers course up my spine. She does not do this in the broad field of forensic pathology, but instead in the narrower subspecialty of serology, the study of blood, and DNA. Bells begin to go off. It is becoming clear that there is some point to all of this, and despite Harry's best guess, it is not cosmetic.

"Dr. Angelo, could you tell the court, as part of your medical examination in the present case did you perform any blood tests on the victims in this case, and in particular, the John Doe, the unborn fetus?"

With the mention of the child, Laurel winces. There is a palpable shudder through her body, and I take one of her hands and hold it under the table. I have not told her about Danny's visit to my office. She has enough to worry about for the moment. We will deal with that over the weekend, and if need be I will ship the boy back to where he came from until this is over.

"We didn't do blood," says Angelo, "but we did do DNA." He explains to the court that after his initial testimony, when questions of paternity were raised on cross-examination, he went back and conducted some tests, "expedited," as he says.

"Could you tell the court what tests you performed and why?"

"I carried out what are known as DNA probes to determine paternity," he says.

"Your honor." I'm out of my chair. I'm complaining about the lack of notice on this.

"We are not talking about exculpatory evidence here," says Cassidy.

Constitutional law in this country requires public prosecutors not just to convict, but to act in the interests of justice. Cassidy is under a strict requirement to share with us at an early stage any evidence that she finds that might serve to exonerate my client. The fact that they did tests and did not disclose them until now can mean only one thing—that these tests do not advance our theory of the case that Melanie had a lover. It is my hope that maybe at best the tests were inconclusive.

"Counsel made the issue relevant," says Cassidy, "when he excoriated Mr. Vega, suggesting, I might add improperly," she says, "that the victim was engaged in some lurid love affair. Now that he has raised this ugly specter, we must deal with it," she says. There is a look of rebuke from Cassidy, which on her face takes on a wicked aspect.

"I'm going to allow it," says Woodruff. He motions me to sit down.

As I do, I turn, and catch Dana out of the corner of one eye through the slot in the door. She is tracking on Angelo on the

stand, and from her expression, she senses what I do. Cassidy
would not be calling this witness unless he was going to do
some major damage to our theory of the case.

We are at a severe disadvantage here and Morgan knows it.
The child and its mother had been buried before our case for
the defense had sprouted a theory. It would have required an
order to exhume the bodies for us to perform any similar DNA
testing. Harry and I had discussed this option at an early stage.
But considering the fact that Jack had his tubes cut and was
presumably firing blanks from his cannon of conception, we
saw no purpose. The child had to belong to someone else.

Cassidy nibbles around the edges for a while, a few preliminary questions to Angelo, and then pops the one we are all
waiting for. Was he able as a result of these tests to exclude
Jack Vega from the population of men who could have fathered this child?

"No," says Angelo. "Not only could we not exclude him,"
he says, "but using a single-locus probe, in which specific
shared genetic factors were analyzed between the dead fetus
and Mr. Vega, I would say there is a very high probability
that paternity does exist."

"How high?" says Morgan.

"Based on the probes, he cannot be excluded from the class
of potential paternity, and in this case the likelihood of paternity based on multiple DNA probes is more than ninety-nine
percent, to be specific ninety-nine point four percent."

I sit stunned at the table. What Angelo is telling the jury is
that as a matter of scientific certainty, Jack is the father of this
unborn child. The look of disbelief must register on my face,
for when I glance over, several of the jurors are studying me
as to effect, an ether of discontent settling over the panel.
Several of the women are looking at me, wondering how, in
the face of this evidence, I could scandalize a victim whose
lips were sealed by death. There is an undercurrent of murmuring in the courtroom, and Woodruff slaps his gavel.

There is no need to manufacture a high point in her case.

Cassidy has gone for the underbelly of our own, and ripped it out.

"Nothing more of this witness," she says.

As I rise I feel like I am supported by limbs of jelly. I struggle to keep the stunned expression of anger off my face. But deep down I have the sense that this is manufactured evidence—something hatched at a midnight meeting, when at a weak moment Cassidy saw their case evaporating. It is scientific evidence we cannot test as to its accuracy or veracity.

"Doctor, there's no chance of error in your tests?" I say. A feeble first strike.

"No." No hesitation. Not "I wouldn't think so," but an absolute, emphatic no from Angelo.

His hairless dome shimmers under the bright glare of the courtroom lights. The look of enigma is in his eyes. We both know that unless I can shake him on this, the motive for my theory of defense is gone. On the eve of our case, I will be left with nothing to talk about, already committed to a scenario of the crime that Angelo, in ten minutes, has completely destroyed. Without some shadowy lover in Melanie's bed, why would Jack murder the mother of his own child? Even the most cold-hearted would not commit multiple murder for the purpose of propping up sympathy on sentencing in another, lesser criminal case. Even Jack could calculate the odds on this and find it a loser.

"Surely there must be some margin of error," I tell him, "as to the percentage or probability?" I say.

"This is not like some political survey," he tells me, "but science. There is no margin of error, plus or minus," he says. "The percentage of probability as to paternity turns on the fact that there are degrees of relatedness between individuals. This would range from no possibility, as where the subject is excluded by blood type, for example, to a very low probability, to a point of near or virtual certainty," he says.

He smiles, waiting for me to ask, but I do not, where along this continuum our particular case falls. He would only gore me with his pike one more time.

"It's very interesting that you've reduced none of this to writing," I say. "Surely there must be working papers?" I say. "Your notes?"

He smiles a little concession. "I can produce my working notes," he says. "They're not with me at the moment."

"Of course not," I say. "I would like to see them."

"No problem. I'll send them to your office."

I can examine these and call him again in my case-in-chief, but Angelo knows I am grasping at straws. Any working papers would be written in chicken scratches that only another physician could decipher, and would be crafted in such general and vague terms that the procedures used in testing could be fleshed out only by resort to Angelo's own testimony. I could spend five grand on a scientific circle-jerk and end right back where I started.

Of course we could run our own tests. Exhume the bodies and do our own DNA, but there is no time and Angelo knows this. Our case opens on Monday. DNA analysis at most labs takes a minimum of six weeks.

I am getting angry. It is written in my eyes.

"Dr. Angelo, are you familiar with the medical records pertaining to Mr. Vega's vasectomy twelve years ago?"

"I've read them," he says.

"Well, then, perhaps you can enlighten the court on how it's possible for a man who's undergone a vasectomy for the express purpose of sterilization to father a child?"

"It happens all the time," he says.

"Excuse me?"

"Obviously you're not aware, but there's a considerable potential for failure with regard to this procedure. Lawsuits filed all the time," he says, "by couples surprised at becoming new parents after the man has undergone a vasectomy."

"Now you're going to tell us that ninety-nine-point-four percent of these procedures fail. Is that right, Doctor?"

"No, actually it's about five percent."

"Pretty rare," I'd say. "Not exactly an odds-on bet," I tell him. "I suppose some witch doctor performed this procedure on Mr. Vega, using a dull stone scalpel?"

"No. It's called recanalization," he says. "The vas deferens, the excretory duct for sperm from the testicles, is normally severed as part of the vasectomy. The ends are tied off. Failure rates often depend on how much is removed and how the occlusion is performed, the tying-off," he says. "If the occlusion fails, the ends of the duct can grow back together and rejoin."

"Did you surgically examine Mr. Vega to determine that this is what occurred?"

"No," he says. "But the techniques used by the physician in his case are no longer considered to be medically on the cutting edge. Please excuse the pun," he says.

A few jurors actually smile at this. Angelo has made a joke. He is mocking me. Unless I can turn this around I should sit down now. But I have dug the hole deeper, damaged our case more by these specifics. The compulsion to fill in just a little, some concession from the witness, some seeming high ground that I can end it on, if only for the illusion that we have gained something by all of this. Like the compulsive gambler, I am driven to win back just a little of my losses, some equivocation that I can build on later, that I can argue to the jury on close.

It is a high-stakes gambit, but I sense that even the most medically disinclined in this courtroom have a singular burning question at this moment. If I passed out a hundred cards for suggested queries, all would come back with this at the top of the list. I could leave it and sit down, but the jury will wonder why. Against this I balance the first rule of the courtroom: *never ask unless you know*. Still, I can hear it murmured in their collective minds. It is overpowering, a single interrogatory in the desperate hope that he says no.

"Dr. Angelo, did you perform a sperm count on Mr. Vega?"

I stand transfixed by the twinkle in his eye as he says, "Yes."

It is like the sensation of hot lead flowing into every orifice of my body, the shuddering realization that I have fallen into the fiery crucible prepared for me by Cassidy.

I could turn and walk away, excuse the witness. But Morgan on redirect would drive this thing through me like a javelin.

"And what did you find?" I ask.

"We found that while Mr. Vega had apparently suffered some scar tissue as a result of the vasectomy, he was able to project a sufficient number of sperm to conceive a child." He delivers this death blow with a smile, the coup-de-grâce.

I stand leaden before him, the shambles of my case arrayed around me. Even the skull of Melanie Vega, skewered by its metal stake on the evidence cart, seems to mock me in its stark silence. Except for pictures of them copulating—Jack and Melanie—Angelo has slammed the door on any doubts concerning Vega's fatherhood of the dead child. In a single sitting he has done more damage than all of their witnesses combined.

It is why Cassidy didn't touch this, the vasectomy or any of its tangents, in her original examination of Angelo. She wanted to wait until I was too far along the path of my defense to change course, until after I had called Jack a killer in front of the jury. It was the trap she constructed for me, and I fell into it like a lamb to the shearing. I had been warned about her, the cunning, relentless style. Her case in seeming disarray, with two judges and the referee giving the bout to the challenger, Cassidy has gone for the knockout punch and connected.

CHAPTER
29

By the time Angelo finishes I am gutted like some bottom fish on a factory ship, filleted in front of the witness box. It is nearly noon, and Cassidy tells Woodruff that the state now rests its case.

As Angelo steps down from the stand, there is a palpable atmosphere in the courtroom, a mood swing of dynamic proportion, that would have oddsmakers offering book that Laurel will never leave this place a free woman.

The apprehension in her eyes as she studies me, unsteady in front of the witness box, tells me that she is not oblivious to this sea change. At one point I find it necessary to actually grip the railing at the edge of the bench in order to steady myself as I negotiate the ten feet back to our counsel table.

It is Friday afternoon, and Woodruff tells me to be prepared to open my case for the defense first thing Monday morning. I think he is taking pity on me.

When I answer him I hear all of this, even my own reply, through a pulsing auditory drone, like the rumbling of an engine in the bowels of a ship. It is the pounding of blood through carotid arteries, caused by the panic now coursing through my brain.

The judge slaps the gavel and the court is adjourned, the jury led out.

The matron is moving on Laurel, whose eyes have not left

me. I arrive just in time to take her hand and exchange a few words.

"We'll have to talk," I tell her. "This afternoon." My voice has an ominous quality, the forbidding tones of a surgeon who has spent some time with his fingers inside of a loved one, looking for cancer, and now must deliver the news.

"I'm not going anywhere," she says. Laurel actually manages a smile before she is led away. A fatalist at heart, it is as if she never expected a different ending.

"Ten-to-one the fucker's lying," says Harry. He's talking, almost to himself, about Angelo, his face flushed, the only one I know who hates losing more than I do. Only in this case the stakes for me are much greater.

"Real convenient," he says. "Eleventh hour they come up with this shit, nothing in the report, bodies all buried." He's throwing papers pell-mell into the evidence box, grousing under his breath.

"There's something we've missed," I tell him.

"What?"

"I don't know. Something doesn't square."

"I'll tell you what *I've* missed," he says. "That bitch with the bumper of my car." He's leering at Cassidy, hissing under his breath as she loads her things into her briefcase.

Lama slides a chair out of her way, opening the passage for Morgan to get between our tables to the swinging gate in the railing.

"Have a good weekend," she says.

"Morgan. You got a minute?"

She stops and turns.

"I may have to talk to you this weekend." I swallow a lot of bile as I say this. "After I talk to my client," I tell her.

She knows what I am broaching, some deal to save Laurel's life.

"I don't know if my client will go for—"

"Don't concern yourself about your client," she says. "Your only worry should be here. Whether I can be persuaded to budge, which at the moment does not look promising,'' she says.

She proceeds to give me a lecture in full view of several reporters taking notes, comments on Laurel's ethics as well as my own.

''She's a bad actor,'' says Cassidy, ''and we both know it. And your antics with her husband, the sealed indictments. You and the judicial wannabe over there.'' She gestures toward Dana, who is fighting the tide of bodies trying to get inside the courtroom. Cassidy makes little noises like tisk-tisk.

''Is there a chance—''

''You can leave a message on my service,'' she says. ''If I don't go anywhere, I'll get back to you.'' With this she turns and they start to walk away, Lama intoning in a voice that can be heard through the courtroom, ''Can you believe the gall?''

It is clear that they intend to make me grovel.

They merge with the crowd heading for the door.

I can actually hear Harry growl. Then he utters a couple of expletives.

''They're lying,'' he says.

''I don't know.''

''Don't be naive,'' he tells me. ''They made it up out of whole cloth. They know we can't check it.''

Harry is of that school of social thought that believes most victories in criminal courts are fashioned from the preponderance of perjury. You spin yours and they do theirs, and in the end the side that is most adept at invention wins; the thought that throughout history truth has withered and died of loneliness in most courtrooms.

It is with this deep thought that I feel the hot whisper of breath on the back of my neck. When I turn I am staring into Dana's eyes.

''I heard what happened,'' she says. She's white as a sheet.

She puts one hand on the nape of my neck and comes up close with her lips, and for an instant I think she is going to kiss me on the cheek. Instead she puts her mouth close to my ear, and in the faintest tones whispers, "Not to worry. I can get you the witness."

I pull away and look into her eyes. She is talking about the man who saw Jack with the killer Lyle Simmons, at the bar across the river.

She ignores the fact that this does not supply motive. Why would Jack kill his wife?

"Where is he?" I say.

"That's not something you need to worry about," says Dana. "All you have to know is that he will be here, in court, on Monday morning, ready to tell you what he saw."

"When did you find him? Why didn't you tell me?" I ask.

As she pulls away, there is an aspect to her eyes, something that tells me not to tread there, that this is forbidden ground.

"You're out of your mind," says Harry. "Don't ask questions," he says. "She's right, what you don't know can't hurt you. All you know is what this guy says. Pure and simple. Real easy," says Harry.

"It's simple. I'm not so sure it's pure," I tell him. I have concerns about this, the fear that this witness is suborned, perjured testimony. It is all too convenient.

It was on her tongue, as well as in her eyes. "I can get you the witness," not "We have found him."

Like Detroit makes cars, I have the sick feeling that this guy, and what he has to say, are manufactured. What I can't figure is why Dana would do this, a woman with a judgeship looming. Why take the risk? She can't hate Cassidy that much.

"And besides," I tell Harry, "we have problems because the witness is not on our list. He could be excluded on those grounds alone."

The state has an absolute right to check him out, to ensure that he's not a ringer, someone with a criminal record, maybe a penchant for lying on the stand, to make certain that he was not on ice, doing time in some human warehouse when he claims to have seen these revelations across the river.

Harry says this is no problem. "They complain, we offer them time to check the guy out. In the meantime we tap-dance with a few other witnesses. Continue to beat out the theme that Jack did it."

"Why?" I say.

"Who knows? Fucker's crazy," he says. "Not the first time some pol went 'round the bend."

"You forget," I tell him, "that the witness is probably lying. That he probably never saw Jack with anybody in a bar. You don't think Cassidy's going to figure this out?"

"You forget," says Harry, "who is offering this guy up to us. The fucking federal government," he says. The glee in Harry's eyes as he says this is something to behold. "Stop and think for a minute," he says. "You don't actually believe they're stupid enough to produce somebody who isn't absolutely bulletproof? If the feds do it, Lama could check the guy seven ways to Sunday and come up empty. They'll probably make him an archbishop or something," says Harry.

He talks as if the government operates a referral service for such things, like a nurses' registry; perjured testimony with references.

"Take my word," says Harry. "There are two things the federal government does well: print money and make up false identities," he says.

His words freeze me in place like a naked Eskimo in an Arctic blast. My eyes at this moment are two big round O's.

"What is it?" he says.

"Something we didn't see. Something you just said."

"What?"

"Identities," I say.

"What are you talking about?"

"The Merlows. We've been asking ourselves from the beginning, what was it that George or Kathy Merlow saw that night?"

"So they caught a glimpse," says Harry. "Somebody doing Melanie. Unless you think we can get Chuckles to let us conduct a séance in open court, they're beyond the pale," he tells me. "Let's concentrate on the other figment," says Harry, "the one that breathes when he lies." He's talking about Dana's witness.

"How can we be so sure they saw something?" I tell him. "What if they didn't see anything?"

"Then somebody went to a lot of trouble to kill them for nothing." Harry's not tracking.

"Maybe it's not what they saw," I tell him, "but who, or more precisely, what they are."

He's giving me a lot of dense looks.

Before Harry can move, I'm out of my chair and down the hall, in the direction of his office, Harry like a shadow.

"Where are you going?"

As I open the door, it is clear that Harry's office is a place waiting for a fire.

There are piles of yellowing newsprint on the floor, clipped-up papers, and leftover scraps, mixed in with briefs and research notes for cases Harry is working on. There are snippets of news stories, articles nailed to the walls with a million push-pins. These range from cartoons to banner headlines, all the stuff that fuels Harry's engine of political paranoia.

I start pitching paper.

"Wait a minute. What are you doing?" Harry is incensed, as if somehow there is a chemical equilibrium to this, some order to the stew of litter that I am upsetting.

Halfway between an ancient issue of *The New Republic* and a molding jelly sandwich I find what I am looking for. Saffron with age and brittle, it carries a dateline from Lexington, Kentucky. I hand it to Harry and let him read.

He barely has time to finish the first graph when it hits him.

"No," he says. "You don't think . . . ?"

"One way to find out," I tell him. "Do you want to make the call or should I?"

CHAPTER
30

My opening statement to the jury is brief, and probably obscure. It is not the blistering assault on Jack that I have honed to a bristling point for the past month.

"In a few moments," I tell them, "you are going to hear testimony and see evidence that for some of you may cause considerable dismay. For others," I say, "it will merely serve to confirm your darkest suspicions about the nature of man and his institutions of justice. This evidence," I tell them, "has come into my possession only within the last thirty-six hours, and in many ways it comes as more of a shock to me than it may to all of you."

Thirty seconds after I call her name, Dana Colby walks through the courtroom door and up the center aisle. She is calm, almost serene, in a dark blue suit, the kind a prosecutor would wear to court, and heels that click on the marble floor.

She walks past me as if I am not here, not a look or whisper of recognition, her stone-cold gaze straight ahead up at the bench.

Laurel is at the table with Harry, asking him questions, why I am putting Dana up. We have not had time to bring her current, and until this evidence is in, I have no idea as to its impact on the jury or the judge.

There is a flurry of activity at Cassidy's counsel table. Among other things, she and Lama are checking our witness list to ensure that Dana's name appears. What was originally intended as chaff on our own list was seen by them as just that. They had forgotten that Dana's name was there. Now they are surprised when she actually appears and takes the stand.

She is sworn and sits, her gaze fixed on the middle distance somewhere at the back of the courtroom. The only hint of any anxiety some mild thumping with two fingers of one hand on the arm of her chair.

She refuses to make eye contact with me, as I have refused to take her calls or see her for two days now, since having her served with the subpoena to appear here. I think she knows, or has possibly guessed what we have.

Dana tried to camp in my office this morning to catch me, a meeting I wished to avoid, so Harry and I stayed away, prepping for court at a coffee shop two blocks down the street until moments before we arrived here.

"State your name for the record?" says the clerk.

"Danielle Elizabeth Colby."

I had not known her first name was Danielle until this moment. Perhaps a measure of just how little I know about this woman.

I move dead center in front of the witness box where she can no longer ignore me, and standing here, we finally confront each other.

"Ms. Colby, would you tell the court what you do for a living?"

"I'm a Deputy United States Attorney." There is a deadpan to her voice, emotionless, as if something has been drained from the woman I thought I knew. There is more than a little pain in this exercise for me.

"Chief Deputy in your office for the Eastern District of this state, is that not so?" I say.

"Yes."

"In a word, you are a federal prosecutor, aren't you?" I ask.

"Yes."

I am leading her shamelessly, but all of this is harmless and Cassidy is anxious to have me get to the point. I think perhaps Morgan has not picked up on the friction between us, and believes that we are working in tandem to do a number on her case.

"Ms. Colby, who were George and Kathy Merlow?"

With the mention of their names she stiffens, like someone has shot a mild jolt of electricity through her chair.

"They were neighbors of the victim in this case, Melanie Vega," she says. "They lived in the house directly next door."

This is not what I am looking for. Dana is adroit. She manages to avoid the question, so I am left to use this to spin a little silk and crawl further out into the web.

"And to your knowledge did they reside there, in that house next door, on the night that Melanie Vega was murdered?"

"Yes."

"Before that night, did you ever have occasion to talk with George or Kathy Merlow for any reason?"

Dana has beautiful eyes even when they are darting in discomfort as they are now. Her tongue searches for saliva.

"I might have," she says.

I nod slowly. I am not enjoying this, and I think she knows it, so she embellishes a little to get me away from the nub of it.

"We lived in the same neighborhood, you see a lot of people," she says. "I might have seen them someplace or other." She makes this sound like some social accident, a rubbing of shoulders that cannot be recalled with precision.

"I see. Might one of these places where you met George and Kathy Merlow have been your office downtown at the justice department?"

Finally we arrive at the point, like a prime number, an issue that cannot be divided by half-truths.

She looks up at the judge. "Your honor, if we could have

a moment in chambers," she says. "There are matters of critical importance, life and death," she says.

Woodruff has heard a lot of things from the bench, but never a witness asking for a private conference in the middle of her testimony.

"Is there something wrong with you physically?" he says. "Are you ill?"

"No, your honor."

"Then you should answer the question," he says. Dana's moment of truth.

"I might have. I can't remember." Truth turns to evasion.

"Surely that is something you would remember, a meeting in your office?" I say. I try to bring her to it gently, as little pain as possible, like a cyanide capsule cracked between the molars.

"I meet with a lot of people," she says. "I cannot remember them all." She writhes and squirms, a futile and agonizing effort to put off the inevitable.

All the while I can see Laurel pumping Harry, a series of heated one-liners in his ear. She wants to know what I am doing. What Dana has to do with all of this.

"Isn't it a fact, Ms. Colby, that the night you met the Merlows outside in front of their house, the night Melanie Vega was murdered, that you were there not as some itinerant passerby but on business?"

"I don't know what you're talking about," she says.

"Isn't it a fact that you went to meet George and Kathy Merlow as a representative of the United States Department of Justice to assure them that they would be all right, that everything would be taken care of?"

She looks at me like I'm smoking some bad weed.

"Who called you?" I say. "Was it your boss, because you lived closer than anyone else? Or did you have some special relationship with them, something like a caseworker?" I say.

"Your honor, I think counsel is confused," she says. "Someone has clearly given him misinformation. Misled him," she says, "for whatever reason."

In all of this there is a lot of protest, but it is not lost on Woodruff that there is neither a denial nor a reply to my question.

"I'm waiting for an answer," I say.

"Your honor." She is still looking up at him, a plaintive appeal falling on deaf ears.

He tells her to answer the question.

She takes it to a level of higher appeal. She turns to me.

"Can't we talk? I thought you cared." She mouths these words in a whisper so low that the court reporter asks her to repeat them. She has missed them for the record.

Dana ignores this.

"At the moment," I say, "what I care about is your answer to the question."

"Fine," she says. There is a transformation that takes place in this instant. It is measured in her eyes, a recognition that anything that might have been between us is gone, vaporized by deceptions now being dragged by the painful process of the law into the naked sunlight.

"You want to know about Kathy Merlow?" she says.

"Yes."

"Fine. I'll tell you. Kathy Merlow was part of what is known as the federal witness relocation program."

"She was a federally protected witness?" I say.

"Yes."

"What was her real name?"

"Carla Leopold," she says.

"How did she come to live in Capital City?"

"She had testified in cases on the east coast, against certain organized crime figures. As a consequence there was a contract out on her life. She was given a new identity along with her husband, and moved to this city in order to protect their lives. It was part of a plea-bargain."

With this there is the low rumble of voices through the courtroom, a stirring in the press rows as a dozen heads come up. Pencils stop their little squiggles. A lot of wondering as to where this fits in our case.

"Your honor, what is the relevance of this?" Cassidy is out of her chair, watching all of this from the railing in front of the jury box. She probably believes Dana and I have concocted this story to provide a defense in a faltering case. What she senses is that the jury is listening. The objection is designed to break my stride.

"Your honor, if I could make an offer of proof, I think it will become abundantly clear that the information from this witness is highly relevant."

"Make it quickly," says Woodruff.

"Ms. Colby. Are the couple known as George and Kathy Merlow dead or alive?"

Dana's face at this moment is drained of all emotion, though this question seems to take her by surprise, that I of all people would ask it.

"They no longer go by the name of Merlow," she says.

"So they have a new identity?"

"Yes." She admonishes that if I ask she will not tell me what it is. I don't ask.

"But they are alive?"

"Yes."

It is what I'd suspected, ever since my conversation with Harry. His cynicism that the government can do only two things well: print money and provide new identities. It was the spark that fired all the little pieces that didn't fit; Clem Olsen's information about the fingerprint on the paint tube and the woman named Carla Leopold, the accountant employed by the Regal International Trading Consortium, a front for organized crime; her "death" nearly two years ago in a fiery auto accident on an east coast highway; and her seeming resurrection on a grassy churchyard knoll in Hana two months ago. It had worked once before, death and resurrection with a new identity, so why not simply do it again? There had been no murder in Hana, only the illusion, to stop me from looking.

But there had been a killer. For this Dana apologizes openly on the stand.

"We knew that he was still active because of the postal bombing," she says. "It was his MO," she says.

Marcie Reed was murdered for a simple reason, to keep her from telling me what she knew—that her friend Kathy Merlow was a relocated witness. Merlow had confided in the one friend she had found in Capital City, and it had cost that friend her life. The people who had come to see Marcie before Harry and I were not Lama and his troops as we had suspected, but contract killers, on the track of Merlow. When they discovered that I was dogging her as a witness in Laurel's case they decided to follow along. What better than a lawyer armed with judicial process to force a witness to ground? One word from Marcie and I would have stopped looking. I would have had a defense much more stout than a mere eyewitness to the crime. I would have known what I now know.

"We knew that he'd been commissioned to do the hit." Dana's talking about the contract killer, and that he was looking for the Merlows. "You were just a little too convenient," she says.

"So you used me as bait?" I say.

"I never thought you would be in any real danger. We tried to get him on the way out at the airport, at Maui. We missed," she says.

Much of this is going past the jury, so I regroup for their benefit.

"Let's go back to the night of the murder. Who asked you to go and meet with the Merlows?"

"My boss," she says.

This would be the United States Attorney for the Eastern District. A Presidential appointee. I am beginning to sense that this thing reaches much higher than I thought. Dana has been burning up the air between here and D.C. I had assumed these were related solely to her judicial aspirations. Now I suspect that even that has some more sinister origins.

"And why did he ask you to go and meet with the Merlows?"

"To make certain that they were all right."

"Because Melanie Vega had been murdered that night?"

"That's right," she says.

"Your honor, this is getting us nowhere." Cassidy is tromping around in front of her table now. "I still don't see any of this as relevant. These people, the Merlows, did they see something or not? I mean, they're either witnesses or they aren't. If they're witnesses, let's put 'em on; if they're not, let's move on."

Cassidy is getting a lot of support from Lama, head nodding like "right on." She still doesn't get it.

"If I could ask one more question, your honor, maybe I could clarify."

He gives me a nod.

"Ms. Colby, why did the federal government move George and Kathy Merlow in the middle of the night, on the very evening that Melanie Vega was murdered?"

"Because we had reason to believe that Mrs. Vega had been murdered by mistake, that the intended victim was Kathy Merlow."

As Dana says this, it sweeps like a tornado over the press rows at the front of the courtroom.

The pool camera at the back of the courtroom is whirring, it's videotape capturing this. I can sense a transformation, from the local to the national angle as some of the gray heads in the press rows turn to each other and look, wide-eyed, wondering at the implications of all of this.

Cassidy is protesting that we have injected elements of evidence that were beyond discovery. She actually moves to strike all of Dana's testimony on grounds that it cannot be verified.

"Records of federally protected witnesses are sealed," she says. "What documentation do we have for any of this? How can the state possibly verify it?"

The fact that Dana has torched her career by these admissions seems to offer little proof of veracity, as least to Morgan Cassidy.

"I might be able to help with that," I tell her. "Documentation," I say.

Cassidy's mouth is a gaping hole, a cavern of silence as I offer this. It is clearly not what she wanted. Before she can speak I'm back from the counsel table with a stapled sheaf of papers handed to me by Harry. He's passing out copies, one set to the clerk and another to Lama at the counsel table, where he is joined by Cassidy.

I show this document to Dana and she identifies it—a list of federally protected witnesses on a computer-generated form, something used by Justice and electronically sent over secure channels to field offices around the country. She asks me where I got this. I do not tell her. It came from a gracious editor at a newspaper in Lexington, Kentucky. What finally brought me to my senses was the news article read to me by Harry months before, the piece about the botched computer sale by the Department of Justice, the weak magnet used to erase the computer hard disks, and the eventual sale of these computers, still containing their highly confidential information, to the public. It was the news article that Harry hung on the bulletin board of the dayroom at the county jail, the one warning snitches to beware.

"Your department had reason to believe that the Merlows were compromised, didn't they?"

"We had reason to believe that a number of relocated witnesses had been compromised."

"Why?"

She confirms the almost laughable folly with the computers. How Justice and the FBI tried to buy them back, even raided some homes and businesses, using warrants, to confiscate some of the equipment. I can tell this gets Harry's ire, all the juices of the original story repackaged and concentrated. In the end the information was too far disseminated for the gov-

ernment to unring this particular gong. So they set about trying
to relocate the witnesses, new identities on a priority basis,
those believed to be most in danger first.

"But they didn't get to the Merlows right away, did they?"
"No."

"Not until after Melanie Vega was murdered?" I say.
"That's right."

"Ms. Colby, I want you to think very carefully. I'm going
to ask you one final question, and I want you to answer clearly
for the court. What did the Department of Justice discover
after the murder of Melanie Vega that so upset them, that
caused them to conceal this information, to withhold it from
an attorney defending his client on charges in connection with
that murder? Tell us," I say, "what was it that they found in
those compromised computer records?"

Everything I have done, the entire foundation I have laid
up to this point, has led to this question.

Dana sits poised in the box, the only person in the courtroom besides Harry and myself who knew that this moment
would come.

"They discovered . . ." Her voice cracks a bit. "They discovered that the street address, the new street address on the
computer records for Kathy Merlow, was wrong," she says.
"A typographical error."

"Whose address was it?"

"It belonged to Jack and Melanie Vega."

There is a palpable roar that echoes through the courtroom,
an audible wave of indignation that rolls through the public
areas of this room—the thought that those charged with justice
would conceal such an outrage. An innocent citizen dead, another on trial for her murder, when the barons of bureaucracy
in Washington have known the truth for many months. Reporters are out of their chairs heading for the cameras in the
hallway outside, visions of the lead on "Headline News."

Woodruff is fanning pages of the computer document on
the bench. When he finds it, he looks at me from on high, a

glazed expression. His glasses fairly slide to the end of his nose before they drop off, where he catches them on the rebound off the blotter on the bench. He sinks back into the tufted leather of his chair. Melanie Vega and her child were murdered because a clerk in the bowels of the bureaucracy in Washington made a typographical error.

At this moment, the expression on Woodruff's face is a hybrid between wonder and fury.

I can only surmise how high this thing goes. There is no doubt in my mind that Cabinet members in Washington will be ducking for cover by nightfall, an attorney general doing mea culpas, insisting that the buck stops at her desk, while she casts for underlings to throw onto the pyres of sacrifice, to appease the gods of politics. It is a scenario we have seen before, staged in other scandals.

As I look at her, drained and worn in the witness box, there is not a doubt in my mind that Dana will figure high on their list of victims. Her dreams of judicial glory are wafting on the winds, like the odors of carbonized wood in the wake of a wildfire.

Woodruff is banging his gavel on the bench, trying to bring the place back to order.

Cassidy is trying to holler some objection or a plea from her counsel table, but cannot be heard. Finally the judge's voice breaks over the din. "There will be order or I will clear the room," he says. "Mr. Bailiff, have those people sit down or tell them to leave."

It takes nearly a minute for what passes as order to be restored, a restless vapor of electricity floating just above our heads.

"Your honor, we, the state, knew nothing about this." Cassidy's protestations from the counsel table.

"Speak for yourself," says Dana.

For the first time this morning I am surprised by the words that pass from Dana's lips.

"I cannot prove that you knew," Dana says. "But your investigator sure as hell did."

What is clear is that Dana is not going down on this alone.

With this Cassidy is floored, looking at Lama with a face of betrayal. If it were anyone else she would not believe it, but with Jimmy's track record to date, instinct tells Morgan not to jump to his defense too quickly.

"Please explain that," I say. Dana is still my witness.

"I mean that as liaison to the FBI in the postal bombing case, Lieutenant Lama was informed that the victim, Mrs. Reed, was a friend of Kathy Merlow, and that Mrs. Merlow was a federally protected witness."

Suddenly there is more than a crack in the door. There is a stillness in the courtroom, the sense that even if they do not know how, a second shoe has just dropped.

"Your honor, this was never disclosed," I say. "Exculpatory evidence critical to our case, withheld by the state," I tell him.

Lama has known since before we went to trial that Kathy Merlow was the target of a hired killer.

I look at Cassidy, and I know in this moment that she is as much victim in this as Laurel and I. Lama has used her in his war with me.

She is protesting that she never knew, that Lama never told her. Jimmy is out of his chair, singing a swan song, telling the court that he didn't understand the significance, his reason that he never told anyone. He wants Woodruff to believe that this, dirt that every cop on the beat would chew on over doughnuts and coffee, a connection with their idols at the FBI, that Jimmy would keep this to himself ignorant of its consequences.

Woodruff does not buy this. The only question, he says, is whether or not there was malice in this act of concealment. The judge is now talking legal parlance, the difference between a mistrial and outright dismissal. For us the distinction is cosmic.

Cassidy is pleading for a mistrial, no hard evidence of any intentional wrong, she says. An oversight. This would give her the chance to retry Laurel, to put us to this agony one more time.

If Woodruff dismisses with the jury in the box, jeopardy would attach. Laurel would be a free woman.

"You would subject the defendant to a second trial?" says Woodruff. This he poses to Cassidy.

She hems and haws. "A question I would have to discuss with my boss," she tells him.

Cassidy simply wants to avoid the hammer being dropped in this way, a judge forcing her to eat crow, feathers and all.

"One question," says Woodruff. "Knowing what you know now, would you, as a professional prosecutor, have brought charges against the defendant, Laurel Vega, in this case?" It is the ultimate issue.

Cassidy hesitates for only the briefest moment, the answer is not on her lips, but in her eyes, an admission that Woodruff reads as well as I. It is in this instant of hesitation that I hear the silence of salvation.

"That's what I thought," says Woodruff. "I will not subject the defendant to the uncertain anxieties of a second trial," he says.

"The case is dismissed. The defendant is discharged. I will make my findings of malice in writing, to be submitted to the parties." As he says these words, there is a baleful smile that passes across Austin Woodruff's face, the kind you see when a judge knows that he has, in the end, dispensed justice.

"This court stands adjourned."

I don't even have time to thank him. There is a throng coming around the railing, Laurel pressed in a sea of bodies. I move to the table.

"What happened?" she says.

"You are free."

For what seems like an eternity, I think she cannot comprehend this, then suddenly she stands, her arms about my neck, the warmth of wet tears on the side of my face. "Can I go to my children?" she says.

"You can go anywhere you want," I tell her. "You are free."

I tell her that Danny is in town. This brings her instantly back to the realm of sobriety. "Where?" is all she asks. I tell her at her apartment. She wants to see him immediately, and asks me to call Julie.

People pushing in with notepads, asking questions, how she feels, whether she thinks justice was done, whether she is angry with the government for not disclosing the truth about the federal witness, whether she is considering a civil suit.

Harry stops her from answering this last in a moment of euphoria. "We are studying it," is all he will say. Harry has his abacus out, wondering if we can add to the national debt.

In this instant of chaos I am pushed away, floating in a current of bodies beyond Laurel's reach as several reporters and some well-wishers get between us.

Laurel shouts, cupped hand to mouth. I cannot understand her.

There is a fleeting image, a face beyond the crowd like a subliminal image on film, something from an arched church window in Hana, and then it is gone. I shake my head, fatigue and stress.

She is shouting again.

"Dinner at Fulton's, six o'clock," she says. "My treat."

I nod, and she is gone.

CHAPTER
31

And so we end on a cheery note, five happy humans sitting around a table in the underground digs of Fulton's, a steak house in Old Town. Outside are flickering gas lamps, cobblestone streets, and broad board sidewalks that front the river where miners and gamblers once mingled in the heyday of the gold rush.

We congregate around a table and toast Laurel and her freedom with after-dinner drinks. She is flanked by Danny on one side and Sarah on the other, and spends much time this evening alternately squeezing and kissing each of them. Julie is on a flight from Michigan, scheduled to arrive at the airport late tonight. I take it as a sign that this, the freedom to hold and love, to bond with the children, is in the end the ultimate reward of liberty, at least for Laurel.

The kids join in salute with some dark fizzing cola from their glasses. Danny actually proposes a toast "to the greatest mother a kid ever had." I give Sarah a squeeze as her expression becomes distant and her eyes misty with this, the knowledge that she will never be able to honor Nikki in this way—what would make this night complete.

Laurel exudes the weariness that comes from victory after great struggle, an emotional release that gives itself up in a kind of quiet and restrained euphoria, as if she might crack like eggshell china if she were to completely let go. After half a bottle of wine and a couple of cocktails the smile seems durably planted on her face, but she is rapidly becoming maudlin. I sense a flood of tears just under the surface. What seven months behind bars and the prospect of death at the hands of the state will do to the normal psyche.

Except for Danny, who arrived on the little Vespa, Harry called taxis to bring us all here, to avoid the designated driver, a pack of drunks out on the town. He does me a favor and takes Sarah home. It is late and she needs to get to sleep. He will baby-sit for just a few minutes, as I have things to discuss with Laurel. Then I will head home myself, to the first restful night's sleep in months.

Laurel and I do Alfonse and Gaston in front of the waiter, fighting over who will pick up the check. When he finally takes her credit card it is only to return three minutes later to inform her that because payment has not been received in several months it is no longer valid. The final humiliation. Laurel is mortified. She leaves with Danny to wait for me outside by the Vespa while I pick up the check, assurances that she can pay me back when she has the means.

It takes several minutes, and finally I climb the stairs to the street level and exit onto the plank sidewalk in front of Fulton's. Second Street in Old Town on a weekend is racing cars and young girls in skirts to the crotch, hitting bars where the boys hang out. But tonight, a Monday, it is largely deserted. A single car, a small van, is parked at the curb in front of the restaurant.

Across I Street at the corner, maybe seventy-five yards away, Laurel and Danny are talking by the little motor scooter with its wooden box, Danny's catchall of possessions on the back. He has parked near a bike rack in front of the State Railroad Museum, a two-story brick-and-glass structure that takes up an entire block adjoining the old S.P. railyard. Laurel has her back to me, and seems deep in conversation with Danny as he works the combination on the chain lock to the scooter.

It is early spring and the Delta breeze has kicked up, putting a chill to the night air. I stop on the corner for a moment to tuck the receipt for dinner into my wallet so Laurel does not see it. She would insist on taking it and somehow paying me back tomorrow.

A janitor is rolling the tools of his trade in a small cart over the rough pressed concrete sidewalk across the street, unlocking the main entrance to the Railroad Museum for his nightly rounds.

I hoof it to the corner and step down a long foot onto the cobblestone street and start to walk. Like a firefly in the tropics it alights on the stone surface a few feet ahead of me and just as quickly disappears. I saunter a step or two to the left, and it appears, only this time it seems to dance off the shoulder of my coat before projecting onto the roadway a dozen feet ahead of me, then, just as quickly, is gone again. It is then that it strikes me—the intense narrow beam, the concentrated red dot of laser light. Before I can think, I take three quick steps to the left, and hear the pop of the silenced bullet as it streaks past my right ear and ricochets off the cobblestone street. Caught by the tenor of metal fracturing at the speed of sound, Laurel turns.

By this time I am in full stride running away from Fulton's, across the intersection, my arms flailing.

"Run! *Go!* Get the hell out of here!" I must look like a rag doll.

For the moment I get dazed expressions from the two of them, Laurel with a hand on her hip, slimmer and rock-hard as if she'd spent seven months in a health club.

But Laurel and Danny have an angle on the shooter, looking behind me. I do not hear the bullet that tears the fabric of my coat at the sleeve and singes flesh, a bloody crease that I reach over and feel with one hand.

By now my feet are flying, as much zigzag as I can do, like a jackrabbit ahead of shotgun pellets, bullets zapping past me. Any moment one will shatter my spine, blast through my chest. The thoughts that race through your mind—Nikki and Sarah.

On one of these forays of evasion I am actually running lateral to the shooter, and in this instant I can see the silhouette of a figure, standing in the open door of the van parked in front of Fulton's. To anyone down the street, from behind it would look like this guy is hunched over lighting a cigarette. Instead he is taking careful aim with two hands. I reverse course an instant before a bullet snaps in front of my face. I hear the sound of metal as it clicks on bricks and flattens itself against the wall of the Railroad Museum, now no more than thirty yards away.

By this time Danny is on his scooter, doing a U-turn and heading out Second Street the other way, under the freeway and toward town.

"Nine-one-one!" Laurel yelling for him to call for help, as she hobbles down the street in heels, heading for the darkness and the open ground of the railroadyard. Danny looking back like he won't leave her. He brakes near the end of the street.

"Damn it—get out of here!" she says.

I take the shooter in another direction, away from them. At full stride I make it to the entrance of the Railroad Museum. I do not know if Lyle Simmons is his real name, or whether like so much of what Dana told me this too was a fiction. But there is no question about who is his quarry here. He is after me. I have now seen him twice, once at the post office and again in Hana. I am one of only two people who can identify him, me and Howard, the guy on the loading dock at the post office the day he delivered the letter bomb. I am wondering if Howard has been dispatched to his maker, the gunman cleaning up all the little loose ends left from Marcie Reed and his botched job on Melanie.

I huddle in the shadows near the entrance of the museum. The place is deserted except for the janitor's cart, which is propped against an open glass door a few feet away. I can see the shooter moving toward me, sliding a loaded clip into the handle of what appears to be an immense handgun, something from the arsenal of a starship, a laserscope and the cigar shape of a silencer protruding from this thing.

This guy has set up his own private shooting gallery, using me as the bouncing metal bunny, at least eight shots that I have counted, on an open public street, and except for Laurel and Danny not a soul has seen this.

He starts to jog, nonchalant, across the intersection, closing the distance.

On my haunches, I move to the cart, push it out of the way. It rumbles across the mottled surface of the pressed concrete into the light of the moon, and suddenly takes two bullets that rip through the plastic bag draped in its center and filled with trash.

He thinks I am using this thing for cover. While he's distracted I slip through the open door into the lobby of the museum and quietly pull the door closed behind me. But I don't hear the latch of the lock as it closes. Then I look. It is a deadbolt, requiring a key. I have no way of locking him out.

The place is shrouded in muted light, and as I watch through the glass door I see the gunman grab the cart, check the back side of it, and fling it to one side. Process of elimination—he looks to the entrance and the closed door.

I slink back into the shadows, turn, rise, and run. I'm looking, but the janitor is nowhere in sight.

I slip around the box office, down a long corridor, and, to my left, another hallway, past the elevator and a stairwell.

I hear him pulling on doors out front. He's gotten them all except the one that's open, making a lot of noise. Last one's a charm as I hear it rattle in its frame, closing behind him.

Then a voice. "Hey, what are you doing? Building's closed. You can't come in here."

"Lookin' fa someone." It's an eastern inflection, somewhere north of Boston, heavy with working-class origins. I have heard this voice only once before, when he delivered the package to Marcie Reed and told her to sign.

"Well, he ain't in here." The janitor again. For a second I think maybe the guy is going to be cowed into leaving.

"What's that?" The janitor taking note. Something's going on.

I hear a flat percussion, muffled, like a lead sinker bounced one time on a child's toy drum. It is followed by another in quick succession and then the sickening sound of something hitting ground, like a sack of oranges off a truck.

The janitor is dead.

I have been hovering around the corner from the elevator, maybe thirty yards from the lobby, and now I move, past a wall of windows that look out on a dark and deserted street. The moon is breaking through clouds above. Across the way the lights of Fulton's and the crowded restaurant, sanctuary that I cannot reach.

Behind me, an ancient steam locomotive, "The Empire," its name carved in lacquered wood, is mounted on rails embedded in a pedestal of mirrors so that the undercarriage gleams in refracted light. It is too bright here, lit up like an arcade. I pick up the pace and put this behind me. Turning a corner, I pass another locomotive, the name "C. P. Huntington" on the side. Suddenly I am off of carpet, my heels on hard wood. I stop to pull off my loafers and carry them in my hand. In stocking feet I slide as I run.

Twenty feet and I enter a great curving room with a cavernous ceiling. The floor turns to concrete, rolling stock everywhere, giant steel dinosaurs looming above me in the shadows. There are four gleaming locomotives at the far end of this room, two exhibits with their doors open, a post office car, and sleeping car, all on rails embedded in the concrete.

It takes me a moment to gain my bearings, and then I realize that I am in the roundhouse, a kind of launching platform for trains. I can see the turntable outside through gleaming glass doors two stories high, under which the rails pass.

Behind me I hear the sound of shoe leather brushing on

thick carpet, slow-moving steps, cautious, uncertain whether I am here.

I turn, and it is then that I see them, glistening in the dampened light of the overhead canisters, sparkling against the shimmer of waxed hardwood, drops of my own blood, four of them between where I stand and where wood turns to carpet. More stain the carpet to the last corner where I can no longer see.

The scratch on my shoulder is not serious, but it has bled, little drops, and like bread crumbs in a dark cavern Lyle Simmons is following them.

No handkerchief. I pull from my pocket the tie which I took off over dinner. I wipe the blood from the back of my hand where it has trickled from under the sleeve of my coat, and using my teeth and my good hand I wrap the tie around the wound on my upper arm and put a knot in it. There is a mild stinging sensation. I take a few steps to separate myself from the last drop of blood. Confident I am no longer leaking, I run at a half-stride past the postal car and a large engine. I negotiate my way around another locomotive and suddenly realize I am running out of building. Beyond this second engine there are two more, then a solid wall.

One of the engines is parked over an underground concrete bay like those used to change oil in a lube shop, only larger. There are stairs at each end of this so that visitors can step down and walk in a cavern beneath the engine to study the undercarriage.

A flash of memories from childhood, when I once played in a schoolyard on a rusting locomotive. I remember crawling through the area between the massive wheels and finding a cavern the size of a small house above the axles, just beneath the barreled bottom of the boiler.

I steer clear of the locomotive parked over the bay. It would be too easy for Simmons to get below me and look up. I would be splayed against a background, a shooting gallery with a metal backstop where he could bounce bullets until one of them hit me. I take the second engine. The numbers 10-10 are stenciled on a plaque leading to a set of wooden stairs that allow visitors to climb up into the cab.

I go around to the other side and crawl through the open triangle created by two of the locomotive's immense drive wheels.

The space is smaller than I remember from childhood, and for an instant sensations of claustrophobia wash over me, thirty tons of steel over my head. My body is halfway into the opening under the wheels. Lying on my back, overhead I can see one of the mammoth drive axles, steel, and the girth of a good-sized tree trunk. I pull myself underneath and do some contortions. I boost myself on top of the axle. I am now lying on top of this like a cat lounging on a branch, with my head toward the wheels on the other side.

I shimmy along the axle to get closer. There are a few slots cut in the massive drive wheels, near where the steam-driven connecting rods fasten to the outside of the wheel. These give me a limited field of vision, back toward the area where carpet turns to hardwood, the end of my trail, the splotches of blood on the floor. I can feel the pulse throbbing in my temple as I check the sleeve of my coat for dripping blood.

As I move under the massive canopy of the engine, suddenly there is a flicker of red light through the slots in the wheel, narrow and intense. I freeze. It is the thing about laser light—concentrated, it does not diffuse over distance. I cannot tell if he is fifty feet away or three. I lie with my head pressed against the inside of the giant steel wheel.

Seconds pass, sweat dripping from my face. I hear footsteps. I look—he is thirty feet away. All I can see are his feet and the bottom of his pant legs, and one other thing—a beam of light. Simmons has some kind of a flashlight and is checking the undercarriage of one of the cars. The man comes prepared. In this instant I know that if I stay here, if the police do not come in time, I am dead.

I watch as his feet disappear up the steps to the post office

car. He is checking the inside. This car is maybe sixty feet
long. Then he will reach the other end, exit, and check the
locomotive next to it, the only piece of rolling stock between
us.

There are only a few windows in the postal car looking out
in this direction, so I take my chance.

I slide off the axle and drop to the concrete between the
wheels. I struggle through the narrow opening on my stomach
and emerge from under the engine on the side away from him.
There are now two engines between me and the postal car. I
move to my right, past the engine with its concrete bay. It is
not until I reach the last locomotive, a mammoth diesel, that
I realize that this thing has blocked my view of a stairway
leading to an overhead gallery, a kind of mezzanine that hangs
above the exhibit hall. Quickly, in stocking feet, I move to it,
around the corner and up the concrete stairs—two flights. I
emerge on an upper level of the museum, bordered by a clear
acrylic railing that is transparent, in full view of the floor below.

For the first forty feet I am able to steer clear of this, until
I come to a bridge that passes between the turntable outside
and the engines assembled below in the roundhouse. The
bridge is only a few feet wide and I must crawl on my stomach
to avoid being exposed by the safety-glass railing.

I can hear his footsteps moving around the engines on the
level below, occasionally flickers of light, alternating red and
white, laser and flashlight. I stop, still as death, for an instant,
anticipating an explosion of plate glass should he see me.

It is then that I see it, a sign over the door at the far end of
the gallery, red letters against white light: EXIT.

There is another way out, a set of stairs at the far end, a
way down to the lobby that Simmons cannot see, a clear path
to the front door and the restaurant beyond.

I crawl on my knees, keeping away from the railing, until
I can stand. I have now worked my way back to the wall of
windows. Somewhere directly beneath me is ''The Empire''

and its mirrored platform. It is then I hear them, not leather this time, but the squeak of sneakers on wood, like two chipmunks in a pissing contest. My first thought is the police TAC squad, part of a SWAT unit.

Gingerly, so as not to get my head blown off, I crawl to the railing and peer through. I cannot see Simmons. Then, below in the shadows, emerging into the moonlight cast from the mirror, I see the moving form. Not some cop in black with a twenty-shot-magazine Heckler & Koch, but Danny Vega, in all of his innocence, whispering my name.

"Uncle Paul . . ."

I could spit, but I could not hit him. He is hugging the walls of an exhibit, trying to stay in the shadows, and giving himself away with his mouth.

"Uncle Paul . . . Are you in here?" Whispers that can be heard fifty feet away.

Then it hits me. The kid has followed my trail of blood from outside on the street into this place. With each step he moves closer to Simmons, somewhere in the darkness out by the giant engines. Then I wonder if he has called the cops. With Danny you can never be sure.

Some way to catch his attention . . .

"Uncle Paul . . ."

For a moment I consider throwing one of my shoes at him, but the clatter would surely give him away. I fumble in my pocket for some change and come up with a few pennies, a nickel, and a quarter.

I look over at Danny. In a moment he will leave hardwood for concrete. From there it is only a few steps more until he mingles with engines in the roundhouse and stumbles across the fiery red eye of death.

I aim one of the coins, a penny, and throw it. I watch as it falls, deflected by a small potted shrub. It lands silently on the carpet near one of the exhibits.

Danny is turning the corner, coming up on the end of the postal car.

Across the way is a mammoth engine, something called a cab-forward, a football field in length, and thirty feet off the ground its curving black metal roof. I throw another coin over the railing, this one at the roof of the locomotive. It bounces off the metal cab, the sound of copper on steel plate, and echoes through the building. I hold my breath.

Danny stops dead in his tracks, looks back toward the engine and up. But when he turns it is the wrong way, with his back to me. I have no choice, I stand in full view, silent but waving frantically with both arms, an island of motion in the sea of stillness around me.

Suddenly an explosion of glass, pebbles of safety glass sting my hand below the railing, dust in my eyes. I step back to clear them, oblivious to the fact that I am now a stationary target. Another bullet snaps by my head and a wall of glass explodes behind me, open to the outside night sky. The Klaxon of a burglar alarm. I hit the floor.

Danny is looking up. He has seen all of this. He lurches forward as if he is going to speak. I press a single finger to my lips, the universal sign for silence, and motion with the other hand for him to back out, to retrace his steps to the entrance, and out.

Danny catches it, looks toward the roundhouse, and suddenly realizes that danger lies in that direction.

He takes two steps, and instantly from one of the displays, pistol in hand, Simmons grabs Danny from behind. The boy struggles, but Simmons has a death grip on his throat, pistol to his temple.

"Move," he says, "and you're dead." His voice is clearly audible. He sees me at the edge of the platform, where I am frozen in place. With the laser he could take his chances, a shot from there. But he could not be sure to kill me. If I fell back onto the platform, he might not get another clear shot. He would have to trek up the stairs, and by then, if I was wounded, I might crawl away.

He surveys his options, the Klaxon ringing in his ears. He

knows he has seconds, perhaps a couple of minutes, no more.

"Come down," he says. "Now. Or I'll kill the boy."

"Don't," says Danny. "He's gonna kill me anyway." Frightened and alone, the kid has the clarity of mind to comprehend his situation.

Simmons chokes off Danny's plea with the grip of his hand on the boy's throat.

"He dies on the count of ten," he says. "One . . . Two . . ."

I look at his eyes, the sign that means what he says. I start to run, retracing my steps, along the gallery, over a small lake of broken glass, in naked feet.

"Three . . . Four . . ."

Headlong for the stairs, one flight, then the other. In the stairwell I cannot hear his voice. I emerge at the bottom. Running through the roundhouse.

"Eight . . . Nine . . ."

"I'm here!" I'm yelling at the top of my lungs, bidding for time.

I haven't rounded the area by the end of the postal car, so he cannot see me or hear my naked feet, my shoes dropped on the floor above. In this instant I expect to hear the sickening sound of suppressed gunfire.

As I make the turn I see him shielded behind Danny, the long reach of the silencer pressed against the kid's head.

"That's good," he says. "On your knees. Now." He's moving quickly, knowing he doesn't have much time.

I drop to my knees and he tells me to crawl forward, into the light cast by mirrored glass under the locomotive, his hand continually on Danny's throat pressing until he is gasping, coughing for air. Then he flings the boy to the floor and tells him to kneel.

"Hands behind your head," he says. "Lock the fingers."

We do it.

All the while he is moving behind us until I can no longer see him, our backs to the blown-out window.

Danny tries to look and catches the side of the pistol against the flat of his cheek. I can hear steel as it smacks bone. The boy lurches as if he will fall forward.

"Eyes straight ahead."

He is behind Danny. I see the boy's face go forward as the pistol is pressed against the back of his head. He's going to kill the boy first.

I tense my body and with hands clasped I throw my shoulder back, crash into Simmons' knee just as I hear the rapid double cough of two fired rounds. A body slumping sideways onto me, the back of its head, hair matted by blood, a stream pulsing from the wounds. He slides across me onto the floor—and as he rolls onto his back, I see the upturned lifeless eyes of Lyle Simmons.

I look back. There in the shadows framed by the moonlit sky, through the wall of broken glass stands Laurel, a pistol and its smoking silencer in her hand.

CHAPTER
32

In the van abandoned by Lyle Simmons in front of Fulton's, police found a small arsenal of firearms, guns for every occasion, as well as loading equipment for ammunition, and the makings for explosive devices—everything someone in the business of killing might be expected to possess.

It was here, in this van, that Laurel told police she first looked when she finally returned from the darkness of the railyard, to find her son's motor scooter dumped in the street and Danny gone. It was in the van that she told police she found the weapon that ultimately saved our lives, the pistol she used to shoot Lyle Simmons.

Danny had panicked. He never made the phone call to nine-one-one, and instead, a half block under the freeway overpass, he turned around and returned for his mother, who by that time was gone. He nosed around for a while, and then, seeing the blood and thinking she might have gone inside the museum, he followed.

Police have now tested both guns, and ballistics reveal that the pistol used by Laurel to kill Simmons matches the bullet found in Melanie Vega. For authorities it is the final evidence required for closure, the last dotting of *i*'s and crossing of *t*'s in Melanie's case.

There are already calls for a Congressional inquiry into the Federal Witness Protection program and the special hazards it presents for unsuspecting citizens into whose midst targets such as Kathy Merlow are dropped. The program has implications for us all, not least of which is the question of how well any of us truly know our neighbors.

There have been news conferences at Justice in Washington where those in power claim no knowledge of any of this—the cover-up that ensued following Melanie's death.

We live in a time where increasingly our national leaders act more like the dons of crime than statesmen where notions of plausible deniability replace the truth, and claims that politicians never knew of the evil done in their own names by others are commonplace. It is the age of unbridled arrogance and video showmanship, where the challenge "prove what I knew and when I knew it" has now become a national motto.

Through all of this, Laurel has shown herself to be both resilient and resourceful, a face of calm in a sea of crisis. When she entered the museum that night it was with a fierce determination to save Danny, no matter the odds. That she was able to save my own life in the process was not lost on Laurel, though she was first and foremost the mother of her son. And, like serendipity, Laurel found an opportunity she never actually considered when she walked through the doors that evening. It was the chance to finally get rid of the gun that had been used to kill Melanie Vega.

The fact is that while Lyle Simmons had been contracted to kill Kathy Merlow, we will never know whether he would have actually struck the right house or not, because he never got the chance. As fate would have it, circumstances intervened and Simmons arrived on the scene a little too late.

As Laurel sits across the desk from me this morning, nearly a month has passed since that night. We are alone in the office. It is Saturday morning, and Laurel has asked that we talk here. Danny and Julie are with Sarah. They have taken her to a show, one of the new cartoon classics with a lot of music and high animation.

On my desk is the final piece of evidence promised to be

delivered by Morgan Cassidy at trial. With the case over, it is a moot point, and not one I am sure Morgan has dwelt on. The police have their killer in a coffin.

But on my desk are the working papers of the medical examiner, Simon Angelo, regarding the DNA and the genetic link between the unborn child and Jack Vega. I had never really bought into the concept of Jack as father in the case, and had wondered whether Angelo has simply reached into his bag of science and pulled a last-minute rabbit from the hat to save Cassidy's case.

I found the answer in an obscure footnote to his working papers, an item not written by Angelo, but printed in small type on a form used in such tests. The projections of probability regarding Jack's paternity were valid, wholly consistent with the results of the DNA probes, but they were premised on a single erroneous assumption—that there were no other males having shared genetic characteristics with Jack. The DNA testing had failed to consider the possibilities of Danny.

It is one of those conversations that people have, lawyer to client. Laurel has asked for assurances of privilege several times before talking, nervous, though I have told her that my lips are sealed, by law if not by blood.

And so she fills in the details that I have only guessed at until this moment.

It was not Laurel who had been at Jack's house that night, who Mrs. Miller had seen in the hooded sweatshirt, but her likeness in all ways including looks. It was Danny.

He had come to talk, and perhaps to actually carry out the desperate and dramatic act of a teenager, not to murder Melanie, but to kill himself.

Danny had known for nearly two months that his stepmother carried his child, a dark secret only he and Melanie knew. It is why she pushed so hard through Jack for custody, a mix of fear and desire. Melanie knew that unless she could keep Danny close at hand, under her wing, in time the boy would crack. He would tell someone, if not authorities, then his mother. Their lives had become a daily act of desperation.

According to Laurel, it is perhaps the ultimate irony that the last act in Melanie's sorry life was one of virtue.

He had found her in the bath when he arrived. I can only imagine the thoughts racing through Melanie's mind in those final moments as Danny, in a state of hysteria, placed the silenced muzzle first in his mouth, then at his temple. Finally, she stood in the tub and pleaded with him to put the gun down. When he refused, she took one step over the side, onto the bath mat, and made a wild swing for the weapon. She grabbed the barrel and they struggled, Melanie half in and half out of the tub. It was a horrified Danny who gently lowered the body of his stepmother, his seducer, back down into the water.

The contested carpet, covered with Melanie's blood and Danny's bloody footprint, was in fact in Jack's house that night—the vagaries of marital settlement agreements, in which every nut and bolt is divided on paper and left to the parties to enforce.

There may be many explanations for what happened that night so long ago, but in the end it all comes down to a single thing, a case of beauty and guile over youth and innocence, a case of Melanie's undue influence over Danny.

"Where did he get the gun?" I ask.

"Where else?" she says. "The source of every vice for the young, a locker at school. A friend of his told Danny some gang members kept the weapon in a shared locker with this kid. So Danny took it."

"I think I met these people," I tell her. The gang-bangers who came to my house that night, the ones Dana chased off with her cellular call to the cops. They had not wanted Danny so much as their gun back. Though they might very well have used it on him had they put the two together.

The weapon had not been in Simmons' van that night, as Laurel had told the police. Instead it was on Danny's Vespa, where it had remained since the night of Melanie's death, the little motor scooter that had been parked in my own garage for months, that Sarah had sat upon and played with, its varnished wooden box padlocked on the back. It was the point of deep conversation between Laurel and Danny that night when I emerged from Fulton's onto the street.

Laurel had had her back to me. Danny had just given her the weapon, which she had placed in her purse, to dispose of in some way, a task she had originally intended to carry out on her trip to Reno months before. In the chaos following Melanie's violent death, Laurel had thrown a few things into a bag for her trip to draw cover for Danny and told the boy to put the rug in a plastic bag along with the gun and place them in the trunk of her car.

The fact that the gun never made it into the bag, Laurel now tells me, was the result of panic and confusion by a teenager.

I think that there was perhaps more design than disorder to this, at least in Danny's mind. The boy had begun to think about what would happen if his mother were caught and charged with the murder. It is true that he sat by anxiously and watched her trial, but in Danny's mind he held the trump card. Until the end, he possessed the murder weapon, and in Danny's limited understanding of the wheels of justice, had his mother been convicted, it would have been a simple thing to come forward, confess the crime, and produce the evidence. I doubt seriously whether police would have bought this.

I can imagine the alarm that raced through Laurel's mind when she stood near the spillway of the Boca Dam, as she now tells me she did that night on her way to Reno, and discovered that the gun was not there. She had intended to load the plastic bag with rocks and dump both the carpet and weapon into the lake. Without the pistol, she knew there was a good chance police could link Danny to the crime. It was for this reason that she kept the rug, washed the blood from it, and made sure that police found it when they arrested her. The rug was intended to keep the cops from looking further for a suspect. She knew Jack would identify it, and she would simply stonewall. Without blood or trace evidence, which she had eliminated by washing it in solvents, the carpet became something, in her mind, only marginally incriminating. It would be her word against Jack's as to ownership. She had never banked on the property settlement agreement, which became the added straw.

As for Jack, it seems the vaunted legislator has taken flight. He is now a fugitive. In a long and rambling letter received by the federal district judge and mailed from another city, Vega said that his sense of survival was more acute than his respect for the courts, or "your supposed system of justice." In the letter Jack vented his spleen against the government for the cover-up surrounding his wife's murder, and wallowed in a sea of self-pity, finally saying that he felt betrayed by the untimely disclosure of his plea-bargain during the trial. He claimed that he had to undergo necessary medical treatment, no doubt plastic surgery to prevent identification while on the lam.

I suspect that he had for some time before this been diverting some of the sludge that we call campaign contributions into a numbered account someplace in a far-off land. The irony in this is that because he bolted before his sentencing, Jack is not technically a convicted felon, at least for purposes of his legislative retirement, which would have been forfeit had he gone to prison.

Checks are being drawn to his next-of-kin, to Laurel's children, of whom she now has custody, and for the first time in years she has an adequate income.

In the end it is Dana who no doubt will take the biggest fall in all of this. Her dreams of a federal judgeship are now cinders, and she has been suspended from office pending completion of an investigation. There has never been a question in my mind but that she was following orders from above. But they are all now clamoring to prevent this thing, the stain of Melanie's death, from climbing higher up the food chain.

Dana did, after all, make every effort to acquit Laurel, to the point of attempting to suborn perjury, not because she was evil, but because she knew Laurel was innocent. In fact she knew nothing. I will probably testify on her behalf when it comes to that.

Loyalties die hard.

AUTHOR'S NOTE

On September 21, 1992, the following article appeared in *Newsweek:*

A CONFEDERACY OF GLITCHES;
UNCLE SAM IS JUST ANOTHER COMPUTER ILLITERATE

When Charles Hayes bid $45 for two truckloads of used government computer equipment in June 1990, he knew he was getting a lot for his money. He didn't know how much, though, until the U.S. Attorney's Office in Lexington, Ky., called in a panic. The computer storage devices held lists of confidential informants compiled by the U.S. Justice Department for federal criminal investigations. The computers also contained the names of people in the federal witness-protection program, people whose lives depend on their whereabouts not falling into the wrong hands. By the time the Justice Department attorneys called, Hayes had already sold the computers again. It seems the government computer technician who prepared the machines for sale tried to scramble all the files using a magnet that was too weak [p. 70].

ACKNOWLEDGMENTS

In writing this work I have received the assistance and encouragement of many without whose help it could never have been completed.

First to my wife, Leah, and my daughter, Meg, for their patience, support, and never-ending love;

Next to my publisher, Phyllis Grann, and my editor, George Coleman, for their tireless efforts, confidence, and boundless enthusiasm;

To my agent, John Hawkins, for his calm counsel in times of chaos;

To Sam Solinsky, for his research and timely news clippings into matters political and legal that helped to make this book authentic in its color and character;

To Dr. Nils A. Schoultz, M.D., for his lifelong friendship and support, for the warm memories of college together at the University of California at Santa Cruz, and in particular for his advice on matters urologic, and especially the facts concerning the odds for success pertaining to the medical procedure known as vasectomy;

To the Honorable Thomas M. Cecil, Judge of the Superior Court of Sacramento County, for encouragement and support, and in particular for his assistance in obtaining color and authenticity pertaining to the state-of-the-art facilities that are the Sacramento County Jail;

To Lance Gima, Assistant Laboratory Director, California State Crime Lab, in Berkeley, California, and Debby Bell, Paternity Testing Coordinator for Meris F.D.L. laboratory, in Sacramento, California, for their assistance on matters pertaining to DNA testing and paternity;

And last but not least to Meg Byrerton, Office Assistant with the California Department of Parks and Recreation, for her assistance regarding the California State Railroad Museum.

SPM